TIMEBORNE

BLADE OF SHADOWS

BOOK ONE

SARA SAMUELS

TIMEBORNE

BLADE OF SHADOWS
BOOK 1

SARA SAMUELS

Published by Sara Samuels

Denver, CO 80237

First Edition

Copyright ©2023 Sara Samuels

All Rights Reserved.

Cover design by Krafigs Designs

Editing by Rainy Kaye

Formatting by Storytelling Press

*"The world is filled with darkness. Come closer, dear reader.
Fear not for I am taking you on a journey."*

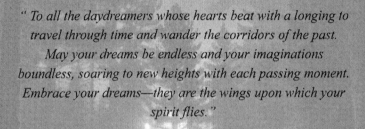

" To all the daydreamers whose hearts beat with a longing to travel through time and wander the corridors of the past. May your dreams be endless and your imaginations boundless, soaring to new heights with each passing moment. Embrace your dreams—they are the wings upon which your spirit flies. "

AUTHOR'S NOTE

Dear Reader,

Thank you for joining me on this adventure. You are about to dive into a series where each book is a crucial piece of a larger puzzle. For the fullest experience and to grasp the evolving story, it's important to read them in order. This sequence ensures you won't miss the unfolding mysteries and the journey of our characters. I've crafted this series with great care, aiming to take you on an unforgettable journey. Start at the beginning of book 1 and enjoy the ride—each book brings you closer together to the big ultimate reveal.

With all my love,
    Sara

CHAPTER ONE

March 2004

It took one look at a creepy porcelain figurine to know my entire ten-year-old world was about to change forever.

You know those disturbing antique dolls, the kind with the eyelids that open and close with a soft tick? Their eyes stared at me blankly when I ran past the shelf they were sitting on at the back of my parents' store full of outdated crip-crap. Each time I saw them, I wanted to rip off their heads, so they would stop looking at me.

And now, Mom was about to get another one. She was standing at the glass counter full of old pocket watches in her and Papa's antique store, *Life after Life Antiques*.

An elderly grandmother-type woman stood across the counter from her, holding a porcelain doll.

I came here every day when I was done with school and had finished my homework. Today, I brought my homework with me. My teacher, Mr. Keys, gave us the assignment to write about something interesting, so I wrote about *Life after Life*. I walked up and down the aisles, sat near Mom, and wrote.

Most of the antiques were interesting. Some were strange, like when a customer brought in an old motorcycle with a trumpet where the exhaust valve should have been. Papa snatched that one right up and said he made a "small fortune on it" when he sold it.

Another one, a colorful metal "puppet theater," had a hand-painted cardboard figure wearing a jester costume on the stage. The jester stood next to a ballerina. A lightbulb at the back of the stage lit the whole thing up. I cried so hard when Papa said he was going to sell it. So, he gave it to me for my eighth birthday a couple years ago. Two years later, I still had it on a shelf in my bedroom. When I pulled it off the shelf, my imagination took over, telling stories about the ballerina and her long-ago life.

I liked pretending about what it was like to live in the past.

And then, there were the coins Papa found at a yard sale. He excitedly showed them to my mom and said, "Would you look at this, Alina? Ancient Roman coins! Think of the money we'll make on these coins!"

When I tried to look at the coins, Papa closed his hand around them. "Sorry, pumpkin, these coins are not for kids."

Later, I found out why; I snuck into the drawer where he had stashed them. On one side was a guy's head. On the other was a naked man with a, you know, that thing between his legs. But all the letters around the edge of the coins intrigued me. They were Roman numerals, something I learned about in school. And holding something supposedly hundreds of years old gave me a thrill.

"My, this one is unique," Mom told the customer, a woman with a scrunched, wrinkled face, jerking me out of my daydreams. She held the doll before her and turned it from side to side.

The doll wore a torn, faded cloak with a hood, like Little Red Riding Hood. But I couldn't tell if it was a boy or a girl. It sort of looked like a boy. Its face was smudged and smeared like it had melted. Limp, black hair fluffed about its head beneath the hood. I couldn't tell if the skin was supposed to be dirty brown or sickly white. And its eyes—those eyes were the worst kind of eyes, tracking me wherever I moved. Whatever it was, the thing looked hideous.

I wanted to run up to her and yell, "Don't get it! Don't get the gross doll!"

"Olivia?" Mom said. She lowered her head to look at me over the top of her reading glasses. "What do you think of this one?"

I was surprised she'd asked for my opinion.

"Me?" I said, pointing to my chest. Mom had made it clear before that she was the expert in antiques.

"Yes, you. What do you think? Should we get it?" She smiled the friendly smile she reserved for me.

I shook my head back and forth like a weathervane. My best friend, Sally, had a weathervane on top of her barn, and when the wind blew, it fluttered back and forth just like I was doing. I didn't want that toy thing, and I didn't want Mom to get it.

"No?" she said.

"No," I whispered. "I hate it."

"I'm sorry, Mrs....what did you say your name is?" Mom said to the wrinkled grandma.

"Mrs. Johnson," the woman said. "Are you sure you won't take it? I'll give you a great deal."

"No, I'm sorry. It just doesn't fit with our store." Mom gave Mrs. Johnson one of her "I'm done with you, and if you keep bugging me, you're going to get a spanking" looks.

Mrs. Johnson got the message, stuffed the horrible toy in the paper sack she brought, and left.

"Wasn't that an odd doll?" Mom said to me and let out a shaky laugh.

I nodded, and she placed her hand on her lower back and stretched as she did when she was tired.

"What do you say to ice cream? I think we can take a break, don't you?" she said.

"Goody! Who will run the store while we're gone?" I said, placing my pen on the lined paper I was using to write my story.

"Your father, that's who. Jack!" Mom called through the door leading to the back. They stored some of the antiques while deciding on prices and cleaning them up.

"What?" Papa called.

"Olivia and I are going to go get some ice cream at *Cool Scoops*. Do you want one?"

I loved ice cream, especially the kind at *Cool Scoops* just down the block.

Papa appeared in the doorway, smiling. As usual, his hair was all messy, and he looked like a mad scientist. "A double scoop of fudge brownie for me, please. In a bowl. With whipped cream on top."

"I want a scoop of fudge brownie and vanilla chocolate chip in a sugar cone!" I said, hopping up and down.

"Then, let's do it!" Mom reached behind the counter for her purse. "We'll be back in a few," she said to Papa, slung her bag over her shoulder, and extended her hand to mine.

I took it, and we exited *Life after Life* to the sound of the tinkling bells that clanged against the wooden door.

Outside, the sky was filled with heavy, gray clouds. A thunderstorm was coming.

Mom said, "Go back inside, and I'll run to the parking lot and get my umbrella from my car."

I raced back into the store and pressed my nose to the glass to watch for Mom.

When Mom returned and rounded the corner, a man approached her from the opposite direction.

The man was dressed in black everything, from his head to his toes. His hair was the color of midnight, long and wavy. He reminded me of that creepy doll. He lifted his head and stared at me in the same way that toy-thing looked at me in the store. Only the doll's glass peepers looked like they belonged on a kitten's face compared to the frigid-blue orbs of evil that stared back at me from this man.

The image of his face branded itself into my mind. I stared, transfixed.

He broke eye contact and approached my mom.

Mom looked up. She seemed to recognize him, and the two began to talk, accenting their words with sharp, angled gestures.

Suddenly, the man lunged at my mother, shoving her backward.

Mom's lips formed an outraged O shape. She thrust her hand into her purse and retrieved a dangerous-looking blade.

I had no idea Mom carried such a lethal-looking weapon.

Assuming some sort of bent-leg fighter's stance, Mom waved the knife at the man's face.

The scary-looking guy matched Mom's stance, and he put his arms out, ducking and dancing out of the way of her blade.

As the man gracefully evaded her attack, mom continued to strike and thrust with her weapon.

SARA SAMUELS

A terrible grin spread across his face as if he were enjoying their fight.

Both of my palms pressed into the glass as I watched, unable to look away. *Please don't let anything happen to my mommy.*

People stopped to stare at the fight, but no one moved a muscle to help. It seemed they were more interested in the outcome than the fact that they were witnessing a vicious act of violence.

Finally, the man seized my mother's wrist and whirled around, pinning her arm behind her back.

Mom kicked her leg backward and landed a blow on his shins.

He let out a grunt and whispered something in her ear. Then, in a lightning-quick maneuver, he whipped a dagger from his pocket and plunged it into Mom's chest.

I let out a scream.

Mom cried out and collapsed on the sidewalk, gently guided by the killer's arms. Her weapon clattered to the ground.

Why would he help her to the ground? It didn't make sense to my ten-year-old brain. None of this made sense.

The murderer crouched, whispered something in her ear, and then kissed her lips gently as if he loved her. Afterward, he grabbed my mother's knife from the sidewalk where it had fallen and tucked both blades into his pocket. He flashed me a wicked evil smile and disappeared like he was never there.

I rushed out the door and ran to my mother's side. I fell beside her body and screamed some more.

A dark, red stain bloomed on the front of Mom's dress.

"Mom! Mommy!" I cried, and tears poured from my eyes.

My father ran out of the store and picked me up. "Olivia, get in the back—*now!*"

"But Mommy…" I blubbered.

"Now, Olivia. Go!" He pointed at the door. "Get in the back and stay there while I call the police."

He reached for his cell phone in his pocket.

"But…" I said, staring at my mom, who was groaning on the sidewalk.

"Now."

I raced inside, ran into the back, and huddled between two crates that had arrived last week. I pressed my hands to my ears as sirens wailed outside and people shouted. I didn't know how much time had passed until Papa returned to the shop.

He looked awful, with pale, sweaty skin and worried eyes.

A policeman came with him.

"Sweetheart? Are you back here?" Papa asked.

I whimpered from between the two crates.

"Oh, there you are. Officer Daily would like to ask you a question. Can you come out here?"

I scrunched my face, tears still streaming down my cheeks. "No!"

Footsteps clattered across the floor, and Papa crouched in front of me. "Sweetheart, you're safe. Officer Daily only has to ask you one or two questions, okay?"

I shook my head.

"Did you see who stabbed your mom?" Papa said.

I shook my head again. I didn't think I could explain how the evil man I witnessed could simply disappear, like smoke wisping into the air.

"Dearie, did you get a good look at him?" Officer Daily said.

I looked at Papa and shook my head once more.

"Come here." Papa opened his arms, and I rushed to him, hugging him tightly. "You're safe, sweetheart."

"But *Mommy*…" I wailed.

"The ambulance took her away. They're going to take good care of her." He turned toward the policeman. "My daughter's pretty traumatized. I think your questions will have to wait."

Officer Daily said something about, "If you think of anything or she tells you anything…" but I blotted out the rest.

I was terrified that the man who stabbed my mom would come for me next.

Papa said, "You must let go of me, Olivia, so I can show the policeman out."

"It's fine," Officer Daily said. "I'll see myself out. You take care of your little girl."

He strode away with clomping footsteps that echoed into the building.

Papa pried my arms from around his neck, stood, and took my hand. "I've got to make a phone call. Let's go into the office."

He led me into the small, windowless office where he and Mom did their paperwork.

I sat on one of the wooden chairs opposite the metal filing cabinets while Papa sat in front of the desk.

He pulled the green plastic phone toward him when it rang and answered.

"She what?" Papa asked after the voice on the other end spoke. He covered his eyes with his free hand, and his chest shuddered. When he removed his hand from his eyes, it looked like he was crying. "I can't believe this. This can't be happening."

He slammed the handset into the cradle with a crash.

Then, he lifted it again and dialed. "Moon Lee. I need you here right away. Alina's been killed."

I started to cry, too.

Within fifteen minutes, Lee's voice came from the front of the store.

I shuffled to the doorway and peeked around the corner.

Lee said, "What did you see?"

Papa said, "I didn't see anything. I was in the store, and Olivia was staring out the door waiting for Alina to take her for ice cream. Suddenly, Olivia screamed and rushed out the door. A moment later, I found Alina on the ground with blood pooling over her body and Olivia crying by her side. Lee, it happened so fast… Lee, you have to tell me, was Alina in any kind of danger? Did she have any enemies that would want to kill her?"

"I can't tell you that, Jack."

"What?" Papa said. "Why can't you tell me? You and Alina were always so close, closer than I was ever with my wife. You and your secret glances with each other. Holding secrets from me, and now she's dead, Lee, dead…gone forever….so I'm going to ask you again—was Alina in any kind of danger?"

"I can't tell you!" Lee said regarding my father with an impassive expression.

"Then, don't tell me." Papa's voice was getting louder like he was mad. "Keep your little secrets. But you're Olivia's godfather. Goddamn it, I'm going to need help raising her! I can't do it alone."

Lee said, "I have a plan. You've got to trust me."

"Why should I trust you?"

I began sobbing so hard I could barely hear a thing.

I only made out the phrases: "Why does Liv need to learn how to fight?" and, "Fine! You think it's important, so fine."

Papa and Lee stalked toward the back room.

Seeing me, Papa crouched and said, "Shh, sweetie, Lee's going to help us."

"I want my Mommy!" I wailed. *Where did my mommy go?* The thought of living without Mom brought a fresh wave of tears. I wanted to hide…run…wake up from this nightmare, throw my arms around my mom, and be comforted by her.

"I know, sweetheart, I know. Me, too." He glared at Lee.

Lee lowered himself to the floor. "Little Moon, listen to me." He pushed my hair away from my snot-covered face.

I took a shuddering breath and looked up at him.

"Do you trust me?" Lee said.

I nodded.

"Good. I'm going to train you to fight. You're going to have to work very hard. I couldn't save your mother, but at least I can try to save you."

CHAPTER TWO

OLIVIA

March 2019, 14 years later

Beads of sweat dripped down my face as I pummeled the boxing bag in the gym at Lee's cabin, deep in the Cougar Mountain woods near where my father lived. Slivers of sunlight forced their way through the jalousie windows that lined the top of the walls.

I'd been at it for over an hour. I was exhausted, but I couldn't stop. I hit left and right, striking my fists rhythmically against the white leather bag. This was a sport I couldn't live without. Ever since my mom was killed, I'd trained like this as often as I could. I had to protect myself and my father. The man who killed my mother could still be out there, waiting to strike when we least expected it.

Or, he could have killed others. Hence, my job was to train people of all ages to defend themselves and make weapons of whatever was available. I taught both groups of children and adults and private, one-on-one sessions.

No one should ever have to experience what my father and I went through.

When my arms and body were officially trashed, I dropped to the bench beside me. I wiped off my sweating face with the towel hanging around my neck. I grabbed my phone from my gym bag and noticed a missed call from my father.

How odd...he usually never calls me this early. Papa is more of a night owl, spending time with his research.

Panic overtook me, and my already thundering heart rate increased. I quickly unlocked my phone and dialed Papa.

"Hi, sweetheart," my father chirped.

I smiled, and my anxiety disappeared. "Good morning, Papa. How are you?"

"I'm doing well, honey. I'm just checking in on you." He paused a beat. "I, um, I thought maybe we could have breakfast today if you're not busy. I made all your favorites."

"That sounds great. I'll be there! What's the special occasion?"

"No special occasion, darling, just a lonely father that misses his only child and dearly wants to see her."

The delivery of his words was cheerful and warm, but something about his request gave me pause.

"Of course. I'll be there. I've got to shower first. Give me an hour, and I'll come over."

"Oh, honey, I'm glad to hear it. See you soon!"

I ended the phone call and headed for the shower. Having breakfast with my father was unusual. I usually had dinner with him or maybe lunch. But breakfast? We seldom had a morning meal together. I always woke up early for training and never had time for morning meals.

I finished the shower, dried myself, and put on my white sunflower dress. It was a favorite dress that always made me feel fresh and free. I grabbed my Glock 22 and strapped it against my thigh. I trained with many weapons, but the Glock 22 was my favorite gun.

I looked at myself in the mirror. The young woman staring back at me appeared capable and confident. Nodding, I thought, *Today's going to be a good day.*

After I climbed into my vehicle—a Forest Green Jeep Wrangler beast of a car—I affixed my mobile phone to a magnet on the dash. Then, I called my boyfriend, Tristan.

Tristan and I had been in a relationship for two years and were madly in love. I would have even gone so far as to call us soulmates. He was the perfect man: kind, sweet, strong, and classy, everything a girl wanted in a man. We were always together; we shared an apartment off 45th street. But this morning, he'd said he had to deal with something for his job as an Emergency Room Technician at Priority One Hospital.

"Good morning, beautiful," he said sweetly.

"Morning, babe." I fit the key in the ignition and powered it up. The engine roared to life with a satisfying growl.

"How was your workout this morning?" he asked.

"It was good. Muscles are destroyed, though, I'm afraid." Stepping on the gas pedal, I navigated down the dirt driveway and headed toward my father's house.

Tristan laughed a deep laugh that stirred my insides to steam. "I don't know how you do it. I'm always dying after our workouts while you seem ready for at least another hour."

I smiled as the Jeep lurched over the uneven terrain. "I must maintain my stamina to match you in other ways, hint, hint."

"Mmm, and you do it so well, babe," Tristan practically purred. "Why aren't you here?"

I frowned. "I thought you had to be at the hospital this morning."

"Would you believe I forgot my frigging work badge?" He made a tsking sound. "I had to drive all the way back here to get it. I'm heading out the door as we speak."

"Boy, that sucks. The traffic can be a bitch in the morning." Except for out here. There wasn't another car for miles.

After Mom died, Papa and Lee moved out of their apartments in Seattle. They settled in an isolated wooded area about thirty minutes from downtown Seattle. Neither could see the other's house, but I could get from one to the other via a quick jog through the forest.

"You got that right. So, what are you up to?" Tristan said.

"I'm heading to my father's for breakfast. He said he misses me."

The conversation paused.

"Did I lose you?" I said.

"No, sorry. Looking for my work badge," Tristan said.

I frowned. Didn't he just say he was heading out the door? "Tristan, you *always* leave it in the same place—on the side stand next to the bed. I saw it there when I left this morning."

"Did you?"

"Yes, did you lose your mind this morning?"

"I must have...I was in such a rush to get to work on time," he said. "And you're right—there it is."

"What a goof you are. Anyway, I've got to focus on the bumpy road here. I'll see you tonight," I said.

"Have a good time eating breakfast while I check in stab wounds and drunks," he said.

My voice softened when I said, "Love you, babe."

"Love you, too," he said in a husky voice.

When I arrived at my father's house, he was peppy and

warm, but something seemed off. I couldn't put my finger on it. But I noticed his hands trembled when he reached for a coffee mug from the cupboard.

I often worried about my father. So did Lee.

When I was a teen, Lee had told me Papa's mental health had always been fragile. So much so that Papa contemplated leaping from a clock tower window at McMont College in Vancouver, B.C. That's where he'd pursued his education in something he only vaguely hinted at over the years. Apparently, he'd presented a dissertation that wasn't well received. He'd been mocked and ridiculed.

People could be so mean.

"Keep an eye on your father, Olivia," Lee had told me. "Your mother saved him from ending his life—that's how they met and married. Now, it's your turn to watch over him."

I never knew what troubled Papa so much that made him want to end his life. Whenever I asked Lee, the only thing Lee would tell me was, "It's his story to tell, not mine."

"Are you all right, Papa?" I said, setting two chipped China plates on the small round table in his kitchen.

A pitcher of orange juice rested on a placemat in the middle of the table and a carafe of coffee.

"What, me?" he said, hurrying to the stove to flip the blueberry pancakes he was preparing. "Fine, fine, never better."

He donned an oven glove and reached in the oven to retrieve a plate of thick, fragrant bacon. "Nice and crispy, just the way you like it."

He waved the plate in front of my nose.

My stomach growled.

"You're such a tease, Papa," I said, grinning at him.

"Just a loving father," he said, setting the plate of bacon in the middle of the table. "Now, sit, sit—let's eat!"

I settled on one of the white-painted chairs, watching my dad as he hustled about the kitchen. His posture was slightly stooped, and his hair was thinning. He was a tall, medium-built man in his sixties, his hair more salt than pepper. Yet, his light blue eyes were always intelligent and aware, missing nothing. New wrinkles had formed on his face, but his mind was still as brilliant as when I was a child. His smile was as bright and warm as the sun.

It was almost painful to look at him sometimes. He seemed so vulnerable. So, I cast my gaze out his kitchen window.

An entire forest of redwoods, pines, and rhododendron bushes surrounded his modest home. Even though this house was near a bustling city, it was completely isolated, protected from prying eyes and passersby.

After Mom died, Papa had always blamed himself for not protecting her and keeping her safe. Fourteen years had passed since her death, but he'd never healed. Finding her killer had been his sole quest. He sold *Life after Life*, quit his university job, and basically withdrew from life in general, trying to solve the crime. The case closed five years ago due to a lack of evidence and not enough information. But I was certain Papa still hoped to avenge Mom's death.

"Here we go," he said, turning away from the stove with a platter of blueberry pancakes. He set the platter in the center of the table and sat down opposite me, smiling. "Help yourself."

I forked several pancakes and strips of bacon and helped myself to some OJ and coffee. Then, I proceeded to shovel food into my ravenous mouth.

"Aren't you going to eat?" I said, between bites of food.

"Oh, I'll nibble a bit." Papa reached for a piece of bacon, broke it in two, and took a bite. "How's your training going?"

"Good, good," I said, shoveling down the food. "Lee's got me on a new cross-training regime. It's kicking my butt."

"Good, that's good. And you're still with your boyfriend?"

I swallowed and glared at him. "Of course, I'm still with him. Why do you ask?"

"Honey, you know I don't like him. He's not a good fit for you. I think he's dangerous," Papa said.

A bemused laugh left my throat. "Dangerous? Hardly. He's the guy who preps patients with gashes, broken bones, and head injuries. I'd say he's more of a hero."

Frowning, Papa stared at his plate.

"Look, I know he's not your favorite, but I adore him." Anger tightened my throat. "And you didn't have me over for breakfast so you could lecture me about my choice in men, did you?"

"Lee agrees with me," Papa said.

I felt as if the wind had been punched from my lungs. Lee was my mentor, trusted adviser, and best friend. "Lee's always nice to Tristan. They even train together."

"He thinks there's something off about your boyfriend. He can't put his finger on it, but something doesn't sit right with him."

"Oh, come on…you got Lee to agree with your jealousy over the time I spend with my *boyfriend?*"

"I'm not jealous. You're a good daughter—the best. You see me all the time, and I cherish each moment," Papa said, his gaze softening. "I just want you to be careful, that's all."

He fell silent and stared out the window.

On the way over here, my phone conversation with Tristan slid through my mind. *He did sound sort of off or something. But dangerous? No.*

I shook my head and focused on my father.

"What's really going on, Papa?" Reining in my anger, I reached across the small table and placed my palm on his bony knuckles.

His head pivoted to meet my gaze. "I invited you here for a different reason."

I paused my fork's progress on the way to my mouth. "Which is…?"

"I've got to tell you something I've never told you before," he said.

I rested my forkful of pancake on my plate. "I don't like the sound of this."

He captured my gaze with his clear, blue eyes. "I haven't always studied history or worked with antiques. My greatest passion was something different."

I chuckled. "So, that's your big revelation?" I picked up my fork of blueberry deliciousness and lifted it to my mouth. "You had me worried," I said through the bite of pancake.

Then, I dragged my finger through the remaining syrup on my plate and popped it in my mouth.

A thud whacked the window. Startled, my head whipped toward the direction of the sound. A snap and crackle of branches followed the whack.

I stood and crossed to the window, peering outside to see what had caused the sudden noise. *Probably a crow who now has a king-sized headache.*

"This isn't funny, Olivia," Papa said in that stern voice he got when he needed to explain something to me.

"Okay. Tell me what you used to do that you never told me." I leaned against the windowsill.

"Before I tell you, I want you to promise me to understand and accept."

I looked at my father. "I will try my best to understand and listen."

"I studied time travel," he said.

My eyebrows arched. "That's interesting."

"I spent my whole life studying it. I have a theory about how it works. I won't bore you with the details, but according to my research, there's a collision of black holes at the time of a solar eclipse. If a baby is born at that instance, they become a Timeborne and can time travel."

"Okay, and you're telling me this because…?"

"Because, honey, twenty-four years ago, on November 3rd, 1994, you were born during the solar eclipse. Two black holes collided the instant you were born. You are a Timeborne, Olivia."

"You want me to believe that I was born during the solar eclipse and that I can time travel?" I let out a laugh. "Good one, Papa."

He glared at me.

"Papa, this is insanity and madness. Time travel is impossible, and I think you have officially lost your mind."

"It's true," he said. "I spent my whole life studying time travel. How can you doubt me? I'm your father."

"I know you're my father, but you've never been the same since Mom's been gone. You shut yourself away from the world and stopped teaching. I think these four walls have made you go crazy and paranoid, creating time travel fantasy stories in your head."

"I'm shocked, Olivia, with your tone and attitude. I didn't expect the outcome to be like this at all. Before I started telling you all of this, I asked you to understand and accept." Papa balled his hands into fists on the table.

"And I promised you to understand and listen," I said coolly. "But I didn't mention anything about accepting. I'm sorry, Papa; I don't mean to hurt or offend you. I just can't believe what you're saying."

"Go to Lee and ask him." Papa pointed toward the window. "He knows everything. He will support my story, and you will know I was right."

"I won't go to Lee and ask him to validate your story, Papa because I'm sure you told him to play along for me to believe it." I puffed up my chest like a cat in a catfight.

"You're tearing my soul into a million pieces right now. I feel like I'm reliving my 1988 dissertation day again." Papa dragged his hand through his hair.

"Then why tell me this today at of all days?" My father's face became stone cold when I said the last sentence.

I tried a different tactic.

"Why didn't the doctors and nurses say something?" Another chuckle left my mouth.

"There were no doctors or nurses," he said flatly. "You were born in a cave…in Peru."

"Wait, what?" I repeatedly blinked, trying to understand what he was telling me. "I was born in a cave?"

"Yes. At the apex of the eclipse. Your mother was searching for an artifact in La Cueva del Fuego. She fell and hit her head, and her water broke. I think it was a moment of destiny—you weren't supposed to be born for another month. But, yes, you were born at the solar eclipse."

I placed my palms on the table. I was stunned at what he was telling me. "Have you been drinking again?"

"No! I haven't touched a drop in months!" He rose and began clearing the table.

I bolted to my feet and grabbed plates and silverware. "So, why are you telling me this crazy story right now?"

I practically threw the dishes in the stainless-steel sink, where they landed with a clatter.

"Because Lee and I think you're in danger," he said, placing our coffee mugs on the counter with a loud whack.

"You and Lee, huh? And you didn't think to come to me and say, 'you're in danger, Liv, and we think it's your boyfriend. Oh, and you're a time traveler.'" I glared at my father.

"What do you think I'm doing now?" he said, his hands trembling.

"You're whacked—both of you." I seized more dishes from the table and took them to the sink. They banged and tinkled against one another as I unceremoniously dumped them.

"Ask him! Go ask Lee yourself!!" Dad pointed toward the door.

"I'll do that," I said.

"Then, go. No one ever believes me. But everyone believes in Lee. He could tell you the sky was made of ice cream, and you'd believe him!" Papa was shouting.

He never shouted at me.

"Why are you doing this, Papa?" My anger warred with grief. I'd never fought with my father, and I didn't like it.

"Because you need to know the truth," he said, the fiercest gaze I'd ever seen emanating from his eyes. "Now go and talk to Lee. Before it's too late."

I'd never heard him talk to me like this. My mom? Sure. He and Mom would have these heated debates, but they always kissed and made up. I stared at him, my heart hurting and my mind swamped with confusion. Shaking my head, I tried to form a meaningful sentence to add to this conversation. I came up blank. Finally, I said, "Thanks for breakfast."

Then, I whirled and headed toward the door.

"Wait!" Papa called.

When I turned to look at him, Papa bolted from his chair, moving with a speed that belied his age.

"What am I waiting for?" I asked, threads of suspicion pulling at my mind.

Papa disappeared into his back rooms. When he returned, he clutched several small leather-bound books. "Here," he said, thrusting the books into my hands.

"What are these?" I said, my brows furrowed.

"They're my journals. I've kept logs ever since I was in college. If you read them, maybe then you'll believe me. Take them home and read them. *Please*, Olivia. I'm begging you."

I squinted at my father, thinking he must have started drinking again. But, deciding to play along, I took the journals. I'd never read them—it just felt too personal.

CHAPTER THREE

OLIVIA

Sitting in my Jeep in my father's driveway, I pounded on the steering wheel. I felt ambushed by both my father and Lee—the two men who had raised me. *What the hell? They both dislike my boyfriend? I know Papa does, but now Lee? Is Papa making up a story to justify his own feelings? And Papa thinks I'm a time traveler? He's lost his frigging mind!*

I was too angry to speak to either of them.

I glanced at the journals by my side. I was afraid to open them. Would I discover the ravings of my father's unstable mental health? Or was he telling the truth?

I powered up my vehicle and drove along the tree-lined driveway, heading for the streets of Seattle. Driving usually calmed me down, so I meandered through the back roads and neighborhoods, aimless in my wanderings. I could have headed back to Lee's underground dojo to train. I was a fighter, trained to teach others to fight. No one should have to experience what I went through as a child. But I was too angry to even do that at the moment.

Why would my parents tell me I was born in a hospital

when I was really born in a cave in Peru? That's sort of a remarkable story. Gives me street cred, you know? A sarcastic chuckle left my lips.

When I arrived in Fremont, a funky, former-hippy, now-somewhat gentrified neighborhood, the traffic stopped.

"What the fuck?" I muttered, still pissed at my father and Lee. But then I saw it: there was a street fair ahead, closing off the main street through this district.

I searched for a parking spot and found one, intending to wander through the booths and maybe distract myself from my lingering sour mood.

White and gray canopies occupied both sides of the street, with vendors selling organic honey, homemade jerky, colorful baby hats, and tie-dyed skirts and T-shirts. No one had worn this kind of hippie attire since before I was born.

Why do they always sell it at street fairs? Trying to offload fifty-year-old inventory?

In a million years, I'd never be caught dead in a flowing skirt and T-shirt covered with swirling colors. When I was not dressed in workout attire, I was usually in jeans and Henleys.

As I examined all the crip-crap for sale, my mood improved. I turned away from a booth selling jewelry made from ocean glass and spotted Lee, dressed in Levi's and a long-sleeved Western shirt, his arms full of bags of organic produce.

He saw me and brightened. "Hey, you! What are you doing on this side of town?"

I covered my abdomen with my arms and said, "I could ask you the same thing. What are you doing out of the woods? You seem to never leave your sanctuary."

He hefted the bags he was holding. "My pal Charley grows the best damn produce. If I know he's here, I always stop by."

I glanced at the dark-green lettuce, vibrant red peppers, and vivid orange carrots poking from the top of one of the bags.

"Huh," I said, my bad mood creeping back into my mind.

"Why the gloomy look?" Lee's face crinkled.

"Are you and my father trying to double-team me?"

Lee's forehead furrowed. "Double-team you?"

He stepped to the side as a mother, two kids, and a baby carriage tried to squeeze through the crowd.

"About my boyfriend… how you both think he's dangerous. And some cockamamie idea about how I might be a time traveler. I think you both consumed mushrooms last night and are still tripping." I tightened my grip on my stomach.

Lee's eyes softened. "Your father is going through a lot. It's the anniversary of your mother's murder."

"Oh," I said, stepping backward. Lee was right. She died on this very day, March 18th. I rarely thought about it, having shoved it into a trunk in my mind and buried it. "I forgot."

"Your father never forgets, Little Moon," he said, using his pet nickname for me since I was born in November during the Little Winter Moon of his people. He transferred one of the bags to his left hand and reached out to pat my shoulder with his right.

"I got into an argument with him, thinking you two were trying to make me crazy," I said, guilt winding its way through my insides like a poisonous snake.

"We both love you." He shifted the white plastic sack he had just moved back into his right hand so he was carrying a balanced load.

"And you don't think Tristan is dangerous?" I said.

"Tristan is becoming a lethal weapon with his training," Lee said, evading the answer. "As are you."

"But you don't think he's dangerous to me, right?" I said, suddenly insecure.

"Hello!" Lee called over my shoulder. "There's an old friend of mine. I've got to say hello to him. I haven't seen him for ages. See you at the gym tomorrow."

"Okay, yes, see you," I said, but he was already moving past me to get to his friend. Shaking my head at his vague answers, I continued to wander.

At the end of the row stood a tent with a sign out front saying, *Psychic Readings. See your past, present, and future.*

"Stupid," I muttered as I approached, intending to walk across the Fremont bridge and look down at the water.

A blonde woman pushed aside the tent flap, her eyes all shiny and bright.

"She's good," she said, stabbing her thumb toward the tent. "If you have any unanswered questions, she'll tell it true."

"Huh," I said, unconvinced.

"You should try it," the blonde said.

It was probably her job to reel in the unsuspecting.

"No, thanks," I said.

"Suit yourself." Blondie shrugged and scurried in the opposite direction from where I was headed.

The tent flap pushed open, and a woman wearing a long-tie-dyed skirt and T-shirt emerged. And here I thought no one wore those kinds of clothes.

I almost laughed. The tie-dyed stand probably stayed alive by selling its wares to other vendors.

The woman pushed back her lengthy, black wavy hair and said, "Would you like a reading?"

Her mascara gave her crazy long lashes that framed her blue-gray eyes.

"Nope," I said with a shake of my head.

The woman was nearly a foot shorter than me. She tipped her head and said, "I'm Aurora, and I can sense you're a skeptic."

She grinned.

"It doesn't take a psychic to determine that half of the people here are skeptics. They're the ones who walk right by your tent," I said with a wave of my hand.

"Walking past my tent doesn't make them a skeptic. It simply means they don't want a reading at this time. Come on in. I'll only charge you half." She inclined her head toward the tent.

"No," I said. "Not interested. Skeptic, remember?"

I started to step past her tent when she said, "I'll tell you something about the man you're going to marry."

And there it was—the perfect cast with the hook landing firmly in the flesh of my cheek. "Fine, but I've only got a few bucks in my pocket."

Aurora shrugged, lifted the tent flap, and waited for me to enter.

I made my way inside the dimly lit tent. In the center sat a small, round table covered with a red tablecloth. A stack of large, colorful cards rested in the middle while two wooden chairs faced one another. Everything about this scene looked like a caricature of what a fortune teller's tent should look like.

Smirking, I sat down.

Aurora sat opposite me and reached for the cards. She shuffled them deftly, like a Las Vegas dealer. Then, she tapped them and placed them in the center of the table, saying, "Cut them, please."

I accommodated her request.

She reached for them again and laid out three cards. Her

hands fumbled as she laid out the third card, and a fourth card fell on the table.

"Oh!" she exclaimed. "A modifier to the spread."

She glanced at me and then directed her attention to the cards. With one long painted nail, she tapped the card to her left.

"This one is the Tower. Its meaning is about upheaval, chaos, and disaster."

My heart clenched as I remembered the day Mom died—that day I never wanted to think about.

"Yes," I said in a strangled voice. "I've had some upheaval in my life."

Aurora picked another card from the deck and laid it on the tower. "Someone close to you died—your mother, I think?"

My eyes narrowed. She's just guessing, right?

"Maybe…" I said as tears pricked my eyes. "Okay, yes."

Aurora leaned under the table and retrieved a box of tissues. She scooted the box in my direction, and I plucked several, dabbing at my eyes.

Then, she tapped the middle card. "This one represents the Moon. See how it's upside down?"

I nodded.

"This position means you're in a period of confusion, fear, and misinterpretation." She picked up the depiction of a moon over a silvery lake and handed it to me.

I stared at it, thinking of the things my father had just told me and the things that Lee had said.

Which one is telling me the truth? Is Papa just grieving today? Or is Papa right that I was born in a cave and can time travel?

The idea seemed preposterous, so I shook my head and waited for Aurora to continue with her reading. When she didn't speak, I blurted, "Okay, so I'm confused about things. I mean, who isn't from time to time, am I right?"

I forced a laugh.

"I'm only the messenger, not the message." She studied the card to her right. "Now this card…this represents The Wheel of Fortune. Its meaning is that of change, cycles, and inevitable fate. This is a good card because it means something big is about to happen. The modifier that flipped out is the Lovers card. There's a man you're associated with or will associate with who will bring you love, marriage, and happiness. And this man is powerful and fierce. He is a warrior—a strong and fearless man."

"That must be Tristan!" I said, sitting up tall.

My father and his foolish notions…

Aurora picked two more cards from the pile next to her. She placed one between the Wheel of Fortune and the Lovers and one to the Lovers' right.

"Here we have the Five of Wands. The Five of Wands represents conflict, competition, and tension. There will be a difficult journey to get to the marriage, but you'll get there." A smile flickered across her face. "The three main cards I picked are Major Arcana. They denote major life events. The Five of Wands is as fleeting as an emotion. But the difficulty the Five of Wands speaks of will occur."

"That makes sense," I said, nodding. "My father doesn't like my boyfriend, but he'll come around. Tristan is a good, good man."

Aurora leveled me with her gaze but said nothing. Then, she focused on the card to the right of the Wheel of Fortune. "Ah, the King of Cups. It seems you have a father who is good and true. He loves you wholeheartedly and is warm and kind. He represents the modifier to the Lovers card and to the

Wheel of Fortune. He's closely aligned to your fate and to your choice of partners."

I frowned. *Is this whacko saying I'm to listen to Papa and his thoughts of Tristan and danger?* I scoffed. How stupid was this to be caught up in the musings of a fortune-teller?

My attention was drawn to the sweat trickling down my neck and the cloying, musty scent of this dumb little tent. And, whatever this fake seer said, one thing was true—my Papa was a good man who didn't deserve my anger. Papa *was* probably just having a tough day. He had never been able to let Mom go.

I pushed away from the table and fished in my dress pocket, retrieving a ten and a one.

"Here," I said, flipping the cash on the table. "It's all I've got."

Then, without giving her a second glance, I pushed my way out into the fresh air and the scents of cinnamon rolls and pizza wafting from the vendors' tents.

I'll head back to Cougar Mountain and apologize to him.

I shoved through the crowds to return to my Jeep and climbed in. Papa's journals, resting on the passenger seat, seemed alive, drawing my attention.

I picked up the first one, which had been warmed by the hot sun in the closed cab. I skimmed the first few pages, reading something about Papa's dissertation in front of a group of distinguished academics.

Papa had written, in 1905 Albert Einstein proposed the theory of special relativity. This theory suggests that photons can travel through space at a constant pace of three-hundred thousand kilometers per second. Not only is this speed challenging to achieve, but it's also impossible to surpass. Yet, across space, particles are accelerating. Then, in 1915, Einstein proposed the theory of general relativity, where gravity curves space and time, and time slows or speeds relative to how fast you move.

So, given these two theories, I've also been studying solar eclipses. These new scientific studies show that two black holes can collide during a solar eclipse. That's the critical moment. And, if a child is born at that significant time during impact, they can travel through time. It's like a gift that's bestowed on them.

A solar eclipse is a mystery to us all. How can the sun and moon connect for a few minutes, immersing us in complete darkness? It only happens every hundred years, and people worldwide wait for and wish to see how the sun and moon join. But imagine if a child, a small infant, was born during the solar eclipse when these two black holes collide. That child would have the ability to time travel. But...! There was a catch. The collision of the black holes also creates an evil power. It was up to the Timeborne to destroy and cleanse the world from the evil born with it.

I looked up from the words, anxiety chewing holes in my stomach. This was worse than I'd imagined. My father was literally insane.

I forced myself to read some more.

Many different nations and cultures believe in this idea and wait for a Timeborne to appear and show to everyone that time travel does truly exist and is possible. The Native Americans believe that their ancestors witnessed Timebornes and the ensuing evil many years ago. The Mayans and Incas witnessed the birth of a child during that critical moment when the eclipse occurred. The child born during this event can time travel during each full moon.

"Oh, my God," I whispered. "Papa." I slammed the journal shut and picked up another one. In this one, my gaze landed on an entry that read, *Peru, 1994. Alina is searching for a sacred artifact. She will be one of the archaeologists presenting at the Archeology Summit in France at the end of the year. She wants something meaningful to contribute, like the importance of the carved cat deities or humans with animal faces found at the Chavín excavation one-hundred and fifty miles east of where we were standing. I've insisted on accompanying her. Someone has to protect her—she's pregnant with our child!*

A shiver shook my backbone. *Mom was pregnant with me in Peru!* My hands shook so hard I had to rest the book in my lap.

Sweat trickled down my neck in my sweltering Jeep. I rolled down the windows and kept reading.

With this entry, I am gazing down at my beautiful child. We have named her Olivia, and she is perfect. Her birth was most extraordinary. As fate would have it, she was born during the solar eclipse in a cave. Funny thing. Lee contacted Alina via short-wave radio before the blessed event. He told her he'd been in a sacred ceremony with his people. The short-wave connection wasn't very good, however. The sound echoed with high-pitched feedback. The words "my ancestors," "ancient artifact," and "la Cueva del Fuego" were discernible, but nothing else.

"So, I'm to search for artifacts in the cave of fire?" Alina had said.

"Yes, yes," Lee said, coming through loud and clear. "Look in la Cueva del Fuego. That is where you are to search."

So, we headed for the mountains as the moon rose in the sky. Alina didn't want to wait.

Inside the cave, Alina's foot caught on a rock, and she tumbled to the ground, her head striking the wall. Alina had been having what she called "Braxton-Hicks" contractions all afternoon. I suspected they were the real thing, and I'd been right. Alina started yelling and crying out with the pain of the contractions. While I tended to Alina's wound, the entrance of the cave, which should have been lit by the dim glow of the full moon, became utterly dark.

And our dear, sweet angel, Olivia, was born at the apex of the solar eclipse. She is a Timeborne! And, if that isn't miracle enough, a black dagger fell near Alina when Olivia arrived. A black-hilted knife with symbols inscribed on both the blade and the handle. It is a wonder.

But now Alina and I are fighting again. She is telling me to stop spewing nonsense to her about time travel and my preposterous theories. She wants me to keep the dagger as far away from her as possible. She says we need to consult with Lee.

I flipped a few pages with shaking fingers. Here I read, we consulted with Lee when we arrived back in the states. Lee took the dagger, saying he needed to look after it. He and my wife kept exchanging looks and glancing at me as if I were insane. I know I am of sound mind.

I pressed my hand to my mouth. Even my mother did not believe Papa. I thumbed ahead and found a passage about Lee getting back to my parents after a month.

Lee told me, "At the time of the full moon if the dagger cuts Olivia's skin, she can travel."

This was huge news! All my research was finally coming to life!

Lee stated, "The cutting of flesh with the uttering of sacred words on the knife will take the Timeborne to another time and century. But it will also release the darkness." Lee insisted on taking the dagger and hiding it away. And we never spoke of it again.

I couldn't read any more of my father's mad ravings. I

shoved the journals to the Jeep floor and pressed my hand to my forehead. I had to go back and check on my father. He had lost his grip on reality if he thought I was a time traveler and Tristan was dangerous.

Forty minutes later, I turned up Papa's tree-lined drive-way. Hopping out of the seat, I hurried toward the house, twirling my keys around my fingertip as I trekked across the slate stones for the front door.

I walked into the darkened house. *How odd. Papa likes to have lights on.* "Papa?"

"He's in here," said a familiar voice.

Chills rippled down my spine as I sprinted toward the front room.

My father sat shivering on the sofa while Tristan, the love of my life, held a gun to Papa's head.

CHAPTER FOUR

OLIVIA

My boyfriend, my heart of hearts, the guy I dreamed of marrying someday, held a gun to my father's head. This couldn't be real.

"Tristan," I said, my voice rushing out in a panicked whisper. "What are you doing?"

Tristan grinned. I'd never seen a look like this on his gorgeous face. Not when we were making love or working out, not when he was mad about something...*never*. It was like I was looking at someone evil—someone *so not* Tristan.

"Baby, stop...Put the gun down...*please*." I glanced at my father, who was trembling on his worn, battered sofa in his living room with books and papers strewn everywhere.

"Not happening, *babe*," Tristan said in an ugly voice. "Your father finally said the words I've been waiting to hear."

"What...what words are those?" I stammered.

I could take down a two-hundred-pound muscle-bound man with one kick or kill a man with a blow to his upper lip, ramming the heel of my hand into his brain. But, as I stood in front of Tristan, who held a gun to my father's head, I felt as helpless as a newborn kitten.

"Tell her, old man." Tristan whacked the side of my father's head with the butt of his Glock.

Papa winced as he jerked.

I cried out, lunging for my father.

Tristan whipped the gun in my direction. "Don't. Move."

"Okay, okay." I threw my hands up, palms facing Tristan. "Tell me what my father said."

Blood seeped from the gash in Papa's head and trickled down the side of his face.

"You're a Timeborne, Olivia." Papa's voice emerged all shaky and weak.

"A…a Timeborne…That's the term for a time traveler," I said, my mouth growing dry.

"And you're going to bring me the dagger, and we're going to time travel tonight, *sweetheart*." Tristan sneered, and suddenly his thick dark hair, lush lashes surrounding his sapphire-blue eyes, and his muscular physique all repulsed me.

A dagger. Papa wrote about a mysterious blade.

"I don't know anything about a dagger," I said, still holding my palms out.

"Tell her," Tristan said with a snarl at my father. He whipped the gun about as if to backhand my father again.

"Stop!" I cried as Papa winced and shielded his face with his arms.

Already, Papa's temple was swollen and purple.

"Tell her," Tristan yelled again.

"When you were born…in the cave in Peru…a dagger appeared by your mother's side," Papa said. He side-eyed Tristan before continuing. "It's black as night and covered with ancient symbols. Your mother insisted we take it to Lee for confirmation about your abilities as a Timeborne. He took it to his people, and they confirmed what I suspected. It's true, Liv. You can travel through time."

I staggered backward, unable to process what was happening. These were all the ravings from his journal. And my father believed them.

I focused on Tristan. "How did you... How did you hear us?"

"You told me you were going to have breakfast here, so I came straight over and hid in the woods," Tristan said. "I hoped that's what your father wanted to tell you since tonight is the full moon."

"You spied on us?" My jaw dropped open.

"I've been spying on you for five years." Using his free hand, he fished in his coat pocket and retrieved a small recording device. "But today, I wanted to hear it firsthand."

He pressed play, and the conversation Papa and I had this morning streamed into the air.

The part where I heard something smack against the window gave me pause.

"That was you outside the window?" I said.

"Yeah. I thought I'd blown my cover. Especially when you walked to the window and looked around. That's when I thought I was screwed," Tristan said, smirking.

"How did you...?" I began.

"Break into your father's home to plant a listening device? Simple, sugar. Your old man has these crying spells...They exhaust him, and he drinks, then he falls into a dead drunk sleep." Tristan coughed up a laugh.

"I haven't...not for weeks, Olivia, I swear it," Papa said.

"I'm so sorry I didn't believe you this morning, Papa," I said.

My head was swirling from everything: the news that I

could supposedly time travel; the evil lurking in my apparently good-guy boyfriend; Lee and Papa holding secrets from me for all these years…

"I should have told—" Papa started to say.

"Shut the fuck up, Jack," Tristan hissed. "Now's not the time for hearts and flowers and kissy-kissy boohoos. You're a weak man."

Papa started to cry, and my heart shattered.

Tristan cocked the gun and clocked my father in the face.

I lunged for Tristan's arm. He wheeled and shoved the barrel in my chest.

"Don't think I won't fucking pull it, Liv," he said, looking at me with cold, dead eyes. "Stand up. *Now!*"

My mind whirled. How fast can I get to my Glock? I can shoot this asshole and be done with it.

Tristan rose and hustled to stand behind me as if reading my mind. He pressed his gun to my temple, then slid his hand down my side. When he reached the hem of my skirt, he tugged it up.

"Surprise, surprise. I know you so well," he whispered in my ear.

I shuddered. This was the man who just last night made passionate love to me, whispering terms of endearment in my ear.

I was just about ready to shove my elbow into his ribcage and break a few ribs, but he said, "Don't try anything, or you're dead, your father's dead, and then I'll go for Lee."

I stilled as he unbuckled my thigh holster, and the Glock fell to the ground. He let his hand linger at my inner thigh.

I wanted to vomit at the touch.

He kicked the gun out of the way and said, "Sit."

When I complied, tentatively perching on a kitchen chair, he loomed over me, saying, "Yeah, yeah, you can kick my ass and all that. But not this time. You try anything with me, even the little stunt you just tried, and your father eats the first bullet. You'll be next, got it?"

"Understood," I said through gritted teeth. "Papa, where's this dagger?"

"I don't know," he said, his cheek red and swelling. "You'll have to ask Lee. He swore to hide it and keep it, and you, safe."

I let out a growl. "You know Lee has no use for a mobile phone. I'm going to have to confront him in person."

"Do it." Tristan waved the Glock at the door.

"Don't you touch a single hair on my father's head while I'm gone," I said.

With a hesitant glance at my father, I pushed to my feet and left, running toward my Jeep. I was inside that vehicle, gravel spraying, before I could shut the door.

Once I reached Lee's, I slammed the brakes, skidded to a stop, and leaped from the driver's seat.

"Lee!" I called, with my hands cupped around my mouth. "Moon Lee! Where are you?"

"Little Moon?"

His voice came from outside, around back, so that's where I headed.

I found him out in the back, chopping wood. Although he was in his late sixties, like my father, his body was firm and virile as he hauled back his arms and swung the ax, splitting the logs in two.

"Little Moon," he said when he saw me. As usual, his Grizzley tooth necklace was in place around his neck.

I'd always been captivated by that tooth with its long, spidery crack running the length of it.

"Lee," I said. "I need the crazy dagger everyone is looking for, *now*."

"What? Why? What's going on?" Lee said.

"Tristan's holding my father hostage, and he will kill him. He wants the knife so he can time travel with me."

"Tristan knows about the dagger and time travel? Who is he really?" Lee said. He rested the ax next to the stump he was using to split the logs. "Is he working with the darkness? Does he have connections with the government? I knew something was off about him."

Lee was spouting everything my father had written about. Could it all be true?

"Lee…Lee. Now's not the time to sort out who Tristan is. He's got a gun to Papa's head as we speak. Are you or are you not going to give me the dagger?"

"It's somewhere safe," he said, his gaze sliding back and forth.

"Well, give it to me!" I thrust out my palm.

"I…I can't…I don't remember where I stashed it. It's somewhere in the mountains," he said, his eyes still shifting back and forth.

I threw back my head and groaned. Something about what he said didn't make sense. If this dagger was so sacred, how could he not remember where he'd put it?

"Are you fucking kidding me? How long will it take to get it?" My father could be dead by the time Lee produced the knife.

"I…Wait. It might be around here somewhere…" He cupped his chin as he pondered, then he snapped his fingers. "Oh, I remember. Come with me."

I followed Lee as he crept across the leaves and debris toward his humble cabin. Still muttering about Tristan, he headed for the small room he called his antique store. It was chock full of antiques from Mom and Papa's old *Life after Life* store and Native American artifacts.

He'd told me that he made a sale or two over the years, but I didn't believe him—no one ever came out here. Inside the room, he wandered about, opening drawers and searching on shelves.

I was aghast. "This supposedly sacred knife has been right under my nose the entire time? And no one thought it might be useful to tell me about it?"

"We were trying to keep you safe, Little Moon." He hefted a pile of old books and said, "Open this box, please."

I crossed to where he stood and pried open the dusty wooden box. Inside, there was an old iron knife. "That's it? That's the knife?"

Lee nodded.

I picked up the beat-up-looking blade and examined it. Then, I squinted at Lee. *Is he lying?* Nothing looked particularly remarkable about the weapon in my hand. "And this will make Tristan or me time travel?"

"Yes. Take it." He waved his hands at me and glanced past my shoulder at the window. "The moon will soon be rising."

I turned and lifted my gaze to the sky. Sure enough, the top of the full moon peeked through the trees beneath a darkening sky.

"Thank you," I said, grabbing the knife.

I raced to my Jeep as Lee called, "Be safe, Little Moon!"

I didn't care about my own safety—I only cared about my father's. Driving at a reckless speed, I raced back to Papa's house.

Once in the driveway, I slammed the brakes again. The tires crunched, sending gravel flying.

I tossed the knife on the passenger seat, opened the glove box, and removed another gun. I leaped from the driver's seat and strapped the weapon to my thigh. *Tristan thinks he knows me so well.* Once my gun was strapped to my thigh, I sprinted into my father's house.

My father sat shivering on the sofa, but Tristan was nowhere to be seen.

"Where is he?" I hissed to Papa.

He inclined his head toward the kitchen. The left side of his face was all bruised and bloody.

Tristan sat at the kitchen table, a bottle of Jack Daniels and a partially full tumbler of amber liquid before him. His gun rested on the table near the whiskey.

"I don't know where your Pa keeps the good stuff, so this will have to do." He lifted the glass and tipped the contents into his mouth.

"I've got your dagger," I said, keeping my distance.

"Do you? Show me." He poured another finger of whiskey into his glass.

"Not until you untie Papa."

Tristan flashed me a narrow-eyed glare. "You're in no position to negotiate it."

"Wanna bet?" My hands balled into fists by my side.

Tristan licked his lips as he studied me. "Have a seat. We have to do the ritual at midnight. We have a few hours to wait."

"I don't want to sit with you," I said. "I'd rather be with my father."

Tristan picked up the gun and pointed it at me. "Sit. Down."

I grabbed the edge of the chair opposite him and pulled it away from the table. I was sitting as far away as possible from this son of a bitch.

Still pointing the gun, Tristan stood and backed toward the cupboard. He glanced behind him, opened the cabinet, and reached for a glass. His head whipped around to face me again. He stepped to the table and set the glass down. With his left hand, he poured whiskey into the glass. Then, he stepped behind me, held the gun to my temple, and said, "Scoot your pretty ass up to the table so we can have a proper drink together, *babe.*"

Huffing out a sigh, I dragged my chair forward.

Tristan waved the gun at the tumbler of whiskey. "Drink."

I seized the glass and tossed the burning liquid down my throat.

"Good girl. I love the way you can hold your liquor. Have another."

"No. And I haven't been a girl for a long time, *boy.*"

"I said, have another drink." He pulled the trigger on the Glock, and a bullet exploded into the floor near my leg.

I shrieked. *Is this guy a psycho, or what?* My hand shook as I poured another glass of whiskey.

"Down the hatch, babe," he said, resting the gun barrel beneath my chin.

With the cool metal against my skin, I took the glass and tossed it back.

"That's the Olivia I know," he said. Then, he sauntered around the table and sat. "Isn't this fun? I always loved to drink with you."

"I wouldn't call it fun. I pressed my palms against the table, trying to stave off the woozy feeling in my head from two quick shots of whiskey.

"Oh, right, right, you're a feminist. I forgot." He chuckled and poured himself another drink.

"What was all that lovemaking we did? Why did you tell me things like how special I was to you?"

"You were special at one point, but duty comes first. I had a job to do, and my job was to watch you. To make things look real, I had to play the part." His face bore no expression.

"You had a job to do? What kind of job?" The thought of anyone putting out a hit on me slammed through me like a punch to the gut.

A cold smile stretched across his face.

"So, you used me and never really loved me?" My heart splintered.

He shrugged.

I felt used like I was a pawn in his twisted game.

At some point, he plucked his phone from his pocket and stared at the screen. "Let's go. Where's the dagger?"

"In my Jeep," I said. My head swam with the drink.

"Go get it," he said. "I've got to take a leak."

I calculated my next move. I could so quickly disarm Tristan—he was drunk. But so was I, and my movements would be sloppy. I couldn't afford to make mistakes. Not when Papa's life was on the line.

"Are you going to release my father?"

"Of course. We'll take your father into the woods to watch what he's waited for his whole life." Tristan laughed. "My God, he's babbled about time travel non-stop for years. He's obsessed with it. I'm surprised he never mentioned it to you."

He took a couple staggering steps and laughed. "Whoo, baby, am I drunk, or what?"

I was so done with this game. My leg whipped out in a roundhouse kick. Tristan sobered too quickly and shot the gun, taking out my father's kitchen window in an explosion of glass.

"Stop fucking around, Olivia or your father's a dead man."

"Olivia!" Papa called. "Are you okay?"

My ears rang from the gunshot. "I'm fine, Papa. I'm

going to go get the dagger and give it to Tristan, and then this will all be over."

Papa sobbed. "I'm so sorry, sweetheart. I should have told you years ago."

"Papa, stop. No regrets. We'll be out of this mess soon, I promise." Keeping my gaze pinned on Tristan, I inched toward the door. "I thought you needed to use the bathroom."

"I lied," he said in a calm, clear voice. "Now, go. I'll meet you out in the woods."

I was furious as I staggered toward my Jeep in the dark. How could this be happening? And, me, a time traveler? No way. I had to be in the worst nightmare of my life, and I hoped I would wake up soon.

"Get a move on, old man," Tristan shouted at my father.

I glanced over my shoulder to see them coming toward me.

Tristan was holding Papa's arm and waving the Glock in his other hand.

I retrieved the dagger from the seat and gripped it tightly. As I approached Tristan and my father, Tristan's gaze fell to the blade in my hand.

His eyes glittered with greed. "So, that's it?"

My father glanced at the knife and frowned.

"Yes," I said. "I'm going to exchange it for my father when we're away from the house."

Tristan's eyes narrowed, but then he turned and shoved my father toward the clearing.

The moonlight streamed down from the sky as we stood in the middle of a stand of trees.

Still gripping Papa's arm, Tristan said, "Okay, hand it over."

"Not until you release Papa," I said. I could accurately

throw this dagger and hit Tristan right in his throat. He'd bleed out in seconds when I sliced through his carotid artery. But he was a madman. He'd see the blade flying and shoot my father.

Tristan released Papa with a shove.

"Now get far away from him," I said.

Tristan sidled several feet from Papa. "Give it here, Olivia. It's ten minutes until midnight."

He waved the gun at me impatiently.

I took aim and tossed the knife to him. It flew in a smooth arc and landed near his feet.

Tristan crouched and picked up the knife. Then, a bitter laugh escaped his lips. "You must think I'm a fucking idiot."

"What do you mean?" I said, my brow furrowing.

"This is a piece of shit." He flipped the dagger toward the ground, and the tip of the blade landed in the dirt.

The knife vibrated back and forth.

"This isn't a sacred knife. It's just a piece of iron rubbish," Tristan said. "There should be symbols lining the blade and the onyx handle, and it should glow brightly as midnight approaches. Where's the real dagger?"

"That's it, Tristan," I said, reeling. "That's the knife Lee gave me."

Did Lee betray me again?

"Well, that lying old fool gave you a fake."

Out of the corner of my eye, I saw the outline of Lee in the woods. He held a blade over his head that did, in fact, glow as bright as the moon.

"I'll go get it. I'll race to Lee's cabin and demand he hands it over to me," I said.

"You'd better move fast," Tristan said. "You've got nine minutes left."

In one swift move, he lifted the gun and fired.

My father cried out and crumpled to the ground.

"You bastard!" I started to race toward Tristan, but he pointed the Glock at my father. "Eight minutes, Olivia. You'd better run as if your father's life depends on it. Wait—it does."

Papa held his leg and moaned. "Go get the dagger, Olivia. Go to a different time. Start a family and leave this time behind."

I sprinted toward Lee, pushing aside branches as I tore through the woods. "Lee! Give me the real dagger!"

Lee swayed back and forth as if he'd been drinking. "I'm sorry I gave you a fake, Little Moon. I'm only trying to do what's best for you."

"I don't have time for your life lesson. Give me the dagger, Lee!" I reached for the knife, but he snatched it away, slicing my hand in the process.

I cried out. A bolt of pain shot through my skin. Blood dripped from my palm, landing with soft plops on the leaves. I sucked the blood from the gash.

"I'm so sorry, Little Moon," Lee said. Holding the knife aloft, he began to chant, singing a beautiful song in a language I didn't understand.

"Ya hamiat alqamar fi allayl, 'adeuk litutliq aleinan lilnuwr waturshiduni khilal alzalami. Dae alshams aleazimat tarqus min hawlik bialhubi walmawadati. Mean, aftahuu bawaabatikum wamnahwani alsafar eabr alzaman walmakan mithl zilal allay."

"What are you doing?" I said.

Beyond him, in the clearing, Tristan stared at me. He lifted the Glock toward my father and fired as my vision faded.

Papa's chest heaved, then dropped like wet cement.

My heart shattered, splintering like broken glass, as a sob caught in my chest. "Oh, God. Papa's dead." The worst pain imaginable bore down on my chest, squeezing until I couldn't breathe.

Darkness continued to close in around me.

Lee slapped the dagger in my hand and pressed my fingers around the handle.

Before I could reply, I slipped from consciousness into a dark, smothering void.

CHAPTER FIVE
OLIVIA

A headache the size of a house squeezed my skull as I came into consciousness. I was disoriented from the smell of ocean air, the sound of crashing waves, and the cold wake-up sensation of water lapping against my feet and legs. Wriggling my hands, I felt what must be sand beneath my fingers.

With a yelp, I opened my eyes and peered around me.

This is strange. I'm on a beach somewhere, surrounded by pristine sand and Caribbean blue water, as far as the eye can see.

I frowned. I must have had a horrible dream about Tristan and my father and some strange notion about time travel. There was no way any of that happened...right? Tristan was a good guy whom I loved with all my heart. And time travel simply didn't exist.

"Wow, what a nightmare," I muttered as I rolled onto my hands and knees. "And I feel like I went on a bender at a party somewhere."

The image of Tristan pressing a gun to my temple in

Papa's house, and Lee in the woods revealing a dagger that shone like the sun blasted through my mind.

Please tell me that isn't real. That was a dream, or this is a dream, but please tell me my father is still alive.

I squeezed my eyes shut, desperate to erase the horrible memory. Then, I became aware of a gash on my hand. The blood was dried, plastered against my skin. I didn't recall such a gash until the image of Lee whipping the glistening black dagger at me rolled through my mind. I dismissed it as part of that horrible dream.

The sun glinted on something black beneath the water that surged across the shore.

I scrambled forward and pulled the object free of the sand. *Oh, shit.*

It was the dagger Lee had handed me before I blacked out. I reached up and rubbed my mouth and my jaw, bewildered. Then, I lifted the hem of my dress and slid the dagger into the leather strap that held my gun. I wriggled it to the outside of my leg while the gun rested against my thigh on the inside.

The cold water lapped at my fingers and wrists, so I scooped some up and splashed my face, attempting to soothe my headache and calm my racing heartbeat. The cold liquid helped restore me, so I rose to stand and studied my surroundings.

I blinked several times. How in the world could I be on a beach?

Slowly, I turned in a circle, looking for clues as to my whereabouts. I saw no sign of life until I looked behind me. I squinted, peering at a man standing several yards away. Behind him, a white-washed city rose up a hill, the kind one saw in posters on travel destinations.

My eyebrows shot high on my forehead. I had no idea where I was. None...nada...*no comprende.*

The guy was wearing some sort of kilt-like garment, with a purplish-red cloak around his neck. A spartan helmet of polished silver rested atop his head while the same silver metal covered his torso in fish-like scales. Reddish-brown curls peeked from beneath his helmet.

This guy looked like he was an extra in an old-time movie about the war in ancient times. And, from the look of it, he had just finished a battle scene, as blood dripped down his arm, falling to the sand in thick, red drops.

Without thought, I rushed to help him.

"You're injured," I said.

He swung up his sword at me.

I put my hands up and pointed to his wound.

"You're injured," I repeated.

He looked down at his muscled arm with disdain as if offended that I'd pointed it out. Then, he spoke to me in a language I didn't recognize.

Lee had insisted that I become fluent in many languages growing up. I'd mastered Russian, Arabic, French, Spanish, Italian, Mandarin, some Aramaic, and some Sioux, and I was somewhat fluent in Latin.

The words spewing from this soldier's mouth sounded like Latin, but there was a dialect there, like a course I took in Medieval Latin.

I struggled to understand it but only picked up words and phrases.

But the gestures he was making with his arms were clear, spoken in the universal language of anger, impatience, or annoyance.

I patted the air before me and tried out my Latin.

"*Auxilium volo*," I said, and then I repeated it. "I want to help."

I pointed at his arm, ripped off the hem of my dress, and mimicked wrapping it around his wound.

His eyes formed slits as he regarded me.

"*Auxilium volo*," I said again. "*Placere*," I added, thinking a friendly "please" might calm this guy and prevent him from having a coronary and me having to perform CPR on the beach.

His eyes remained slits, but he lowered the sword and thrust out his arm.

I wrapped the strip of fabric around his injury, then looked up as several men, dressed in the same fashion as the wounded guy, pushed a young woman toward the beach.

The woman cried and screamed as she was shoved to the sand. Her dirty blonde hair hung in a matted, disheveled mess around her face, and her garment, which consisted of miles of fabric draped around her frail body, looked old and torn.

The men were all laughing and jeering.

I didn't care who she was or what she'd done—no one should be treated in such a manner.

"*Prohibere! Sinite eam!*" I raced toward her. "Stop! Leave her alone!"

The men fixed their attention on me. One of them, a man with hair the color of shadows at night, elbowed another and said something, and they all laughed. Shadow-hair stepped from the group, his chest all puffed with pride, and leered at me.

"*Rursus a te?*" he said, grabbing his crotch through his kilt.

"I sure as hell don't want a turn," I said.

Before he could react, I performed a roundhouse kick, clocking Shadow-hair in the face.

His head whipped to the side, and blood spurted from his mouth.

The young blonde woman looked from me to them, and then scampered away.

When Shadow-hair righted himself, his face bore blotchy red marks and the muscles in his jaw ticked with strain. He shouted something like, "Get her!" in Latin.

The remaining four men grabbed their weapons and stormed me.

I whirled, ducked, shoved, and kicked, landing several blows.

One of the men lowered his body and rushed me like a bull. He slammed into me, taking me to the sand.

The air rushed from my lungs as I landed. I opened my mouth to suck in air, but nothing happened. My eyes seemed to swell in their sockets, practically bugging out of my face. As I struggled to recover, the men descended on me with chains. I tried in vain to resist as they bound my arms and legs and hauled me to my feet.

I thought I caught the words, "She must be from Caledonia? Do you think she's a spy? She's highly trained!"

Another said something that I interpreted as, "Take her to the emperor. He'll know what to do."

The wounded guy, whose arm I wrapped, joined the others. He gave me a suspicious glare, yet I caught a touch of... curiosity? Compassion? There was something besides the stoic soldier peering at me.

I looked at him questionably.

He re-directed his gaze and resumed his impassive stare.

Whoever he was, whatever this was, wherever I was, I was in deep shit.

I tried in vain to comprehend what was going on, but I

came up with a big fat nothing as I was hauled through the dusty streets to my unknown destination.

CHAPTER SIX

OLIVIA

I was wholly disoriented and utterly freaked out as I stumbled through this foreign city.

Paved roads, as well as passageways made of packed earth, crisscrossed in every direction. Yet, there wasn't a car, truck, or motorcycle to be found. Instead, men rode horses or lumbered next to donkeys laden with baskets. Some men tugged carts down the street. Women dressed in long, simple gowns made of pale muslin or linen hurried past, hauling children by their grubby little hands.

The men wore shorter garments that looked like tunics, with sandals covering their feet, bound to their legs with straps crisscrossed along the shins.

In the distance, a two-story structure consisting of stone arches spanned the length of a wide river.

That looks like a...I squinted. It appears to be an aqueduct. That's impossible.

Several hills surrounded me, each bearing some sort of stone-like temple—the kind I'd seen in drawings of ancient Rome.

My heart battered at my ribs as my mind struggled to make sense of my surroundings.

Where was I? And how the hell did I get here? The only answer was through time travel, but I refused to entertain that as a possibility.

From the looks of it, I seemed to be in ancient Rome, but I refused to accept this as my reality. Perhaps I'd been drugged, and I was having a *terrible* trip.

Behind me, one of the soldiers yanked a bag over my head.

I yelped when the scratchy fabric slid over my face, plunging me into darkness. The heavy cloth smelled foul, like someone's unwashed underarm, and effectively smothered me. As I was dragged along, I found myself gagging, but I didn't throw up. Unable to see where I was and unable to slow my steps, I lurched and stumbled, ushered on by the men who gripped me by both my arms.

I was pushed and shoved along, stumbling up a set of smooth stairs. I was half-dragged, half-lifted up a steep stairway. Then, we must have entered through a doorway since the air inside felt cool, not the blazing heat outside. My footsteps struck the smooth ground without stirring puffs of dust. Perhaps it was a stone floor or even tile. The sound of five men and me tromping through this building echoed against the walls, creating a cacophony of noise.

The men talked to one another, but I could only interpret fragments of their words in my freaked-out disposition. I made out things like, "What kind of attire is she wearing," followed by lewd laughter. Another man said something to the effect of, "If the emperor doesn't want her, I can make good use of her," and again, the lascivious laughter rung against the walls.

A door creak sounded, and the men's voices all hushed. I

TIMEBORNE

was pushed and shoved forward until I was jerked to a halt. Then, the two men at my sides thrust me to my knees which cracked against the unyielding floor with a painful thud.

A loud, clear voice bellowed into the air.

To the best of my ability, the male voice said, "What have we here? Where did you find this scantily clad female? Is she some sort of prostitute?"

"We found her by the beach, your excellence," one of my captors said. "We think she's a spy...perhaps she hails from Caledonia. She has been trained to fight like a man."

The smell of my putrid, fear-laced breath mixed with the horrible odor of the fabric bag covering my head. Dry heaves rocked my belly, and I gagged and wretched without throwing up from my position on the floor.

All around me, a din of jeering, hooting voices bashed against my eardrums.

"Reveal her to me," the pompous-sounding male stated.

The bag was whipped from my face. I sucked in the fresh air, scanning my surroundings. Two rows of men sat to my right, all sporting short-cropped hair and clad in flowing white garments. An imperious attitude radiated from each one. They looked much like the depictions of Roman senators from my history books.

To my left stood an unruly group of what must be citizens, both male and female. They were dressed in various clothing, all pale in color, and they appeared more ordinary than the men on my right.

Before me stood an ornate gold throne with a cruel-looking man seated upon it. He wore a toga, draped to create a wide band across the chest. Religious icons were interspersed across the garment. A jeweled diadem graced his salt and pepper hair.

Behind him, thick, heavy red curtains hung from the wall.

Veined marble lined the rest of the room, and the ceiling was crafted from some sort of blood-red stone, polished to a glimmering shine.

Two warriors stood by his side, staring straight ahead, their expressions impassive.

The king, emperor, or whatever studied me with a sneer upon his face, which looked carved from stone. "This wench is your so-called spy?"

He let out a brash laugh, much like donkey's bray.

The senators all laughed with him, and then the citizens joined in.

The noise was deafening.

The emperor pounded the end of his staff against the tile floor. It let out several loud cracks, and the men and women grew quiet.

The emperor cocked his head and coolly regarded me.

"She can't be a spy. She's more of a goddess," he said, almost reverentially. With a lift of his chin, he said, "Unchain her."

The soldier next to me said, "Your excellence, we can't do that."

"Can't or won't?" the emperor said, regarding him with a gaze that could melt steel.

"She's...she's..." the warrior stammered. "She's deadly, your grace. She'll kill you."

"Amuse me," the emperor said.

The warrior's Adam's apple bobbed up and down in a hard swallow, but he turned to the guy on my opposite side and nodded.

The two warriors eyed each other warily as they worked to unchain me.

Once the chains fell to the ground with a loud clang, the

five soldiers who brought me here drew their weapons and backed away from me, assuming a fighting stance.

I stood, glancing at the emperor while assessing my surroundings. My anger built. I'd been betrayed by Tristan and dragged through the streets in this strange land like a dog. I drew strength and power inside myself, channeling it the way Lee had trained me to do.

"Never behave in predictable ways," he used to tell me. "If they expect you to punch left, punch right. If they expect a kick to the neck, kick their kidneys instead. Be watchful and wary, sizing them up. But *always* do the unexpected."

The Emperor narrowed his eyes at me. Without tearing his gaze away, he said, "Where is this so-called deadliness of which you spoke? She's merely standing there like a deer in my chamber. Are you idiots trying to convince me that she fought with you?"

No one said a thing. Instead, they shuffled their feet, appearing sheepish.

The emperor continued to assess me, a puzzled expression on his haughty face. He leaned forward as if about to rise. "Bring her to my bedchamber. We'll see what kind of deadliness she shows me in bed."

A chuckle left his throat.

That was my signal to attack. I whirled, kicking the guy to my right in the juncture between nose and lips. That spot was one of the weakest.

Blood spurted from his face as his body slumped to the ground.

Nailed it. I continued to whirl, kicking and striking with coiled fists.

Their swords whooshed as they attempted to slice my skin.

On either side of me, the crowd roared with excitement.

I dodged away from one warrior's sword, and he impaled the guy attacking me from the other side.

Two down, three to go. I lunged for one of the fallen soldier's swords, swung it over my head, and thrust it into the neck of the red-faced guy racing toward me. *And that's three.*

There were only two left.

They exchanged secretive glances like they had a plan.

Too bad my plan would be superior to whatever they came up with. Grinning, I wiggled the fingers of my free hand in a come-hither fashion. Then, I two-hand gripped the sword, took aim, and let it fly. It slid through the gaps in one of the soldier's steel-plated armor and sliced him clean through the belly.

He fell to his knees as blood spurted from his wound.

The "fans" were screaming, shouting, roaring with excitement.

A glance to my side revealed the emperor on his feet, yelling, "What are you waiting for? Kill her!"

One of the warriors next to the emperor's throne had allowed an expression of…concern?… to crack his stoic face.

I shook my head and focused on my opponent.

He produced a knife with a blade the length of my hand.

That distraction of the warrior to the emperor's right cost me precious time. I looked back too late to stop my opponent from charging me. He slammed into me. I landed flat on my back, his blade poised at my throat.

I could be dead in two seconds flat. All he had to do was shift his hand to the right.

I seized his wrist and held it taut, but the sharp blade against my skin left me trembling. My muscles shook from the strain.

The warrior on top of me was muscular and massive. I could barely breathe from his weight. He leered at me, sweat dripping from his face onto mine. He thought he was victorious.

I grimaced, my face contorted in a rictus of control. *Can't. Let him. Win.*

With a mighty shove, I thrust his hand away, wriggled out from beneath him, and rolled him onto his back.

The crowd gasped, then cheered.

No doubt furious at being bested by a woman, this guy looked pissed. I snatched the knife which had fallen near his head. Without hesitation, I slit his throat. Then, I powered to my feet and held the bloody knife high.

The room fell into utter madness as the audience cheered and stomped their feet.

I glared at the emperor, who had assumed his seat again while he stroked his jaw.

"Marcellious!" he said, and the warrior to his left trained his attention on him.

The emperor waved his hand in the air.

Marcellious stepped from the marble platform onto the floor, his sword held high.

I was exhausted, but I gathered my strength and assumed a crouch.

The five men I'd vanquished lay scattered on the floor like bloody dolls. They had fought with haste, thinking to best me with size and speed.

This Marcellious guy seemed strategic.

Keeping my gaze trained on Marcellious, I inched toward one of the fallen guard's swords and retrieved it from the floor.

We faced one another as we circled like we were in a high school wrestling match—only this was anything but high school. My opponent wanted my head skewered at the end of his sword.

I'd prefer *his* head rolling across the floor.

Marcellious was a giant of a man, and he was ripped with muscle. He had a rugged jaw lined with stubble, chiseled cheeks, and dark, shadowed irises flecked with gold and full of secrets. His broad shoulders, thick biceps, and muscular thighs made me wonder if he power-lifted horses in his spare time. He was genuinely handsome, the kind of man who would grace the covers of GQ, Vanity Fair, and Esquire if he lived in my time. But I got the feeling there was something sinister lurking beneath the surface. Marcellious was, in a word, deadly.

The way he undressed me with his eyes unnerved me. He was no doubt contemplating how dead he wanted me before he had his way with me.

My eyes narrowed, and a grin spread across his face.

Moon Lee had taught me to always exploit my opponent's weakness.

Marcellious' weakness was sex.

He moved toward me and swung his sword.

I ducked out of the way and thrust my knife at his side.

He swung again.

I ducked and thrust again.

We continued this cat and mouse play for several moves. Each time, Marcellious' gaze fell to my breasts or dropped even lower to the V between my legs.

He wanted me.

I hooked my leg behind his knee, and he buckled, stumbling backward. Righting himself before falling, he let out a curse and lunged into me.

Using two hands around the hilt of my sword, I hit his blade with a loud clang, knocking it out of his grasp.

With a grunt, he barreled forward and wrapped his arms

around me, clenching his sweaty torso against me as he tried to wrestle me to the ground.

I dropped my free hand, letting it brush the front of his loincloth near his cock.

He hissed, faltering, giving me the break I needed to shove him away.

Our gazes met, and his eyes were hooded and dark.

I licked my lips.

Keeping his eyes pinned to me, he inched toward his sword. In a lightning-fast maneuver, he snagged the sword and lunged at me so fast I didn't have time to react. He slid behind me, his sword to my neck. My breath hitched.

He licked the shell of my ear and whispered, "Your fighting skills arouse me. I want you, you beautiful creature."

I let my head fall backward, brushing the side of his face with my hair.

"Well, that makes two of us," I whispered.

Then, I elbowed him in the gut.

With a snarl, he spun me around and jabbed the tip of his wicked sharp sword into the hollow of my neck.

I threw my sword to the side, appearing defeated.

He thought he'd won, so he lowered his weapon, dropping it to the floor with a clang. He raised his arms and turned in a circle, victorious.

The senators, citizens, and the emperor cheered for his success.

He stalked toward me, grabbed my face in his meaty hand, and kissed me.

The kiss was disgusting. But I did what I must, stroking his face and trailing my fingers down his thick neck.

Then, I bit his lip hard, drawing blood.

Jeers and laughs rang out in the throne room.

His head jerked back, and he gritted his teeth. He licked

the blood from his lips, and then shoved my back against the wall.

"You bitch," he spat out.

"I'm sorry, I'm sorry, I'm sorry," I said, forcing myself to cry. "You win. I surrender myself to you."

"Ha!" He seized my wrist and raised my arm high, dragging me into the center of the room.

The audience went wild, screaming and shouting.

Fool that he was, he released me and bowed to the audience, claiming his victory.

I scrambled behind him, leaping on his back and wrapping my arm in a chokehold around his neck. I clasped my hands together behind his head and bore down against his carotid arteries, squeezing with all my might in a rear-naked choke. I held it for longer than was "safe," squeezing with all my might.

Marcellious swayed, trying to bat me off him. He fell to the floor, unconscious, and I leaped out of the way.

I turned and faced the emperor, panting as I tried to catch my breath.

He was on his feet, a look of rage on his face.

"Roman," he said. "Finish her off!"

The guy who had thrown me off my game with his oddly caring expression thundered toward me, sword drawn.

There was no size up with this warrior. He was cunning, he was strong, and he was fierce. I leaped and somersaulted, grabbing a sword from one of the dead men, and jack-knifed to my feet. My tiny little knife was nothing to this guy, and I wanted an even advantage. We were caught up in a battle, with steel flying at one another.

My limbs were weak with fatigue, and my moves were sloppy. This Roman guy could quickly finish me off, but he didn't. *Why not?* I was exhausted. I was confused. I didn't know why I was here.

Our sparring probably looked pathetic. He was clearly the cat, and I was the tiny mouse, so tired I could fall over asleep, just like Marcellious.

Roman darted behind me and wrapped his beefy arm around my neck. My sword hung at my side.

This is it. This is the point where I die.

Instead, his lips pressed next to my ear, and he whispered, "Let me help you. Stop fighting with me."

"I don't trust you," I hissed. "I don't trust a soul here."

I summoned the remaining strength and jabbed my elbow into his armor-covered torso. My sweaty arm slid right off the slick metal, and he seized me again.

He whispered, "If you don't stop and let me help you, you will die. Please surrender to me, and I will help you however I can. You're injured, you're hurt, and you're bleeding."

I glanced at him and then at my blood-covered hands.

His luminous eyes conveyed a depth of compassion that unnerved me.

He was right. I was so weak right now he only needed to blow my way, and I'd collapse. And yet, I didn't want to admit defeat.

My body didn't give me much choice. I fell to the ground, and the surrender was only partially fake.

"*Ego deditionem!*" I shouted, then ground my teeth together. "I surrender!"

Roman crouched down as if to grab me. He whispered in my ear, "You are the champion of this fight. I'm impressed by your unparalleled skills and your cunning moves and strength. I want to know how you knocked out Marcellious. And I've never seen anyone fight with such grace."

The audience cheered and applauded Roman.

Marcellious returned to consciousness and staggered to his feet, clutching his head.

I sank into despair and utter disbelief.

How did I get here? How can I get out? This is not happening! I can't believe I just killed five men for the first time.

Roman's large, sweaty hand curled around my wrist, and he yanked me to my feet, facing the emperor.

The emperor praised Roman with vigor. "*Bravo! Bravo!*"

The audience continued to cheer and yell. He pumped his hands, palm down, and the room quieted.

"Who are you?" he asked.

Panting, I said, "I'm no one."

"Who are you?" the emperor repeated with a growl. "Where did you come from? Are you a spy from Caledonia? You do look like a Scottish woman, especially with hair like the color of fire and eyes of the color mixed gold."

"No," I said, wiping my mouth with the back of my hand. I pulled it away and eyed the blood covering my fingers.

"How did you learn to fight like that?" he asked, resuming his seat on the throne.

What can I tell him? My godfather in Seattle, Washington, taught me? If this is really ancient Rome, Seattle doesn't exist.

I swallowed and said, "I grew up in a village far from here. My father taught me how to fight. But he's…he's dead."

The image of my father crumpling to his knees after Tristan pulled the trigger flashed before my eyes. I forced myself not to tear up or show emotion of any kind.

"Where is this village?"

"It's in the north," I lied. "But the entire village has been wiped out by the enemy."

I sniffled, and it wasn't fake. I was still thinking about my father.

Oh, I had to shut down this emotion fast. If I yielded to my feelings, I'd get killed. There was no guarantee whatsoever that this Roman guy would protect me.

The emperor rose and stalked toward me.

Roman stepped back, and the emperor made a lazy circle around me, a haughty smile on his face.

A musky scent wafted from his skin. He circled me like a cat about to rub his face all over my breasts.

I stiffened, keeping my expression neutral.

"You're exquisite, my dear," he said, inches away from my mouth.

His breath smelled like an old man, already starting his morbid decay.

"A real jewel. But, alas, I have too many mistresses. Roman!" He snapped his fingers in Roman's direction. "You take her."

"Thank you, your excellence, for your kindness," Roman said. "But I'm in no need of a mistress right now."

"Then, Marcellious, you'll take her." The emperor pointed at Marcellious, who could barely hold himself upright.

Roman, who stood in my line of sight, stiffened. His lips pressed together, and he eyed Marcellious.

Then, he turned to the emperor and said flatly, "I've reconsidered your excellence. I'll take her for myself."

"Good," the emperor said, pleased with Roman's decision. "Take her away."

He dismissed me with a swish of his bejeweled hand, climbed on his dais, and settled on his throne.

"What is our next order of business?" he asked the men in white robes. Clearly, he was done with me as if I had provided the afternoon entertainment.

Roman gripped my biceps and forced me to walk. His

face resumed its former stony impassive expression as he shoved me out of the throne room. He ushered me across the most immense room, consisting of a spacious courtyard surrounded by a colonnade. Gigantic paintings and frescoes covered the marble walls. My footsteps echoed through this cavernous space.

He said nothing as he guided me out into the blazing sun, heading toward several horses who stood, resting beneath trees.

I didn't have the strength to ask him where we were going.

When we stood before a handsome horse, as golden as the sun, Roman said, "Climb on."

The horse shifted side to side, having awakened from his drowse by our presence.

I stared at the saddle and the giant beast who wore it. Four stubby prongs emerged from the corners of the saddle, but there were no stirrups.

"How?" I said, perplexed. "Do I back up several meters, run, and make a flying leap?"

He frowned. "Climb on."

I waved my hand at the saddle. "There's no stirrup."

His frown deepened, and he placed his hands on the saddle and vaulted into position.

I was impressed.

He reached his hand to me.

I took it, and he lifted me—yes, *lifted* me—into the air.

I managed to scramble onto the horse in front of Roman.

He threaded his arms next to my waist and reached for the reins. I leaned against his armor and promptly passed out from fatigue.

CHAPTER SEVEN
ROMAN

How had my day started out so normal and ended up so bizarre? It was a day like any other, serving the emperor and his needs. But then a female was dragged into the throne room, and she single-handedly destroyed the emperor's closest guards. Now she rested before me, slumped like a wheat bag against my chest.

I couldn't leave her in the care of Marcellious—he would destroy her. But I wracked my brain as to what to do with her, what to say. She spoke an odd form of Latin which was challenging to comprehend. But her command of weaponry was unparalleled.

Where did she come from, that she fought like a man with the beauty of a goddess? Her shining hair held the color of a sunset, trailing down her shoulders and tickling my cheeks when the wind whipped it against my face.

A wound on her palm gave me pause. It was red and swollen as if infected, and angry red snake-like streaks surrounded it as if seeking other places in her body to attack.

All these thoughts ruffled my typical stoic facade as my horse Tempestas picked his way through the streets, heading for my home. I could face down an army of the most formidable opponents but an hour in this woman's presence had me questioning my own sanity.

I kept Tempestas at a steady walk instead of his usual hurried prancing gait. We passed the stone and brick shops that made up the town, by the forum where goods were sold and meetings were held, and made our way past the temple, where we worshiped the gods. The public baths were in the building next to the temple. I could use a good long soak, but now was not the time. Then, we arrived at the far end of town where all the homes were located, and Tempestas maneuvered up the cobbled street, heading for my dwelling.

Steadying the woman on top of Tempestas took some work as I dismounted. Once my feet were on the ground, I gathered her in my arms and rushed toward the door.

"Amara!" I shouted, racing through the wooden door to the atrium. The living quarters, sleeping quarters, and kitchen all surrounded the lush flora in this section of my modest home.

I found Amara, my sweet, elderly housekeeper, standing near the brazier in the kitchen. She stoked the coals in the bottom of the metal cooking device before flipping what smelled like a roasted rabbit. A brick cooking stove had been built against the wall, but she preferred this smaller, more manageable source of fire.

"Amara, please help me!" I hurried to her healing room, where all her herbs were stored.

Amara followed, entering the room behind me.

I presented the limp woman like she was something I'd found in the market.

Amara's eyes widened, and she ambled toward me in her stoop-backed gait. "Who is she? What's happened to her? Where did she come from?"

"I don't know who she is or where she came from, but she's in our care and protection now. She's killed several of the emperor's guards as if she were sent by the gods," I said. "If you were there, you would have been shocked by the entertainment she put on for the citizens. It was as if she was a gladiator fighting for her life."

Amara's eyebrows rose high on her forehead. "A woman doing such a thing? That's unheard of. Remove her clothes at once."

I took a step backward, balking. "I don't think that's appropriate. Wouldn't it make more sense if you were to undress her? I am, after all, a man."

I was no stranger to the temptations of a female, but respect had been instilled in me from an early age. And simply stripping her bare seemed completely disrespectful.

"You've seen a woman's flesh before. Quit being a prude and take off her clothes," Amara said. "I need to tend to her wounds and see if there are others."

My face and neck flushed with heat as I peeled the flimsy garments from her flesh. When she was stripped of her clothes, I sucked in a breath. She had to be the most exquisite woman I'd ever laid eyes on.

Her body was generously curved yet strong and well-toned with skin that'd been kissed by the sun. Her face, with its bow-shaped red lips and long brown eyelashes, appeared angelic in repose. It was nothing like the fiercely focused woman who fought and killed five men. The silken strands of her fiery hair begged to be caressed. The image of a goddess in the temple came to mind. She was a mystery, a temptingly beautiful woman who arrived at a bad time in my life.

Who was this woman?

There was something odd strapped around her leg. I removed a strange metal device from the inside of her silken thigh and turned it over in my hands. A mysterious-looking dagger was strapped to her outer thigh.

"Here." I thrust the unusual weapons at Amara. "Take these and put them aside for me to deal with later. Then, tend to her needs. I shan't stand around and stare at a naked woman."

I folded my arms over my chest, averting my eyes from this lovely beauty. Already, she had captivated my attention and aroused my curiosity.

"No, you shall not," Amara said. "But we need to move her to a place of comfort. Lay her on the *lectus cubicularis* in the guest room sleeping quarters."

I hesitated. I didn't want to touch the bewitching woman lying on the table, but I was the one who put her there, so…

I stooped, lifted her in my arms, and strode to the sleeping quarters. I laid her on the chamber bed, in a room next to mine.

Amara entered carrying a bucket of water, rags, and herbs.

I left her to her healing and exited to remove my guard's uniform.

Three days had passed since I brought the warrior goddess-woman to my home. She had been under Amara's constant care. All her cuts and bruises had been healing nicely, except the wound on her hand. It didn't show any signs of lessening. Instead, it was filled with pus that Amara had to drain daily. The flesh surrounding it festered as if angered.

She awoke at times, mumbling and incoherent, then

slipped into her nightmarish realms where she'd writhe and struggle against unseen enemies.

For three nights, I'd laid in the quarters next to hers, suffering from a restless longing to know who this woman was who slept so close to me. What brought her here? Where did she come from?

Today, as I did every day when I returned from my duties, I made haste for her chamber, eager to find out if she had awakened. She still slumbered, breathing slow and even, a goddess by her own rights in a trance that couldn't be explained.

Amara kneeled before her, dabbing at the gash with a wet rag.

"How is she?" I said, folding my arms and leaning against the doorway.

Amara had dressed the goddess-like woman in a linen stola. It draped along her curves in a manner that stirred me most uncomfortably. I stared at the rough stone wall behind her, unwilling to be affected by this strange creature.

"No better," Amara said as she dabbed at the ugly wound marring the woman's otherwise perfect skin.

I crouched next to her chamber bed and cupped her palm in my hands. Her skin was hot as if it'd been held over the flames. I examined the gash, noting a purplish-green discoloration. I'd seen that color before. Someone had poisoned this beautiful young woman. But why?

"Amara, your husband has healed wounds similar to this," I said.

Amara frowned. "What do you mean?"

I lifted the woman's palm to Amara's face so she could examine it. "Look at the colors. They look much like the marks of poison Gaius treated before."

Amara squinted at the gash, her frown deepening. "We could try to heat a knife to white hot and…."

"That's exactly what I was thinking," I said.

Amara nodded, dropped her rag in the basin, and exited the room.

I stroked the woman's gossamer hair splayed around her head like flickering flames. *So beautiful.* The hair was a marked contrast from her too-pale skin. If we couldn't extract the poison, this beautiful creature might die. That thought was unthinkable. Since our destinies had collided, I must find out who she was and where she came from.

A short time later, Amara returned, bearing a knife on a ceramic platter. "I've heated it. Use this rag to pick it up, or you'll burn your hand."

She indicated a towel draped over her arm.

Carefully, I picked up the blade and pressed it to the swollen gash.

The woman gasped and bolted upright, sending the knife clattering to the floor. Her agate-colored eyes blinked and tracked the room. She squeezed my hand, leaving nail marks on my palm, then collapsed, unconscious once more.

And we had no more answers than we did when I arrived.

CHAPTER EIGHT
OLIVIA

I traveled through hellish landscapes in my mind for an untold period. Blood rained down from the skies and washed on the shores of my inner landscape in crashing waves. Armor-covered men screamed and urged their galloping horses toward me while waving their swords in grand, sweeping arcs.

At times, I felt the warmth of water pressed to my brow, neck, chest, and arms. My right hand felt enormous, like it was the size of a basketball, left out in the sun too long. The warm water continued to be applied to my skin. But then I slid back into nightmares, leaving the soothing sensation behind.

Finally, I awakened, and my hand no longer felt hot and huge.

A woman hummed next to me, and that same sensation of warm water pressed into my skin.

I sucked in a gasp of air and opened my eyes, blinking rapidly as if I were caught in a windstorm.

Oh, God. I was in a strange room with all these ancient-looking artifacts: elaborate ceramic vases, a colorful fresco painted on the wall, and an exquisite pattern of tiles on the floor.

This had to be a dream or a museum. I shook my head. I didn't know what it was. At least it beat the nightmare I'd been wandering through.

"Easy child," a wispy voice said, like rattling autumn leaves.

Gnarled hands with swollen knuckles and papery dry skin patted my face.

I pushed the hands away and hastened to sit upright.

"Who are you?" I said to the kindly-looking woman. "Where am I?"

The woman put out her palms. "We're not here to hurt you. What's your name?"

My heartbeat thundered in my ears. I didn't know where I was, but I had to get out of here. My mind was reeling.

"Please tell me your name. There's nothing to fear. I'm Amara," the old woman said.

"I…" I said, my gaze darting around the room like a hummingbird. "My name is Olivia."

Amara gave me a warm smile.

"What a beautiful name, Olivia. Where are you from?" she said, speaking in the manner reserved for children or the insane. "What do you remember?"

A flood of memories pushed through my brain, tumbling like rushing water over rocks. "I was eating breakfast with my father. He told me many strange things and then warned me about my boyfriend, Tristan."

"Boyfriend?" The old woman frowned, but I continued to speed talk.

"Tristan kept me a prisoner at my father's house, and then we went out into the woods to meet with Lee. And then,

Tristan killed my father." All the memories collided against one another as they escaped my mind and fell from my lips.

"Shh," Amara soothed. She hugged me gently.

Feeling her embrace comforted me.

"Lay back," she said. "Clearly, you've had a shock of some kind."

"I… I can't lay back. I've got to…."

"Shh. Let me take care of you. You need to be bathed and tended to." She leaned down, retrieved a cloth from a water basin, and wrung it out. Then, she began washing my arms.

Her touch was soothing and gentle, and I melted back into the strange bed and closed my eyes.

She lifted my head and smoothed my hair over the side of the bed.

My eyelids fluttered open.

Amara held a flask and poured some kind of liquid into my hair that smelled of lye or animal fat. The fluid drained into another basin Amara had placed on the floor. She massaged the interesting substance into my scalp, and my eyes, heavy with exhaustion, closed.

The feeling of being cared for by this elderly woman was so sweet, that I yielded to her ministrations.

When she was done, she rinsed my hair and then massaged some sort of fragrant, sweet-smelling oil into my hair. "Your hair is so long and abundant—do you ever think of cutting it?"

I squeezed my eyes as thoughts of my mother flooded my brain.

"No," I whispered, allowing my eyes to open. "My mother's touch is still held at the end of my hair. I can't bear to cut it."

"Where is your mother now?" Amara asked as she peeled

back the plain-looking garment I'd been dressed in and proceeded to wash my entire body.

"My mother is dead." The memory strangled my heart, squeezing it into a tiny ball.

"I'm sorry. Any other family?" Amara stroked me with sure, firm hands.

"No," I said, unwilling to share too many details.

Amara dabbed the warm water against my skin. "Your body is so beautiful, child. You've been blessed by the gods."

I said nothing, lost in the confusion of where I was and where I'd been.

The sound of a door opening and closing whispered into the air, and far away footsteps clattered into the house.

I tensed and pressed my forearms into the bed, lifting my torso. Quickly, I shielded my body with my hands.

"That must be Roman," Amara said.

"Roman?" Panic shot through my veins. "Who's Roman?"

Images of being in a throne room and killing several men came rushing into my mind. I covered my mouth in horror.

I've killed five men. I can't believe I've killed.

Some tall, imposing warrior had dragged me away from the palace and hauled me into his lap while on his horse, and now I was here.

I glanced at my hand, which had been wrapped in soft linen. *Did I damage it when I killed all those guards?*

"Did Roman… Did he bring me here?"

Amara dressed me in a soft, draping dress. "Yes. He brought you here, and I've been caring for you. Will you excuse me a moment?"

She shuffled from the room.

"She's awake," Amara said, from the other side of the

closed door, a smile in her voice. "Would you like to speak to her?"

"Bring her to my room in twenty minutes," Roman said. Then, his footsteps echoed through the house.

To his room…? Wasn't I given to him by an emperor?

I rocketed to my feet, rushing for Amara as she stepped into the room. "I won't do it! This is some kind of horrible mistake. I'm not a whore. I refuse to be his mistress! I'm not that kind of woman!"

Amara's eyes widened to the size of the ceramic basins she used to wash me. "Child! He would never! He's not that kind of man!" She gestured to me. "Come with me. He would like to speak to you—nothing more."

Somewhat mollified, I followed her.

We entered a large room, vast compared to the one I had awakened in.

The bed was high off the ground, covered with a rich purple bedspread embellished with gold accents. Carved cats sat staring sternly from the corners of the bed while a footstool rested beneath. The legs of both the bed and the footstool were intricately carved from ivory and gilded with gold leaf.

Colorful depictions of horses and dancing maidens covered the walls. The floor consisted of tiles polished to a gleaming shine. A simple writing desk sat in the corner. Exquisitely carved oil lamps hung from the wall, providing a soft glow from the lit wicks.

"This is Roman's room? It's beautiful," I said, brushing my fingertips on the bedding.

"Yes. This house is the emperor's one concession to Roman," Amara said, her lips pulled down in a frown.

"Concession?" I said. "To what?"

"It's not my place to say. He'll be back shortly. I must

tend to our meal." Amara shuffled from the room, leaving me to ponder the seemingly ancient furnishings and the so-called "concessions" the emperor had made.

I crossed the room to Roman's writing table. Several pieces of parchment and a delicate sheet of wax inscribed with Roman numerals sat stacked in the middle of the table. A reed pen sat next to the documents and a small pottery object. The pottery was small enough to fit in the palm of my hand. I lifted the little lid to find what looked like ink inside. Replacing the cover, I stared at the writing. I couldn't make it out except for the single phrase: 207. A.D.

My hand flew to my mouth. This had to be some kind of joke. There was no way I could be here, wherever this was, in 207. A.D.

Before I could come to terms with this latest discovery, a male voice said, "The punishment for invading one's privacy is fifty lashes."

I whipped around to see the same incredibly handsome man who had dragged me from the palace. He radiated confidence as he stood in the door, a teasing smirk playing at the corners of his mouth. His short, wavy hair, the color of a night sky, appeared disheveled, while his jaw was lined with a day's worth of dark stubble. His body was pure power, stocky and muscular, wrapped in bronze skin. The man before me was a weightlifter's dream, unlike Tristan, who worked out for hours and never developed any bulk. The bluest eyes I'd ever seen, flecked with leafy green, holding shadows and secrets, stared back at me.

"Where I come from, the punishment is much lighter—a mere slap on the hand might suffice." I moved away from his desk, studying him the way a cat might check its prey.

"Here, a slap on the hand would never suffice." Like a

lion, he stepped into his room with grace and lithe power. "My name is Roman Alexander. And you are…?"

"What do you care? Why do you need to know?" I said.

His thick eyebrows arched. "Excuse me? Here in Rome, we practice such a thing as manners."

Rome? What the hell? I'm in Rome?

My body trembled, but I willed myself to stay calm. Rule one in fighting was this: never let your opponent see your weakness. I must present myself at all times as unshakable.

"Where I come from, we can never be too careful around our enemies."

"Enemy? I am not your enemy." Roman sat down at the edge of his bed. "If I were your enemy, we would not be having this conversation—you'd be dead."

A shiver cascaded up my spine, but I held myself in check.

Can I really trust this guy? I was unwilling to let down my guard.

"Your name?" he said again, sweeping his powerful arm toward the bed, indicating I should sit next to him.

Sitting next to him felt too close. I leaned against the wall. "Why should I tell you?"

His jaw grew rigid, and a tic started pulsing at his right eye. "Because you recognize the importance of being polite to the man who brought you home and cared for you. How is your hand, by the way?"

"My hand?" I lifted my palm and found it wrapped in a white linen cloth. I unwrapped the linen cloth and stared at my hand. A pinkish scar cut across my skin, but it was no longer swollen or hot.

"Yes, your hand. I suspect you were poisoned. For days, your hand wouldn't heal until Amara, and I pressed a heated blade against your skin to stop the poison from spreading further into your body."

The memory of a blade slicing through my skin cut through me, and I yanked my hand in the air. "Poisoned? Who would do such a thing?"

I pictured Lee in the darkened woods, illuminated by a brilliant moon, slicing my hand with a knife. *Did Lee poison me? He was my mentor, so why would he do such a thing as poison me?*

"I can't say. I barely know you. I don't even know your name." A faint smile tugged at his lips.

I let out a long sigh. "My name's Olivia James."

"Are you a spy, Olivia?" He said this casually, conversationally, but I could sense the serious intent behind his words.

"No." I folded my arms across my chest. "But I do want to go home…*immediately*."

"I see," he said, smirking. "How would that be possible? You told the emperor you don't have a home. Something about your entire village being burned to the ground."

I blanched, shrugging with a haughty sniff. Lying was on my list of Do Not Dos, and already, I had lies stacked against me. "I have a home."

"Can you tell me where it is?" Roman leaned forward and unclasped the sturdy leather sandals adorning his feet and shins. Then, he lifted his legs to his bed.

He was tall, probably six-four. And stretched out the way he was, he reminded me of a lion resting in a tree, languid yet able to claw one's eyes out with a single swipe of his mighty arm.

"Sadly, no." I cast my gaze at the floor.

Roman pursed his lips. "I'll repeat it again, Olivia. I am not the enemy, but *you* could be. And yet I let you into my home, given you care. Have you considered that?"

I glowered, not making eye contact. I was not used to being treated this way, especially by a man.

"Here is what I propose. I won't expect much from you, but if you follow my rules, you'll get more freedom. You've just killed five men. That's unheard of for a woman. So, I think you can understand I can't just let you go."

I lifted my head and flashed him a squinty-eyed glare. "I could just as easily kill you."

Roman barked out a laugh. "I could have killed you, and yet, I didn't, did I?"

The question hung in the air between us. In my opinion, it didn't deserve an answer.

I pushed away from the wall and sauntered to stand before him. "How about you just let me go? I promise to not cause you any trouble."

He swung his legs off the bed and rose, standing nose to nose with me. Heat poured from his powerful body.

My heart pounded in my chest, surprising me.

If I were a weaker woman, I'd be intimidated by his stance, but instead, I held tight to the strength, skill, and values taught to me by Lee.

"It doesn't work like that here," he said, crossing his arms over his chest. His muscles bulged in chiseled lines in an impressive display of strength. "The emperor gave you to me."

This sentence sliced through my calm poise.

"In my land, we're equal to men. I'm not yours to keep!" I lifted my hands as if to shove him but held myself back.

"Go ahead," he taunted. "Do it."

"Do what?" I said, shaking out my hands as if that was what I intended to do.

He laughed. "Good one, Olivia. You're wise not to shove

me. How about I help you out? We found something on your person you might want back."

"What? Give it to me," I said.

He skirted around me and headed to a small box that looked like a treasure chest in the corner. Stooping, he opened the box and retrieved two objects.

When he turned around, he held my Glock and my dagger.

"Give those to me!" I lunged for my weapons, but he lifted them in the air, out of reach.

I'd have to hop up and down like a monkey to get them from him. "Where did you get those?"

Roman swung the weapons behind his back. "Like I told you, they were strapped to your thigh. How about you tell me what they are?"

I couldn't tell him anything. Suppose this was ancient Rome? In that case, I'd be viewed as insane if I told him the type of weaponry we used in the 21st century or revealed the nature of the dagger.

"I'll do nothing of the sort," I said. "Not as long as you treat me like an animal."

"An animal? That's how you regard our kindness?" He didn't wait for an answer. "Instead of insulting my house-keeper and me, you've *got* to let me help you, Olivia."

"Why should I?"

"Because you *need* my help," he said. "And the emperor has left you in my care."

"But—" I protested.

He held up his palm. *"Stop.* Listen to me. Here's what's going to happen. You're going to help Amara with her chores. If you rebel, you will see an ugly side of me. I'm warning you once, and I won't warn you again—*don't push me.*"

"Are you threatening me?" I leaned toward him, my

hands coiled into fists. I knew I should back down and play it cool. I was in a foreign land, a strange culture, and I didn't know the rules. Any wrong move on my part might result in my death or imprisonment. But it was hard to shake the values I'd honed daily in my 21st-century reality.

"Don't even try to fight me," he said in a deadly voice.

"Or, what?" I said, crouching. I whirled in a circle and swung my leg, intending to land a roundhouse kick on his abdomen.

He batted my leg away, caught my wrists, and slammed my face against the bed. "I'm a Praetoria to the emperor. You'd best treat me with respect."

My mouth closed, and I remained silent, my labored breath panting against the purple bedding, which smelled of musk and man.

Pinning my arms behind my back, he said, "If you follow my orders, I will help you. If you try to escape, I'll hunt you down, and then we'll see which one of us is the deadliest of the two."

A chill rippled up my spine.

"Okay," I whisper.

"Okay?" he said.

"That's what I said. Now let me go."

"Amara!" Roman bellowed, releasing me.

I rolled on my back and jack-knifed to my feet, sidling away from him. No one had ever maltreated me in such a manner, and I didn't like it. I wanted to punch this bastard and hurt him…but I had to hold my ground.

Amara shuffled into view. "Yes, Roman?"

"Please escort Olivia back to her room," he said.

"Come with me," Amara said.

"It's right next door," I snapped.

Roman seized my shoulder, bearing down with his strong

fingers. "Apologize to Amara, *now.* She's the one who's kept you alive all these days."

I sighed and softened my gaze toward Amara. "I'm truly sorry. I'm out of sorts. My head hurts, and my heart hurts, and I'm utterly confused. But I'm sorry to have taken it out on you."

Amara nodded and extended her arm toward the doorway. "Please, child. You need rest. I've prepared the draught for you, and you'll feel better in the morning."

Contrite, I exited.

Once I got to my room, alone, I paced.

"How am I going to get out of here?" I muttered to myself. "I can't focus. All I want to do is run away…but where would I run? I don't know where I am or how I got here. What am I going to do? And this Roman guy—he's bound to be my undoing. How can I trust him?"

I slumped on the chair in the corner. I was utterly bereft, with absolutely no ideas as to how to escape.

A lone tear tracked down my cheek as fatigue drew at my limbs. As I drifted into slumber, powerful arms lifted me and gently placed me on the bed.

Roman stroked my long hair, smoothing it against the pillow.

I was too tired to open my eyes.

As I continued to drift, the last thing I heard was Roman's voice. "Why are you here at this time in my life? Why now?"

I wished I knew the answer to those questions. But at this moment, all I could do was fall into a heavy, dreamless sleep.

CHAPTER NINE

OLIVIA

Amara sounded like a little bird as she hummed and twittered about the kitchen while I was behaving like a two-year-old having a tantrum.

"You've got to let me go, Amara. I've got to get back to my people," I said as I kneeled on the floor, scrubbing the tile with rags and a water basin.

She had kept me so busy I could scarcely think, but I managed to find enough time to whine.

Amara grew scarecrow-still with a knife in one hand and a skinned rabbit with its head, tail, and paws chopped off in the other. "If you leave, dear, it will be my problem and a horrible one. You leaving will displease Roman, and I will be the one who had let you go, don't you see?"

I huffed out a sigh, dipped my rag in the cool water, and wrung it out with all my might. "So, besides scrubbing floors, what other kinds of tasks will I be doing?"

In the last three days, I'd scoured every square inch of this lovely home, including the small pool in the atrium.

Amara smiled. "Today, we're heading to town and shopping for food."

"Really?" A grin formed on my face. The thought of getting out of this house sounded delightful.

"Yes. We'll head out as soon as the rabbit stew is finished." Amara turned back to chopping the rabbit to pieces.

I let out a sigh. As soon as the rabbit stew finished might be hours. In the meantime, I'd continue scrubbing tile.

As predicted, we left the house nearly two hours later. At least the scouring helped me keep some tone in my body. I hadn't been able to work out for days, and I was already feeling slack-muscled.

I relished the sun beating down on my face as we strode along cobbled streets toward town, carrying baskets for our foodstuffs. I'd been cooped inside Roman's stone dwelling too long and had barely set foot outside.

As we passed the houses where villagers lived, there was a disparity between wealthy and poor people. Roman's home seemed like a palace compared to the poorly built tower blocks, which looked like slum apartments. Adults and children spilled from the towers appearing haggard and thin. An instant sense of protectiveness overcame me, and I hurried Amara through this crowded area.

We approached a column-lined street with stone buildings on either side. Vendors crouched beside their goods, selling meats, fish, cheeses, produce, olive oil, and baskets of colorful spices. I tugged Amara out of the way of a herd of goats. The goats bleated as they hurried through the crowd in front of their owner.

Chickens squawked and beat their wings against their basket prisons while mongrel dogs raced through the streets looking for an easy snack.

A skinny-looking kid, maybe thirteen, ran toward us, his eyes bright.

"Miss! Miss!" he called.

Do I know this kid? Is he going to try to harm us?

I stepped in front of Amara to protect her.

The kid slid to a stop in front of me on his sandaled feet. "I saw you! I watched you down at the beach!"

A fuzzy memory of waking up on a sandy shore and being accosted by warriors swirled through my head.

A few people turned and stared at me.

"I, uh...I don't know what you mean," I said, hoping to not draw more attention. Although I was dressed in a white stola, covering me from head to toe, I was sure I stuck out with my height and long, red hair.

"I want to be like you!" The kid was all gangly legs and arms attached to his skinny body. Bruises covered his upper arms and the side of his cheek, and I grew alarmed.

These were the kids I taught back home—those who were abused and needed to learn to defend themselves.

"Anthony," Amara said, a reproving expression on her face. "Where are your manners?"

She glanced around nervously. Then, she gestured for us all to move to the side of the walkway so people could pass by.

"I'm sorry...it's just that I'm so excited to meet you, miss. Can you teach me to fight?"

My heart hammered inside my chest. I didn't want to draw undue attention to myself

"Keep your voice down," I hissed. "And, no, I can't teach you to fight."

Not only did it seem like a bad idea to teach this young guy to fight, it also didn't fit with my plan to escape as soon as I could find a way out of here. Despite Roman's warnings, I was desperate to find a way back home.

I put my arm around Amara's shoulders and guided her down the road. "Let's continue with our errands, shall we?"

The kid lunged at me and grabbed my upper arm.

"Please. You've got to help me. I live with a bad, bad man. See these bruises?" He gestured to the purple and yellowish markings on his arms and cheek. "He did this to me because I didn't clean up the house on time. He dragged me into the road. *Please.* You've got to help me."

As I hesitated, torn between my desire to help and my need to stay out of trouble, a man bellowed through the crowd.

"Anthony!"

His voice ripped through me like an ice-cold wind. I knew that voice. It belonged to the warrior I did a blood choke on in the emperor's palace—the warrior called Marcellious.

Marcellious thundered through the crowd like a bull, yelling, "Don't you dare touch my son!"

He seized Anthony's arm and flung him out of the way.

The kid whimpered, stumbling backward into the arms of a female villager.

"How dare you?" Marcellious stormed toward me. He looked all wild-eyed and steaming with rage. Before I could react, he backhanded me. My head whipped to the side, and blood sprayed in an arc from my lip.

I did *not* see that coming. I assumed a fighting stance and prepared to lay into Marcellious.

In a low growl that no one else could hear, Marcellious said, "You've humiliated me in front of my emperor. You've disparaged me in front of the senators and in front of the people. Not this time! Not in front of my family, too!"

He lunged at me, grabbing my forearms. We wrestled about, unable to take the other down. Then, Marcellious' leg shot out and hooked the back of my knee.

I fell to the ground with a loud "Oof."

I rolled to the side and lunged to my feet before he could kick in my head. I seemed clumsy today, sloppy, and the wound in my hand decided to make a painful reappearance.

Marcellious swung his fist and clocked me in the ribs.

I doubled over in pain. I landed a punch at his jaw, but it caused the gash in my palm to throb.

Marcellious countered with a stinging blow to my cheek.

Now, it seemed the entire village had crowded around us, come to watch a trained warrior fight with a mere woman. If social media were alive today, this fight would be seen worldwide. And I would no doubt be shamed. Women in this time were not supposed to fight.

Amara hurried toward us.

"Amara, no!" I yelled.

Marcellious landed another blow to my abdomen, knocking the wind from me.

"Marcellious, stop!" Amara cried in a voice as clear as crystal.

Marcellious turned to face her. "This is not your fight."

"Nor is it yours. Don't let your anger kill her. She's in our charge, not yours."

I was panting, hurting, and unable to find my bearings. I was doing a shitty job of protecting myself, that was for sure. Yet, I marveled at Amara's bravery.

How is it that Marcellious has stopped because of her words?

Marcellious seized the back of my dress and twisted it. He yanked me upward until I was barely on my tiptoes.

The fabric tightened around me like a noose, making breathing difficult. As I stood in his grip, flailing my arms, Marcellious roared.

"I was the king of the arena. I *was*. And this wench tried to best me. She and I are not done. I shall not rest until victory is mine!"

A horse clattered through the crowd. People screamed and shouted as they maneuvered out of the horse's way.

I looked up to see Roman on top of Tempestas, his mighty steed, and he looked mad.

He leaped from the horse and powered toward Marcellious, sword in hand.

Marcellious released me.

Roman thrust the tip of his sword at Marcellious' throat, staring him in the eyes.

I stumbled forward and fell on my palms, tearing open the flesh of my wound.

"Let her go. She's not your problem," Roman said.

Marcellious stood stock still, his hands in the air. Sweat poured from his skin as he faced down Roman. "So, you're going to save your whore, is that it?"

Anger rushed through my veins.

"I'm no one's whore!" I lunged to my feet and leaped onto Marcellious' back. "Take back your words, you asshole!"

The crowd gasped and shouted, but I couldn't make out the words.

Roman lowered his sword, slid it in his scabbard, and hauled me from Marcellious' back. Then he dragged me toward Tempestas and threw me over the horse's back like I was no more than a sack of flour.

He mounted Tempestas, picked up the reins, and guided us away from the crowd without another word.

And I, draped over the horse for all to gawk at, knew I was in for some trouble.

CHAPTER TEN

OLIVIA

Humiliated, draped over Tempestas on my belly, I silently fumed as the horse cantered home. I was behind Roman, but I didn't dare attempt to fling myself from the horse. I'd likely further injure myself or, worse, if I survived, be stoned to death by the villagers. As far as I could tell, there wasn't a friendly face in the crowd.

When we arrived at Roman's home, he reined the horse to a stop and said, "Get off."

I slid to the ground and landed on shaky legs.

"Get in the house at once," Roman said. "And wait for me there."

"But…" I started to protest but stopped when I saw his dark expression. I'd never been more frightened by a man in my life. Fists by my side, I charged toward the front door, flung it open, and slammed it shut.

It closed with a satisfying bang. I leaned back against the door, strategizing. Roman had utterly humiliated me, leaving me ready to burst into tears or cut off his head.

When footsteps clattered outside, I stepped away from the door and whirled around as he crossed the threshold.

"How dare you humiliate me like that? I was able to handle myself just fine," I said, glowering.

Roman slammed the door shut. The entire room shuddered from the impact. "Are you serious? Look at you. You're bloody and bruised. Even your hand is bleeding again!"

Fire blazed from his intense Caribbean-sea-colored eyes.

I flung my arms into the air. "And you shamed me in front of the entire town."

Roman charged me, seized my shoulders, and backed me into the wall. "You made a promise to me. What you did today is *wrong*. You have no right to dishonor a guard of the emperor."

His neck was corded, and the arteries pulsed with blood. Heat radiated from him like a furnace.

I stabbed his sweaty chest with my finger. "Don't you dare talk to me like that. I'm a well-respected woman where I come from."

Roman leaned into my touch. "A well-respected woman wouldn't say the things you say. She wouldn't act like a man in public or in private, and she sure wouldn't fight an esteemed guard of the emperor."

His voice emerged raw and menacing.

"Get your hands off of me," I said, pushing against his chest.

He released me. "Go get cleaned up."

"No!" I spit out the word.

"Then I'm keeping your weapons." He turned as if I was dismissed.

I grabbed his arm. "You can't do that to me. Those things are *mine,* and I need them back immediately. They're dangerous, and they can create chaos if they get into the wrong hands. And I don't trust you with them."

He pried my fingers from his biceps. "You don't have much choice in the matter, do you?"

Flinging my arm away, he sauntered down the hall.

I stormed past him, pushing my way to my room, where I slammed the door right when he walked by. Then, I flung everything that wasn't tacked down to the floor: clothes, vases, basins. I didn't have a voice here in Rome.

The door flew open and Roman stormed inside the room. He grabbed me and pushed me face down on the bed, his knee in my back and his strong hands restraining my arms. "This is *my* house, my room. You are not to defile it!"

"You don't understand why I'm so angry. You're letting an innocent child be abused by a monster. Anthony only wants to be taught to fight. He asked me to help him protect himself from his father," I said as best I could with the side of my face pressed into the musky-smelling bedding.

"Is that what started the fight?" Roman said.

"Yes! I can help him—I can help Anthony defend himself from his father."

"Marcellious is not Anthony's father, and he's definitely not your problem." He applied weight to the knee, which jabbed into my lower back.

"But he's a *child*. You saw the bruises on his face and arms. He's probably got other injuries, too. I can help him."

Roman removed his knee from my back and released my arms.

I flipped on my back lest he changed his mind and pinned me to the bed again.

"I'll consider your request," he said. "I'll tell you when I think you're ready. In the meantime, you cannot go anywhere unless Amara is by your side. You're to conceal your hair and do not make eye contact with anyone under any circumstances except for Amara. Understood?"

I gritted my teeth and nodded. I abhorred being treated like a child under a man's thumb.

Apparently satisfied with my answer, Roman pivoted and stalked toward the door. "And clean up this mess at once."

Now I really felt like a toddler. I wanted to wail and batter my fists at him, but I held myself in check until he was gone. Then, I picked up a piece of clothing, wadded it into a ball, and threw it at the wall.

It landed with a dull, unsatisfying thud.

"I mean it, Olivia," Roman called from wherever he was.

Asshole. I ground my teeth together, but I did what was requested—I cleaned my goddamned room.

After this encounter, weeks went by, with me accompanying Amara to the village to procure supplies. I kept my head down each time, talked to no one, and avoided eye contact. If the villagers recognized me, they didn't let on. And every day, Anthony approached me.

"Please, miss," he begged, groveling at my feet.

"Go away, Anthony," I said every time.

Today, he begged me to help again. I noted fresh bruises on his neck, and he had a black eye, nearly swollen shut. Something inside me snapped.

"Did he do this to you?" I exclaimed.

Anthony dropped his gaze to the ground. "Yes."

I ground my teeth together and beseeched the sky for answers. "Where can we meet in secret?"

Hopeful, shining eyes stared back at me. "We can do it on the beach before mother wakes up. Marcellious is never home. He lives at the palace."

I frowned, glancing at Amara's back as she dickered with a vendor.

"How does he do this to you?" I gestured at Anthony's wounds.

"He makes surprise visits to check and see if Mother has a lover and if I've done my chores. His visits are random… always unexpected."

"Does he arrive in the morning?" I said.

Anthony looked up at me with haunted eyes. "Rarely."

"But he has come in the morning before your mother gets up?"

The kid swallowed.

"Not good…" I said.

It was risky all around. I could escape the house after Roman left and before Amara got up. Roman left at dawn, and Amara awakened an hour or so later.

"We can meet immediately after dawn breaks, but only for forty-five minutes. No one in my household can see me leave."

Anthony nodded.

Amara glanced over her shoulder at me.

"What are you doing?" She hurried over to us. "Anthony, you must leave her alone. You'll get her in terrible trouble."

Her gaze snagged on his injuries. Lifting Anthony's chin in her bony hand, she turned his face back and forth. Tears glistened in her eyes.

Finally, she released Anthony and said to me, "Don't make me regret this. You can work with the boy in the late afternoon. But you must stay in the shadows and not allow yourself to be seen by anybody. And you *must* get home before Roman arrives at eight in the evening. I'll tell him you escaped without my knowledge if he catches you. I won't take the blame."

Her milky brown eyes took on a fierceness I'd never seen.

"Understood. I agree to your terms," I said solemnly. My head pivoted toward Anthony. "Where can we meet in private?"

He thought a moment, then said, "There's a private cove I go to at the beach. No one is ever there. That's where we can train."

I nodded. "Okay. I'll meet you there tomorrow. Now, go!"

I shooed him away with a sweep of my hands.

Amara and I finished our shopping, but an uneasy tension passed between us. Still, I was thankful she'd agreed to let Anthony learn how to defend himself.

The following day, the one after that, and the one after that, I scurried down to the beach, feeling like a skulking criminal. I relaxed when Anthony and I climbed the sharp rocks to the private cove. That was when we trained. That was when I was focused, and my mind was clear, untroubled by anything. I taught him to defend himself, never attack, using the principles of Aikido.

Anthony was a quick study. He picked up the techniques effortlessly.

When our hour was over, I snuck home, staying in the shadows, keeping my head down.

Every night at eight, Roman strode through the door.

I took out every bad thing that'd ever happened to me on Roman. And he seemed to do the same, constantly jabbing at my foul moods and closing himself into his room to dine alone.

Clearly, he was miserable with my presence.

Obviously, I was distraught about being stuck in Rome. I'd been betrayed by Tristan, so deeply hurt by him I couldn't seem to recover.

I was confused by Lee's actions before I'd been hurled into the past.

In my mind now, all men were to be mistrusted. I knew Roman was only trying to help me, but how did I know whether he had ulterior motives for me?

And Amara was distressed over the constant tension from Roman's and my private war.

The only person who was happy with this arrangement was Anthony.

But I still couldn't trust that Roman wouldn't find out. He was too skilled of a soldier to let something of this magnitude escape his watch. The question was not *if* he found out...it was when.

CHAPTER ELEVEN

OLIVIA

Time blurred into a monotonous rhythm as one day bled into the next here in Rome. Each day I rose, scrubbed floors, helped cook, scrubbed some more, went to the village with Amara and shopped, and returned home exhausted before it was even early afternoon. And, in the late day, I snuck from the house to help train Anthony.

He'd grown so much that he'd become an excellent sparring partner. If Roman noted my toned muscles, he said nothing.

Still, I had no answers about how I could ever get back home. The thought of being trapped here filled me with melancholy. But, on, I trudged through my days.

As we were shopping in the market, however, Amara was interrupted by a female villager. The two huddled together, with me standing self-consciously to the side.

Finally, Amara turned back to me, and the other woman scurried away.

"Here," she said, thrusting the basket she was carrying into my hands.

"Why are you giving this to me?" I was already burdened with the bulk of the goods we'd purchased.

"I'm to go help a villager give birth," Amara said.

"Now?"

"Yes, now. You're to prepare Roman's meal for him. I'll probably be gone overnight." Her lips pressed together as if she was perturbed.

"You will?" I squeaked. The thought of being alone with Roman without Amara's attempts at softening things made me uneasy.

She grabbed both my forearms. "Yes, Olivia. I deliver babies. The villagers count on me for providing this service to them. And, since you're here, you get to prepare Roman's food."

I blew out a breath from between pursed lips.

"And you two…." She released me and waggled her finger at me. "You two are to be civil with one another. Don't burn down the house. Don't even talk to one another if you can't hold your sharp tongue. I'll return when I can, and I want to still have a home to live in, understood?"

She gave me a stern glare.

I nodded. Amara had become like a mother to me since I'd come to Rome. We shared an easy camaraderie with one another, and I felt comforted by her presence—at least until Roman returned home. Then, I became tense and nervous whenever he was in the room with me.

"I'll do my best," I said.

"Do better than your best," Amara said. "Your best has produced nothing but stress and trouble so far."

The lines on her face deepened.

Shame pooled in my belly. I was disheartened to witness the effects Roman's and my fights had caused on this dear, old woman.

"I'll really try, Amara."

A flash of hope lit her eyes. Then she said, "Oh. One more thing. There is a tincture in my healing room on the counter. Pour some of it into a vial and give it to Roman when he retires. It helps him sleep."

"Roman needs herbs to sleep?" I said.

"Yes. He suffers from a sleeping plague," Amara said. "Don't forget. Promise me."

"I promise, Amara."

Amara nodded before she turned and hurried through the crowd to deal with a woman in labor.

As usual, I kept to the shadows and avoided looking at anyone as I speed-walked home. I let the tension fall from my shoulders when I closed the door of Roman's house behind me. I set the baskets on the atrium floor and leaned against the door.

I savored the peace and quiet that permeated the house. It wasn't often I had the chance to be alone besides my room. With a sigh, I carried everything to the kitchen and put it away.

As the day wore on, the rooms in this house began to feel hollow, my increasing loneliness echoing against the walls.

While chopping vegetables, I thought of my father and how I'd belittled him and his time travel story. I wished I'd listened more and told him I believed him, embracing everything he told me. Time travel was not only possible. I'd done it. Instead, I'd rushed through our meal and didn't give him the time of day. Then, perhaps, I'd still be with him, and he'd be alive.

I scooped the vegetables into a sturdy ceramic pot to be placed over the coals.

A rumble of thunder boomed outside, startling me. A torrent of rain followed.

The booming noise shattered awake the memory of my mother's murder, like ripping a bandage from an unhealed wound. The face of the man who killed Mom loomed before me, leering at me, and my hands began to shake.

His eyes were the coldest I'd ever seen. And the way he'd looked at me—I knew I was his next victim.

Who was that man? He seemed to know my mother. They argued as if they were acquainted before he drew a knife and plunged it into her heart.

I was crying to match the rain pattering overhead. Fat tears dripped down my cheeks and spattered on the floor. I missed my mother. I missed my father. I missed Lee, and I missed home most of all. Wiping my eyes with my sleeve, I caught sight of Roman, leaning in the doorway, studying me.

"Is everything all right?" he said in a gentle voice.

"I'm fine." The words launched from my mouth like a grenade. I longed for someone to hold me, embrace me tightly, and tell me that everything would be okay once I could escape this nightmare.

Roman sauntered toward me. "It doesn't look like you're fine."

His kindness was almost worse than his rage. It reached around my heart and squeezed more tears out.

"I said I'm *fine*," I blubbered. When I looked up again, Roman stood before me, all six-four handsomeness and brawn.

My heart jackhammered against my ribs.

Stay away, stay away, stay away, I silently told Roman.

My hand shot out when he reached for me and slapped I him hard.

He jerked back, surprised, touching his face with his hand.

"Your dinner will be ready in a minute, my lord," I said, adding a mock bow.

"I don't want your damn dinner. You can eat here by yourself," Roman said.

"I've been making this stupid meal for you, weeping my eyes out, and you're going to walk away?"

Roman whirled, his mouth opened as if to retort.

In frustration, I picked up the knife I'd used to chop vegetables, hauled back my arm, and threw it toward the wall.

He jutted out his hand, catching the blade and hissing as the sharp edge sliced his palm. In one swift move, he flung the knife across the room, where it clattered against the wall and fell with a tinny clang to the tile floor. Blood dripped from the gash in his hand.

I gasped and pressed my hand to my mouth. What had I done? I didn't mean to hurt Roman. My hot-headed temper needed to be reined in before I did any more harm.

"You need to stop this. I'm sick and tired of your threats and your behavior," Roman said, his face contorted with fury.

I tugged up the hem of my stola and retrieved a small kitchen knife I stole to hide on my body. I never went anywhere without a weapon.

Roman stormed toward me, grabbed the knife, and threw it at the wall. This one landed with a thwack and clattered to the floor, near the kitchen knife.

His voice lowered to a deadly hiss as he stood shaking with rage. "You've got to figure this out. I'm the *only* person who has helped you. I've never touched you or done anything to you, but you're about to unleash an ugly part of me." He seized the bowl I used to hold the chopped vegetables and smashed it on the floor. "Clean this up. I'm done with you."

He whirled and powered away from me.

Trembling, I lowered to the floor and picked up the

pottery fragments wet with Roman's blood. I resumed sobbing, but this time it was for myself.

Where were all the lessons and manners I'd learned about behaving around others? Roman was right. I'd let go of all my values and become a horrible person. Roman and Amara had only shown me kindness, and I'd pushed them away. If Lee or my father were here, they would tell me I'd failed as a person. I was angry at myself, as well as ashamed. I had to apologize to Roman.

After cleaning the floor, I scooped water from a bucket into a shallow basin and grabbed a few rags to carry into Roman's room. I entered his bedroom without knocking.

He sat at his desk chair, holding a cloth over the gash.

I crouched before him, resting the basin on the floor, dipped a rag in the water, and wrung it out. Then, I took his hand and washed it.

"I'm so sorry, Roman. I didn't mean to lash out at you, slap, or even wound you with the knife. Ever since I came to Rome, I have felt lost and confused. I just lost my father and feel so lonely and helpless here. I'm going through a lot, and I don't understand why I'm here. I have everything jumbled in my head, and I have been taking out my anger on you. It's wrong, and I'm sorry." I lifted my gaze to his. "You're right. You and Amara have shown me nothing but kindness since I arrived, and I've behaved unthinkably. I've mistreated you and disrespected you. I'm truly sorry."

My eyes moistened with tears.

His lips pressed in a stern line, and then he let out a long sigh. "Why don't you tell me about yourself? I still know nothing about you. I'm a good listener even if I don't understand you. Please, share your heart with me, and I will try to help. Why are you so hurt and angry?"

CHAPTER TWELVE

OLIVIA

Crouching before Roman in his bedroom, cleansing the gash I'd inflicted on him, I found I was at a loss of words for once. The wicks of the oil lamp flickered and danced against the wall in a golden glow.

Roman allowed me to tend to his wound. Luckily, it was not too deep and began to clot.

Finally, he said, "You're angry, you're hurting, and you're not allowing yourself to grieve your father's death. You have to grieve and express your emotions. If you don't allow yourself to mourn, the darkness will consume you, and you will lose yourself in it."

I looked away from him, and my tears resumed falling down my face. The anger and sadness I'd locked away all these months consumed me, and I didn't know how to deal with it. As the weeks had passed, I'd tried to numb myself, ignore my feelings, and continue with my life. But with each passing day, it had become more challenging. I'd only focused on the hardships, the hell, and the pain here in Rome. I'd lost myself in rage and grief with no family and no friends.

A gentle hand landed on my arm, caressing me. I looked up and locked eyes with Roman.

Care and concern looked back at me from his brilliant blue-green eyes.

I started to wipe away my tears, but he caught my hand in his, stopping me. As we studied one another, my heart skipped a beat, and my breath caught in my throat.

"Don't wipe away your tears but allow them to fall freely," he said, his gaze tangled with mine. "Long ago, someone once told me that speaking about your pain unburdens your soul. It makes you feel better. Can you allow yourself to speak of your sadness?"

He let go of my hand and crouched next to me, never releasing my eyes.

A small smile emerged on my face. Roman wanted to listen to me. He wanted to hear of the terrible nightmares I carried in my heart of the night I lost my father. Just thinking about my father made my heart hurt, and the pain and sadness tore my soul. I'd never discussed my personal life with anyone besides Lee. Not even Tristan knew of my deep and complicated life. And now Roman, a stranger, wanted me to share my most profound sorrow and emotions about that night.

Part of me wanted to share my entire life story with him. But another side of me—the stubborn side—insisted I carry that burden with me, continuing to eat me alive. But, as our eyes locked, I wondered if maybe Roman was right. Perhaps if I shared some parts of my life, the pain would be less heavy and bearable.

"I don't know where to begin." My gaze trailed to look at the flame of the oil lamp.

"You can start anywhere you want," he said softly. "I'm here to listen and help you if I can. But most importantly, I'm here to make your burden bearable and allow you to grieve and express yourself."

With a shuddering sigh, I began. "I fell in love with a man I cared deeply about. But I was so enamored of him that I never noticed the dark mask he wore. It all started with my father wanting to have a morning meal together. I came to my father's house, and he began telling me of...." My gaze flicked up to Roman's and then fluttered away. "Of what he believed and had studied his entire life. And then he told me the man I was with was dangerous and not to be trusted."

"Were you married to this man?" Roman said.

"No, I was not married to him." I narrowed my eyes, wondering how he would regard this admission.

"You lived with him without being married to him?" Deep lines furrowed Roman's forehead.

Tired of crouching, I lowered my rump to the floor and leaned against the wall. "Yes. In the village where I come from, you don't need to be married to live with a man you love and care for."

I waited for his reaction.

"So you were lovers?" he said, the lines of confusion deepening.

"Yes," I said. "It's complicated. It was allowed in my village. It wasn't seen as a way to punish the woman."

Roman held out his palms. "I'm sorry, I didn't mean to upset you. I just want to understand better, that's all. I won't question you again. Please continue." Could I really do this? Could I really share things that had occurred in a time and place that didn't yet exist? My heart told me yes, it was safe to share.

"My father believed that Tristan—the man I was with— was hiding things and wasn't being honest. I defended the man I loved and told my father he was crazy and losing his

SARA SAMUELS

mind. I was with Tristan for two years, and my father surprised me with his suspicions. I was caught off-guard."

"So, this Tristan, the man you were with, was not telling you the truth," Roman said.

"Yes. I became angry. I think you can tell I have a temper." I flashed Roman a wan smile.

"I have seen it many times, now," Roman said, returning the smile, one eyebrow lifted in amusement.

I nodded. "I yelled at my father and left his house, shouting cruel names and hurting him deeply. I regret my actions." I pressed the heels of my hands into my eyes and took a deep, calming breath.

"Where was your mother at this time?" he said.

I lowered my hands from my eyes and flashed him a furious glare as anger ripped through me. Remembering Mom's death—how she was murdered by the dark man, killed without mercy—was an excruciating memory. That day had haunted me nearly every waking hour of my life.

"She was murdered," I said. My teeth clenched together.

Roman wiped his palm across his mouth. "I'm sorry for your losses, Olivia. You bear much pain and sorrow. I, too, know what it feels like to lose people you love. I have lost many dear people in my life, and I know it won't end. It's the circle of life."

Rage boiled inside me. I clenched my shaking fists.

"You don't understand, Roman. Both my father and mother were *murdered*. I was sleeping with Tristan. I shared my body and soul with him. I loved him and cared for him." My voice rose. "And when I witnessed who he was, I was heartbroken. I hated him to the point that when I see him again, I will torture him, destroy him, and then slowly kill him!"

Roman held his hands to me, drawing me up to face him. "But the pain will remain right here."

He reached out a fingertip and drew a circle over my heart.

The touch soothed my fury somewhat.

"And your father will still be dead and gone," he continued. "Vengeance will never be the key to anything. You will only feel emptiness and pain. You might kill Tristan, but your father will remain dead, and nothing will change that."

I yanked my hands away from his gentle embrace, furious at his kindness and his reasonable words. How dare he suggest that I could not exact revenge? As anger seized my heart, so did the awareness of what Roman had done for me tonight.

Roman had listened to me. He had allowed me to share my burden without judgment. And here I was, about to rage at him again.

Roman drew himself up to his full height. "If I knew how to find this man who has betrayed you, I would exact revenge for you so you would not have to carry the burden of grief or the life of this man on your shoulders."

"Noble words, Roman. But that's all they are," I shot back, unable to reel in my anger. "You'll *never* find Tristan."

"Be that as it may," Roman said, his voice rising. "I only want to help."

The arteries in his neck engorged with blood as he glared at me.

"You're right," I said, holding out my palms. "I'm sorry. Thank you. This conversation has helped me greatly. Sharing with you has lifted some of the grief I've carried for so long."

"You're welcome," he said, crossing his arms over his muscled chest.

We simply stood, facing one another, our gazes tangled in confusion.

If we were in Seattle, in my time, we'd no doubt hug. But here in Rome, I had no idea the protocol for "making up after a fight with the guy who lets you live at this house." So, instead, I departed, telling him I'd bring him his dinner and his sleeping draught.

Once that was done, I made way for my own bed. I had no idea what tomorrow held, but I knew I'd better mind my manners. My fate here was uncertain, and I certainly didn't want to end up in worse circumstances. I had to figure out how to escape.

CHAPTER THIRTEEN

OLIVIA

Alone in my bedroom, I tossed and turned on the feather mattress, unable to fall to sleep. It seemed that everything had changed between Roman and me. Inside, there was a new spaciousness where sorrow, rage, and grief once lay. He no longer felt like a stranger to me. Tonight, I'd let my walls slowly tumble down.

Roman was right. Talking through my experience made it easier to bear. The pain was still there. My father was dead... my mother killed... Lee wasn't here. I only had Amara and Roman in my life. They were the only family I had left.

How can I make it back home? I still didn't know where Roman kept my gun and dagger. Even if I could find them, I had no idea how to get home.

I closed my eyes. Could it be that I have a purpose here in Rome? What purpose could that be, though?

Everyone here was rude, bitter, and barbaric. I grew up different—civilized and well-mannered.

After hours of tossing and fretting, I finally drifted into a tortured sleep. A short time later, I was awakened by the sound of yelling. As I came to consciousness, I tried to adjust to my new surroundings. I still couldn't get used to this place. Every time I awakened, I believed I was still dreaming. But the dream always became a reality.

I was no longer in the 21st century but deep into the past.

I tossed the covers aside and rolled from the bed. Padding across the room, I cracked open the door and peeked through the tiny hallway.

It was dark and quiet. Did I imagine the shouts?

I exited my room and headed toward the kitchen.

A violent scream erupted.

Gooseflesh covered my skin as I paused in the darkness and waited.

The scream sounded again, and it was coming from Roman's room.

I raced down the hallway, skidding to a stop in his doorway.

Roman thrashed in his bedding, shouting things like, "I couldn't save them. They wouldn't let me!"

The oil lamps continued to burn, throwing shadows around the room.

"Roman," I said, shaking his shoulder. "Roman! Wake up! You're having a nightmare."

His eyelids fluttered open. He struggled upright then stared at me with unfocused eyes. His arms shot out, and he wrapped his hands around my throat.

I bit his wrist.

He yelled, releasing me, and shook his arm. His eyes cleared as he came to consciousness.

"What are you doing in my sleeping quarters? Leave at once!"

"You were shouting," I said. "You were having a nightmare."

"Oh, gods." He squeezed his eyes shut.

I placed my hand on his forearm, and he yanked it away, lying down and rolling away from me.

"Do you want to talk about your nightmares, Roman? They seem intense and dark," I said softly.

"Leave me alone, Olivia. My nightmares will haunt me until I die."

"Roman, please. I shared with you. Please tell me what's troubling you. What nightmares do you have?" I glanced at the floor, finding the sleeping draught untouched. I reached down and picked up the vial of liquid. "You didn't drink your sleeping herbs. Is this why you need them? They keep away the nightmares?"

I waved my hand in a circle around his head.

He backhanded the glass container from my grip, and it flew across the room, shattering against the stone wall.

My mouth fell open as I stared at him.

"It won't help," he said with a groan. "Nothing helps. My demons will never release me."

"Amara says they help you sleep."

"What the herbs do," he said, keeping his back to me, "is force me into a sluggish unconsciousness. I awaken each day feeling like I've been crushed by boulders. Last night, I thought…"

"Roman…" I placed my palm on his shoulder.

He was covered with sweat.

"Go away, Olivia," he said. "Leave me be."

"What if I don't?"

He stayed silent, my hand on his shoulder, for several long breaths.

One of the oil lamps fizzled out, darkening the room.

Roman let out a long sigh and rolled on his back. He patted the bed, and I sat by his side.

His expression was one of anguish. It broke my heart to see him this way.

"Okay… I will tell you." His Adam's apple bobbed up and down as he swallowed. When he turned to look at me, his eyes appeared tormented, red with fatigue, holding nightmares and ghosts. "I came to Rome when I was twenty-one—that was nine years ago. I became a merchant. I set up a stall in town, but times were hard. I sometimes stole food to survive. A vendor caught me stealing apples, and the Vigiles captured me and threw me into prison. It was a horrible place, crowded with men. The prison was windowless and soulless. Disease spread throughout the small space. We were given little to eat and fought like mongrels over each scrap. No place to piss or defecate save for the floor, so the room smelled like hell."

"Oh, my," I said, repulsed.

Roman stared vacantly at his own private nightmares. "I pleaded with the guards to set me free." His troubled gaze turned to me again. "They laughed at me and called me weak. But they must have seen me fight for survival in the prison because one day, I was released. They told me I had two choices—continue to be a slave for the rest of my life or become a gladiator and win my freedom."

He let out a long sigh. "I chose to be a gladiator. My first fight was with Marcellious. You can imagine how weak I was…."

His face was lined with shadows in the oil lamp light, giving him a hollow appearance.

"Oh, no!" I brought my palm to my mouth.

"Yes. It's true. Marcellious fought mercilessly. He broke every rib in my body, leaving me for dead. I lay on the ground, gasping, waiting to die to the jeers and shouts of the citizens of Rome. But Amara's husband, Gaius, found me.

Somehow he took me to the barracks…and he healed me." Roman took a shuddering breath. "I didn't want to live. I wanted to die. I was in so much pain."

"But you did live," I said, resting my hand on his muscular thigh.

He sucked in a breath but didn't resist my touch. "I knew of Gaius through Amara. She shopped at my stall and bought goods from me. She often told me of her husband and his healing powers."

"So, what did you do? How did you end up so strong, a trained warrior?" I said, stroking his muscled leg with my thumb.

"Gaius, he…" Roman stared into space, lost in his own world. "He told me I could best Marcellious if I trained hard. He said I had potential. So, I took his advice and mastered many skills. I bested men twice my size in the coliseum and became known for my prowess. You see these marks?"

He lifted his tunic over his head to reveal dark symbols, like tattoos on his skin. His chest was rippled with muscles. "I had these branded into my flesh each time I killed one of my opponents."

I gasped and fingered one of the symbols. "You had these branded?"

"Yes. It was painful, but it was necessary. You see, to train as hard as I did, I had to accept a position of servitude to the emperor. The emperor would not allow a person as powerful as me to be on his own." Roman shook his head. "Instead, I was placed in his charge. Did I want that? Not in a thousand years. But I'd be hunted down and slaughtered if I didn't accept. That was made clear to me."

I withdrew my hand.

"I had a friend… His name was Marcus. He was my closest friend. We fought together, side by side. There were none more powerful than us, but we loved each other like brothers. Fighting as we did, we thought we would earn our freedom from the emperor and be sent from his palace to live our lives in peace." His eyes narrowed, and his face hardened. "However, Marcellious had other plans."

He turned his head toward me, and the look of abject misery in his gaze frightened me.

"Marcellious was jealous of Marcus and me. He hated our success in the arena and the attention we garnered from the emperor. I only had to kill one more opponent to gain my freedom. I was elated. I couldn't wait to be free of the emperor. He's a ruthless dictator." Roman's lips pressed together in a hard line. "I often went to bed at night, my skin bloody and raw, whipped by the emperor's slaves."

His lips worked around and around.

"Marcellious, the conniving man that he is, convinced the emperor to only release me on one condition. The condition was the cruelest of all. I was to fight Marcus to the death in the arena."

"Oh, my God," I said. I sat still, listening, but inside, my hatred of Marcellious grew, festering like a poisonous seed.

Roman slid a suspicious glance my way. "Who is this god you invoke? I've not heard an expression such as that. Our gods are many, and we don't call them forth in such a manner."

"I'm sorry," I said. "It's just an expression where I'm from. I'll refrain from using it. Please continue."

I swirled my hand in a circle.

Roman resumed staring into space. "I told Marcellious I refused to fight my friend. He informed me that the emperor had known I would say this. So he declared that if I did not fight my friend, he would have me fight several wild beasts in the coliseum and I'd surely lose my life. Again, I refused. I would rather die than take the life of my best friend. He had a young child and a wife who depended on him." He let out a shuddering sigh. "But, when I told Marcus about the plan, he insisted we fight. 'Slay me,' he said. 'Hack off my limbs. You must choose your freedom. All I ask is that you take care of my boy.'"

A thick silence stretched between us.

Finally, Roman whispered, "And, so I agreed."

I was unable to speak. I couldn't imagine what it would have been like to kill my best friend. I tried to imagine killing Lee, my godfather and mentor, to gain freedom from servitude. The thought was simply unfathomable.

Roman continued talking in a tone that was as dead as his friend. "Marcellious watched the fight. It was brutal and heartbreaking. I couldn't believe I was slaying my closest ally." He rolled his lips between his teeth before saying, "I killed Marcus with a swift and honorable death. Afterward, I threw my sword to the ground, fuming with rage. I shouted out to Marcellious who stood by the emperor, 'Are you happy now? Is this what you wanted? You might have been the king of this arena once, but now I am the king of the arena.' I headed for the box where the emperor sat, intending to claim my freedom. Only he…he said to me…" Roman's voice cracked. "He told me I was free of my duty as a gladiator, but now I was to be his guard. He said no man as ruthless as to kill his best friend could be allowed to roam freely."

The silence blanketed me. I felt heavy, barely able to coax my lungs to inhale.

Roman turned to me, and his eyes were void of life. "Now you know my story. I had to kill Marcus to gain my freedom, but even that was taken from me. My only concession was that I was allowed to live here with Gaius' wife after he died.

Normally, a guard in the emperor's employ is given little time away from his servitude."

He drifted off in thought.

"I had to tell Anthony that I took his father from him. But, still, I could not care for him. Marcellious took Lydia, Anthony's mother, as a lover before we even laid Marcus to rest. I'm haunted by my past. Tortured. I have no one to confide in, save for you, now. My family, like yours, has been taken from me. Even my twin brother—I don't know where he is."

"I didn't know you had a twin brother. Do you look identical?" I said.

"No, we don't have the same features," he said. "I don't know how to find him. I've been living in my own nightmares for years."

A beat of silence stretched between us.

With another long sigh, Roman said, "Now you know my life. Every day I work with a monster, and then I come home, and you yell at me. I hope from now on we won't hold onto anything, and we're partners in this and we can help one another."

I nodded. "I want that, too."

Our gazes entwined, and it was as if we were plunged into our own private bubble of intimacy. I eyed the impressive tattoo on Roman's chest. Besides the branding, he boasted an elaborate pattern covering his heart, shoulder, and upper arm.

Roman was perhaps the most handsome man I'd ever laid eyes on. There was a nobility to him and enormous power that attracted me. Since Tristan, I trusted no one. I had to stay away from love and focus on myself. Falling in love with Roman would be my undoing, and I wouldn't let that happen.

I was from the future, a Timeborne. He was from Rome, and I didn't plan to stay here long.

I yanked my gaze from his and stared at his jaw.

He rolled his lips between his teeth and studied me. Then, he said, "I know you're training Anthony."

My stomach clenched. Was this where it got ugly between us again?

"I had to do it, Roman. I couldn't just let Anthony be abused. Marcellious is a vicious man. You can hate me or fight me all you want, but I'm proud of training Anthony. He's growing into a powerful young man who will be able to protect himself and his mother."

"You're a skilled fighter," he said, looking at me squarely. "And I'm honored to have met you."

I narrowed my eyes, touched by his words.

"I would like to train with you. If we're to be allies, we need to know one another's strengths and weaknesses. I know you fight well, but you're not using your full potential when you fight—I can sense it," he said.

Inside, I bristled, ready to strike out at him. Instead, I took a deep breath. "To learn from a warrior such as yourself is an honor."

His hand came to rest on my thigh. For some reason, whether it was the day's fatigue or the new bond we'd forged, I melted by his side.

I ignored my earlier admonitions not to get close to Roman. We laid still until his breathing became deep and even. And then, I, too, succumbed to slumber.

At some point, strong arms cradled me and took me to my room. But I never fully awakened, feeling safe for the first time since arriving in Rome.

But Rome was a brutal land. How long could this feeling possibly last?

CHAPTER FOURTEEN

OLIVIA

I awoke as the fingers of dawn crawled their way into my sleeping quarters. Clatters and clangs rang from the kitchen, indicating Roman's presence—Amara never made that much noise. I decided to prepare his breakfast before he left for the palace, so I rolled from the bed, shrugged on a clean stola, and hurried down the hall.

When I entered the kitchen, he looked up, holding a basket of ground wheat, an expression of wary vulnerability on his face.

"Good morning," I said. "Here, let me help."

I glanced into the bowl before him and saw the ingredients for wheat pancakes, a staple here in Rome. I added water to the mixture and crossed to the brazier, where I stoked the coals Roman had lit.

"I'll bring this out to the triclinium. Go on out there and relax."

Roman cocked his head, then flashed a small smile before departing.

When I'd prepared several pancakes with dates and abundant fresh cheese on the side, I headed to the dining room to serve him.

He was already lounging on one of the couches in the manner in which we dined at night, sometimes. Apparently, this was a sign of wealth, but Roman and Amara didn't seem wealthy—they were more of what I'd call middle class in the century I was born. But perhaps their status was what Amara referred to as the emperor's "concession."

I handed him the plate, and he reached for it. Our fingers brushed together, and I let out a small gasp. Our eyes locked, and something new passed between us…something intimate and altogether awkward.

We both looked away at the same time.

"Did you sleep well?" I asked, sitting on the couch opposite him.

"I did, thank you." He shoveled food into his mouth with his fingers. "And you?"

"Yes, after we each spoke, I slept very well." I stretched out on the couch and propped my head in my hands. "So, when should we start training?"

"Tonight, after the evening meal. Will that work for you?" He lifted his gaze to mine.

"Of course." I smiled. There was newfound ease in conversing as if we did this every day.

The front door clattered, and then Amara shuffled into the room, looking bone-weary but radiant. "We did it. Athena has produced a son for her husband."

She beamed.

"Excellent," Roman said, sitting up. "A son is always welcome."

I ignored the slight on the female gender as he polished off the last of his meal and glanced at me.

"Thank you for breakfast," he said warmly.

"You're welcome," I said with equal warmth.

Amara's head swiveled back and forth between us. "You haven't killed one another, the house isn't burned to the ground, and, dare I say, you're acting pleasant to one another. What, pray, did you do last night?"

"We resolved our issues," I said.

"We've agreed to be allies." Roman stood, set his plate on the couch, and then met my gaze with affection. "I'll see you tonight to train."

He exited the room.

"Allies? And training?" Amara said. "Did something happen between you two last night? Did Roman kiss you?"

She shuffled to one of the couches and nearly fell on top of it, appearing exhausted.

"Oh, no." I sat up, waving my palms at her. "Nothing like that. I'm not ready to give my heart to anyone."

"You'd make a good pair," Amara said, adding a secretive smile. "You're both strong. And you're as beautiful as he is handsome."

I blushed, suddenly obsessed with staring at my blunt fingernails. "Oh...I'm just not ready to be with a man again...My heart is healing."

"Pity," Amara said. "He needs to sire children. He'd make an excellent father."

This comment really made me blush. I never dreamed of having children with Tristan, thank God. But the thought of carrying Roman's child made my insides flutter.

"Do you have children?" I asked, hoping to redirect the conversation.

"Not anymore," she said, her expression bruising with sorrow. "You remind me every day of my daughter, actually. She was good-hearted and strong. Quite capable as are you."

She rubbed her eyes with her fingertips. When she withdrew her fingers, damp spots circled her eyes.

"What happened to her?" I said.

"She's with my husband now," Amara said tiredly. "They're in the heavens with the gods."

I sensed the pain in her words, so I didn't press her further about that topic but chose a new one. "I've meant to ask you —in the marketplace when I fought Marcellious...."

Amara flashed me a wary gaze.

"You were the one who made him stop. I thought he would kill me—but *you* got him to stop. Do you know him?" I pressed my palms into my thighs.

"I do know Marcellious. He wasn't always cruel. In fact, he used to be a good man." She brushed her palms together as if ridding herself of memories. "My husband was also a good man but left this world too soon."

She added, "I think you and Roman should get together and try."

A shiver launched up my spine. I shook my head at the pleasurable sensations coursing through me.

"I can't, Amara. I just can't."

Amara stared at the floor. "I see. I think if you cooperate with Roman, he'll let you go. Which would be a pity...." With a groan, she pushed away from the couch and crossed to stand before me. Grasping my chin with her bony fingers, she said, "You're a good woman, Olivia. I'm glad to see you and Roman have made peace. At least consider what I've said. You and Roman would make a wonderful couple. Now, I'm going to go rest. Please take care of the household while I slumber."

She released me and shuffled away, her back more stooped than ever.

Throughout the day, I considered Amara's words.

I couldn't give in to any feelings between Roman and me —I just couldn't. But, when he strode through the door at eight, I found that my knees got weak, and my heart beat faster.

Shut this down, Olivia!

He seemed awkward, pausing as if I'd held him back with some super-human power shield.

"Olivia," he finally said.

"Roman." I ducked my head. "I'll be ready to train after we eat."

"Good, good," he said, continuing his stride.

We all ate and talked at the evening meal, speaking of nothing save for the weather and other incidental things. Amara filled us in on Athena's birthing process, which seemed to make Roman uneasy.

I smirked at his discomfort. Big, strong man who kills countless men can't deal with the blood and guts of birth...

After Amara and I cleaned up, I headed to my bedroom to prepare for training.

I donned the stola I'd modified to train with Anthony. It had no sleeves, and it made for suitable training attire when I tucked the chopped-off draping into the belt. It was loose and fluid.

I made my way into the back garden. Roman was already there, practicing with his sword. And, like the devil he was, he was shirtless.

Good grief. How could I focus on my moves when he was standing there all shirtless and wearing some sort of leather kilt?

He grinned as if he was well aware of his effect on me.

I should peel off the stola, and then we'd see a reaction. I chuckled at my wanton thoughts.

"I brought a sword for you," he said, inclining his head toward a sleek, deadly-looking blade.

I glanced in the direction indicated. Holy Moley. When I trained back home, we usually didn't use deadly weapons.

I picked up the sword and hefted it up and down.

"Too heavy?" he said, his grin broadening.

I held the polished handle with two hands and swung it in an arc back and forth. "This will suffice."

Roman whistled. "Think so?"

"Watch me."

We parried and thrust, practicing different techniques. He showed me his typical "bludgeon your enemy moves" while I shared my finesse skills. Then, after a brief rest, we practiced hand-to-hand combat.

Our bodies glided over one another, slick with sweat. I taught him some basic Aikido moves, and he quickly mastered them as if he'd been doing them all his life. He gripped my forearms when he effortlessly rolled backward in response to my attack, drawing me down to the ground.

Surprised, I balanced on his sweaty chest, trying to keep myself at arm's length.

"I've never seen this technique result in a takedown," I said, panting. "Nice move."

He said nothing as our gazes locked.

I stared into twin pools of ocean blue and, as if magnetized, my mouth opened, and my head lowered.

Roman stared at my lips.

When I was barely an inch away from his face, his hot breath puffed against my skin.

I swallowed as I looked down at him.

"Olivia," he said. "I…"

Slowly, I shook my head. "We can't…."

"No," he said, but neither of us made a move to disentangle.

His powerful body beneath me was rock solid in all the right places. He gripped my wrists as if clinging to his remaining self-restraint.

At this moment, I wanted Roman so bad that I was blinded to any other impulse. I was utterly consumed by his strength, power, and skill as a fighter. His incredible good looks were the cherry on the sundae. No wonder the artists of this land carved such splendid statues of men. Roman, the man, lived in these times.

Yet, how would we fare in a fight if we were this smitten with one another? We'd be dead, that was what. Disgusted, I climbed off him with a groan and brushed off my stola.

He rolled onto his belly and climbed to standing. "The emperor is having a birthday party. Have Amara see to your attire. I'd like you to be my guest."

I was stunned. "You want me to be by your side at the emperor's party? Won't my presence cause a scene?"

Roman waved his hand dismissively. "You'll get to see me fight. The emperor wants entertainment, so entertainment he shall get."

He leaned over to retrieve his sword and twirled it deftly in his hand as if the moment we'd just shared didn't exist.

"And who will you fight?" I said, picking up the sword he'd brought for my use.

"Marcellious. The emperor thinks it's funny. He knows Marcellious has blood lust in his heart for me. That's why I thought it useful to train with you. Your style of fighting is unlike any method our warriors employ."

His gaze tangled with mine, and I fell into a space where the only two people who existed on this planet were Roman and me. It was an utterly electric sensation.

"So," he said, breaking eye contact. "Will you do me the honor and join me at the party?"

His mouth set in a firm line.

"I wouldn't miss it for the world," I said, staring at his lips. I'd almost kissed that mouth. I still wanted to. And the feelings beneath that desire scared the life out of me. It seemed that I was falling in love with Roman Alexander... And I was not sure if he felt the same way.

CHAPTER FIFTEEN
OLIVIA

Amara had been fussing over me for hours, preparing me for the feast at the emperor's palace. She'd washed and oiled my hair and body and dried me lovingly. Then, she bade me sit in my sleeping quarters while she fetched the gown she'd made for me. I felt so loved by Amara that when she left the room, a few tears escaped my eyes as I thought of my own mother.

From what I remembered of her, Mom wasn't nearly as domestic as Amara. Still, then, other choices had been available to her. Who knew the role she might have played had she lived in these difficult times?

In the 21st century, Mom was a passionate academic and an enthusiastic archaeologist—or, at least, she had been. Papa had told me many stories of the archaeological digs they'd been on together, in Peru, Greece, even Rome. After I was born, their excursions ceased.

Still, she often played a game with me at the *Life after Life* antique store. "We're going to be archaeologists today, Olivia," she'd tell me. She'd show me a picture of something small from the store catalog, like a tiny blackbird egg ceramic scent bottle or a silver-tipped smelling salt vial. When I memorized it, she'd say, "when you find it, we'll discuss what it is and how it was used, okay? Now, you head in the back, and I'll hide the artifact you're to look for today, alright?"

I'd nod eagerly and scamper into the back.

Mom would conceal the object on one of the numerous shelves throughout the store. After it was hidden, she'd come and get me and tell me if I found it by lunchtime, we'd go and get ice cream.

"Oh, goody!" I'd squeal and set off on the hunt.

As I matured, I realized what a valuable activity that was. Mom was clever at hiding something, and it often took me hours to find the object. She'd give me hints and clues if I got stuck or frustrated. As I roamed the store, I'd carefully push aside and wonder about the treasures Mom and Papa had procured throughout the years. Then, when I'd find the object, as I always did, we'd discuss how it had been created and what it was used for. No amount of bookwork in school could teach me the kind of history I'd learned in *Life after Life* with my mom as the teacher. And she'd engendered in me a love of ancient cultures.

Had it all been preparation for being a Timeborne? Sadly, I'd never know the answer to that.

I blinked away my tears when Amara bustled toward me, carrying a long, rustling swath of fabric.

"I can't wait to see this on you," she said, her own eyes glistening.

When she held a garment before me, I gasped, rising from the bed.

"Oh, Amara! This is exquisite!" I reached for the stola, which had been dyed a soft green and edged with gold.

Another simpler garment dyed the color of red wine, still hung on her arm.

"Put this on first," she said, handing me the wine-colored garment.

I took it and set the green stola on the bed. I slid the simple dress over my head and let it float into position. Then, I donned the stola.

Amara pressed her hand to her mouth. "You remind me so much of my daughter, Olivia. I feel as if your presence has been a gift to me. You've let me have a piece of my daughter back."

I nearly blubbered at her statement, but I held myself back. "And you've been like a mother to me, dear Amara."

I reached for her and fell into her arms, crying.

Amara eased back and said, "Wait. We have one more item." She hurried away and returned a moment later carrying what looked like gold chains. She wound them around my waistline and stood back. "You're such a beautiful woman, Olivia. Wait until Roman sees you."

"Wait until Roman sees what?" His deep, throaty voice rang through the hall.

When he appeared in the doorway, my knees nearly buckled.

He'd dressed in a short purple toga flecked with gold thread. His muscular arms were bare, as were his powerful legs. He stood, mouth open, staring at me, transfixed, all brawn and power.

When he managed to close his mouth, he said, "My dear goddess, you put Athena to shame by your beauty."

He crossed the room in two quick steps, took my hand, and pressed a kiss to my palm.

His warm lips grazing my skin felt more intimate than any encounter I'd ever had.

"You're exquisite, Olivia." He released my hand and looked deeply into my eyes.

"Thank you," I said, blushing madly.

Roman seemed to zip up his reaction. He took a step backward, nodding at Amara. "You've done a fine job preparing her for the celebration."

Whoa. What just happened? One minute he was warm and open; the next moment, he became stiff and unyielding.

Amara's eyes shone. "You two look splendid."

She clasped her hands together.

Roman's lips pressed together firmly. Then, he turned to me and said, "Are you ready?"

When I stepped outside Roman's home, I was greeted by, of all things, a red chariot. Tempestas and another horse stood hitched to the open-backed cart.

"Is this what we're heading to the palace in?"

"Yes," Roman said, smirking. "Is this not to your liking?"

"No, it's..." I searched for words. "It's wonderful. I've just never ridden in a chariot before."

His eyebrows stitched together, but he said nothing as he helped me into the cart. He joined me, and we stood, bodies pressed together.

I held onto the metal rim as Roman took the reins.

With a soft cluck, the horses lunged forward. Roman urged them into a trot, and our bumpy ride began.

Once we arrived at our destination, Roman helped me from the chariot, handed the reins to a boy, and pressed a coin into his hands. Stooping to look the lad in the eye, he said,

"You'll get one more when I return, as long as my horses are in good shape."

"Yes, sir," the boy said solemnly, slipping the coin into a hidden pocket inside his tunic.

Roman held out his forearm, and I placed my palm on his warm, muscled arm. As he escorted me toward the palace, his countenance grew somber.

"Are you alright?" I asked.

"This is where I *work*, Olivia," he said grimly. "The only saving grace is that you're by my side."

He drew his arm across his body and pressed his palm on my hand.

We approached the palace, lit by torches and looking like a scene out of a fantasy tale. People were dressed in luxurious garments, and candles and torches illuminated everything. Ordinary townsfolk gawked and hid in the shadows, much like my 21st-century culture gawked and fawned over England's royal family. I felt as if I were in a dream.

I had been so traumatized when I'd arrived in Rome and had been dragged to the palace with a bag over my head. I had no idea how magnificent this place was. We strode through an elegant atrium, down a corridor, and entered a vast triclinium the size of my apartment back in Seattle.

Marble columns lined the dining room, and colorful frescoes adorned the walls and ceiling. Candle-lit chandeliers draped from overhead, highlighting the gilded sconces and mirrors that hung on the walls. Statues of male nudes and women dressed in flowing gowns stood as sentinels along the sides, watching over the revelry already in full swing.

Tables had been set up on either side of the room while a scantily clad aerobatic ensemble pranced and leaped in the center.

To my virgin eyes, it looked like Cirque du Soleil on steroids.

Female servants glided about, carrying trays of meats, cheeses, fruit, and wine. A buxom beauty with flaxen tresses sauntered toward us, carrying a tray bearing a flagon of wine and several gold goblets.

"Would you like some Mulsum wine?" she said to Roman, not sparing me a glance.

"Olivia?" he said, pulling me close in a protective gesture.

"Only if you want some," I said.

Roman reached for two goblets and held them out for the servant to fill. Then, he handed one to me and looked deeply into my eyes. "Thank you for being here."

"Thank you for inviting me," I said as a shiver of pleasure shot through my belly. A cloak of intimacy surrounded us, making me feel alone with Roman in this palace overflowing with people.

Roman's eyes grew hooded as he studied me. He stepped closer, and I thought he might kiss me. Did I want to be kissed? Before answering that question, he circled his wrist with mine and lifted the goblet to his mouth.

I did the same, giddy with the intimacy each touch of this handsome, provocative man evoked in me.

"To us," he said, tipping the goblet to his lips.

"To us," I said, not really understanding what that meant to Roman but savoring the many feelings coursing through my body. I sipped the warm, honey-infused wine, lowered the goblet, and unwound my arm from his.

A booming voice interrupted us. "Roman!"

As Emperor Severus approached, dressed in a full-length gold-threaded toga, a chill launched up my spine.

"Emperor," Roman said, bowing his head.

"I see you've brought the woman I gifted you. Is she serving you well?" the emperor said, beaming.

Oh, how I wanted to take that man to the ground. Every muscle in my body tensed, preparing for a fight.

"Olivia has become an asset to our household, yes," Roman said politely, touching my shoulder in warning.

When I glanced at him, he gave a subtle shake of his head.

"Excellent!" the emperor said. "Come, come. I'll show you where to sit."

He strode toward the front, where the largest of all the tables sat. Several women cooed as he approached. The emperor swept his hand to the right, indicating the table closest to his.

"This table shall be yours. Marcellious shall dine across from you." He gestured to the table opposite ours. "Now, sit! Eat! Be merry!"

Severus sailed toward his gilded seat placed between the many women.

Their trills and coos grew louder.

When the emperor graced his seat, the women's hands fell upon him like turkey vultures feasting upon their prey.

I scanned my surroundings, alert for any threats.

"Olivia?" Roman said.

He held out his hand and guided me to our seats.

Sitting at this feast of feasts, being served copious amounts of food and wine as if I were an extra on an extravagant movie set, I felt ten kinds of awkward. I'd never been schooled in "partying with the emperor," so I observed as much as possible. Mostly, it looked like any sort of behavior was acceptable.

Women sauntered around, their breasts bared, while men

flashed their cock at times, regaling the bare-breasted women. Laughter, jeers, and shouts filled the room.

It was as 21st-century historians described it: utter debauchery.

While the acrobats pranced and tumbled, I ate small bites of the various dishes. There was pork, and lamb roasted to perfection, falling from the bone. Dates, goat cheese, puddings, and pastries were in abundance. And although the wine was watered down as a sign of what a "civilized culture" should drink, I consumed enough of the sweet wine to catch a slight buzz.

While Roman and I made small talk, most of the time, his attention was drawn to one of his fellow warriors. They snuck glances at me, as they engaged Roman in conversation. As a result, I felt like I was an exhibit, nothing more, during the meal. But Roman seemed to sense this as his hand kept sliding under the table to squeeze my thigh or hold my hand. I took comfort in these small acts of kindness.

As the evening progressed, lines of stress formed around his eyes. Was he worried about the fight? Whatever it was, I found myself offering him comfort and support, whether it was a smile and a shy glance or stroking his solid thigh.

The emperor lurched to his feet when servants began to clear the tables.

"Fellow citizens," he bellowed. "It is time for tonight's entertainment—the *gladiator* fight."

A din of noise erupted in the room.

Severus waved his hand at the acrobats and shooed them away.

They pranced, hopped, and tumbled from the floor, leaving me with an eyeful of Marcellious, directly opposite us.

My gut rebelled at the sight of him, threatening to expel the contents of my stomach.

Roman's body grew rigid.

The two men locked gazes in a war of wills.

Several warriors surged toward both Marcellious and Roman.

The emperor climbed onto the table, stepping on a platter of the remains of meat. He swept his hand toward Marcellious. "Esteemed Praetoria Marcellious Demarrias shall fight as Secutor!"

Roman seemed to pale, and his features grew pinched.

I frowned as I studied him. "What's going on?"

With as grim an expression as I'd ever seen on his face, he said, "You'll see."

"Tell me," I said, placing my palm on his forearm, but my words were drowned out.

The crowd cried out and applauded as the men climbed on Marcellious' table and drew him up, holding his arm high.

Marcellious yanked his arm from their grip, leaped to the floor, and pumped his arms up and down. He swaggered up and down the length of the massive triclinium, egging on the guests.

Some people hissed and booed. Some called out his name as he seemed to soak up the adulation.

The emperor grinned. "And my esteemed Praetoria Roman Alexander shall fight as Retiarius!"

Same as with Marcellious, several warriors climbed on our table, spilling platters of food and goblets to the floor. They hoisted Roman up with them, holding his arm in the air.

The clamor of noise grew louder as cheers and shouts filled the room, echoing off the marble walls.

Roman leaped to the floor, threw his hands up, and urged the crowd on.

I could barely hear myself think.

The warriors surrounded Marcellious and Roman and swept them away.

The drunken citizens surged toward a door at the opposite end of the room in which we'd arrived.

Three of the women who sat with the emperor approached me and took both my arms.

Laughing gaily, they guided me forward.

"Wait! Where are we going?" I said.

"The emperor says you are to sit with us," a pretty blonde said.

"We're going to the Colosseum, of course," a brunette said.

They kept laughing and tittering as we proceeded, smashed against all the other sweaty, smelly partygoers as we rushed forward like a mighty sea of spawning salmon. We trekked down a long passageway, propelled forward whether we wanted to or not. I felt suffocated, trapped as I was pushed, shoved, and maneuvered ahead.

Finally, I was ushered through a richly decorated archway and deposited at a marble podium at ground level in the Colosseum. Blonde girls one and two and brunette girl took their seats. The emperor arrived and took his place between them while several other well-dressed men, presumably senators, took their places in adjacent podiums.

Torches lit the arena, and people continued to fill the enormous Colosseum.

I gaped at my surroundings. I'd seen the Colosseum when I'd trekked to Rome in the 21st century, but only the remnants of it. Here, at this moment, the arena stood intact in full glory.

"So, tonight, you shall see what my Praetoria Cohors consist of," the emperor said, leaning toward me. He picked up a flagon someone had deposited at the table before us and poured some wine into a goblet.

"No, thank you," I said, trying to push the goblet away.

"I insist," he said offhandedly, filling his own golden goblet to the brim.

"May the best man win!" He lifted his wine glass high.

May the best man win? Icy fingers of dread squeezed my stomach. I thought this fight was for show?

A heavy wooden gate opened at the far end of the arena, and a man appeared out of the shadows. He strode onto the sand covering the arena floor, dressed in a shiny bronze helmet with two circular eye holes, bronze manicas, or arm guards. His legs were covered with metal greaves, and he carried a sword in one hand and a six-foot-tall scutum shield in his other hand, which had been decorated with a crest. A subligaculum, or loincloth, covered his hips, and a wide leather belt known as a balteus held the loincloth in place.

I knew this because Papa had purchased and sold a gladiator uniform for a nice sum after Mom died. I used to imagine what it would have been like to fight in such a cumbersome uniform.

I squinted at the gladiator, trying to determine if that was Roman.

The man seemed much stockier than Roman, so I guessed it to be Marcellious. He seemed to move laboriously as he circled through the arena, swinging his sword in mighty arcs to the cheers and whoops of the crowd.

The arena doors closest to us parted, and another man stood in the shadows.

That's got to be Roman. My heart soared at the sight of him until he stepped out onto the sand.

I pressed my hand to my mouth.

His uniform provided no protection at all. This was why he'd become so tense when the emperor made his declarations of the fight. Apparently, this was the uniform of the Retiarius. There was no helmet to guard his head. Instead, he stalked, helmetless, bare-chested, around the arena, carrying only a trident and what looked like a net. One metal manica covered his left arm while a galerus shoulder guard had been strapped in place by leather. A loincloth covered his hips, yet his feet and legs were bare.

This hardly seemed like a fair fight. Roman was, in essence, at the mercy of his opponent, with only his moves, wit, and speed to work with.

When Roman stalked before the emperor's podium, he barely glanced at me. He secured his net in the waistband of his loincloth, rendering his left hand accessible. His jaw seemed to be carved out of marble and his eyes of glass. If I hadn't been living with him for the past six months, I'd think him the stuff of legends.

The two men gradually tightened their circles until they were within stabbing distance.

The cacophony of sound all around me was nearly unbearable. I pressed my hands to my ears as my eyes stayed glued on Roman.

Marcellious made the first move, charging at Roman, sword drawn, letting out an ear-splitting yell that carried over the shouts and jeers of the audience.

Roman thrust out his trident.

Marcellious lifted his shield and knocked away the blow as if Roman wielded a fork. Then, he lunged, trying to skewer Roman.

Roman dropped to the ground and somersaulted backward in an Aikido roll, landing on his feet.

The crowd let out a collective, "Oh!"

When Marcellious charged again, Roman slid out of the

way, capturing Marcellious' wrist with his free hand and propelling him forward.

I taught him that move. I grinned.

Marcellious stumbled in his clunky gear, nearly losing his footing.

The audience guffawed and jeered.

Marcellious stormed toward Roman, swinging his sword like a battle-ax. Roman tried to dodge, but the blade caught him in the shoulder.

I let out an uncharacteristic scream. Sure, I was used to fighting, but not like this—not in a brutal life and death exhibition involving someone I deeply cared about.

Roman's head snapped to look at me. Marcellious charged again, grazing the tip of his sword against Roman's chest.

Oh, dear God. Please don't let him be distracted by me.

I vowed to stay silent until the fight was over. Roman *had* to be the victor.

The crowd yelled at the sight of blood trickling from Roman's shoulder and torso.

Roman wiped some of the blood with his thumb and licked it. He removed the net, swung it overhead like a lasso, and then released it.

"Come on, come on, *come on*," I yelled. "Get him!"

The net sailed toward Marcellious' head, and I shot to my feet.

"Yes!"

Roman yanked, but the netting simply slid from Marcellious' shiny helmet.

"Oh, come *on!*" I cried. I stabbed my forefinger at the emperor. "This is unfair. How can you let them continue?"

The emperor laughed. "Such good fun, isn't it?"

I returned my attention to the fight as Roman lost his footing and fell to the ground.

Marcellious towered over Roman, his sword poised at Roman's neck.

"Stop this fight!" I screamed at the emperor. "Stop it at once!"

The emperor laughed and took a swallow of his wine.

"I thought this was just for show!"

"What do you think a gladiator fight is?" He gave a wicked smile.

"Not a fight to the death. It's supposed to entertain, not end in someone dying!"

The emperor shook his head and pointed to my seat. "Sit down like a proper woman."

"Like hell, I will!" My attention snapped back to the fight.

Roman managed to force Marcellious away with his trident. He rolled and jackknifed to his feet.

Marcellious knocked away Roman's trident and charged again.

Roman hesitated, and Marcellious' sword sliced his forearm.

I gasped.

They continued to fight, sometimes with Marcellious appearing victorious. Sometimes Roman seemed to dominate.

But, as they fought, Roman's movements seemed off. We'd trained far harder than this. Sure, we weren't fighting to the death, but Roman seemed clumsy and unsure with his footing. His mind was somewhere else.

Unwilling to watch him get killed, I stormed from my seat and fled the Colosseum, racing down the long, dark corridor. I sprinted into the triclinium where we'd feasted, nearly slipping on the food and drink which covered the marble floor.

The servants caught enjoying the remnants of the lavish meal, jerked and scurried about as I zipped through the dining room.

I didn't care what they did. I *hated* Rome.

When I reached the entrance, my vision was blinded by tears. I stumbled outside and found Tempestas and the other horse unharnessed from the chariot and loosely tied to a tree.

The boy Roman had paid to watch over them lay curled in a ball next to them, deep asleep.

I flung myself inside the metal cart and huddled on the floor, sobbing.

"I just want to go home! This is too much!" Lifting my head to the starry sky, unsullied by 21st-century pollution or city lights, I beseeched whatever god or gods might be listening. "Please give me a sign! Please tell me a way out! Rome is a cruel, savage, and barbaric place, and I don't want to live here anymore."

When no sign came, I collapsed on the metal floor, utterly overwhelmed.

In the distance, the cries and shouts of the crowd continued.

I lay there, numb, until the sound of footsteps roused me. I leaped to my feet, fearing an intruder.

Roman dragged his feet toward me, limping. The beautiful purple toga he'd worn had been tied around his waist like a loincloth, leaving his chest bare. His torso was lined with bloody cuts, and his cheek was swollen and bruised. A wicked-looking gash marked his left shin.

"Oh, God." I rushed toward him. "You're alive!"

"Where did you go?" he said, in a voice lined with fatigue. "I thought you left me."

"No! I just couldn't take it…the fight…it was so unfair."

"Who said anything about this being fair?"

I caught his face between my hands and caressed his stubbled cheeks. "You told me this was for entertainment. The way you described it didn't sound like a fight to the death."

Roman took one of my hands and kissed my palm. "Severus demanded we fight. He said it was just for show. But, of course, he wouldn't have minded had one of us killed the other."

He shrugged.

"So, Marcellious is still alive?"

Roman nodded. "Wounded, as am I, but still living."

I shook my head. "I couldn't just sit there and watch you get killed. What happened to you? We trained so hard together, but it looked like you lost your edge. Marcellious may have had the advantage of armor, but you had all those skills you learned. Why didn't you fight the way you were supposed to?"

I held his shoulders as I searched his eyes.

Roman let out a long sigh. "To be honest with you, Olivia, I was distracted."

"Distracted? With what? What could have possibly been more important than fighting for your life?" I squeezed his arms.

The look he gave me scorched me to my soul. "You."

"Me?" I staggered backward.

"Come here," he said gently.

I stepped closer, and he clasped my hands, drawing them up and holding them against his sweaty, bloody chest.

"I need to tell you something," he said.

That powerful magnetism we shared cloaked us in our own magical world. The magnetic pull between us felt potent and thick, drawing us toward one another.

"What is it?" I breathed.

"I have fallen madly in love with you, and I can't hide my feelings for you any longer."

His eyelids grew heavy, weighted by the lust and heartfelt emotion that poured from him in waves.

All the air seemed to whoosh from my lungs. I blinked a few times, unsure of how to respond. I'd never been with anyone as powerful, beautiful, or handsome as Roman. It made all my experiences with sex and love up to this point seem insignificant.

He lifted my hands to his mouth and gently kissed the tip of each finger. "I can't keep these feelings inside."

"Roman…" I started to back away.

Before I could finish, he captured my lips in a dominating, passionate kiss, crushing his mouth to mine. His lips ground against mine, stirring intense desire, and flames licked at my skin.

Our tongues vied for control, thrusting into one another's mouths. The dance of his tongue was like his fighting style—direct, focused, intent on domination.

I writhed against his steel-like body, intoxicated by the full strength of his muscles. The contact between our mouths and the electricity rippling between us was overwhelming. I was sucked into a vortex of longing.

He groaned, and the sound vibrated against my lips. His commanding presence showed me how fiercely he wanted me with one hand hooked around my neck.

He seized my ass with his strong hand, digging his fingers into my flesh, drawing me toward him to feel the rigid heat in his loins. All the while, our mouths stayed connected, inhaling one another in lusty abandon.

This was no gentle kiss—this was a claiming. Did I want to be claimed by Roman? The way my body responded, the answer was a huge yes.

We wrenched apart, and my head dropped back. My entire body trembled with arousal.

"Look at me, Olivia," Roman said in a low, intoxicating voice.

I lifted my head to meet his scorching gaze.

"I want you. I desire you, body and soul. I want to have you in my bed, make passionate love to you, and make you pant with desire, leaving your body on fire," he said. A smile of victorious satisfaction spread across his face. His tongue darted out to lick his lips. Roman trailed his fingers down my neck with our eyes locked, revealing a tender side to him that was almost too much to bear. Dominant Roman was one thing, but tender Roman made my knees want to buckle.

He caressed my arm and drew tiny circles at the tender pulse point on my wrist. Then, he brought my arm to his lips and kissed the same place.

I shivered as pleasure and need throbbed through my veins, drowning out the whispers.

With one arm hooked behind my waist and the other holding my forearm, Roman worked his way upward, one slow, sensuous kiss at a time.

I couldn't stop this. I didn't want to stop this. Any lingering doubts I may have had about loving Roman wisped into the night sky like coiled smoke.

He kissed my collarbone, then proceeded up my neck.

My head lolled backward as his lips pressed against my jaw.

"Roman," I breathed.

He let out a low chuckle. "You're the most beautiful woman in the world, Olivia."

My lips parted, hungry for more of his mouth.

Unlike the claiming of a few moments ago, he slanted his head and brought his lips to mine in a carnal kiss. He worked his mouth in a circle against mine, teasing, exploring, accompanied by deep, satisfied groans. His hands worked the muscles of my back like a large cat might do, a lion, kneading me into pliant, yielding flesh.

His hips thrust into my belly, sliding up, then pulling away. Every movement of his body painted an image of what it would be like with him inside me. If I were to let that happen, I had no doubt I'd be wrecked. No man would ever touch me the way Roman did.

I inhaled deeply, savoring the earthiness, the passion, the intensity of Roman Alexander. He was not a man to be trifled with. His body was pure muscle, honed to perfection by hours of training. He had killed and would kill again. But now, his mouth and body rolled against me, into me, like an ocean wave, rocking me.

Drawing back slightly, he said, "You're so beautiful, Olivia. You have captured my heart. For so long, I thought my heart was incapable of beating the way it beats for you."

His warm breath puffed against my swollen lips.

I blushed, my heart pounding against my chest. "I can say the same about you."

He brought his hand behind my head, and neither of us moved for a few seconds. We just breathed into the other's mouth, more connected than I'd ever been. He tasted of blood, love, and possibility. Touching him was like finding honeyed water in a barren landscape.

Then he began another insistent circle, working his hips into my belly as his mouth played with mine.

I was on fire, completely, madly intoxicated by Roman. I brought one leg up and hooked it behind his thigh, drawing him closer. I simply couldn't get close enough to him. I wanted more of Roman...so much more. I craved him with a yearning so strong it threatened to consume me.

He caressed my thigh, sending electric shockwaves through my entire body.

He worked my strap down over my shoulder and stroked my skin. He kissed my neck and my collarbone.

I wanted to explode. His kisses, his touch, had my body in flames. I didn't want this to end.

How far were we going to take this?

I was ready for anything.

Something sharp pierced my shoulder. I yanked away from the kiss, and my head whipped around.

To my absolute horror, I saw an indistinguishable person, dressed entirely in black from head to toe. The only thing I could see were the eyes that radiated pure evil.

My childhood nightmare came back to life.

Someone who looked exactly like my mother's killer stood before me.

CHAPTER SIXTEEN
OLIVIA

For a few terrifying seconds, I looked into eyes so dark no amount of light could pierce the blackness. My limbs were frozen, and I was right back in my childhood, a ten-year-old girl watching the man who was about to kill my mother.

This can't be happening.

Roman broke the spell, charging toward the blackness, fists cocked. Shouting out a curse, he swung his arm toward the darkness, but his fist seemed to disappear into a black mist.

All the strength drained from my limbs as I watched, helpless. I began to yell at myself from a distant corner of my mind. *Pull yourself together! Gather your strength. Fight!* But my mind continued to float like a balloon far away from my earthly form.

"Olivia!" Roman said. "Come back to me. Fight it. Fight it now! Don't lose focus."

I blinked, my forehead creased in confusion. "What?"

I came back into my body with a thud. I whirled my leg in

a roundhouse kick. My foot connected with a whole lot of nothing.

The black form reappeared, its outstretched hands reaching for my throat.

I ducked out of the way and kicked again.

Once again, my foot flew through nothing.

How can this be happening? How can it simply disappear?

Claw-like fingers clasped my neck and began to squeeze.

Roman seized the cloaked darkness from behind. The black shape disappeared and then reappeared at my side.

It leered at me.

I charged it, shoulder down, ready to connect with its belly. But it dissolved into thin air, and I kept on going, propelled by momentum, until I stumbled to a stop.

The thing appeared opposite me, as solid a shape as I was, and grinned.

I picked up a stone and hurled it at its head.

The rock flew through where the head should have been and bounced on the ground.

I stared, stunned, at where the person should still be standing. There was nothing there.

"Olivia!" Roman pointed behind me. "Look out!"

I whipped around.

The human shape wielded a knife with a blade so shiny I could see the moon reflected in it.

The shape disappeared and reappeared behind me, and its blade pressed to my neck.

Roman raced toward the apparition.

The blade disappeared. I whirled around right as Roman brought his double-fisted hands down on the dark shape's head.

The head wisped into nothing, then the creature reappeared. The blade reappeared at my neck, held from behind.

I brought my hands up to push the arms wielding the blade, but they met with nothing. I dropped my arms by my side.

"What are you doing, Olivia? Why aren't you fighting?" Roman continued to stalk around the dark shape, his eyes scanning and searching.

"There's no point," I said, feeling the sharp blade pressed into my flesh. It was the strangest thing—it was like the knife was held by a vibrating, pulsing ball of energy.

"Of course, there's a point. You'll be dead any second if you don't push back!" Roman looked anguished.

"Come on. You've seen this thing. It simply disappears when either of us tries to punch, kick, or shove it." My shoulders sagged. How had it come to this? From one intoxicating, lust-driven moment to greeting death the same way it had snatched my mother from my life…

"Don't you see, Roman? I've lost everyone in this life. There's no point in living anymore." One lone tear pushed itself from the corner of my eye and tracked down my cheek.

"But you haven't lost everyone. I'm still here. Don't you remember what I just told you? I'm in love with you, Olivia. I won't lose you." Roman's eyes pleaded with me, but it was no use.

I had to say goodbye to him. Maybe we'd meet in some other lifetime. "Thank you for making me feel like a woman again. Thank you for making my last memories with you so special."

The "I love you" phrase hung on my tongue, but I couldn't say it—I just couldn't. Another tear pushed its way free.

The blackness continued to pulse behind me. Why didn't it just slice my neck and get it over with? It was like it was playing with me, a cat with its prey.

I swallowed as the blade pressed harder against my throat. Maybe the damn darkness was getting a hard-on at the thought of killing me, and it had to enjoy the moment. The very thought disgusted me. I pushed my hands backward, hoping to feel something solid, but instead, they just floated through this vibrating nothingness.

"We would have to lose one another eventually, Roman," I said, thinking of what it would be like for him when I found my way back to Seattle and left him.

Roman shook his head as his hands fisted by his sides. "I won't lose you. You mean so much to me. You showing up here in Rome and being gifted to me by the emperor. You were meant to be here…with me. Don't you see that?"

"You're making things up. We all do that when we're caught up in the thrill of romance."

My relationship with Tristan was a perfect example. I had only seen what I had wanted to see. What an idiot I'd been.

"Olivia, I won't lose you. I care too much for you. I can't lose you now. I refuse to let you go," Roman said, crouching.

"Roman, you have to let me go. I have nothing left to lose. I'm done fighting. I'm done trying."

"I'm sorry, Olivia, but I have no choice. I have to save you. Even though it might hurt you, I hope you can forgive me."

I started to cry out as the blade sliced into my neck.

Roman whipped out an ancient-looking gun from his loin-cloth and shot the darkness from the side.

It exploded into nothingness, and the knife landed on the ground with a thud.

I fell to my knees and palpated my neck, ensuring my

head was still attached to my torso. My hand came away bloody, but I didn't seem to be spurting blood.

My gaze snapped toward Roman.

The weapon he'd used, what looked to be a dueling gun from the 1770s, hung by his side, a wisp of smoke coiling from the barrel. I was shocked to my bones.

"What the hell just happened?" I lunged to my feet and stormed toward him, palms outstretched. When I slammed my hands into his chest, he stumbled backward. "Where did you get a gun?"

"I can explain where it came from," he said, tucking the gun into his loincloth.

"You *lied* to me. You're a fraud. You knew my weapon when you showed it to me, didn't you? But you pretended not to know." I backed away from him, holding my hands up to block him if he chose to approach me.

"Let me explain, Olivia," he said, stepping toward me.

"Don't come any closer," I hissed.

He stopped and held his palms out. "I'm sorry I didn't tell you everything."

My jaw dropped open. What was Roman saying? What was this "everything" he hadn't shared with me?

"Don't touch me. Stay away from me."

His hands dropped to his sides, and his jaw slackened. His eyes glistened as he looked at me.

"I can't do this anymore. I won't be betrayed again." I pivoted and ran, kicking off the lovely sandals Amara had placed on my feet. Tempestas' head jerked up as I ran toward him. Quickly, I untied the horse, tore my dress apart, and flung myself over Tempestas' back.

The horse reared and whinnied, but I hung on, digging my heels into its flanks.

The horse took off at a gallop while I clung to its sides with my legs.

I couldn't stay here. I couldn't stay in Rome any longer. I didn't have a plan or know if the next town or the town after that was any safer. I only knew I had to get away as far as possible.

But sadly, I had nowhere to go.

CHAPTER SEVENTEEN
OLIVIA

I reined the galloping horse to a skidding stop outside of Roman's home. I'd never rode a horse in the black of the night, but Tempestas knew the way. Hurling from his back, I flung the reins over his neck and stormed toward the house. Crying, I fumbled my way down the darkened corridor, feeling my way to my room.

Once I entered, I lit one of the oil lamps and began flinging my few clothes and belongings on the straw mattress. Then, I gathered everything together and tied it with a stola.

When I whirled around, Amara stood in the doorway in her nightgown, eyes bleary as she stared at me.

"What happened, child? Is Roman okay?" She came toward me, a bundle of motherly concern.

"Yes, Amara. He's alive and well, but I have to leave. You can't stop me. Don't even try." I grabbed the tied heap from my bed and started to push past Amara, but she seized my arm with surprising strength.

"Wait! Tell me what happened. Maybe I can fix this." She looked at me with a kind of desperation I'd never seen before.

I shook my head. "I can't, Amara. I just can't. I love you deeply like a mother, but...."

A sob burst from my throat.

Amara scanned my shredded gown. "What happened to your stola? Did someone rape you? Is that what this is about?"

Fury replaced the desperation.

I dropped the bundle and seized her shoulders. "I learned something about Roman that he should have told me. He betrayed me, just like my last boyfriend. I can never trust him again. He is a liar, a man hiding behind a mask. I'm tired of the betrayal."

Amara's eyes filled with tears.

Her sympathy was just too much to bear. I grabbed the clothing and raced from the room.

When I exited, Tempestas stood in the yard. I mounted him, flung my belongings in my lap, and took off.

Before I knew it, I found myself at the beach. I galloped through the surf, lit by the moon, and wept. I didn't have a plan or know what to do or where to go. But at least I had left Roman behind.

The thought of losing Roman tore at my heart with so much grief, that I thought I would die from the pain. That was the problem with loving someone, wasn't it? This was what I'd hoped to spare him and me both by not giving into love. Why was it I got stabbed in the back by the people I cared most about? I was cursed. I would die alone in this miserable world.

Another horse galloped toward me, with a man driving it.

I whirled to face him, bringing Tempestas to a stop in the surf.

"Go away!" I shouted as Roman pulled his horse to a halt, splashing water droplets on my face.

"We need to talk about what happened. Let me explain."

"What's there to explain?" I pulled back on Tempestas' reins, and he backed up, then spun in a slow circle. "You lied to me about everything. You hid your true self from me, making my life miserable. You betrayed me. How could you possibly have had a gun?" It seemed preposterous, but could Roman have traveled through time?

"I didn't betray you. I just didn't tell you everything to protect you."

"Protect me? I'm capable of protecting myself. I don't need a bodyguard."

Tempestas reared slightly, then backed up and repeated the movement.

I clung to his sides with my legs.

"Please calm down. Please come off the horse and let me explain," Roman pleaded.

"Explain what? How much of a fake you are by telling me your sad story of how you became a gladiator? How tortured your life was? You're a coward, a phony, and a disgusting bastard."

"Everything I told you that night was true. I just didn't tell you a few minor details."

"How is having a dueling gun minor?"

"Olivia, I'm still the same man who saved you, cared for you, and has grown to be deeply in love with you."

"Don't you dare tell me you love me!" I spat the words from my mouth. "You should have let me die and spared me the pain I'm going through right now. I should never have let you in my heart!"

Tempestas pranced and reared.

"Olivia, you've got to listen to me. You're in danger. The darkness found you—it found us both. We're both in danger. Right now, you're frustrated, angry, and hurt. Get off Tempestas and come with me so we can talk things out."

A flash of fear pricked at my spine. What does he mean the darkness found us both, and we're in danger? How does he know?

I reined Tempestas away from Roman and kicked him. We took off at a gallop.

Roman's horse caught up with us in seconds. Galloping by my side, he reached for Tempestas' reins, seized them, and somehow managed to bring both horses to a stop without killing us.

"You've got to listen to me, Olivia! Now that it's found you, the darkness won't cease until it kills you. The gun didn't kill it. It only made it go away temporarily. But it will be back, and it will *kill* you!"

"I don't want to hear this—any of it! There's got to be another explanation."

Roman threw back his head and let out an exasperated growl. "Damn it, Olivia! I'm so sick and tired of this. You've got to trust me. I know what I'm talking about. I know you're angry, hurt, and upset. I know you want to tear me apart, but right now, you have to trust me."

"How can I trust someone who has been lying to me this whole time and concealed his true identity?" I flung myself off Tempestas, away from Roman, and stomped through the surging surf.

Roman didn't follow me. Instead, he sat on his horse, clutching Tempestas' reins, and watched me in the moonlight.

I stormed around, letting the waves push me, falling to my knees and getting up, only to fall again from the force of water.

"Come home, Olivia."

"It's not my home," I sobbed. "I lost my home a long time ago."

"It's late. You're frustrated and tired. Please come home and I will explain everything to you," Roman said gently.

I could barely hear him over the pounding waves. "I said no. The only thing I need to do is get away from you. I don't need you."

A stony expression, all shadows and hard lines, crossed his face. "You do need your weapons, though. And I have them."

I stared at him, mouth agape. "Those things are mine!"

I powered toward him, racing out of the surf.

"You know where to find them. They're at home," he said, then he wheeled both horses around and took off at a gallop, speeding away from me.

I fell to my knees in the sand. My beautiful stola, the one so lovingly prepared by Amara, was destroyed. It hung in tattered rags on my body. But the worst part? My heart had been utterly demolished.

I dropped my head into my hands and wept. I cried for everything I'd lost and every confusing mystery I couldn't solve. I cried for my mom…for Papa…for Lee. But most of all, I sobbed for the loss of Amara and Roman, the two beautiful souls who had cared for me in this strange land.

At some point, I grew quiet and simply watched the waves crash on the shore, rushing to meet my knees before being pulled back into the ocean again.

When the sky began to grow light, I picked up my body and began to walk, destination unknown. My eyes were puffy from crying, and I was sure I looked a fright as I staggered along. Without being fully aware of my movements, I blinked when the familiar white home I had come to cherish came into view.

Roman's house lay straight ahead.

Roman stood like a sentinel outside in the yard, waiting for me, his arms by his sides. His expression was utterly dejected, marked by lines and deep grooves in his face. Blood still oozed from his wounds.

"You came," he said softly.

I said nothing to him. Instead, I brushed past him and entered the house, closing the door behind me.

CHAPTER EIGHTEEN
OLIVIA

When I returned from the beach after my confrontation with Roman, I was at odds with my feelings for Roman and my desire to get back home. Seeing Roman standing out front in the dim light of pre-dawn, his limbs hanging limply by his side, blood oozing from his wounds had stirred an impulse to care for him and tend to his injuries. But the fresh gash of betrayal he'd sliced through my heart by not telling me who he was overruled any thoughts of kindness. I was furious and hurt. And talking to him was the last thing I intended to do.

In the atrium, Amara stood near the pool, wringing her hands. She took one look at my tattered appearance and blanched.

I plucked at the torn, shredded dress and said, "I'm so sorry, Amara. The dress was lovely."

I probably looked like a version of Cinderella who had been bombed.

"No, no," Amara said, waving her hands in front of her. "You don't need to apologize...not for anything. I'm only grateful you came back."

She fluttered toward me with her arms outstretched, like a bird flapping its wings. She enveloped me in her arms, hugging me hard.

I returned the hug, sniffling a little at her warm embrace. I loved her so much.

Amara eased away from me and said, "You should go clean up and rest. I'll prepare breakfast."

Gratitude filled my heart. "Thank you. As of right now, I need some space and time to think things through. I might not come out for a while."

"Take whatever time you need, child. I'm so glad you returned. We thought we'd lost you. Now, go rest. We'll be fine." She shooed me away from her.

I dragged my weary body down the hall and clomped toward my room. Inside my sleeping chamber, I came to an abrupt stop. My gun and the dagger had been placed on my bed.

I nearly wept at the sight of them. I raced to the bed, picked up the dagger, pulled it free from its leather casing, and inspected it. It glistened like it had been polished to a sheen. Had Roman done that? Now that I had it, could I use it to escape Rome? I had no clue how the process of time travel worked save for a full moon had to occur.

It drove me crazy to have the tool to time travel, but not the knowledge as to how to do it. Was I to simply stand in the full moon's light and wave the knife about? And how did I know where I'd end up?

I checked the gun. It had been polished as well. I popped out the magazine and counted my bullets. All twenty were present and accounted for.

Unable to hold myself up any longer, I peeled off my tattered clothing, dropped it on the floor, and fell naked between my sheets. I clutched the Glock and the dagger to my chest and closed my eyes. *Bliss*.

As I lay there, my mind tried to wrap itself around all the things I'd experienced last night—a party at the emperor's palace in ancient Rome. Never could I have imagined such a scene when I was growing up in 21st-century Seattle. I'd watched Roman and Marcellious fight in the Colosseum—the very Colosseum that had housed numerous fights between gladiators, criminals, and wild beasts.

And then there was that kiss. Oh, that kiss. Just remembering it brought swirls of excitement to my belly and core. When our lips had connected, time and space fell away, leaving us as one giant pulsing heart.

Then I'd been assaulted by a thing not of this world. It made no sense how it appeared as a human one minute; the next, it disappeared like wisps of smoke. Roman had tried to save me from that dark freakshow that wanted to kill me. No matter how hard we had tried, nothing had worked. That was, until Roman pulled out that gun and shot the darkness, making it burst into particles and vanish.

How I needed Lee and Papa here to give me answers.

But I couldn't ask Roman for help now. He had lied to me. He'd betrayed me. And I could not, would not forgive him for that…could I?

Yet, Roman had taken me in and saved me from the emperor when I'd arrived. He and Amara had cared for me when they'd found me bewildered and afraid. And now, Roman and I seemed to share an intimacy far deeper than anything I'd ever dreamed of experiencing.

Dammit, I was so confused. Papa had said I could slip through time during the full moon. But no other instructions had been provided except for muttering some sacred chant.

I finally fell into a dead, exhausted sleep.

When I awoke hours later, I washed and donned fresh clothes before heading out to find Amara.

Amara was in the kitchen preparing the evening meal. She stopped stirring a fragrant stew and smiled warmly at me. "You look so much better. I trust you slept well?"

"I did." I averted my eyes from her warm gaze. It hurt too much to take in her kindness when my heart felt like a vacant hole. "Where's Roman?"

"Serving the emperor, of course," Amara said, bustling about the kitchen.

"Doesn't he ever get a day off?"

Amara frowned. "Roman is one of the Praetoria Cohors. He gets to live at this home. That's the only concession the emperor would make since he denied Roman his freedom. We are very fortunate to have Roman's presence here each night."

"Because otherwise, he'd live at the palace?" I said, sidling toward the brazier.

"He would still be a slave, subject to the emperor's whims. Most of Severus' Praetoria Cohors die in servitude. They serve the emperor for life. There is no escape."

Imagining having no absolute freedom saddened me. How horrible life was in these times. And yet, we lived in harmony with the seasons. There were no mobile phones to distract us, no television, internet, cyberbullies, or television news to sway us or reinforce our political leanings. At times I treasured the simplicity in which I currently lived.

Yet, here, there was a brutal realism to life. It was considered "just" to take a life or to enslave one. In fact, the gladiator fights, literal fights to the death, were seen as a sport—good entertainment.

I shook my head to rid my mind of these awful thoughts.

My life in Seattle had become a thing of the past. I didn't want that to be true. I had to find my way back home.

I studied Amara. She never complained…about *anything*. Instead, she toiled away from dawn until nightfall, doing what she must do to care for Roman and now for me.

I shouldn't take out my confusion on her.

Roman, however, was another matter.

"Can I help you?" I asked her.

"Yes, please. Chop those vegetables and put them into the pot."

I picked up the knife I'd thrown at Roman several weeks ago. A wave of sadness washed through me. I wanted to move forward with Roman, but I couldn't seem to move past the betrayal. I had to get away from here.

"Amara," I said.

"Yes, dear?" Amara stayed busy chopping the legs from a small hare for a stew.

"When is the next full moon?"

Amara turned to look at me. "It's two weeks from now."

"Two weeks?" The words slammed into me.

Amara looked at me, her eyebrows drawn together in a quizzical expression. "Why? Is something important to happen during the full moon?"

I couldn't meet her gaze. "No, I was just wondering."

I continued to chop the vegetables before me.

When Roman came home, he went straight to his room and emerged to eat.

We avoided one another, speaking when necessary, like me saying, "Are you finished?" and him saying, "Yes, thank you."

At least we were polite.

Other than that, we never even glanced at one another.

After dinner, Roman excused himself and retired to his room.

Amara and I cleaned the kitchen.

When fatigue tugged at my limbs, and all the chores had been finished, I fell into a dreamless sleep. I awoke before dawn when the front door closed with a bang.

Roman had made sure to leave before I rose. Whatever. I didn't want to talk to him either. Even though he had answers I desperately wanted, I refused to ask him.

Amara and I said little as we buzzed around the house, cleaning and preparing food.

In the evening, Roman returned while I was in the kitchen.

"Olivia," he began, but I shook my head and scurried toward the door.

His sigh made my heart sink.

At dinner, I served his food and removed his plate when he was finished, but we did not speak. Inside, I felt dead.

I went to bed at day's end and slept restlessly.

Would I ever speak to Roman again? Probably. It was only a matter of when.

In the evening, Roman strode through the front door and came right into the kitchen. "Olivia, I—"

"I don't want to hear it," I said, putting up my palm.

I tried to glide past him, but he caught my arm. A whoosh of excitement cascaded through my belly at his touch. My heart raced, and heat rose on my face. I yearned to touch him and kiss him madly. Not speaking with him these past couple of days had wounded me, but I wasn't ready to give in to my feelings.

"This time, you *have* to listen. Where's Amara?" he said, his jaw set in stone.

"In the triclinium," I said.

"Fetch her."

"What if I don't want to?" I said, my snark returning full force.

"This isn't about you. Go get Amara." He pointed to the door. Then, he let out a labored sigh. "Please."

I held back the statement on my tongue of, "You go get her," and pushed past him.

When I returned with Amara, Roman stood like a statue with his arms folded over his chest.

"I'm being deployed," he said.

My frozen heart jerked back to life. "Deployed? As in, to war?"

"Yes, I've been promoted to a Centurion to oversee a band of men. We're being sent to a war zone to command an army." His mouth pressed into a firm line. "I'm to be in allegiance with Marcellious."

"But you both despise each other," I said, declaring the obvious.

"This is a war we're talking about, Olivia," Roman said without looking at me. "One's disagreements with others don't matter when we fight the same enemy. Amara, you've been asked to come as the healer."

"Oh, dear," Amara said.

"You can't ask that of her. Amara shouldn't be in a war zone," I said hotly.

"Yes, bastard that I am, I've been the one to choose this," Roman said with a roll of his eyes. "I can think of nothing more appealing than to drag my housekeeper into an environment of danger."

"Olivia," Amara said, placing her hand on my shoulder. "If the emperor says you are to do something, you do it. Refusing his order could mean your death."

"You're serious?" I said. "If a civilian says no, he simply kills you?"

"Yes. That's the way of it," Amara said. "Of course, I'll come," she said to Roman.

Roman nodded.

"So, then, what about me? I'm to remain here all by myself?"

God, I sounded like a child. But the truth was, I was scared to death that I might lose both Roman and Amara in this ghastly war.

"You're to accompany me as my assistant, dear. A healer needs helpers," Amara said. "When do we leave, Roman?"

"At dawn." Roman caught my gaze, and our eyes locked for the first time in two days. A look fraught with indecipherable meaning passed between us. Then, he broke eye contact, saying, "I'll be dining alone tonight. I'll see you both at daybreak."

CHAPTER NINETEEN

OLIVIA

We traveled by foot and on horseback to reach a port in Italy. I went with Amara and a few other women, whores of the soldiers who traveled separated from the men. At night, we formed encampments within an enormous circle of warriors.

I didn't see Roman once during that time.

When we were close to the port, we set up our last camp before boarding the ship. Then, in the whispering light of dawn, the other women and I were escorted aboard one of the numerous wooden vessels via a rickety gangplank. Men, their skin black with grime, urged us onward with leers and shouts.

Ignoring their lecherous taunts, I stayed behind Amara, clutching her hips lest she fell.

The gangplank next to us bowed from the hundreds of soldiers, weighted with armor as they tromped onto the ship.

I managed to briefly catch sight of Roman.

Our gazes locked, and the world fell away for one halting second. There was no thought in my mind about betrayal—only the powerful bond between us.

I was shoved forward by the woman behind me, and

Roman was propelled ahead by the other sailors. And again, only deceit and lies hung between us as I watched him climb onto the ship.

I might not see him again until we reached landfall in Caledonia, the country I knew as Scotland. Would that be so bad since we weren't even on speaking terms?

Amara and I were housed below deck in filthy, windowless rooms with the other women who accompanied us on our journey. As the days wore on, I spent most nights awake. Eyes wide and bleary, I listened to the satisfied outbursts of the men mingled with the cries of the women whose sole purpose was to provide pleasure for the sailors.

The oarsmen occupied the deck above us. Day and night, they tirelessly dipped their oars into the water, moving in unison to propel the boat forward with a din of grunts and grumbles.

All the women were expected to prepare food. We toiled endlessly, readying salted beef or pork and biscuits, rendering them palatable with the olive oil stored in amphoras throughout the ship. The men would clamber downstairs to retrieve the food barrels and distribute them to the others.

Amara and I ate only enough to sustain ourselves. We were both often seasick, so we felt it best to minimize our food intake.

One week into the trip, the shouts and frantic cries of the men on the uppermost deck alerted us that something big was about to happen. All the women huddled in one room. Our boat seemed to move swiftly, and then a loud crash split the air. The ship shuddered and groaned as if struck by an earthquake.

Cheers and shouts replaced the yelling.

Then, the ship seemed to be moving in the opposite direction, followed by another resounding crash.

"We're going to die!" one of the whores cried out.

"I'll find out what's happening." Although we'd been forbidden to set foot on the top deck, I sneaked upstairs. Once topside, I peered over the railing to find a neighboring ship, its hull blasted open, and most of the oars ripped apart, sinking into the sea. From what I could tell, the Roman sailors had boarded their ship and were scrambling back on board our ship with prisoners. Countless other ships surrounded us, both ours and presumably those of "the enemy." Several enemy ships had been struck by our vessels. Wood and screaming men bobbed about in the water in a horrifying tableau of the effects of war.

Unable to bear witness, I fled downstairs.

"We won this battle," I told the other women. "Don't worry. We're going to be alright."

In truth, I knew nothing of the sort. Had Roman been responsible for all this death? Had he given the orders to ram the other ships?

I hated Rome. And most of all I despised Roman Alexander.

By the time we made landfall in Brittania, many days later, with several more bone-shattering battles under our belts, Amara and I emerged from the ship's bowels emaciated, gaunt, and miserable. I helped her debark the boat and made our way to where the men had assembled. Everyone stank of sweat and bodily fluids. What I would have given for a hot shower at that moment.

Roman strode toward us atop Tempestas, leading two horses. "Olivia, are you alright? I've been worried sick about you."

"I was below deck. Are you telling me you couldn't take a moment to come downstairs and check on me? At the very least, you could have seen to Amara. She and I were so sick we barely ate in two weeks." I practically vomited the words out. I was so furious.

Roman set his jaw and handed the horses to Amara. "Take these. The emperor issued the order to let the healer ride to our encampment. And I'm sorry for the treatment you endured on the vessel."

He didn't spare me another glance.

As we rode, at least we were surrounded by fresh air and sunshine. I felt much like a mole torn from its underground tunnel system. Light and fresh air were foreign to me at this point. I'd surely be dead by now if I weren't so strong.

Several of the whores hadn't made it. Their dead bodies had been dragged upstairs and now probably lay at the bottom of the sea, being consumed by marine life.

I stayed silent during much of the ride, musing about Roman. Before, I'd been obsessed with thoughts of the connection between Roman and me. Now I was obsessed with how disconnected we were. But, in my heart of hearts, whispers of love pushed through my anger. I still didn't know what to do. Yet, the big question looming in my mind begged to be answered. Was Roman a time traveler? If so, where did he come from? Was Roman even his real name? And then I wondered what he knew about the darkness. He seemed familiar with it as if he knew its motives—where it came from and what it searched for. How could he know so much?

Roman dropped back a few times from the front, where he rode behind the emperor in his litter hoisted on the backs of his servants. As Roman approached, I resented him for being so hale and healthy. He was now a commanding officer, and apparently, the officers feasted on the ship. At the same time, the rest of the men ate the hardtack we prepared.

During the ride, he tried several times to speak to me.

"Olivia, I need to talk to you," he'd say. Or, "Olivia, please let me explain."

Or he would try to hand me food he seemed to have in abundance.

I met all his requests for conversation or his generous food sharing with icy silence until he rode away.

Only after he departed, my heart would hurt as my shields fell away. Before Roman told us about being deployed for war, I was planning to time travel during the full moon. But now, with war on the way, that thought had vanished from my mind. Like Roman, I had fallen into a world of duty, where I did what I must instead of what I wanted to. So much for free will in this century.

I simply couldn't leave Amara and Roman at such a difficult time.

"Child, I wish you would tell me what happened," Amara said to me as she rode by my side.

"I can't tell you, Amara. I really can't." How could I? She didn't seem like a time traveler…did she? Could she have crossed the centuries with Roman? At this point, I was too paranoid to trust anyone.

Amara had begun to revive from all the fresh air and clean water we had on land. We stopped near a creek from time to time and drank until our stomachs were bloated. We also dipped into the fresh flowing stream and rinsed off two weeks of living aboard a ship. Then, we'd make sure to fill the leather bladders we'd been given with water to carry with us on our journey. Although my clothes stayed damp for an hour or more, I managed to doze a bit in the saddle and, by day's end, glimmerings of my own restoration pushed through my fatigue.

We reached a plateau as the sun hung heavy in the sky, falling toward the horizon.

All around us, there were horses, men, and activity.

Same as before, we were instructed to erect our tent in the middle of the men.

Amara and I worked quickly to prepare our humble dwelling for the night and the tent where she'd tend to the injured. I couldn't wait to fall onto my meager bedding and sleep without being tossed and pitched about by the whims of the sea.

I was startled when Roman approached me.

"Making sure I'm okay? I'm fine," I snapped at him. "Or have you finally realized you need to check on Amara from time to time?"

I threw back the flap of Amara's and my goatskin tent and started to step inside. He seized my arm.

"Help me erect my tent," he said, but the pleading in his eyes told me this had nothing to do with me helping him. Roman was desperate to connect with me.

"Your hands work as good as mine. Or, wait, don't Centurions have servants to help them?" I jerked away from his touch.

I felt cruel and vicious when I entered the tent, closing the flap behind me. Why couldn't I at least talk to him and hear him out? I just couldn't. I'd been so badly hurt by Tristan. And Roman held secrets as to why he had a gun. I'd felt so alone here in Rome until I began sharing with Roman. But still, my trust muscles were as trashed as my physical muscles used to get after training. If I were to talk to him, I was afraid I'd start to cry. And that would make me look weak, something I wouldn't tolerate. But deep inside my heart, I knew my walls were ready to crumble. And, if I were honest…I needed Roman. I was becoming emotionally attached to him, which scared me more than anything.

CHAPTER TWENTY

ROMAN

As stars began to punch through the sky, one by one, I stood outside Olivia's tent, my head bowed, unable to come up with a way to resolve the tension between us. Onboard the ship, I'd been under Severus' thumb and his maniacal thirst for blood. The man was insane. Our every waking hour was spent seeing to his whims, whether in battle or in servitude. Yet, I desperately wanted to check on Olivia and Amara in the few moments I had to myself.

The emperor had other ideas. I was either under his constant scrutiny or being watched by Marcellious. I had no doubt that he'd gleefully tell the emperor I'd sneaked downstairs if only to rid me from his life once and for all. I couldn't even head downstairs under the guise of needing release with a whore.

Severus had brought several women for his, the officers', and the commanders' enjoyment. But all such congress with his women was to be conducted in the lavish parlor his servants had erected within earshot of his opulent lodgings on the ship.

The emperor's behavior disgusted me, and I refused to

partake in his so-called "generosity." In my mind, it was more of a perversion.

I'd have moved heaven and earth to see to Olivia—but I wanted to keep my own head while on the ship, so I hadn't dared to risk his wrath.

Now, though, when I had access to her, however, limited, she refused to speak to me. How could I expect to command an entire army with so much tension between the woman I loved and me? I was a lovesick fool.

Amara emerged from her and Olivia's tent as I turned to head back and see to my quarters. She rushed toward me.

"Roman," she called.

She gestured for me to lower my head to hers, so I brought my head to her level.

Cupping my ear with her hand, she whispered, "You've got to fix your relationship with Olivia. You got yourself into this. I don't know how but I'm sure it had something to do with your behavior."

I sighed. "I've tried. What else can I do? I've tried to talk to her multiple times, but she refuses and pushes me away."

"I don't know what happened, but Olivia is heartbroken. She quietly cried every night onboard the ship. When she slept, she'd call out your name. Only during her waking hours did I see this stony silence she holds before you. Fix it." She stood back and glared at me.

"But how?" I spread my arms wide.

Amara stabbed my chest with her fingertip. "Use your heart. Woo her. Make her feel special. She *needs* you, Roman, but she's too stubborn to let down her guard."

A weighted silence hung between us. I still didn't know what to do.

Amara huffed out a sigh. "Tell you what…after Olivia and I eat and prepare to retire for the night, you can return and speak to Olivia. I'll watch for you. You will come and speak with her and make amends."

A spark of hope bloomed in my heart for the first time in weeks. Maybe Olivia and I could repair this thing that had torn us apart. I longed to feel her lips on mine again and tell her all I knew.

Back at my tent, I waited to give Olivia and Amara time to prepare their dinner and eat. I made and remade my bed to keep myself occupied. At last, I muttered something about needing to see to the Emperor, for the benefit of my tent mates, and slipped into the night.

Grunts, groans, and laughter issued forth from the emperor's tent. I shook my head and padded toward Olivia's tent. I used my night senses to guide my way as darkness smothered the land. Many under my command were already snoring.

As I approached the women's quarters, Olivia's voice rang out.

"I'm utterly exhausted, Amara. I've got to sleep. I can't stand upright any longer."

"Yes, child, you must. I have to retrieve something out of my healing tent. I'll be back in a few minutes to prepare you for slumber," Amara said.

"You're too kind to me," Olivia said, exhaustion evident in her tone.

It broke my heart to hear her sound so fatigued. She must have experienced a kind of hell in the bowels beneath the oarsmen. The bottom of the ship was usually a rat-infested pit. But there was nothing I could do while sailing. Tonight, though, on dry land, I intended to pierce her walls.

Amara slipped out of the tent, scanning for me.

"Over here," I whispered. My heart pounded in my chest at the thought of seeing Olivia.

Amara rushed toward me. "Go!" she whispered. "We've

eaten well and are ready for sleep. I think she'll be receptive to you."

I nodded, swallowing hard. Silently, I made my way to the door and pushed back the soft leather flap.

Olivia stood in the diffuse glow of an oil lamp, clad in a stola with her back to me. Her long hair, bound in a plaited braid, hung down her back, ending in coiled tendrils. The lamplight danced across her tresses, lighting them like a flame.

I was so captivated by her I nearly lost my resolve.

"Can you please unbraid my hair, Amara? I'm so tired I can barely lift my hands." She lowered her head as if it were too heavy to hold upright.

As quietly as I could, I padded across the floor. Standing behind her, I placed my palms on her shoulders and massaged her tense muscles.

"Olivia," I breathed.

A long, deep sigh left her lungs, and she seemed to sway from exhaustion or a swoon from my touch.

I hoped it was the latter.

Tentatively, I nuzzled her cheek and slowly began to unbraid her luscious silken tresses. I gently took the braid apart and massaged her hair. It smelled of creek water and fresh air—much more pleasant than the unwashed scent when we climbed from the ship. As far as I was concerned, her scent was entirely intoxicating.

"I'm not your enemy, Olivia." I let my callused palms caress her silken arms, reddened by the day's sun but no less beautiful. "I don't want to fight with you. I'm here to make peace with you."

She leaned into me, letting her head fall back against my shoulder.

"I knew your true identity when I met you. I just couldn't

tell you what I knew." Stroking my hands up and down her skin gave me tremendous pleasure. I could barely contain my excitement but knew I had to move slowly with her.

Olivia pivoted in my hands. When she looked at me, fierce radiance shone from her eyes.

"Why couldn't you tell me?" she said, but none of the poison she spat at me for the last few weeks fell from her lips. "For months, I've felt utterly alone."

As I studied her, my heart swelled with love for her. Placing my palms on her shoulders again, I caressed her collarbones with my thumbs. "I felt I had to."

"I want to know the whole truth, Roman," she whispered.

"And you shall. I want to tell you. I shall share everything with you. But first, I need to say something." I cupped her face between my hands. I was hungry for the touch of her... the taste of her...the everything of her. She'd become more essential than food.

"What?" Eyes closed, she nuzzled her cheek into my palm. When her eyelids fluttered open, a magnetic intensity pulsed between us.

"You're the first person I've ever loved," I said, gazing deeply into her eyes. "I know I hurt you by not telling you everything, but my feelings for you are real. I deeply love you and care for you. Not speaking with you or holding you tore my heart into pieces. I can't live without you."

She sucked in a breath, and her eyes glistened. "I... I don't know what to say."

"You don't have to say anything. I just want you to know that."

She nodded, and her lips parted.

The heady current of electricity connecting us drew us together. My body was on fire for her—I wanted her heart and soul. I slanted my head and lowered my lips to hers, hovering millimeters apart, savoring her nearness. Her breath warmed my mouth with soft puffs of air. I drew closer... closer...

From outside the tent, a soldier hollered, "Roman Alexander."

Olivia jerked back.

I threw back my head with a groan. "What?"

"Marcellious needs you at once, sir," the soldier called.

"I'll be right there."

"I'll inform him at once," the soldier said.

I brought Olivia's palm to my mouth and pressed a gentle kiss to the center. "Promise me you'll wait for me. I'll be back soon. Please don't leave. I'll tell you everything."

Olivia licked her lips. "I promise I'll be here when you return."

Those were the words I needed to hear. I vowed to return as soon as I could. Only, entrenched as I was in the vagaries of war, I had no idea when I'd get another chance.

CHAPTER TWENTY-ONE
ROMAN

The second I stepped inside Marcellious' tent, I knew there would be trouble. Maybe it was the set of his shoulders or the smirk across his face. Or perhaps it was just that he had requested my presence. Either way, I calmed my breathing and prepared myself for the worst.

"Centurion Demarrias," I said formally, deliberately making eye contact.

"Centurion Alexander," he replied coolly. He sauntered across the tent to stand directly in front of me.

My eyes never left his face. "What did you need so urgently? Is there a battle to be fought even though we're nowhere near our destination?"

He met my gaze with brutal intensity. "Where were you? Were you, perhaps, with *her*?"

I bristled at his question, not wanting him to even *think* of Olivia. "To whom are you referring?"

"Come, come, Roman. You know of whom I speak. Tell me… have you *fucked* her yet?" A wicked leer crossed his face, creasing it with shadows in the lamplight.

"That's not the nature of our relationship," I said, anger coiling in my belly.

"Est alquid quo tendis, et in quod derigis arcum?" he said with a sneer.

My face remained placid even though I was filled with fury. Of course, there was a point to my life, only I hoped it would someday be away from here.

"You have no balls," he said, adding a cold laugh. "If she were mine, I would have fucked her good and hard, thousands of times. She would be carrying my babies by now."

A tic pulsed in the skin above my right eye. Why was Marcellious getting to me? I dealt with his ugly taunts daily, letting them slide down my back like mud. So, why now did he affect me? Was it because I was holding back?

"Surely, you called me here to speak of other things, Centurion Demarrias. Get to your point." I loosely crossed my arms over my chest.

"You really should participate in the emperor's lust-filled follies," he said, matching my stance. "The most delightful decisions get made when you're balls deep in one of his whores, side by side with Severus. He'll agree to anything when he's in the throes of an orgasm."

I frowned. Where was he heading in this conversation? "Such as?"

Marcellious laughed. "There's been a change-up in the troops. You'll no longer be overseeing Cohort VI. You'll be training Cohort IX—you remember, the ones we took as slaves?"

He gave me a challenging glare, watching for my reaction.

My fury reached a tempestuous level, and I wanted to tear Marcellious from limb to limb. *I* had been assigned to work with Cohort VI, the best of the best. Severus knew I was a better fighter than Marcellious. And, I was soon to be promoted to Primus Pilus, the highest-ranking and most respected of all the Centurions. I would be in charge of Cohort I, the elitist of the elite.

And now I'm to work with trainees and new recruits, the scum we'd captured while at sea?

"I don't believe you. Why should I take orders from you when you're in the same league as I am?" My fingers itched to wrap around Marcellious' throat and throttle the life out of him.

Marcellious' smile sliced through my belly like a cold, stiff blade. "It seems I've been promoted."

Snakes began to writhe through my insides.

"Don't you want to hear of my new promotion?" His ice-like smile couldn't possibly get any colder.

I said nothing, trying to quash my desire to destroy Marcellious Demarrias.

"I'll tell you since your tongue seems to be tied in knots. I'm to assume the role of Primus Pilus." His eyes narrowed, still waiting for my reaction.

It couldn't be. Any promotion was to be given to *me*. I'd earned it. Marcellious had done nothing to gain the respect granted to Primus Pilus. It took every ounce of strength I had to not kill Marcellious, right here, right now.

"I see," I said, my tone dead.

"You're to start training Cohort IX at dawn," he said, still poking his sharp stick of changes at my insides.

"Will that be all?" I could barely restrain myself. If I didn't leave soon, I feared doing something I'd regret.

"I suppose."

At least Marcellious looked deflated at my non-response to his news.

"You're dismissed," he said to me with a wave of his hand.

I took one long, deep breath, pivoted on my heel, then strode from the tent.

A few tents were still lit by oil lamps, guiding my way as I wove through the camp. No way could I go see Olivia—I was too hot with rage. Instead, I picked my way away from the encampment until I was well away from earshot. Finding a tree near a bubbling stream, I pummeled it with my fists until my knuckles were bloody and raw. I released my anger with shouts and cries until I was spent. Then, I returned to the encampment and beelined toward the emperor's tent.

I stood outside the door flap, listening to his disgusting cries of pleasure and the whores' tittering laughter. When the sound died down, I threw open the flap and entered.

"Care to tell me why Marcellious was promoted to Primus Pilus instead of me?"

"Centurion Alexander," Severus said, nestled between three bare-breasted women, their hair in various states of disarray. "This fine wench to my right hasn't yet been given a turn on my cock. Would you like to do the honors?"

"No, thank you. Why was Marcellious promoted to Primus Pilus instead of me?" I stared at the leather wall ahead of me.

The emperor let out a long, labored sigh. "Centurion Demarrias informed me that you've been dallying with a certain red-haired someone."

"I've done nothing of the sort, my liege." The rage I'd spent on the tree returned triple fold, shooting flames through my veins. I glanced at the wretched ruler.

"Pity," the emperor said, frowning. "She's a lovely one. Still, it's his word against yours."

His gaze flicked toward mine, daring me to contradict him.

I resumed staring at the wall.

"I'd be willing to change my mind, however, if I got a turn with her." A slimy smile flashed across his face.

Never would I agree to such a thing.

"No," I said simply.

"You know I could have her if I wanted her," he said.

"I do, sir." I swallowed back my fury. My limbs began to shake.

"It's your choice, then. You accept your assignment or bring her to me, and I make you Primus Pilus. Unless I decide I really want her. I simply take what's mine to take."

All I could see was red. My breathing came so fast that I feared passing out.

"Thank you, my liege," I said through gritted teeth. "I accept my role as trainer of Cohort IX."

"It's settled then." Without another word, he climbed on top of the woman to his right, the one he'd offered to me.

I left the tent. My hands were too bloody and beaten to take out my rage on another tree, so I stormed back to my tent and fell onto my bedding. I barely slept a wink.

By dawn, I'd forced my emotions into the recesses of my mind. I woodenly put my eighty assigned soldiers, the weakest of the weak, through their skills. First, I had them walk through the lowlands of Caledonia with forty-five pounds of weaponry strapped to their bodies, all while dressed in full armor. Their armor alone weighed nearly twenty pounds.

They groaned and complained until I, on horseback, had to punish the loudest complainer for all to see. I used a whip to mark his back, taking out some of my anger on him. I hated doing it, but I had to do my job. Severus no doubt had spies everywhere, monitoring my every move.

After the whipping, the complainer fell to his knees, and I forced him to get up and continue walking.

After that, the whining ceased.

Cohort IX completed eighteen miles in just over two hours—it was far too slow.

"Tomorrow, we run the entire time," I stated.

A collective groan rang out.

"And again the day after and the day after that. I won't cease until you show me you can best your walking time by half an hour." Tempestas pranced back and forth, as restless as I was.

An officer by the name of Quintus accompanied me. I'd had him prod and jab the slowest men with a wooden staff honed to a point. Quintus was a cruel man who took pleasure in dispensing punishment to others.

"That's enough," I'd commanded him when he bloodied several soldiers' arms. Even I couldn't stomach his cruelty.

"But, sir..." he'd protested.

"I said, that's enough!" I'd kicked my horse and proceeded up the line.

When we returned to camp, I spied Marcellious training the elite Cohort I in the field next to the encampment. His men all moved with grace, agility, and power. They were ready for battle. My men needed weeks of training—weeks we didn't have.

Marcellious grinned at me, and I flashed him a wicked leer. Marcellious and I were the same age but two very different soldiers. He was violent and cruel. I was reliable, loyal, trustworthy, and skilled.

Since I'd been given the dregs of men to train, I'd be ruthless with them until they showed signs of strength and cunning. We'd train to be merciless in our attack. I'd work them so hard they'd be able to best these elite warriors under the command of Centurion Demarrias. Then, we'd see how much Marcellious wanted to gloat.

One of my men, Quintus, sauntered ahead, weaving between the tents.

"Quintus!" I called.

"Yes, sir," he said.

"Assemble these men in the clearing at the far end of the encampment. I shall return shortly."

"But sir?" he protested.

"What is it?"

"Aren't we done for the day?"

"We're done when I say we're done. Now *go.*" I stabbed the air with my finger.

I didn't want to know what form of brutality he'd use to assemble them. I galloped down the side of the camp and then had my horse pick its way toward the center, where the women were staying. I was desperate to see Olivia and tell her I hadn't forgotten her. I hoped she hadn't given up on me.

But none of the women were here—not even the whores.

Puzzled, I assumed they'd gone to gather supplies for a meal.

I wheeled my horse and raced back for the assemblage.

The men looked ragtag, at best, in lines as wiggly as a worm.

"Quintus!" I bellowed. "Straighten them out into orderly lines, or I'll see to your demotion."

My rage was tireless today.

Once the men stood in rigid lines, I said, "Quintus, you shall fight this man."

I pointed at a man near the front of the line with my sword. He'd shown promise during the march.

Then, I navigated my horse back and forth in front of the lines. "You're to use wooden swords and wicker shields for your battles."

Many of the warriors appeared to relax at this news.

Clearly, they didn't know the faux weaponry weighed nearly twice as much as their metal counterparts. They'd find out once fatigue drained their limbs of the last of their strength.

"Get your weapons from the supply tent." I pointed to a large canopy erected for this purpose.

Quintus and the other man tromped toward the canopy and returned with the wooden weapons. The untrained soldier staggered under the weight of the fake sword to the dismay of the others.

While Quintus demonstrated, I trotted up and down the line, ensuring all eyes were trained on the front.

Then, all weapons were distributed, and the men began their practice.

Quintus and I rode among the trainees, offering suggestions, berating the ignorant, and complimenting those who showed promise. All the while, I kept scanning the tents for signs of the women.

Had they been "recruited" to serve the needs of Severus?

The thought of Olivia in bed with the emperor sickened me, nearly threatening my stomach to expel its contents. The visual stirred my anger to new levels, which I took out on my recruits. I'd indeed be loathed among the entire camp by nightfall.

After I was done with the one-on-one battle, and the men could barely move, we practiced training in the manipular system.

This system involved a four-line organization, with the younger, less experienced at the front, and the older, more experienced at the back. The *velites* would be light infantry armed with darts and thrusting swords. The *hastati* would be given a short stabbing sword. The *principes* would carry large shields and good quality armor, and the *triarii*, the most experienced, would eventually carry even larger shields and the best armor available—if they lived through this terrible war, that was.

While training in this formation, their job was to keep their ranks precisely, without opening or closing too much. They were never to crowd the others or allow too much space between them for the enemy to penetrate. Once penetrated, disorientation and confusion would ripple throughout the Cohorts, leaving them defenseless.

These men were, for the most part, imbeciles and cowards. It was a mystery to how they'd been soldiers for the other side.

I had my work cut out for me.

Disgust rolled through me as I observed them. I could have had more success with rats than these men. I was sure Marcellious found my plight laughable.

I'd laugh when I shaped these men into skilled and deadly warriors.

After a break for our midday meal, they returned somewhat restored. We worked on doubling the ranks, followed by doubling again and forming four deep. Then, we practiced the triangle formation and the circle or orb.

I was disheartened by the time the day of training had ended. After seeing to my horse, I dragged myself back to my eight men *contubernium*, those with whom I'd supposedly bond during our battles, and flopped on my bedding.

I covered my eyes with my forearm, not wanting to speak with anyone. The only thing I could think about was Olivia. Had she given up on me? I'd told her I'd return shortly. How could she know I'd be dragged into a cesspool of deceit at the hands of Marcellious? He knew my weakness—Olivia—and he would indeed exploit me at every turn.

How could I ever survive these long weary months of battle? Worst still—how could I protect Olivia in the process?

CHAPTER TWENTY-TWO

OLIVIA

wo days later, consumed with worry, I paced back and forth inside Amara's and my leather-walled tent, my hands balled into fists by my side. An oil lamp filled the space with golden light.

I was in the middle of a war encampment of all things, surrounded by ruthless warriors. But the one I wanted desperately to see hadn't yet shown his face. I'd waited for him the last two nights until sleep clawed its way into my brain. I looked for him this morning when the sound of hundreds of warriors marching footsteps awakened me. I kept my eye out for him throughout the day. I even sneaked toward the training ground.

But all I saw was Marcellious, looking pompous and arrogant as he put his men through their paces.

Where is Roman? He said he'd only be gone for an hour when he left me two nights ago. Now it's been two days. Where could he be? I hope he is safe.

My mind was all over the place, the very mind I'd trained to remain calm and collected in stressful situations. It bounced back and forth between one tragedy and the next.

First, it landed on the betrayal with Tristan, creating a firestorm of fury in my gut. Then, it landed on my father's slumping form after Tristan shot him. This thought pushed tears into my eyes.

Papa. Is he really dead? Perhaps he lived?

No. It was too much to hope for. Papa was gone, and I'd never see him again. I couldn't even say I was sorry and tell him he was right about *everything*.

Next, my restless thoughts turned to Lee, my mentor and friend. Had he been the one to poison me and the dagger? How could he do that to me? We were friends. At least I thought we were friends. Could I really trust anyone?

Needing comfort, I burst from the tent and entered a world of darkness. I tread softly toward the healing tent where Amara had gone. When I opened it, I spied Amara, hunched over a table covered with dried herbs as she sifted through them with her fingertips.

"Amara," I said, my voice plaintive.

She looked up, blinking in the dim light. "What is it, child?"

"It's Roman. He said he'd return to speak to me two nights ago, and he hasn't. Do you...do you think something happened to him?" My voice quavered as I spoke.

Amara let out a long sigh. "Child. He's at the mercy of the emperor. I'm sure the only thing that would keep him away from you is Severus." She whispered the emperor's name as if saying it loudly might conjure evil spirits. "I can prepare a sleeping draught for you?"

She gestured toward the many herbs before her.

The thought of being drugged didn't appeal to me. What if Roman finally returned? I wouldn't want to be in a stupor.

"No, Amara, thank you. That won't be necessary." I

inhaled deeply and let my anxiety go. "Just talking to you has helped."

A warm smile crossed her face, and she held out her arms.

I took a few short steps and welcomed her embrace. Amara was my comfort when things were hard and my friend when things were calm.

"Thank you," I said when I eased back. I kissed her soft, wrinkled cheek. "Thank you for understanding."

"Of course, Olivia. I love you."

"And I love you back." I pivoted and exited, heading back for my tent. But my pacing resumed.

Another hour passed, and then another. I'd kept up my relentless pacing the entire time, unable to relax into slumber. I was too wired.

When footsteps stormed in my direction, I lifted my stola and grabbed my knife from its sheath around my thigh, thinking an intruder was coming. I crouched with my hands in a fighting stance and readied myself to take down whoever was coming.

The tent flap whooshed open, and I charged—straight into Roman's arms. He wrenched the knife from my grip and threw it on the ground.

I pounded his muscular chest with my fists. "Where have you been? I have been worried sick thinking the worst happened to you!"

Stripped of armor, clad only in his loincloth, he looked wild-eyed and fierce, as if the day had unraveled him, leaving him bare-boned and desperate. His elaborate tattoo covered his heart and his shoulder. The inked symbols ranged from simple to artistic, full of detail. Scars marred his skin yet only added to the beauty of his tattoos. His face looked as if it had been carved from granite, severe and unyielding yet beautiful.

"What's wrong? What happened?" I dug my fingers into his shoulders, seeking answers in his eyes.

"Olivia," he growled. "All I want right now is comfort from a woman. All I want is you."

He seized my face between his large hands and crushed his lips to mine, dominant and commanding. His hand gripped the back of my head, his fingers clenched.

If our last exploration was a claim, this one confirmed what we both knew. We both wanted each other.

There was a desperation to this kiss. It seemed as if I were demanded to provide the anchor to him lest he fell into insanity. And, at this moment, no was not an answer—he was driven to be with me. And I didn't care; I wanted him with singular focus and unwavering desire.

The taste of sweat and blood lay on his lips, begging to be cleansed.

I'd never tasted anything so arousing. I licked and sucked, taking what he offered, willing to consume his pain and transform it into something glorious.

Roman's body was taut and commanding with hard muscle and heat. He pushed his thigh between my legs, widening my stance.

I opened to him, like letting go into the wild wind of our passion, allowing it to carry me to lands unknown. Our bodies crashed into one another, driving hard to get what we needed. And I needed him, as much as he needed me.

It felt like a tempest was in the tent with me, consuming me with the kind of passion no 21st-century woman could ever imagine.

My entire body burst into flames of unchecked longing. I'd wanted him for so long but had buried my desires. No more. I yielded to him, kissing him back with a fury. My core flooded with wet heat.

I'd been catapulted into this unforgiving land without my consent or knowledge. This kiss, this act of communion, was a way out for us. Through our bodies, we could leave everything outside of this tent behind. For a few stolen moments, the world would be ours to command.

I grasped Roman's stubble-covered jaw with my hand and took control of the kiss, letting him know we were equals. I would not be his subservient lover.

He pried my hand from his face and laced our fingers together.

I wrestled my hand away from his and placed it behind his neck, digging my fingernails into his solid muscle. I had to let him know I could yield to him, but I could also dominate, just like he did.

He growled into my mouth.

I bit his lip, tasting blood.

He drew back, blinking at me. The sanguine fluid that pumped through his veins smeared his mouth and chin. His eyes narrowed as he assessed me. Then, he wiped the blood from his face with the back of his hand.

I captured his hand and sucked the blood from his skin. I owned him at this moment. Then, I hooked my fingers behind his neck, drew his forehead down to mine, and met his fierce gaze.

"You don't possess me," I said.

"I don't want to possess you," he replied. "But I intend to devour you and give you pleasure, unlike any other man. I want to mark you and make you mine forever."

I leveled him with a steely gaze. "I know the passion that you will give me; no man will ever satisfy me. Only you can make me burn for you. I hunger for your touch and mouth. My heart beats for you…."

His lips curved into a wicked smile.

Lowering his head, our mouths locked once more.

He ground his lips against mine while he made animal-istic grunts and groans, which vibrated against my skin. He sucked my lip and bit me until I tasted blood. Then, he kissed my neck while his hands fumbled with my stola, practically tearing it from my torso until my chest was bare.

I became savage with a kind of passion I'd never experienced. My civilized side, the manners, and the culture I'd been raised with buffeted out the tent as my desire grew more intense.

I kissed his chest, salty with his sweat and musky with his manliness, raking his back with my nails, marking him. I lapped at his skin with my tongue, drawing his scent into my mouth.

He tasted of blood and battle and unchecked need.

"Olivia," he said, his voice husky and raw. He dropped his mouth to one of my breasts, sucking my nipple into his mouth.

Exquisite pleasure rippled through me, and my head fell back. Ecstasy warred with pain as he continued to suck my tender flesh. A howling ache escaped my mouth in a long, loud moan. I wanted him to suck me into his soul.

Roman's hand flew to my mouth to stifle me.

My teeth clamped down on the flesh between thumb and forefinger.

He let out a grunt and yanked his hand away. Then, he released my nipple with a loud pop, and we both staggered back, panting, wild with desire.

His body, this muscular form that could slay men and slaughter an entire army if he so chose, stood taut like a beacon of desire.

"My goddess, you're beautiful," he said in a voice so low and seductive it sent shivers through my core.

"I've never seen a sexier man," I said.

This delicious, magnetic force buzzed and hummed between us, insistent on us erasing the space.

We lunged toward one another, grasping and clawing.

He seized a handful of my hair and held me firm.

I dug my fingernails into his shoulders, piercing his flesh.

Unexpectedly, we both seemed to slide into a fluid, dreamy landscape, as if sucked from one dimension into another.

My hands fell from his shoulders, and my breathing slowed.

He reached out to trace my collarbone, then stalked around me, his fingers still tracking my skin.

I extended my limb as his callused fingertips trailed along my inner arm, coaxing shivers up my spine.

"Olivia," he said with what could only be called reverence.

Our palms connected, then our fingers. I let my arms drop as Roman slid behind me.

He placed his hands on my shoulders and stroked my back and waist. He wriggled his hands into my stola and urged it down my hips and thighs, where it landed in a pool of soft fabric at my feet. Then his palms caressed and squeezed my ass.

Had any man ever touched me with such adoration? Such intensity? Such seduction? The answer was a big, fat no.

Longing flooded my insides. I wanted Roman deep inside me.

He must have sensed my need as his fingers trailed between my thighs and made their way up to my slippery, wanting flesh.

Spreading my legs, I moaned as he stroked me. I was wet, so wet, and consumed with desire. My hips undulated into his touch, inviting him, coaxing him to keep touching me. I wanted him to take me places I'd never been. To take me out of here. To draw me into our own personal galaxy, away from the hell that awaited us outside of these leather walls.

I gripped his muscular forearm with my hands, unwilling to let him stop touching my slick flesh. His arm was rigid, a post I could anchor against as I sought release.

Roman seemed to sense my need. He clutched my ass with his free hand as he caressed me with the other. His fingers slid and swirled, pushing into me, then emerging to circle the swollen nub of flesh. His gaze bore into me, beseeching me to let go.

I was close to coming…so close…but I didn't want this moment to end. I felt like I stood on a precipice.

Then, Roman placed his hand on my shoulder and spun me around. His lusty eyes glittered as we both stood, facing one another, completely naked.

His cock hung thick and heavy between his legs, inviting me to ride him hard and deep. A wicked smile crossed his face as he lifted my hands and laced his fingers with mine. Then, he pushed me backward until my feet touched my feather-filled sleeping mat.

Roman lowered his mouth to mine and kissed me, long and deep, urging me to drop to my goatskin.

Once I was on my back, he spread his bulk over me.

Everything about Roman felt safe, yet commanding. Passionate, yet soft and sensuous.

Pressed against my body, he looked into my eyes with a sweet smile in place. "Olivia, from the day you walked into my life, you're all I think about. You're the reason I breathe and the stars in my sky. I wouldn't want this any other way. You're the love of my life, and I love you endlessly."

I felt myself split apart by his words. My heart cracked

wide. This thing between us had grown to epic proportions and now begged to be released.

I drew his face toward me and captured his lips with mine.

He didn't fight me—he let me take control.

My hunger for him grew enormous. Intense longing filled my veins as our lips ground against one another. Our moans became a symphony, sending our desire out into the heavens. We were caught in a spell of our own making, twisting us together with unyielding force. No way would either of us emerge from this connection unscathed. We were being unraveled, thread by thread, cell by cell.

Roman reached between us, grasped his rigid cock, and fit the head into my core.

"This is where I belong. Only this can ease the ache I feel," he murmured as he pushed himself deep.

I groaned, adjusting to his size and his intensity.

His eyelids lowered as he kept his gaze pinned to mine, slowly rocking his hips.

I lifted my legs and hooked them behind his thighs, and his eyes rolled back in a swoon.

"My sweetheart," he uttered, finding my eyes. He laced his fingers with mine and held my arms over my head. Then, he began this rhythmical dance of thrust, kiss, thrust, kiss.

Our bodies crashed together then withdrew, over and over, like stormy waves.

With my hands pressed into the animal hide, held in place in his powerful grip, he sucked and nibbled my lips.

His thrusts were hard, focused, and demanding.

With each thrust, both pain and pleasure shot through me. His length filled me, slamming against my insides. My core stretched wide, burning my skin, to accommodate him.

But the feeling of his rigid erection stroking against my

swollen clitoris, again and again, stoked my pleasure. I felt caught between two warring sensations—one said, "resist," and the other said, "let go."

As the intense sensation between my legs grew, I wrapped my legs around his hips.

We were two coiled rods of intense light and smoldering heat, fused together by our passion. Each time Roman thrust into me, I opened to him, wider and wider. The more I opened, the harder he drove into me. And each time he withdrew, I let out a whimper of need. Intense sensations swirled through my belly and danced along my spine.

Roman's hips began to buck wildly. With his mouth still fused to mine, the vibration of his grunts hummed into my face.

And then, unable to hold back, he tore his lips from mine. He let out a growl, and his movements became more insistent, driving into me ferociously and splitting me apart. My orgasm built like thunder, reaching its crescendo. I cried out when I came, but Roman's hand flew to my mouth, stifling my screams of desire. His hand was replaced by his mouth, devouring me, capturing me as my screams of pleasure let loose into his throat.

With his mouth smothering my cries, he let go of his own release. His hips bucked, and he growled in satisfaction like a rutting lion. When he finished, he dropped his forehead to mine.

Eyes closed, he uttered, "You are my life. My love for you is eternal. You captured my heart, my soul. I want you to be mine forever."

The sound of his voice echoed through the chambers of my heart. His words touched me in a quiet place deep inside of me.

We both lay silent, breathing hard. Then he rolled off me, his slick heat sliding from my core.

I missed him already. My body felt raw and open. This had been the best sex of my entire life, and now I wanted more of him.

He gathered me in his arms, drew me close, and then kissed the top of my head.

"My beautiful Olivia," he said into my hair.

I felt sated, at peace for the first time in a long time— maybe ever. No man had ever made me feel this way. Our souls were fused, complete, whole.

I wanted this moment to last forever.

But my questioning mind stirred from its slumber.

"I need to know the truth, Roman. I need to hear your story. Are you a Timeborne? I want to know everything about you—the whole truth."

Roman said nothing as he stroked my arm with his warm fingers. Finally, he said, "Yes. Like you, I am a Timeborne. And I shall tell you everything."

CHAPTER TWENTY-THREE

ROMAN

An exquisite sensation rolled through my body as I lay sated with Olivia in her tent. I'd never before felt this way. Olivia was a passionate and sexual woman. As lovers, we were equals. We were snug in our own universe, and the rest of the world had fallen away beyond the walls of this tent. There was no place on earth I'd rather be than here, with Olivia tucked by my side.

"Are you happy, my love?" I said.

"I'll be happier when you start talking and tell me your story," she grumbled, but a smile tugged at the corners of her mouth.

I let out a quiet laugh. "Oh, my impatient one." I kissed her silken hair, inhaling her scent. "The question remains, though. Are you happy?"

"Yes, I'm happy. At this very moment, I feel at peace, pure bliss, satisfied, and more importantly, happy to answer your question. I'm happy that you are here with me, Roman. Now talk before I want you again inside of me...."

She stroked the hair on my belly with her fingertips.

I could feel my cock stirring again, eager to be inside her.

SARA SAMUELS

But she needed answers, so answers she would get. I grasped her fingers, brought them to my mouth, and kissed them, lest they roam into areas I couldn't control—not after plunging deep inside of her. I knew I'd never get enough of her.

"I will tell you everything," I said, "but we have to speak softly. We can't let Marcellious know where I am. Marcellious watches me like a hawk. Even though you were given to me by the emperor, Marcellious is hell-bent on ensuring that I stay apart from you. I'm free to meet my needs with a whore, but not with you. I don't know why this is."

I let out a long sigh as my stomach twisted into knots at the thought.

Her expression transformed into one of outrage. As she opened her mouth to protest, I turned and stifled her with a searing kiss, capturing her mouth with mine. I loved the feeling of Olivia's mouth pressed against mine. Her lips were like a new country, a land of beauty and wonder, begging for discovery. I teased her with my tongue, thrusting the tip of it inside to dance against hers.

She countered by sucking my tongue between her cheeks, eliciting exquisite pain.

I wrapped my hands around her firm, womanly body, clutching her to me, all curves and muscle.

I loved that she gave as much as she took. She yielded and then took command. She was the most mysterious woman I'd ever known.

When I withdrew, her eyes were soft, filled with a desire that matched mine.

"We could take this in another direction," I teased, running my hands across her breasts.

She groaned and closed her eyes. When she opened them, she said, "I want that with all my heart. But, even though I want that, we may not get another chance. I need to know your story. Who are you? Where do you come from? Tell me."

I frowned as the memories I'd shoved into the corners of my mind resurfaced. It had been so long since I'd recalled them. When I'd arrived in Rome, I'd been confused, tortured by my circumstances, and desperate for answers. And answers could not be found in my past.

"I was born on October 17, 1762."

"October 17, 1762," Olivia said, her voice drifting into the tent like a sigh.

"Yes. I had a relatively normal childhood. But when I turned eighteen, Britain's colonies who had traveled to the United Colonies rejected its imperial rule. There were many political and military struggles in my country and that of the Colonies between 1765 and 1783." I stroked Olivia's arm, lost in thought. "I was a hellion…a troublemaker. I'd been raised by my mother, Elizabeth, and I suppose I was taught manners and how to behave in polite society. But I became involved in the politics of the time and wanted to make a difference. So, I told my mother I was going to fight for my country, and there was nothing she could do about it."

My frown deepened. "It must have hurt her deeply, but I had to find my way and fight for what I knew was right." I coiled a long strand of Olivia's hair around my fingertip. "Mother begged me not to go. She said, 'I forbid it! I can't lose my only child. You're my only son. I lost your twin brother, and I won't lose you. Please stay.' She went on and on, begging with me and pleading."

I grew silent, the memories as fresh as the day they occurred.

"And then what happened?" Olivia said softly, stroking my chest.

"What do you think?" A mischievous smile curved my

lips as I looked down at her, nestled in the crook of my arm. "I won."

Olivia scoffed. "I imagine so."

"Here's where it gets fascinating," I said.

"Oh, this whole story is interesting," Olivia replied. "Because it's *your* story."

Thrilled to have her by my side, I pulled her close to me and closed my eyes. But then, the memories took over and spilled from my tongue.

"The year was 1780. Mother and I had been fighting for months. Finally, she took me aside in one last attempt to prevent me from joining the military. She told me I was apparently a bastard, conceived illegitimately.

"'But I love you, nonetheless. You're my world, Roman, and I can't let you fight in some foolish war,' she said.

"She told me that the one who gave his seed was a powerful sheik my mother had an affair with. That's why I have such bronze skin, contrasting with my blue eyes. My mother's eyes were the color of the sky, with hair like summer wheat. Yet, my father was an Arabic man with sun-kissed skin." I wrinkled my nose. To this day, through all the strange encounters I'd had, I still couldn't fully comprehend that I was the son of a sheik and, more importantly, that I had been conceived out of wedlock. The bastard who gave me life should have married her.

"So, her parents found out about the affair, and they disowned her. They shunned my mother, leaving her with only her maid. Mother and the maid—I think her name was Mary. Mary and Mother headed to the Americas. This was before the war when I was in my mother's womb." I shook my head. Thinking of my mother brought sadness to my eyes. Still, after all I'd endured, I missed her with all my heart.

"When they arrived on Colony soil, they paid for a

carriage to take them to Philadelphia to hopefully start a life there. Mother felt like she had nothing left in London. But no sooner than their adventure began, a group of natives called Kiowas attacked them. They killed the carriage driver and took my mother and her maid to do unimaginable things to them, no doubt." I shuddered at the thought of my poor mother in the hands of those horrible men. "Mother thought her life would end on that day. But, miraculously, the Sioux tribe fought off the men who attacked her and Mary. His name was Dancing Fire."

Olivia's hand stopped stroking my abdomen.

I looked at her curiously before continuing.

"Dancing Fire brought them to his tribe and took care of them. The tribe welcomed them, fed them, and clothed them. But Dancing Fire fell in love with my mother. It was easy to see why. My mother was a beautiful woman." I grew wistful thinking of her.

"I'm sure that's true, Roman, because you are a very handsome man," Olivia whispered. "The mixed blood that you carry makes you even more attractive.

I smiled at her. She looked so lovely in the light of the oil lamp, with her naked form pressed beside me, that I began to grow hard again. "Must we continue this discussion? I'd rather be deep inside you, making passionate love to you and exploring other realms."

A wicked grin curved upon Olivia's lips as her palm landed on my rigid heat. "Keep going. Your reward will come soon enough. Think of it this way—the more you share with me, the more I'll share with you." She laughed as she stroked my hot flesh. "Now, keep talking."

I let out an exaggerated sigh and continued. "My mother made friends with one of the tribeswomen. They were both pregnant and due to give birth at around the same time.

Mother found it fortuitous to share her pregnancy with another woman. But one day, the chief took her aside. He said he had something of major importance to share with her. The chief had never spoken directly to Mother, and she grew alarmed. But when she got to his dwelling, he welcomed her and made her feel safe. He asked her to sit across from him, so she did so and waited for him to speak." I glanced at Olivia, wondering how she was receiving my story. She seemed rapt, so I kept going.

"The tribe did everything ceremoniously. They prayed over the animals they killed in a hunt. They prayed over the food they put in their bellies. And, on this day, the chief filled his prayer pipe and slowly smoked it, sending his prayers to the wind as he blew out each lungful of smoke. Mother described how her mind felt altered when he finally spoke. He told her a story of the solar eclipse and how, if a child were born during this time, a tunnel of darkness would split in the heavens, and the child would become a time traveler."

Olivia gasped, and her hand stilled on my cock.

"What is it?" I said.

"Nothing. Keep going."

Frowning, I continued the tale. "Mother became hysterical. She said, 'no, I don't want that. I don't want my child to leave me and to be lonely.' The chief began to placate her, saying things like, 'it's only a folk tale,' and 'it might not be true.'" I scoffed. "To my mind, he sounded manipulative, but on October 17th, 1762, I was born during a solar eclipse. Here's the part that makes me furious. Mother birthed twins. The midwife whisked them both away. The tribe was greedy, and they felt it wrong that my mother could keep two time travelers all to herself. The chief pulled the midwife aside and told her that Mother had to be fooled into thinking only one of her babies survived."

My stomach clenched as I recalled this next part. "My mother's friend birthed a stillborn on the same night as my mother. Her dead baby was taken from her and presented to my mother as the dead twin. The live twin was given to the friend to raise, while my mother was handed her the other twin—me. The tribeswomen cooed and fawned over me, telling Mother it was a blessing to have given birth to such a hale and hearty child. 'The other twin must have been sickly,' they told her.

"Mother was distraught for her dead child but elated to have me. And then they showed my mother the dagger that appeared at the time of my arrival. I have a dagger, too. Like yours." I inhaled sharply and let out my breath in a long, slow stream.

Olivia and I remained quiet as the memories swirled in my brain. I hadn't recalled them for years—they were too painful. But I had to share it all with Olivia if we were to trust one another.

"There's more, isn't there? This isn't the end of the story." Olivia placed her hand over my heart.

"Yes. There's more." I shifted, rolling to my side and urging Olivia to do the same. I curled around her back and whispered into her ear. "Dancing Fire took care of my mother as if she were his wife. He loved her deeply. He told her that I was a Timeborne but that he would protect her and keep us both safe if she married him. All this talk about birthing a time traveler proved too much for Mother. She denied his request, telling him that he was nothing but a barbarian. 'I won't raise my child to be a savage,' she said. 'You keep the dagger. I shall return to England and raise my child to be civilized. I'm a lady of culture and manners.'

"Dancing Fire berated her, telling her, 'if you were any

sort of lady, you wouldn't have opened your legs to another and birthed a bastard.'"

Another sigh left my lungs. "She was outraged and hurt. Yet, she must have hurt Dancing Fire with her declarations, but she was terrified to lose me. Later, he promised to keep the dagger safe with him. 'Life works in mysterious ways,' he said. 'Someday, your son might need it.' Mother swore she'd never return. We moved back to England, and that's where I grew up." I nuzzled Olivia's hair. "Mary, however, stayed behind."

Olivia rolled to face me, looking into my eyes. "So that's why your mother didn't want you to go to the United Colonies."

I nodded. "How she begged me to stay. She said, 'I'm telling you this story, so you don't return to the Colonies. You must never return. What if you meet Dancing Fire? What if you find the dagger? What if I lose you and never see you again?'"

My chest grew weighted with sorrow. "I am a stubborn man. Did her pleas stop me? No. I left her without an apology. I never saw her again." My gaze locked with Olivia's. "There is more to tell. Are you ready?"

She nodded somberly.

"I've got to relieve my bladder. I'll be back." I rolled away from her and got to my feet.

Could I really do this? Could I relive the entire past that brought me to this moment? Could I share my story with her? As I strode from the tent and let myself out into the night, I knew I had to tell her everything. Only then could I truly love her as she deserved to be loved.

CHAPTER TWENTY-FOUR
ROMAN

Some strange bellowing beast let out his night cry in the hills of Caledonia as I stood in the darkness outside the tent, collecting my thoughts. The sound was plaintive, like a call from my past, reminding me not to lose myself in telling my story. I was sharing all to grow closer to Olivia, not to tear open unhealed wounds.

Tonight was a night about transformation. Our intimate sharing earlier had already shifted my heart, anchoring my soul. I would never be the same after opening to Olivia.

When I felt somewhat collected, I entered the tent.

Olivia had pulled a blanket over her hips and legs, leaving her lovely torso bare. Stirrings of heat and desire filled my loins as I gazed at her. I'd travel through time again and again if it meant finding Olivia.

A soft smile curved her lips as she patted the bed. "You were gone a while."

"Just needed to gather my thoughts. This next part is… you'll see. I swore I'd never re-live this part of my past again." I tread across the floor lined with goat hides. Olivia and Amara's tent was simpler than the one I shared with my

SARA SAMUELS

fur-lined *contubernium*. I should be the one assigned to simple surroundings. Olivia and Amara deserved the comforts bestowed on me.

"You're sharing it with me, though." She lifted the covers as I crawled onto the bed with her.

"Yes," I said, settling beside her warm, soft body. "I'm sharing it with you."

Turning her face toward me with my fingertips, I dropped my mouth to hers for a sensuous, heartfelt kiss. I couldn't get enough of her.

When I eased back, I said, "Okay, let's get this telling over with so we can move to other things."

A mischievous smile crossed my face.

Olivia laughed. "Remember what I said. The more you share with me, the more I share with you."

She drew her hand across her beautiful breasts.

I hissed. "Point taken." I tucked her against my shoulder. "Let's see. I left off with my stubborn declaration that I would be joining the military to serve Britain, correct?"

"Yes," Olivia said.

"My captain was vicious. When we arrived in the United Colonies, his orders were to shoot without mercy. To kill anything that moved." I rolled my lips between my teeth, deep in thought. "It's odd, isn't it? I'm with a similar tyrant."

Olivia let out a sigh, but no words left her lips.

"Anyway, our captain insistently prodded us to kill more, be better than we were. He berated us constantly. I hated him as much as I despise the emperor. Captain Braddock was a cruel man with no morals, save those of the devil. I often fantasized about murdering him. But, of course, I could never do such a thing."

"Why not?" Olivia asked.

"I wasn't the man I am today. I was eighteen years old

when I joined the army. I was weak with no muscle on my body. And then…" My gaze drifted into a blank stare. "I got lost one night while on night guard duty. You have to understand, I was young. I thought I knew so much, but I knew little. I knew nothing about this strange land I found myself in or much about anything if truth be told. Same as with my mother, a band of natives attacked me. And, same as Mother, I was saved by the man I later learned to be Dancing Fire."

Olivia's forehead creased deeply.

I cocked my head, studying her. Then, I continued my tale. "I was full of bravado and arrogance. 'I'm going to kill you,' I told Dancing Fire. 'I'm a soldier in the Britain military, and I'm going to kill you.'

"Dancing Fire laughed. 'You barely know how to hold your rifle. In fact, do you even know where it is?' I stammered something about of course, I knew where it was, but then he produced my rifle from behind a tree and trained it right at my heart. I thought I was a dead man. But Dancing Fire said, 'You remind me of someone I used to know a long time ago—a woman. Do you know a woman named Elizabeth Alexander?' He lowered the gun as I struggled to comprehend what he was saying. I was shocked to hear my mother's name. 'You must be the one who cared for her,' I exclaimed.

"Dancing Fire's face grew somber and sad. 'Yes, that was me.'"

I glanced at Olivia. "I wanted nothing to do with this man, but I didn't want to go back and be berated by Captain Braddock–I had to find my way back on my own. Then, when I saw Braddock, I could pretend I'd been doing my duty all along. I said to Dancing Fire, 'So tell me—how can I get back to the other soldiers? I'm afraid I'm lost.'

"Dancing Fire closed his eyes and grew very quiet as he

stood before me. When he opened them, he said, 'You don't have to fight. You're going to die tomorrow.' I scoffed. How could he know such a thing? Was he a fortune-teller? A soothsayer? I said as much and demanded he returns my rifle to me at once. Again, he laughed. He gave me a look…I'll never forget that look. It cut right through me. Then he said, 'Don't you see? Our meeting is destiny. I can give you your rifle, and you can head back to see one last rising of the sun…or….' His gaze turned shrewd. 'You're a weak man. You'll never survive tomorrow. Stay with me and learn how to fight with honor and bravery.'"

I cast my gaze at Olivia. She lay nestled into the crook of my arm, her brow deeply furrowed.

"Keep going," she said. "What did you do? Did you stay and fight with Dancing Fire?"

"Of course." I shrugged. "What other option did I have? It was either fight for a madman and risk the chance that Dancing Fire's prophecy might be true, or stay with the savage. That seemed like the safest option. Honestly, I'd begun to think I was fighting for the wrong side. I was even considering defecting and fighting for the Colonies, which would make me a traitor in the eyes of Captain Braddock and all under whom I served. Then, I'd surely be a dead man."

Olivia shifted in my arm, adjusting her position.

"I followed Dancing Fire to his village. Over the next few years, he taught me how to fight and hunt with a bow and arrow. He taught me to be a clever fighter and to exploit my enemy's weaknesses."

Olivia sucked in a breath.

"As time went on, I wondered what became of my captain. When I asked Dancing Fire, he said, 'He probably thinks you're dead.'

"One day, Dancing Fire took me aside and said, 'I must

tell you something you need to know.' We'd been hunting, and he gestured to some boulders by the side of a creek, indicating that we sit and talk.

"I almost dreaded hearing what he had to say, especially if it had to do with my mother."

"'Did you know you had a twin brother?'

"'Yes, Mother told me,' I replied. 'She said he died during childbirth.' Dancing Fire went on to say what I mentioned earlier—the tribe wanted a time traveler of their own, so they'd lied to my mother. He asked if she had told me I was a time traveler.

"'She mentioned it,' I replied. 'I dismissed it as pure folly and an impossible theory.'

"Dancing Fire told me my twin brother had time traveled six years ago. I, of course, accused him of lying to me. 'You're crazy. That can't be. You must have killed him so you can say anything about him to fool me into believing the time travel story.'

"But the thought that he's out there…" I swept my arm in front of me. "That my twin brother might be out there…"

I shook my head, unable to complete my thought.

Olivia stroked my chest, offering comfort.

I smiled at her, but then my face grew hard at the next memory. "Remember I told you about the darkness?"

Olivia nodded. "But there's a lot I still don't understand."

"Dancing Fire told me about a darkness called Balthazar. That's the most powerful of them all. He said this darkness is set to destroy us and that it's growing every day, stronger and stronger. He urged me to go find my brother, telling me that, together, we're powerful enough to destroy Balthazar."

Olivia gasped, turning her face toward me. "Are you kidding me? So, not only do we have to contend with our own darkness, which I still know nothing about, but we have to contend with the baddest of the bad kind of darkness? Meaning, there are other 'darknesses' out there?"

"Yes," I said. "And I have to find my twin brother. Which is impossible, given that I know nothing about him or anything. I don't know where to begin." The same bitterness I carried ever since I time-traveled to Rome welled in the back of my throat. I pulled my arm out from Olivia and sat in her bed. "Dancing Fire said it would be easy for me to find my twin. He said a twin's soul connection is sacred. All I had to do was time travel." I spat the words from my mouth.

"He said the dagger acts as a guide. It knows where you need to go to save someone." I sighed and shook my head. "I've been looking for my brother ever since I arrived with no luck. I've encountered nothing but dead ends. Instead, I became a gladiator, I met you, and now we're at war.

"Dancing Fire trained me how to fight in the Native American ways. I lived with him for three years, and during my three years, I had never fought with him like I did that day. I was angry. He showed me my dagger and explained to me how it worked. Finally, he said, 'Go and find your brother and bring him back to me.'

"I replied, 'I don't believe any of this madness. It all sounds crazy and unrealistic.'

"The next day, I went out into the woods, alone, trying to clear my head. Captain Braddock found me.

"'Well, well, well,' he said. 'I can't believe my good fortune. It seems I found a traitor.' He trained his rifle on me and said, 'Remember what I told you about killing without mercy? Watch and learn, son.'

"I was chilled to the bone, frozen in place.

"Out of the corner of my eye, I spied Dancing Fire in the woods. He held the sparkling dagger aloft in his hand, like a welcoming beacon. I didn't want to time travel, but with the danger I was in at that moment, I had no choice, so I nodded. It was either that or die by a bullet. Dancing Fire's aim was true, and the blade sliced my hand as he mumbled some sacred scripture. I ended up in Rome with my dueling gun in my back pocket."

I dropped my head into my hands. I'd held onto this story for so long, it made me weary to re-live it.

Olivia pulled her woolen blanket around her and got to her feet. "I can't believe this. I can't believe you're a time traveler. And from the year 1762. That's crazy. How come, if you haven't been able to find your brother for such a long time, you haven't time-traveled again and left this miserable world?"

I scrambled to my feet and stalked across the tent to face her, seizing her shoulders in my hands. "You think I want to stay here, in this damn forsaken place filled with death, pain, and torture? You think I've just been biding my time as the emperor's plaything?"

My words had edges as sharp as the dagger.

"Maybe... I don't know," Olivia said, wriggling from my grasp. "Why didn't you leave and time travel?"

"I don't know the ancient scriptures!"

She let out a frustrated growl. "That makes you and me both. How are we ever to leave this place? Tell me something useful. Tell me who and what this darkness is? I still know *nothing.*"

She began pacing, around and around like a restless tiger.

"Olivia. Stop. Listen to me." I seized her arm and whirled her to face me. I cupped her face in my hands and caressed her to calm her nerves and worries.

"What?" she snarled.

"Have you thought that maybe I stayed, waiting for you?

Maybe a part of my soul knew I would meet you if I stayed in Rome."

"That's a romantic notion," she said, sighing.

"I told you I'd tell you all I know. Stop pacing and listen to me." I tipped her chin up and gently kissed her mouth, coaxing her to be present with me. Her body softened, yielding to my touch, opening to me like a flower in the summer sun.

But when I released her, she gathered up her tension, drawing it around her like a cloak.

She threw back her head and groaned. "How can we fight something as elusive as the darkness? It's there one minute, the next it's not…." She shook her head, loosening tears from her eyes.

"Please, let's sit." I led her toward the three-legged wooden stools in the corner.

We both sat, facing one another, panting hard. "Here's what I know. For people like us—the Timeborne—the instant we're born and the dagger falls by our side, the darkness is created. The darkness appears human-like. It starts to kill people. When it finds you—the source of its creation—it wants to kill you. The only way to kill it is with our dagger. But it's hard since it moves like something not of this world. The darkness can kill us with any weapon that is at its disposal. It can be anything—a gun, a knife, a bow, and an arrow…you name it." I swallowed and took Olivia's hands in mine. "Your darkness is biding its time killing random people. Then, once it finds you or comes near attacking you, it starts to kill people you love and care about the most."

"Where is your darkness?" Olivia asked.

My throat became clogged with emotion. "My dark-ness…" I rasped. "My darkness killed Amara's husband. That's how he died. He was killed a few months before you came, and I haven't seen my darkness since that night he was killed. My darkness is somewhere roaming around Rome, killing innocent people. I, too, don't know how to find it and kill it."

My chest compressed as if my entire Cohort chose this moment to sit upon my chest.

"Oh, Roman," Olivia breathed. She leaned forward to comfort me, but I wanted nothing to do with her care.

"Stop." I held out my palm to her. "It's my burden to bear, not yours."

I felt angry with myself that Gaius died because of me, because of my darkness. I was disgusted that I couldn't save and protect him, and Amara was left without a husband. I hated myself every day for this.

A heavy silence hung between us.

Then, gazing into my eyes, Olivia said, "Your burden is my burden. Your pain is my pain."

I stood stunned, shocked by her words. Longing burned through my soul for this woman who had captured my heart. She was my destiny. My soulmate. I wanted her to be the first thing I saw each morning and the last thing I saw each night. I wanted her to occupy my dreams and fill my veins with each heart beat.

I gathered her in my arms and brought my mouth to hers, hungry for her kiss. I couldn't get enough of her.

Her lips parted, opening to me, and wild tremors pulsed in the artery of her lovely neck. I kept my thumb pressed softly to her blood vessel, celebrating the life that throbbed through her. And, as she opened to me, my cock grew rigid with desire.

Each time we connected seemed more potent, more scorching than the last.

When at last we wrenched apart, Olivia's eyes shone.

"Roman."

She breathed my name like a prayer.

I wanted to lower to the ground and rest my head upon her feet like a supplicant. I worshipped her.

"Yes, my love?" I clasped my hands with hers.

"We share everything now, Roman. What we shared tonight, body and soul, can never be undone. We can't undo the past, but we can move forward together. We have each other now, and nothing will change that. Like you said, the dagger serves as guidance. It guided me to you. It wanted us to be together, and here we are. Who are we to question fate? Our destinies were entwined from the moment we were birthed. I know this to be true." She spoke with conviction and intensity.

"And yet the fact remains. We must find a way to vanquish the darkness," I said.

"So, what can we do?" Olivia's words emerged as a harsh whisper. She withdrew her hands from mine and massaged her temples.

"I don't know. I wish Dancing Fire were here to answer all my questions. He was like a father to me for the three years I lived with him. I never knew my father, so he was both a mentor and a father figure to me. He danced every night by the fire. He even walked through the fire and rubbed the coals on his skin. Dancing Fire is the name he earned. But his childhood name—the name given to him to describe his personality—was Moon Lee."

Olivia stiffened. "What did you say?"

My forehead creased. "I said Dancing Fire's childhood name was Moon Lee."

"Oh, God," Olivia said, pressing her hand to his mouth. "It can't be. Describe him for me."

"Okay," I said, drawing out the word. I gave her a few of

his physical characteristics, then said, "He wore this necklace. He never took it off. It was a—"

"It was a tooth, right? A huge tooth with a spidery crack running through it?" Olivia's face flushed.

"Yes, that's correct. But how did you know?"

"Because my mentor, my friend, and my godfather, was known as Moon Lee. I think Moon Lee is the exact same person you know…I think Moon Lee is a Timeborne as we are. And he is a part of our destiny as we are of his."

CHAPTER TWENTY-FIVE
OLIVIA

The truth about Moon Lee hung in the air like a firecracker right before it detonated. As I faced Roman, the world around us held its breath, waiting to exhale. How was this possible? How could *my* mentor have been the one to save Roman's life and send him to Rome? The thought seemed preposterous.

We studied one another, both of us trapped in mysteries.

Since Roman had shared with me, my attraction for him had only grown. He was a Brit, born of a powerful sheik, now living in ancient Rome. He'd fought in the War of Independence then lived with Native Americans—with *my friend and mentor,* Moon Lee. Lee had transported him through time with the dagger. And our sacred blades had guided us both here, to this time for some impossible-to-fathom reason.

Roman had been trained as a gladiator to fight to the death, and his muscles marred with battle scars showed it. He was like a warhorse, powerful and strong. He could kill without mercy. Yet somewhere, maybe living with his mother in civilized London, he'd learned how to please a woman and possess impeccable manners. I could surely testify to that. My body ached from where we'd collided together. And I felt cleaved by our connection in ways poets and mystics spoke of and people worldwide, at any time, longed to experience.

But our passion didn't seem like the kind of thing that I could share with anyone. Was the same true for him? Could all his lovemaking skills come from the union he and I shared?

A part of me was afraid to admit that I had fallen in love with a warrior.

"Where did you come from? What time were you born?" Roman said, jostling me out of my musings.

I thought about what to say. "I was born in a place that didn't exist in your time or this time. I was transported from my home in 2019 A.D."

"2019!" Roman exclaimed. "What was your world like? I can't even imagine."

"I'm afraid you'll find my description unbelievable." I sank to my bedding, holding out my hand for Roman to join me.

We sat facing one another, Roman's legs crossed and mine tucked demurely beneath me.

I said, "We have these contraptions called computers which send messages worldwide instantly. Things with wheels called cars and trucks, like chariots, but powered by motorized engines. They transport us at high speed. And we have trains that travel even faster which carry many people. The roads of Rome were the precursors to our freeways and highways.

"Giant contraptions with wings carry people across the land in the air, like birds. Rockets fly through the heavens. And so many people. We are crammed into towns and cities in great looming buildings that tower in the air."

Roman's eyes grew wide as he listened. "And how did you know Moon Lee?"

The oil lamp sputtered out, plunging us into darkness. I sucked in a breath before I answered him.

"He was a friend of my mother's when she met my father. There were always close, my mother and Lee. They were the best of friends. When Mother was…" I swallowed a lump of emotion that had lodged in my throat. "When Mom was killed, Papa begged Lee to help raise me and teach me how to defend myself."

"So Moon Lee is the mastermind behind your fighting skills?" Roman asked.

A single shaft of moonlight shone through the seam between the door flap and the tent wall, casting his face in shadows.

"Yes, Lee taught me everything I know. The languages I speak, my knowledge of weapons, my fighting style."

Roman nodded. "Your time sounds wondrous. I should like to see it for myself." A frown darkened his face. "And I should like to go there and kill the man who betrayed you."

"Tristan," I said with a sneer. The very thought of him sent rage shooting through my gut. "Don't make promises you can't keep."

Roman's face grew solemn and fierce. "You have my word, Olivia. I shall hand you his head on a platter. He shall suffer for his betrayal."

The thought of Roman presenting me with Tristan's head launched a shudder up my spine. And yet, such imagery was not uncalled for in the times in which we currently resided. Heads on platters just weren't the norm in the 21st Century. But bloodshed still existed at that time.

"I promise you, if we ever land in my time, you will have

to fight me for the right to serve justice to Tristan. He killed my father, he lied to me, and he betrayed me."

"And for that, he shall pay." Roman's tone was absolute.

Far away, across the camp, a faint shout bellowed into the night sky. "Roman Alexander!"

"Gods, help us. It's Marcellious," Roman hissed. He leaned over, snagged his loincloth from the tent's floor, and got to his feet.

"Get dressed," he said as he wrapped the sturdy cloth around his hips. "He can't see you like this, and he can't find us together."

I searched for my stola hastily, found it in a crumpled heap, and pulled it over my body. Then, I tried to smooth my mussed hair. It would take a week to get out all these tangles.

"So, what next? How can we possibly know if the man who sent us both here is Moon Lee?"

"We can't know unless we see him face to face. We can only suppose." Roman lowered to the floor to affix his sandals to his feet.

Then, he crawled toward me like a powerful beast.

"Olivia," he whispered, placing his large, warm hands on each of my feet.

Shivers cascaded up my legs. I felt grounded to the earth… and to him.

He clasped my ankles and lowered his forehead. "I worship you. You are my goddess."

I stood there in a swoon. How could this mighty warrior be at my feet as my supplicant, adoring me? Especially when Marcellious was looking for him?

He began kissing my feet like feathers drawn across my skin.

"*Roman!*" Marcellious' slurred voice sounded closer, but he was not upon us yet.

"Gods, it sounds like he's been drinking." Roman's warm breath puffed against my ankles. He swept his hands up my shins and continued his trail of kisses. "I worship every part of you."

His rough palms drew shudders of delight as they rasped upon my skin.

My entire body flooded with exquisite sensations. Desire ignited, hot and hungry as if Roman had placed a torch to my insides.

"Roman Alexander, where are you?" Marcellious slurred.

A dull thwack rang out as if he had struck someone's leather tent.

"Sir, how may I be of service?" a sleepy-sounding male said in a faint voice.

Roman kissed his way up my thighs and proceeded to my belly, kissing me through the cloth of my stola. His strong hands gripped my hips as he balanced on his knees.

"I adore your beautiful body, your mind, your heart…" He rose to a crouch and kissed my sides. His hand swept down to the juncture between my legs and stroked me through the linen.

Fire shot through me. I could orgasm from the mere touch of this man through my garment. I'd never been this responsive to a man, ever. It was like I was now wired to Roman, the lightning to his rod, the wave meant to crash upon his stone.

"So, you haven't seen him tonight?" Marcellious said from his location just past my tent.

"No, sir, I have not. Not since he dismissed us earlier." The soldier sounded groggy.

My breath caught in my throat. Marcellious could be fifteen or twenty yards away—which was fifteen or twenty yards too close.

"Roman," I hissed. "You've got to leave."

"Not until you hear my promise." He placed his mouth over my right breast, through the fabric, and sucked.

I gasped.

"Oh, God," I whispered, clutching his head with my fingers.

After a long suck of my nipple, making me ache with need, he released me and proceeded toward my shoulders.

"I swear to you, Olivia," Roman said, on his feet now, nibbling and sucking my neck. His fingers slowly, sensuously kneaded my breasts.

I arched into his hands, craving more, more, *more.*

"I swear that we shall find a way to return to your home when this war is over." His teeth grazed my neck's throbbing artery.

A wave of pleasure crawled up my spine. I dug my fingernails into Roman's back.

"Roman!" Marcellious' voice was closer.

"Roman," I hissed. "You've got to go. *Now.*"

Ignoring my pleas, Roman said, "I don't know how long this war will be, or when it will end. But end it shall." He nuzzled my jawline, and his hand found its way back to my core. "And when it does, we shall scour the land for the ancient scriptures. We shall find a way."

"We could run, Roman. We could run away and find a way to time travel. Or, we could live in other lands." I writhed against his hand, close to orgasm.

"We'd no doubt be caught and put to death, my love. Now, shhh." He pushed the tip of his nose into the shell of my ear.

"My beautiful flame," he whispered as he fondled me. "Always and forever, you shall be mine."

The pressure he exerted on my clit was perfect. My hips

kept rocking, pushing into his hand, begging for release as Roman's fingers worked me around and around. I didn't think I could hold back; I couldn't stop the orgasm if I wanted to. I bit my lip and sucked in a breath as an exquisite sensation shuddered through my body, sending me rocketing into the sky.

Roman's low laugh of delight fell from his mouth. "You're so beautiful when you come."

"Now, where could he be?" Marcellious sounded maybe ten yards away. "I'll find you, you bastard."

A muffled thud, followed by a grunt, made it sound like he had fallen to the ground. He let out a few curses.

I started to moan, and Roman's mouth captured mine in a searing kiss. The kiss ended too soon as Marcellious' voice grew closer still.

My legs were wobbly, shook to the bone by the intensity of the release still rocking through me.

Roman took my face between his hands. His gaze flicked toward the door and then back to me. "Promise me. Promise me we'll fight this together and that nothing shall break us apart."

"I'm getting mad, now, Roman," Marcellious shouted from somewhere near Amara's healing tent.

I curled my fingers around Roman's hands. "We are lovers now, as well as allies. We're together now. And nothing will break us apart."

"I shall find a way to come for you every night. Nothing and no one can keep me away from you." Roman's hands dropped from my face, and he whirled away from me, crossing the floor. He placed one hand on the tent flap and cracked it, peering into the night. Over his shoulder, he whispered, "Let's hope he's too drunk to see my escape."

Like a ghost, he slid from the tent.

I sank to my knees, unable to hold myself up any longer. I stayed fixed in place, listening, tense, hopeful that Marcellious wouldn't find Roman. My heart hammered against my ribcage, seeking escape.

Roman's voice boomed from somewhere in the distance as if he'd sprinted to the other side of the encampment. "Marcellious!"

"Roman? Where are you? I thought for sure you'd be with *her*." Disappointment filled Marcellious' voice.

"You're drunk, man," Roman said. "Don't you have better things to do than to check on my whereabouts?"

Their voices blurred into a fade as they headed away from me. I fell back against my bedding, closed my eyes, and tried to wrap my mind around everything I'd heard and experienced tonight. There was far too much to take in. At last, I had to surrender to sleep, floating on the memories of my mighty, handsome warrior and lover, Roman Alexander.

Tomorrow would come soon enough.

CHAPTER TWENTY-SIX
OLIVIA

Months of this ceaseless, god-awful war continued. When Severus fought and won, the encampment would celebrate far into the night with plenty of drink and whores. When Severus fought and lost, the nightly revelry would ensue with an undertone of rage against the emperor's actions. But no matter the outcome, debauchery ruled through the night.

Amara and I would huddle in our tent, unable to sleep. Then, Roman would arrive, and Amara would excuse herself to the healing enclosure.

To avoid Marcellious' petty scrutiny or the emperor's childish wrath, Roman had to carefully choose the timing of his arrival. Sometimes he'd enter in the middle of the night. Sometimes, he'd slip into my tent right before daybreak. But he kept his word that he came every night without fail.

I hungered for his visits.

The war had taken its toll on us both. We were both fatigued beyond belief. Dark circles ringed Roman's eyes as they must have lined my own. Roman often arrived with the fury of battle coating his skin. His eyes were haunted, espe-

SARA SAMUELS

cially when the emperor commanded that all should "slaughter without mercy, be they men, women, or children." At times like those, Roman's need for comfort was overwhelming. We'd slam into one another, grasping and clawing to find solace.

Our lovemaking was so joyous, so fulfilling. It kept us each going. Coming together in heart, body, and spirit proved our nightly escape from the wretchedness of the war. For just a few sweet moments, the only thing that existed was Roman and me, moving in harmony.

Amara's and my waking hours were spent tending to the wounded. Men, their bodies sliced and gashed, would be carted in, slung over the shoulders of another, or carried on a litter. Sometimes, their intestines would spill from open wounds, or bones would protrude from their skin. A few of them survived, thanks to Amara's skillful healing ways.

Most died.

Amara and I would place coins on their eyes and mouth to pay Charon at the River Styx. Charon was a greedy god who would only provide safe passage if paid to do so. Then, we would beseech the goddess Morta and Charon to deliver the fallen's soul to the underworld. We'd have soldiers carry the dead to the forest, where animals could feast on their decaying bodies.

Every few weeks, we packed up all our belongings and trudged to our following battle site. At those times, I had to search for Roman among many soldiers. He'd never openly approach me, but I'd feel the burn of his scorching gaze seeking me out from atop Tempestas. We'd make eye contact and revel in our connection for a few blissful seconds.

Then, someone would require his attention, and the spell would be lost.

The Caledonia soldiers employed clever tactics in dealing

with the Roman army. After the emperor's earlier victories, the Caledonian guerrilla fighters brutally slaughtered many Roman soldiers. But Severus, blood-thirsty and hell-bent on triumph, forged on.

On one particular day, when we'd set camp in the highlands of Caledonia, I returned from bathing in a stream and entered the healing tent.

"Olivia," Amara said in a hushed tone. Her gaze skittered around the tent like ears might be pressed to the leather walls outside.

"There's no one outside if that's what you're afraid of, Amara," I said. I dabbed at my wet hair with a piece of linen.

"Good." She approached me and huddled close. "One of the soldiers came in for treatment while you were gone. He told me Severus had ordered a slaughter of all residents in the nearest village. I'm so sick of the carnage the emperor is responsible for. I'm convinced he wants genocide. We must go and warn the villagers. Please tell me you'll join me. I'll say I need healing herbs that I can only find in that village if anyone questions us."

Standing hunched over, Amara looked frail and helpless.

"Of course, I'll come. I wouldn't dream of allowing you to go by yourself. Who will protect you?" I flashed her a saucy smile.

"Thank you, dear. We must be quick about it." She scurried about the tent, gathering her satchel and a basket, presumably for picking herbs along the way if we found some.

And then we were off.

We skirted past some Roman soldiers, ready with our story should the need arise. They mostly ignored us, save one man who eyed me like he could eat me. I'd cut off his balls with my ever-present dagger if he even tried.

We trekked through some of the most stunning scenery I'd ever experienced. Surrounded by lush beauty, we walked in a world of wonder: streams with small waterfalls and endless miles of green. Overhead, a hawk circled, the late afternoon sun dancing along with its wings. In the distance, a herd of small deer grazed.

How could the world be so beautiful when war wreaked havoc in parts of the land? It made no sense.

I lifted my gaze to see clouds of smoke on the horizon. "Amara, look! I think we're too late."

Amara gasped and brought her hand to her mouth. Her eyes glistened with tears. "Those bloody bastards. The emperor is a cruel, cruel man."

Amara had cursed. Amara *never* cursed.

I grasped her hand, and we both hurried toward the source of the smoke.

As we approached the village, flames shot from the remaining structures. Smoke spewed into the sky, clogging the atmosphere in billowing clouds. Villagers raced past us, clutching their few belongings, tears streaking their faces.

"Turn around. Don't go there," a woman with three small children urged us. Her eyes looked soulless like the soldiers had taken her spirit and held it for ransom. "The Romans have decimated our homes."

Her snotty-nosed, grubby little kids wailed and screamed by her side.

Amara stooped and patted the cheeks of one of the children, a boy of maybe ten or eleven. "You be in charge of your mother. You're the man. You know what to do—find somewhere safe to hide."

The child regarded her with wide eyes, wiping his nose with the back of his hand. He stopped crying and nodded, a somber expression on his face.

"Do you have a favorite place to hide?" Amara said, placing her hand on his shoulder.

"Yes," he said in a small voice.

"Take your mother and your two sisters there. *Run*!"

The boy's expression turned fierce.

"Mama, come," he commanded. Then, taking the hand of one of his sisters, he ran, his family right beside him.

"You're such a kind soul, Amara," I said as we hastened toward the village.

"People deserve to be cared for, not slaughtered." Her face looked grim.

Inside the boundaries of the town, we were met with carnage and destruction. Homes continued to burn, and dead or dying bodies lay scattered on the roads. Scores of men's bodies lay slumped near a wall with blood soaking their clothes as if they had been lined up and killed, execution-style. Even dogs had been slaughtered, their tongues hanging from their lifeless mouths, their sightless eyes staring into the beyond.

My heart sank at the destruction Severus' army had brought here. And to what end? How could wiping out men, women, and children help *anything?* I was beside myself with rage and sorrow.

Amara and I scurried among the bodies, searching for the living to offer as much comfort as we could.

My heart ached at all the devastation. People stared up at us, their faces frozen in horror or absence of hope. From what I witnessed, it must have been a nightmare of epic proportions to have Severus' army sweep through the town and cause such devastation.

A part of me shuddered at the thought of Roman as part of all this destruction.

A woman wailed from somewhere. "Help me!"

Amara cocked her head like a tiny bird.

The same woman's voice cried out again. "I'm birthing my baby. Help!"

"Oh, dear." Amara shuffled toward the voice.

"Amara, no! What are you doing?" I caught up to her and seized her upper arm.

I was met with her fiercely determined expression, much like that of a hawk.

"A woman is in labor, Olivia! I must help." Amara yanked her arm from my grip and hastened away from me.

With a sigh, I joined her. We followed the cries and moans until we reached a partially burned dwelling.

Amara rushed inside, with me close on her tail.

Furniture lay strewn on the floor, broken or charred. Gingerly, Amara stepped over and around the rubbish, as did I.

In a back room in the same state of disarray, a petite woman writhed on the floor in agony. Her eyes grew wide with fright when she saw us.

"Don't hurt me!" she shouted, scrambling backward.

"I'm not here to harm you," Amara said, in the broken English she'd picked up while on the campaign. "I'm a midwife."

The woman slumped to the floor in relief.

"Olivia," Amara said, her gaze sweeping the chaotic room. "Find a somewhat clean cloth. And water. We need water."

She spoke in the calm, practiced voice of one who had delivered countless babies and was now ready to help bring this child into the world, even if soldiers stormed the room.

I rushed through the house, turning over broken furniture, and searching everywhere for a source of clean water and cloth. Finding nothing that wasn't damaged, torn, or filthy, I raced outside.

Maybe a neighboring house has something.

Once my feet struck the ground beyond the small dwelling, I froze.

Ahead of me stood the darkness, its black cloak swaying side to side as if in slow motion.

"Olivia," it hissed.

Standing in a backdrop of flaming destruction, the darkness looked like my most terrifying nightmare here to haunt me.

I couldn't move, trapped in that fight or flight terror instinct. *Come on, Olivia,* I urged. *Move!* My cheeks stuck to my teeth as the moisture drained from my mouth. *What did Roman say, the darkness can be killed with your dagger or can be distracted by a gun?* My Glock was strapped to one thigh and my dagger to the other. But my limbs were rigid as if I were cast in stone.

The darkness swayed in a circle as if it, too, were rooted to the ground.

I frowned. Something was different about this darkness since the last time I saw it.

Taking a deep breath, I rolled my shoulders. "You think I'm afraid of you? Do you think you can just come here and kill me? Think again. I will destroy you."

I barreled for the shape, expecting to blast right through it. Instead, I met with an unmoving object, slamming my shoulder into it. *What the...?* I reared back, ready to head butt it, but it slowly dissipated into the nothingness I'd expected.

My head was wrenched back with a sharp, jabbing twist of pain.

The darkness behind me had my hair clutched in its fist.

I stared at it from my bent over backward position, wrapping my hands around its bony wrist.

The eyes that stared back at me, even the face, were distinctly feminine.

"Olivia." The darkness faded from view.

My head whipped around to find it again.

The whisper-hiss came from behind me, and I whirled around to face it.

It slowly emerged from nothingness, like ink dropped into cold water.

I lifted the skirt of my stola and retrieved my Glock. I had twenty bullets left, so I had to make each shot count. My hand shook as I brought up the gun. This was preposterous— I'd trained my whole life to keep my cool in dire circumstances, but fighting this…this *demon* unnerved me.

"You think you're so strong," the darkness rasped. "You're nothing but a child, play-acting with your puny weapons. You're *weak* inside. *Weak.* You can try to kill me, but you will only fail. You're not strong enough to defeat me, let alone Balthazar. Balthazar is my ally. He'll protect me, and then he'll come for *you.*

"You see, the moment the Timeborne is born, the darkness is created, and I, Olivia, am your darkness. I crave bloodlust, and I demand more for each human I kill. But killing my Timeborne gives me eternal life, and all I want is to kill you and destroy you."

Her menacing words shook me to my bones, making them vibrate in fear beneath my skin and muscles. This had to be some strategy the darkness employed to rattle me.

"You think your words scare me? You have no idea who you're messing with. If Balthazar is your ally, tell him I will kill you and destroy him." Sweat trickled down my forehead and into my eyes, stinging them.

I blinked to stop the irritation before I took aim and pulled the trigger.

The bullet whizzed straight through the darkness.

It stood there, still swaying side to side, laughing a cruel, wicked laugh. "You think shooting with your gun will weaken or kill me? You are pathetic, Olivia. If Balthazar were here, he would surely kill you painfully and slowly."

My jaw dropped open. The skin on my body frosted over with more fear. I was in over my head, and I had no other recourse.

Out of nowhere, Amara rushed into view, her hands bloody and bright blooms of crimson staining her stola.

"Olivia. Both the child and mother didn't make it. They've both gone to their maker," she said between sobs.

The darkness stiffened, and I swore I saw it—or *her*— smile beneath her dark hood.

"Amara! Stop! Go back inside!" I rushed toward her.

The darkness swept in front of Amara and plunged a dagger into her heart.

Amara dropped to the ground.

"No! No, no, no, no, *no*." Panic and dread overtook me as I skidded to a stop before Amara's fallen form. "What have you done?" I shouted to the darkness as blood seeped from Amara's chest.

It leered at me, then disappeared with a pop.

I fell to my knees before Amara, my knees jabbing into the stones and gravel beneath me.

"Amara. Stay with me. I'll find help somewhere. What do you need? What do you do to those soldiers when they come to you bleeding out? You stop the bleeding. That's it. You stop the bleeding." I babbled in a stream of frantic words as I pressed my palms, one over the other, to her wound.

Her sticky life essence continued to drain from her body,

pooling around my fingers. This wasn't working. No amount of pressure would stop the bleeding and even if I had one, there was no place to put a tourniquet to staunch a chest wound.

I wriggled to free my stola from beneath my legs and bunched it up, stuffing it into her wound the way Lee had taught me.

Amara's eyes fluttered shut, and she groaned.

"This can't be happening. I can't lose another mother. Do you hear me, Amara? I need you. Please stay with me. You *can't* die." Streams of tears trailed down my cheeks as I blubbered. My tears dropped onto Amara's chest, combining with the blood to create a pinkish smear.

Slowly she opened her eyes and lifted a hand to my cheek. She regarded me from far away as if she'd already begun her journey along the River Styx.

I clung to her cool, blood-covered hand, pressing it against my skin. "You can't die, Amara. Please don't die. I can't go on without you."

"Stop crying, my dear child." Her eyelids drifted closed again and a sweet smile formed on her face. "I can see them. My daughter and husband are beckoning to me. I'll soon be with them."

"No, Amara. You have to stay with Roman and me. We need you. *I* need you. What will I do without you? Please don't leave me, please, please, *please*." I felt like the knife plunged into Amara had also ripped my heart apart.

In her drifting voice, she said, "Promise me you'll stay with Roman. Promise me, Olivia."

She dragged her eyelids open again.

"I promise. I love Roman so much, Amara. Nothing will separate us." I kissed her wrinkled, bony hand over and over. The metallic tang of her blood filled my mouth.

"You and Roman are so good together. You were destined to be joined in this lifetime."

"Amara, you were meant to stay with us. We both *need* you."

"You'll be all right, Olivia. You're strong. So very strong. You have a great destiny ahead of you. You'll carry on without me." Amara's words grew so faint that I had to lower my ear toward her face.

"Don't say those things, Amara. The soldiers need you. Roman needs you. We all need you." I squeezed her fingers, clinging to the hope that if I held onto her tight enough, she wouldn't die.

Her hand grew limp in mine and her eyes focused on something I could not see—probably that blasted river the god Charon traversed across in his wooden boat.

I sobbed, and I raged, dropping my head to her chest. "Amara, no. I won't let you go. Please don't leave me."

Anger surged through me, and I stormed to my feet. I felt as if a void opened inside me, a hole that my mother had left when she'd died, and Amara had once more restored. My grief grew like a tidal wave crashing through me. I picked up whatever I could find—stones, wood, rubble—and threw it.

"I couldn't save her from the darkness," I blubbered, tears and snot smearing my face. "I couldn't save my mother or my father, and I couldn't save Amara. I'm a fucking loser."

I whirled around like a crazy person, searching for the darkness.

"Where are you?" I hissed. "I'll tear every limb from your body. I'll fucking destroy you."

The stench of smoke and decay wafted into my nose from the gruesome carnage left behind by Severus' army.

A mother and her young children hurried past, eyeing me warily.

It didn't surprise me that they were frightened of me—I felt so unhinged I was afraid of myself, too. I sprinted down the street, searching for the darkness. I looked in abandoned homes and I darted behind buildings. I tore apart rubble and ruin with my bare hands.

But the darkness was right by saying I was weak. Amara was gone forever, and now my heart was shattering into a million pieces. I was worthless. The warrior inside of me was dead. I couldn't save her; I'd failed again, and the darkness had won.

Finally, as nightfall began to shroud the land, I dragged my weary body back to Amara's prone form.

There, I curled against her stiff form, already consumed by rigor mortis, and sobbed until I could cry no more. My vengeance would come soon enough.

CHAPTER TWENTY-SEVEN
ROMAN

Dirty and exhausted, I trudged across the dark encampment heading for Olivia's tent. I needed her comfort badly. I longed to hold her and kiss her passionately.

At that moment, I didn't care who saw me. If I had to, I'd beat whoever wanted to stop me to a bloody pulp, the same way I'd struck down countless men in the last few months.

I was sick of this war. Sick of the things I'd done as a soldier and would have to continue to do if I stayed here any longer.

Severus's insane thirst for blood and vengeance grew, and so did his cruelty.

Today, he'd ordered us to storm a village of innocent people and cut down every single one.

I managed to get away with not slaughtering women and children but killed more than my fair share of men and teen boys.

Some of them stared defiantly down the blade of my sword as I struck them. Others trembled as I plunged my knife into their chests or sliced off their heads. I hated myself for being a part of this bloody battle. And I despised Severus.

As I approached Olivia's tent, I was discouraged to find it dark. So was Amara's healing tent. I hastened toward the leather-walled dwelling where Olivia and I had shared so much passion these last months. Throwing back the door flap, I found it cold and empty.

I raced to Amara's healing space. No one was inside.

A feeling of dread gripped my insides. Something was wrong. I rushed through the encampment, nearly colliding with Marcellious as he stumbled free of one of the whore's tents.

He adjusted his loincloth, tucking his cock inside. A leer spread across his face.

"I've got her warmed up for you," he said in a slurred voice. "Fuck! I forgot. You don't *do* whores. You spend your time with the warrior bitch."

I grabbed the nape of his collar and hefted him into the air.

He spat at my face.

As his spit slimed down my cheek, I roared, "Where is she? Do you have something to do with her disappearance?"

A confused expression colored his features. "How the fuck should I know where your bitch has gone?"

"She's *not* my bitch." I shook Marcellious. "She's more woman than you could ever hope to hold. And it's a simple question. Do you or do you not know where Olivia and Amara are? Their tents are empty."

"Can't even keep track of one woman, let alone two." Marcellious scoffed, but something strange shone in his eyes.

Concern? Impossible.

Disgusted, I shoved Marcellious away from me.

He stumbled and fell back on his ass, yet it brought me no

satisfaction. Since he smelled like a distillery, I probably could have blown on him and caused him to fall.

Out of the corner of my eye, I noticed someone staring at us from a few yards away. I whipped my head in his direction.

It was one of my legionaries, a sneaky bastard named Cassius Quintus. He seemed to always know more than he said, like he kept his ears to everyone's business. He'd make an excellent spy—*if* he could be trusted to not spill secrets to the person he was spying on.

"Quintus!" I barked out.

"Yes, sir," he said, straightening his spine.

"Have you seen the healer, Amara, or her assistant, Olivia?"

He shrugged.

I charged in his direction, and he seemed to shrink inside his skin. "It's a yes or no question, Quintus. Have you seen the healer, Amara, or her assistant, Olivia?"

I reached out to grab him, but he shoved his hands in front of his face.

"I might have seen them."

I let out a growl. "Where might you have seen them?"

"I saw them leaving. They were headed toward that east-side village we set siege to today."

I caught his jaw and dug my fingers into his bones. "And you didn't think to stop them? Didn't you think it might be dangerous for two women to travel to a place of destruction without a male escort?"

Quintus whimpered. "I'm sorry, sir. I'm not in charge of the women. I didn't think it my place, sir."

I released his jaw and batted the side of his head. "We're all to protect Amara and Olivia. They're ours to protect."

I stormed to the place beneath the trees where we kept the horses and whistled for Tempestas.

Since it was dark, I could only hear him approach.

I circled behind him, took off at a sprint, and placed my palms on his hind end as I vaulted onto his back.

Tempestas galloped away before I uttered a word. He knew when I mounted him this way, I meant business.

Holding onto his mane with one hand, I urged him east, in the direction of the village.

His hooves struck the ground with fury as we rode through the darkened landscape. I prayed no holes would catch his leg and send him and me hurtling to the ground.

When we entered the still smoldering village, I dismounted, found an intact house beam, and lit the end from the embers. Then, I mounted Tempestas again, and we rode through the streets, using my torch to guide us.

Tempestas picked his way around dead bodies and the scorched remains of the village. Our carnage here had been absolute. No one was left untouched.

Disgust roiled in my belly, threatening to dispel the meager contents I'd consumed today.

I searched for hours, my torch long since extinguished. Tempestas wandered up and down streets and then retraced the same route we'd seen a thousand times. There was no sign of Olivia or Amara anywhere.

What had happened to them? Had a marauding troop of Caledonians taken them?

Utter despair filled me. Fighting in this war was hell. But, if I were to lose the two people I loved the most—Amara and my beloved Olivia—I feared I should take my own life. I would have nothing to live for.

Finally, dawn crept along the horizon to shed its light on a terrible new day.

As I turned Tempestas to head back to the encampment, I spied a woman in the distance, cradling another body. The woman keened for the loss of whomever she held. And her hair—no one had hair as radiant as my love.

How had I missed seeing her? I'd combed every square inch of this village many times.

I squinted at the body she cradled. A chill crawled across my body—the body she held was Amara.

I kicked Tempestas' flanks, and he reared and surged ahead at a gallop.

Olivia didn't look at me. Instead, she kept up with her keening and rocking, keening and rocking.

"Olivia," I said as I reined my horse and leaped from his back. I crushed her to me, with Amara's dead body between us. "What happened?"

"I couldn't save her. I couldn't save Amara. The darkness. The darkness came, and I couldn't stop it," she sobbed hysterically. "It killed her mercilessly. It's all my fault, and now she's gone, gone, and isn't coming back. Roman, this is all my fault. I should have protected her, but I failed. I failed…"

With one hand on the back of her head, the other wrapped around her back, I held her tight. "I've got you, Olivia. I'm here now," I said, but I felt anything but soothing.

A mountainous wall threatened to burst inside of me, letting loose a storm of rage and sorrow. Amara was dead, killed by the darkness, just like her husband. I was angry. I wanted to kill, lose control, and go into a fucking rage. But I had to keep myself in control. Olivia needed me, and I needed her.

"The darkness," Olivia wailed, her tears wetting my shoulder. "It looked like a woman. She tormented me, saying Balthazar was coming after us. But I shot at it. I shot at it like you told me to do, and the bullet just zipped right through it, and it stood there, smiling when it saw Amara. And it attacked before I could get Amara to safety. It pulled out a blade and plunged it into Amara's heart. Oh, Roman. It was brutal. The darkness killed her like she was an animal."

Her wails tore through my heart, and the walls came tumbling down. I let out a cry of anguish, and fat tears streaked my face. I couldn't remember the last time I'd cried, and I didn't want to be shedding tears now. Amara was like my mother. She was the closest person in my life before Olivia arrived. She cared for me like a son and fed me like a mother. Nursed me back to health when I was wounded.

My heart was bleeding.

Olivia pulled away from me and studied me, shock all over her face. "Roman."

She reached out to touch my face, no doubt to comfort me, but I wanted no comfort. I shoved her hand away and abruptly stood, fighting back my emotion.

"We need to bury Amara. We need to put her somewhere to send her to her maker, not in this gods-forsaken village which I had a hand in destroying."

My chest heaved with the uncontrollable force of all the emotions I'd buried for so long. Stumbling around, I searched for something, anything with which to lay Amara to rest. The tears kept falling. I couldn't hold them back.

Muttering like a madman, I dug through rubble and ruin until I came across a cloak. I wrenched it free and staggered back to Olivia, who still clutched Amara.

She seemed sobered now, as if my outburst of emotion had allowed her a measure of peace.

I, however, was not peaceful. I felt ashamed to appear so weak.

"Let's lay Amara out on this cloak," I said, not meeting Olivia's eyes.

Without a word, she gently rested Amara's small frame on the fabric. Her stola was covered in blood—the blood of our dear friend, Amara.

I let out a ragged sob. I had killed countless men. I'd killed my best friend Marcus and never shed a tear. Amara's death was different. She was my mother in Rome, the same as I lost my real mother.

Olivia's face revealed anguish as she witnessed my foolish display of emotion, but she stayed quiet.

Together, we lifted Amara's tiny body.

"Where are we going?" Olivia said, her voice hoarse.

"To the woods. Amara would want to be set to rest in nature," I said heavily. "Tempestas, come."

The horse eyed me, then followed.

As we trekked through the village, I set another beam on fire, balancing the cloak carrying Amara with one hand.

Olivia eyed the burning torch but said nothing.

We approached a small stream, its waters sparkling in the sun.

"Here. Let's lay Amara to rest here." With a mighty thrust, I secured the torch to the ground.

Olivia nodded, and we slowly lowered the body.

"Go find kindling... anything we can use to burn the body," I said.

Olivia's eyebrows flew up, but she didn't speak. Instead, she resolutely turned and headed for the forest, as did I.

We both returned bearing an armload of firewood and kindling. We dropped it all on the ground near Amara.

Tears continued to track down my face, dripping to my shoulders. I felt broken... wholly gutted. But I managed to fish three coins from my pocket and place them on Amara's eyes and mouth. Then, I began stacking wood around her lifeless form.

Olivia watched me, then assisted me, carefully, lovingly placing the wood and small branches in position.

Once we were done, she ripped the blood-stained bottom of her stola free, leaving her legs bare. She gently placed the tattered, blood-soaked fabric over the top of the pyre.

I tugged the torch free from the ground and stood by Amara's side.

Olivia took my free hand in hers, and I lost it, sliding into grief so strong it threatened to consume me. As I placed the tip of the flame on the stola, I was wracked with violent sobs.

"To Amara. May you rest in eternal peace with your husband and daughter," I choked out. "You were my mother here in Rome. Thank you for everything that you have done for me. Healing, inspiring, and teaching me to be a better man. I will never forget you. You will remain in my heart forever."

"To Amara," Olivia said in a quavering voice. "You were like a mother to me as well. You welcomed me with open arms. You replaced the hole in my heart and repaired it with your motherly love and support. I will never forget you. Forgive me for not saving you. I will keep my promise to you, and I promise I will avenge your death. I'll miss you with all my heart." Silent tears began to drip down her face. She was heartbroken.

We stood there, hand in hand, watching Amara's body burn.

When nothing was left, I released Olivia's hand and called for Tempestas, who grazed nearby.

Olivia turned to face me, "Roman, I'm sorry...I should have protected her and saved her."

I said nothing. What happened to Amara wasn't Olivia's fault. It was a matter of time before the darkness would come and kill her. If not during the war, then it would have come after. The darkness was always watching us, ready to strike and break us.

Olivia touched my face, but I put my palm out to stop her. I was in pain and her touch only caused me to be angrier with myself because I wasn't there to protect Amara and Olivia.

I mounted Tempestas, then helped Olivia behind me.

She wrapped her arms around me, pressed the side of her face to my back, and we took off, heading for the encampment. By the time we were near, I had my emotions under control. Either that, or there was nothing left to emote.

As we neared the edge of the tents, Marcellious emerged from one of his cohorts' enclosures.

He swaggered toward me. Great. He's the last man I want to see, ever.

"Well, well, well," he said with a cocky smirk. "I guess you think it's all right to not show up for your duties."

Anger boiled in my gut at this soulless cur.

"Olivia," I said in a fierce, clipped tone. "Dismount."

She slid from the horse, and I followed suit. Then, I stormed toward Marcellious and captured his throat in my hand.

Eyes wide, no doubt sensing my fury, he grabbed my wrist with both hands. "You son of a bitch!"

"Amara has been *killed*. We have laid her soul to rest at the edge of a creek. I can't function with your bullshit. Leave me alone before I have no mercy in killing you, right here and right now." I released my hold on him.

"Amara's been killed," Marcellious repeated, visibly paled. His Adam's apple bobbed up and down, giving a curt nod before wordlessly pivoting and striding away.

I turned toward Olivia to see confusion written all over her face.

"Come," I said. "Let's retreat to your tent."

I held out my hand to her, and she took it.

After turning out my horse with the others, we hastened toward her leather-walled dwelling.

Once inside, I slumped on her sleeping mat.

Olivia lowered next to me. "I don't understand how Marcellious, this fierce cold-blooded warrior, showed empathy when you said Amara was killed. He looked shaken."

"I don't know, and I don't care." I was beyond tired and, at that moment, felt incapable of coherent conversation. I dragged my hand through my hair. "I'm only glad that he turned and fled, or there would have been bloodshed."

Olivia and I remained silent for a few taut seconds.

She was the first to shatter the fragile quiet that stretched between us.

"I saw the darkness, Roman. I saw it." Her face looked pale, bruised by grief.

I let out a long sigh and said, "Tell me everything that happened. From the beginning."

Olivia picked at her frayed hem. "Amara heard about the slaughter from one of the legionaries. She begged me to come with her to warn them."

I regarded her with eyes that felt dull and lifeless. "You know you are forbidden from leaving the encampment."

She flashed me a defiant look. "And you know how I feel about the emperor's rules."

Our gazes collided in a war of wills.

Finally, I huffed out another sigh and said, "Please continue."

It was useless to be cross with her about anything.

Her attention flew to the floor. "When we got there, we were too late. The village was already in ruins. A woman cried out in labor, and Amara—you know what fierce compassion she possessed...." A wan smile lit Olivia's face. "She insisted on helping the poor woman. So, we found her, and Amara sent me out to fetch water and a clean cloth. That's when I saw it... The darkness."

She rubbed her mouth and jaw.

"The darkness didn't immediately attack. It just stood there, trying to torment me." She nodded at me, then continued. "And I remembered our conversation about a bullet distracting it, so I shot at it. The darkness said I was pathetic and weak. Then Amara came out. Her hands were covered with blood, and she looked so bereft. She said neither the woman nor the child survived."

Her eyes welled with tears. "I couldn't save Amara, same as my mother. The darkness killed both of the women I loved." She began to babble. "The darkness was a woman, Roman. It was distinctly female. It was a woman, and it killed Amara. But my mother was killed by a man. The darkness that killed my mother was a man. I saw him. His eyes were the darkest blue, and his hair was long and black. His clothes were black, and he had no cloak.

"And I couldn't save Mom, and I couldn't save Amara. I can't save anyone," she wailed, gesturing frantically with her hands.

"Olivia, stop. Listen to me." I grasped both of her hands. "The darkness only kills two types of people. The time traveler or someone the time traveler loves. So, either the darkness killed your mom because you loved her or your mother was a time traveler."

Olivia jerked back as if I had struck her. "I don't know if she was a time traveler," she said, yanking her hands out of my hold. Then she began to speed-talk once more. "I don't think so. How could she be? I mean, she might have been. I wouldn't know. I was only ten years old when my mom died. Lee and my mother were best friends. Maybe it was Lee's darkness that killed my mom, or maybe my mother was a time traveler. When the darkness approached her, she seemed to know it. They spoke for a few minutes, looking as if they were familiar with one another. And then they started to argue. My mom talked to him for two minutes before he struck her with his knife."

"Wait," I interrupted. "Amara was killed by a female?"

"That's what I said."

Olivia's wet gaze and swollen face broke my heart.

"And she spoke to me. The darkness called me weak. She said her ally was Balthazar, and he was powerful and would support her and come for me next." Olivia rubbed her palms together.

"Your mother had to be a Timeborne, Olivia. No normal person would talk to the darkness and have a conversation unless they knew who they were. The darkness conversed with you because it knows you. If Amara was a time traveler, the darkness would torment Amara, too, but instead, it killed her."

Olivia continued to speed-talk in frantic circles. "My mother, a Timeborne? That can't be. It can't be true."

I couldn't process any more information. I was beyond tired and exhausted. I bolted to my feet. "Enough!"

Olivia paled and ceased talking.

"Talking about Amara and your inadequacies to vanquish the darkness won't bring her back," I said, frustration boiling up inside me. "She is gone forever. You must stop blaming yourself and repeating how you couldn't kill it. I *know* you couldn't."

I was wracked with so much shame and grief, and I knew I was wrong in taking it out on Olivia, but I couldn't stop myself.

I stormed toward the door flap.

"Where are you going?" Olivia cried.

"Away from here. I have to get away."

CHAPTER TWENTY-EIGHT

OLIVIA

I sat in shock, watching the door Roman had just blasted through to get away from me.

The last twenty-four hours had been gut-wrenching. Now, the one person I had left in this world to comfort me had yelled at me and cast me aside. Furthermore, he wanted nothing to do with me. He'd pushed away any attempt at comfort, connectedness, or care.

The level of grief he'd let loose at Amara's death astounded me, rendering me speechless. I'd witnessed Roman in various ways, but none as anguished as he was today. Maybe it was wrong of me to say anything to him about the darkness killing my mother. That was when he'd reached the breaking point. But blowing up at me and charging out of the tent left me not only with an ache the size of the sea surrounding Caledonia but too many questions to hold in my brain.

I pushed to my feet slowly, as if I weighed a thousand pounds. Questions poured through my mind.

Could my mother have been a time traveler? If so, was that her darkness that killed her, or that of another, someone she loved? If so, who did she love? She loved Lee. Was Lee a time traveler? He'd have to be if Roman and I were guided by his actions at different times. But, why wouldn't he have told me if that were the case?

I couldn't come up with a single answer.

Amara drifted into my mind. I still couldn't wrap my head around her loss. It made no sense. I should walk across to the healing tent and have a conversation with her or help her grind herbs with her mortar and pestle.

More tears leaked from my eyes. I loved Amara with all my heart. And now she was gone. Since coming to Rome, she'd been the one to guide me and offer both comfort and wisdom until Roman and I could sort out our issues and become lovers. And, even with that joining, her guidance had proved invaluable. She'd known in her heart the kind of man Roman was—and she'd known we'd make an excellent match. I had Amara to thank for even considering Roman a suitable partner since I'd arrived in this time broken and mistrusting.

"You have a great destiny ahead of you," Amara had told me.

How did she know? It was probably the way I fought. She knew I was different than others. She felt it inside her heart.

My soul ached as memories of Amara surfaced. She'd taught me to prepare meals using the devices employed in the 3rd century, such as the brazier or the cooking trough. I'd learned the value of keeping our home clean and honoring it as our temple, not just a house in which we lived. She'd been wise beyond belief. And she hadn't shoved me away when I'd been an angry, uncooperative bitch.

When that line of musing ended, I slumped to my bedding. My eyes drifted closed, and I fell into a heavy slumber where I dreamed of blood raining from the sky, covering everything.

When I awoke midday, muzzy-headed and void of feeling, my stomach burned with hunger. Numbly, I prepared some grains and legumes from Amara's and my meager stores, cooking them over a tiny brazier just outside the tent. Once the food was done, I ate it, tasting nothing. I'd sunk into apathy, shock, and grief so deep I didn't know how I'd crawl out of it.

How could this have happened? I'd fooled myself into believing everything would be okay through my passion and love for Roman. The truth was that I'd been cast here without consent as a fucking Timeborne, which I'd never believed in. And I'd come to live in a brutal period I wanted nothing to do with. Now Amara was dead, Roman didn't want me, and it was *all my fault.*

I sunk into the kind of melancholy associated with a dissociative fugue. There I sat, filthy, my heart battered, my hair in matted tangles, still dressed in the stola I'd worn when Amara had been killed. Her death was as hard and painful a moment as losing my own mother. The feeling was unbearable. My soul was completely broken and shattered into a million pieces. The pain that I felt inside was numbness and void.

I rocked back and forth. It was the only thing I could think to do.

The sun passed across the sky, heating the tent to boiling. Amara and I would typically throw back the tent flaps and air the place out. But Amara wasn't here, was she?

The sun began its descent, and the tent was filled with stuffy air since it hadn't been aired. I didn't care. I continued to sway back and forth.

Darkness wrapped its fingers around the leather

surrounding me, and still, I sat, numb and grieving. When I was completely enveloped by nightfall, the door flap parted, and someone entered. I didn't care who it was. It could be Marcellious coming to rape me for all I cared.

A deep, gentle voice met my ears. "Olivia?"

Roman. I said nothing, continuing to oscillate.

Soft footsteps tread away from the tent, then returned, bearing light.

Roman entered again, wielding a torch he'd presumably fashioned from a branch in my kindling pile and my or another's embers from their braziers.

"Olivia!"

I looked at him with tears in my eyes.

He knelt beside me, and I turned away from him.

I didn't care. I was too far gone.

"Leave me, Roman," I said.

He placed his strong hands around my waist and pulled me into a powerful embrace.

"Olivia, let's get you cleaned up. Come on, sweetheart." He hauled me to my feet with a firm hold braced beneath my arms. Then, he guided me outside and pitched the torch to the ground since we had enough moonlight with which to see.

Wordlessly, he led me to the nearby stream. Holding my hand, he helped me enter the water until I was hip-deep, then scooped me up and dunked me.

The shock of the cold water brought me to my senses.

"Are you trying to kill me?" I spluttered, clinging to his neck.

"Anything *but*, my love. I'm trying to bring you back to life. No sense apologizing to someone who is catatonic." Gripping my shoulder and the back of my head, Roman smiled down at me.

I blinked the water from my eyes, shivering. "You want to apologize to me?"

"Yes." He regarded me with unblinking blue orbs, filled with tenderness. "I behaved like a bastard yesterday. I was beside myself with grief and rage over this terrible war."

"Me, too," I said in a small voice. The shivers became more violent while Roman stood there like he was in a hot bath.

"Let's get you warm. This garment has got to go." He peeled the torn stola from my body, released it into the water, and hefted my naked form in his arms. Then, he splashed his way out of the creek, planting kisses on the top of my head and my cheeks. "I'm sorry, beloved. About everything. More than ever, we need each other now that Amara is gone. We need to mourn together, grieve together, and heal together. And, we have to get out of here. You will have to be the one to search for sacred scriptures since I am still in the emperor's employ."

Pressed against his bare torso, my skin began to warm.

Roman kept to the shadows, silently padding like a big cat through the night. When we got to my tent, he shouldered aside the opening, carried me inside, and, almost reverentially, placed me on the bedding. He searched for a covering and wrapped me tightly, pulling me against him. "Do you agree to stick together? I was a fool to push you away."

"Yes," I breathed, clinging to him.

"Good."

"But I don't know where to search for sacred scriptures, especially since I'm forbidden to step away from the encampment," I said, more than a touch of resentment coloring my words.

"Well, I have news. The war is at an impasse. I'm being sent home with the emperor, Marcellious, and a few others.

The emperor will leave many of his cohorts behind and return when his health has improved. His health has been failing him." A sneer pulled at Roman's lip.

"We're being sent back to Rome?" A tiny burst of hope, like a match lit in a canyon, flickered in my chest. "And we can leave all this war behind?"

Roman sighed. "For a time, yes." He stroked my back with his callused palm. "Many of the cohorts are disgruntled. Some crave the bloodshed and gore sought by Severus, but most are disgusted by what we're asked to do. I think Severus senses that and knows if he remains here, major unrest might mean his death. So, basically, he's running home until he can make a plan." He nuzzled my nose with his.

The tiny light inside my chest grew, stirred by my arousal.

"I have some ideas of where to search for sacred writings. But, first…" Roman dropped his lips to my mouth and kissed me. With grinding insistence, his lips conveyed everything I needed to hear at this moment.

Pushing against my mouth, moaning, he filled me with strength and hope for our future. As the kiss deepened, the pain of rejection he'd left me with dissipated like smoke into the sky. Our skin and flesh began to disappear as our souls reunited.

Roman wrenched away and murmured against my lips. "I'm so sorry for yelling at you."

A trail of kisses fell upon my jaw.

"You didn't do anything. We were both angry and in shock at what had happened. I don't blame you for putting your rage on me. You're fighting a war and killing people, and with Amara's death it has made you even angrier."

More kisses landed on my neck.

"Please accept my humble apologies," he whispered before his mouth ghosted across my collarbone.

"Oh, Roman," I said, digging my fingers into his thick, lush hair. "I forgive you. How could I not? Amara would want us to be happy together, not angry with one another. She wanted us to be together more than anything."

If any part of me was still clinging to apathy, it began to burn, making way for the blazing heat of passionate desire. I wanted Roman more than I'd ever wanted him before. It was like our love for one another deepened each time we came together.

Finally, Roman threw back his head and groaned. "I have to get back to my cohorts. I asked them to assemble so I could tell them who their new Centurion would be. They're probably wondering where I am."

I sighed. I wanted him here, with me, but, soon, we would be together, in Rome, away from all the madness of battle.

"All right." I stroked my fingers across his lips. "So when are we to depart?"

"At dawn."

I jerked my head back. "Dawn? Did anyone think to inform me or was it to be a surprise? Or does the emperor not want me to go with you?"

Already, I'd reverted to my snappish behavior.

"What do you think I'm doing here? I sneaked away from my duties, so I could inform you. Without Amara, the emperor doesn't require your services," Roman said, pushing to stand. "And, if I don't get back to the cohorts, I'll be without a head on my shoulders."

"Go, go!" I scrambled to my feet and shooed him away. But, before he left, I brushed my lips across his.

Still clutching the covering around me, I watched him slip through the shadows. I caught the sound of a rustling nearby. Sinking into my battle stance, I called out, "Who's there?"

A crash and a thud followed, and a man stumbled to his feet.

I could barely make him out through the shadows of night.

"Who's there?" I called again.

No one replied, but a man who looked like Marcellious righted himself and brushed off his legs.

"Marcellious?" I said, disturbed. "Are you spying on me?"

"It seems I am," he said in a smug-sounding voice, slurred from drink.

"Did you learn anything useful?" I scoffed.

"Indeed, I did," he said, stepping into my line of sight.

"We spoke of nothing important," I said as a chill washed across my scalp. I quickly recalled Roman's and my conversation.

What did we say of any value to Marcellious? Should I go warn Roman? Roman had mentioned sending me to search for sacred scriptures. How could that be of value to Marcellious?

"Why the hell are you spying on us? Don't you have whores to fuck?"

"That gets so tedious," he said, adding a sour chuckle. "I'd rather listen to you and your dog, Roman, fuck."

I gritted my teeth together. Marcellious was trying to bait me, nothing more.

"You're pathetic," I said, with a wave of my hand, turning to head inside the tent.

"We'll see," he said, adding a cackle that made my hair tingle.

I had a bad, bad feeling about whatever Marcellious was up to. How long would I have to wait to find out what it was?

CHAPTER TWENTY-NINE

OLIVIA

Being aboard the ship again was far more treacherous than before. Without Amara to comfort me, I huddled below deck, cold and afraid. The whores slept beside me, and the men visited them, but I didn't see Roman for days.

However, the ship moved swiftly, propelled by men eager to return to their wives and families, if they had them, or away from the blood-fest of war. We didn't stop to ram other ships the way we had on the way north, but instead, kept a steady course, past the horn of Gibraltar and heading north-east for the shores of Latin Italia.

A gaudy tent had been erected on the deck again for the emperor's pleasure, the same as before.

Finally, as I lay exhausted from a bout of seasickness, my heart crying out with loneliness for Amara and Roman, familiar hands brushed along my face. Roman's huge body settled next to mine.

He smelled of the sea and his manly scent, stirring my senses. "I'm sorry, my love. I couldn't escape the emperor's demands until this moment. He's kept an eagle-like watch over me."

I shivered. *Should I tell him how Marcellious had spied on us the night before we left?* I hadn't had the chance to speak to Roman since then, what with all the preparation for departure.

Hooking my leg over his hip, I was delighted to feel his cock stirring through his loincloth.

"Are you here to comfort me in that manner that only you can?" I palmed his growing erection through the linen of his garment.

Roman groaned. "If only I could steal time for comfort. I have only a few seconds to spare before the emperor comes looking for me."

"Why is he so diligent?" I frowned.

"I wish I knew." Roman pulled me close. "I'm afraid I'm unnerved by it. He and Marcellious have spent much time together in his private chambers, and I don't think they're merely sharing a whore. I think they're up to something."

I worried my lip with my teeth. "Remember our last night in Caledonia when you came to apologize to me?"

"Yes, what of it?" Roman rocked his stiff erection against my belly, sending a cascade of pleasure rushing through my hips.

"After you left, I caught Marcellious outside our tent, spying on us."

His hard heat began to soften. "Why didn't you tell me?"

"Oh, could it be that I was kept back with the whores on our departure, and you've been busy day and night with whatever keeps you occupied as a Centurion?"

Roman sighed. "Of course. I'm sorry. But what did he say?"

"He said he heard things that would be useful to him. I

didn't know if he was merely baiting me for a reaction or what?" I stroked the pulsing artery of Roman's thick neck.

"I don't recall saying anything that could be used in any way." Roman's brow furrowed into a frown.

"Nor do I...except for the bit about sending me to search for sacred scriptures."

Roman's frown deepened. "That might make him question us, but it's hardly a reason for suspicion. What's he up to?" He pulled away, sat up, and dragged his hand through his hair which had grown long and unruly. "Listen, Olivia, I must give you something of mine. If Severus and Marcellious are planning anything, I need you to keep it safe."

He retrieved a black-hilted knife from beneath his loincloth.

I stared, eyes wide, at a dagger that matched the one I had. It glowed faintly but not as strong as it did during the full moon that landed me in Rome.

Roman gently placed the dagger in my hands and searched my eyes. "I need you to protect the dagger."

"Nothing will happen, Roman. We're traveling back to Rome. It's better than the battlefields."

"I know, but after what you told me about Marcellious, I have to ensure it's safe and hidden."

I nodded at him and tucked away the knife with my own dagger.

Roman looked intently at me. "I need to get back topside. Severus was just finishing up with his whore and will pop out of his tent any moment and ask for me. I'll stay alert and see if I can find anything out."

After a quick kiss on my lips, he hastened from the room.

A sense of dread filled my veins. I had experienced moments of worry since discovering Marcellious outside my tent but hearing about the emperor's scrutiny of Roman sent me into a full-blown panic attack. I paced my quarters, wearing blisters on my feet. When it came time for sleep, I lay on my bedding and fretted all night, listening to the groans and lusty utterances of the whores and their soldiers.

I saw no more of Roman the rest of the journey, and my worry grew. I sneaked upstairs when I could to scout around for my lover. Only when I spied him practicing physical agility skills on the rocking, swaying deck could I calm. Then, I retreated to my hovel below the stairs, in the dark, rat-infested rooms reserved for the women.

When we finally docked in Italy, I was hustled upstairs, across the deck, and down a gangplank by a surly guard.

Roman, looking as fatigued as me, descended the forward gangplank simultaneously. Even his shoulders were rounded and stooped. He didn't look like the mighty warrior I knew him to be.

Once my feet touched land, I pushed through the throng to get to Roman. Rules and restrictions be damned.

Our gazes crashed together, and he opened his arms wide for me.

Several armed guards came up behind him and grappled with his arms, pinning them behind his back.

Roman fought and wrestled with the guards. "What's this about? Take your filthy hands off of me."

The emperor emerged from the crowd. He stepped up to Roman in a dainty walk, much in the manner of a woman. "Roman, Roman, you bloody bastard, you're being charged with treason. I have been led to believe that both you and your witch are spies."

I covered my mouth to stifle a gasp.

"What? This is preposterous. I live and serve for you, my liege," Roman said. The cords of his neck bulged, and his face was mottled red. He sought my gaze. "Olivia."

I tried to reach him, but two guards seized my arms, wrenching them behind my back.

"Roman!" I screamed. "Roman!"

I watched in horror as the guards placed shackles around Roman's wrists and led him away.

"No!" I cried. "Let me go, you assholes!"

People jostled about everywhere, eager for a glimpse of the drama unfolding around me.

Marcellious' voice shouted over the melee of the throng. "Release the bitch."

The guards let me go.

I stormed toward Marcellious and shoved him.

He stumbled backward but didn't fall. "I'd be careful, you know. I'm being promoted and have the exclusive ear of Severus."

My skin rippled with fear. "I don't care what privileges you enjoy. Whatever you told the emperor is a lie. All lies."

Marcellious leered at me. "Are they? I merely repeated what I heard in your tent, and the emperor came to his own conclusion."

Frantically, I searched for Roman.

In the distance, I could barely make out his back.

"Roman," I screamed again.

Marcellious seized me from behind and wrapped his stinking hand around my mouth. He hissed in my ear. "I knew you were a spy and a traitor the moment I laid eyes on you."

My hand shot back, and I tried to grab his balls. I was too weak, though, and my movements were sluggish as Marcellious jerked out of my reach.

"Don't worry. You'll get to touch them."

I spun my head around and spit.

The spittle only landed on his shoulder.

"I'll never touch your balls except to slice them from your body," I growled.

He grabbed my upper arm and shoved me forward. "Let's go. I have a chariot waiting."

"What? Why? Where are you taking me?" Icy fingers of dread frosted my skin.

"To my chambers, of course. You, my dear, are a spy. But I managed to cut a deal with the emperor, and he granted permission for you to be mine. I always wanted to fuck a redhead. With Roman out of the way, I'll get my turn, too."

My anger flared. It took all my strength, but I kicked Marcellious in the stomach.

He grabbed a handful of my hair and punched me.

CHAPTER THIRTY

OLIVIA

When I awoke, my nose was assaulted with unfamiliar smells.

Where am I? I opened my eyes and focused on my surroundings. I lay on a bed covered with a feather mattress. Care had been taken to place a pillow under my head. I glanced down to see my long hair had been combed, fanned across my chest like some kind of art.

The thought of someone combing my hair while I was unconscious launched a shiver up my spine.

My wrists and ankles were chained to the legs of the metal bed, secured by heavy metal cuffs. With a groan, I lifted my head and looked around the room.

The devil himself sat watching me from across the room. I was in Marcellious' private space—I had no doubt.

My temper flared, and I gathered the chains around me to flail, to punch, anything, but I was helpless and unable to move. The unyielding metal bindings dragged my aching arms and legs to the mattress.

"You son of a bitch," I yelled.

His face was calm with a devil's smirk as he lounged

against the far stone wall. Pushing away from the wall, he strode toward me.

My temper was on fire.

Marcellious was a ruthless, barbaric man.

"We have a problem," he said coolly when he stood inches from the bed.

"What? The fact that you've captured me against my will?" I growled.

A terrible-sounding laugh emerged from his throat. That same wicked smirk formed on his face once more. "No. It's far more complex. From the first moment you were brought to the emperor's palace and you fought me, I had this strong desire to possess you…to own you. But when I kissed you, and you attacked me, I knew I wouldn't settle for a mere kiss but something far more than that."

He stroked his jaw as if we were talking about the weather.

"And here's the disturbing part. I will not rest until I conquer and break you," he said, with cold snake-like eyes.

I recoiled from his words. Marcellious was beyond crazy —he was a sick man with disgusting intentions.

"Where's Roman?" My heart pounded like a drum. Roman had to be okay. I didn't think I could live without him.

A cruel smile curved Marcellious' lips.

"Roman is dead as wild animals devour his dead body," he said.

"You're a liar," I said, tugging my arms. The sharp metal of my bindings dug into my skin.

Marcellious crouched and placed his long finger on my lips.

"Shh," he hushed.

My stomach lurched. I was repulsed and disgusted with

his touch. Yet, I had to use his desire to touch me against him. Lee had drilled it into me: *Use any weakness you can find.*

I opened my mouth and lowered my eyelids as if his touch aroused me.

Marcellious cocked his head, studying me intently. Gently, he stroked my lips. Then, he slid his dirty finger into my mouth.

I wanted to gag at his taste, but I stifled that impulse. Instead, I bit his finger.

He hissed and yanked his hand away from my mouth. Yet, his expression was steel, with no emotion. He grabbed a handful of my hair and cupped my face with his other hand.

"No pain will ever hurt me. My heart is stone. I feel nothing," he said with a sneer. "And nothing and no one will ever break me. Never again."

He let go of my face and hair and walked away from me.

"Where the hell is Roman?" I asked again.

Marcellious regarded his fingernails. He removed a knife from a sheath on his belt and began picking the grime beneath his nails.

"Your beloved lover is fighting for his life in the arena. He won't be alive much longer. You see, his final match will be with me." Lowering the knife, he lifted his head to make eye contact with me. That evil smile spread across his cheeks. "I will be the last person Alexander will ever see. I will plunge my sword into his heart, and you will be mine."

A shudder rocked his body as if desire and violence evoked the same arousal in him.

Our gazes still warring with one another, I said, "I will *never* be yours. I would kill myself before you ever lay a hand on me."

A cold laugh left his lips. He replaced the knife in its

sheath. "You won't kill yourself. That's too easy. Why don't you *fight* me instead?"

The impulse to engage in battle hit me hard.

When I first came to Rome, and the emperor's Praetoria caught me, I fought for my life. When I was deposited on the emperor's throne room floor, I killed five men to save my own life. During the emperor's celebration, I battled when the darkness attacked Roman and me. Whenever my life was at risk, I fought with all my power.

Lee's voice rang in my ear. "No matter how hard things might get, Olivia, never give up. Fight with grace, don't give in to your enemies, and never show weakness."

My original goal was to get home at whatever cost. But now everything changed—Roman had captured my heart. Amara had been like a mother to me; now she was gone because of me. Roman was a Timeborne like me, and his problems had become mine.

There were still many mysteries to solve, and I wanted to solve them *with Roman*.

I studied Marcellious, speculating on why he was the way he was. I believed he was a hurt and wounded man with many scars. I wanted to know more about him and find out why he became this way.

"Why do you hate Roman so much? What has he done to cause you so much pain and hatred?"

Marcellious' face transformed into one of rage. "Roman destroyed my life!"

"How so?" I said calmly.

Marcellious threw up his arms. "I was the *king* of the arena, and he stole my glory."

I shook my head. "I don't think that's it. Your hatred runs deeper than that."

"I ruled in the arena. It took me ten years to win victory

after victory, and my soul was blackened when I received my freedom. I craved the blood-lust," he said through gritted teeth, his body shaking. "My life in the arena was filled with the exultation of pain and darkness."

Marcellious let his head drop back as if in the throes of ecstatic release. But then he straightened and met my eyes. "Roman came along and, in a short time, he *destroyed* my honor. He became the best of the best. Worse, he could have killed me in a fight, but instead, he let me live. I despise him for that."

I shook my head. "I don't think that's it."

My intuition was nudging me to go deeper, to probe as far as I could into Marcellious' motivations.

"Roman has managed to obtain everything I wanted," Marcellious said, his nostrils flaring. He clenched his hands into fists. "He got it all. And I got nothing. I lost everything in my life that I held dear." He began to pace. "He got to live away from the emperor's palace while I am forced to live in residence here. He got Amara. And then…"

He stood at the foot of the bed I was chained to and fixed an ugly sneer on his face. "And then, he got *you*."

His demeanor changed as his tongue darted across his lips, and his cock stirred beneath his loincloth.

I became repulsed, but I had to press on.

"All this hatred you have for Roman is because of jealousy? How can you be envious of how easily he gets what he wants in life?" I said, all while thinking how hard Roman had to strive to prove himself and how much he hated being in servitude to Severus.

"I had a woman once," Marcellious said, gazing at my legs.

"What happened?

Marcellious stared blankly before him.

I didn't want to lose his attention. I had to keep him talking, so I tried a different subject. "How did you become a gladiator?"

Still staring into space, he said, "I was a fifteen-year-old boy with no life. I killed to survive. I became good at slaying men's lives. I found my place in society by murdering and torturing. It made me feel alive." He inclined his head as his eyes focused on me. "And then I met *her*. She changed me for the better, if only for a short while. She was my whole life."

His tone had become wistful as if he spoke from a dream.

"Who was she?" I asked.

He shook his head. "It doesn't matter. She's gone, and she's never coming back."

"Maybe if you share more about her, it will help."

His eyes narrowed as he regarded me. "What are you doing? What are you up to?"

"I'm trying to help you. Somewhere deep in your heart, you have some good left in you. No one is born evil. They are created. But you have no one to guide you. You seem lost."

His eyes turned flinty, and he glared at me. "There's nothing good left in me. And there's no way you can help me, so stop trying. I pity you for even thinking you can change me." He scanned my entire body, and again, his cock stirred. "Oh, how I shall break you, Olivia. It will be my pleasure to make you mine and have you scream my name every time I give you pleasure."

I couldn't help myself—I shuddered in repulsion. I had to get his mind away from his lust-filled thoughts about me. "What about Anthony's mother, Lydia? I thought she was your wife."

Marcellious waved his hand before him. "She means nothing to me. She's a means of quenching my needs, nothing more. I don't care for Lydia. The only woman I ever cared for was *her*."

His gaze grew soft as he directed his attention inward.

Whoever this woman was, she was special to him.

"Marcellious." I spoke his name softly to try to coax him out of his memories.

He blinked and resumed his focus on me.

"What?" he snapped.

"Tell me where Roman is. Tell me, and I will try my best to heal you and help you be a better man."

Marcellious' face hardened. "You can't help me. No one can. I'm beyond help or healing. The only one who can help me is my father, and he's far, far away. He's gone." His hand drifted through the air like a leaf and floated to his side. "Gone, gone, gone."

"Who's your father?" I struggled to sit up, then gave up and collapsed back to the feather mattress.

"Gone, gone, gone," he repeated. His footsteps echoed against the walls as he circled me. "Everyone is gone."

"Marcellious, you're speaking in circles. I don't under-stand you."

He shook his face at me. "You're not supposed to understand!"

He stormed from the room.

The energy of a typhoon hung in the room.

"Whoa," I muttered. "What the hell just happened?"

I lay still on the bed, staring at the door he'd vanished through. My heart thundered in my chest.

His footsteps pounded the hall outside the door. The door exploded open and Marcellious, bare-chested, powered into the room. He stood as tall as Roman, over six feet. His eyes were the color of dark secrets, whereas Roman's were sky bright. But his attitude and behavior diminished his appeal.

Where Roman's face was elegant and spoke of nobility, Marcellious' face bore a perpetually cruel veneer. His nose had a slight sideward tilt as if it had been broken many times, and his complexion was swarthy. Tattoos covered his back, torso, and his arms, while scars split the inked symbols in many places, giving them a gruesome appearance. His muscles were chiseled, but nothing about him appealed to me.

A sheen of cold sweat frosted my skin. Was this the point where he'd rape me and take what he thought was his? I'd kill him if he even attempted it.

He spun around to show me his back.

Dumbfounded, I stared at the ugly scars marking his back, distorting the tattoos all over his skin. Roman had blemishes as well, but nothing compared to what Marcellious had.

"Do you see these marks?" he demanded. Without waiting for a response, he continued. "These are all the lashes I endured for my crimes."

My heart broke for his suffering. "Please let me help you, Marcellious."

He whirled around.

"No," he snarled. "I'm going to kill Roman Alexander. And then I'll make you *mine*."

There was nothing I could do, chained to the bed as I was. My heart sunk into a pool of despair beneath the mattress.

I asked, "Do you have any siblings?"

"No," he replied in a dead tone. "I only have my father… *had* my father."

He reached up to stroke a necklace that hung from his neck.

I'd been so stunned by his naked flesh I hadn't noticed the necklace. Gooseflesh popped all over my skin. The pendant looked like the one Lee wore.

"Where did you get that?" Unable to use my arms, I nodded at him.

"Get what?"

"That necklace."

"This?" He frowned.

"Yes, that. Where did you get it?" My mouth became dry as chalk.

"I stole it from Marcus. He was a friend of Roman's." He swayed where he stood as if he might fall over.

"You got it from Marcus?" My mind scrambled to make sense of what he was saying. *Was Roman's best friend a Timeborne?* "So why did Marcus have to die?"

"Because I couldn't bear Roman's bond with Marcus. I trusted no one and could never make a friendship like that. They were inseparable like brothers. They dominated the arena together and I wanted to destroy their happiness. My hatred for Roman is so deep that I will do whatever it takes to kill him." Spittle sprayed from his lips.

The depth of Marcellious' hatred and jealousy was something I'd never seen in my life.

He moved away from me and began to hum, staring into space. His arms drifted by his sides as if he were waltzing through the water.

"What are you humming?"

Marcellious kept on humming, ignoring me. Clearly, he'd lost his mind.

"Marcellious, stay with me, here. Tell me what the song is. It's so beautiful." It sounded familiar, but I couldn't place it.

"No," he said as if he stood far, far away from me. Then, he began to say words in a sing-song voice. "Ya hamiat alqamar fi allayl , 'adeuk litutliq aleinan lilnuwr watur-shiduni khilal alzalami. dae alshams aleazimat tarqus min

hawlik bialhubi walmawadati. Mean , aftahuu bawaabatikum wamnahwani alsafar eabr alzaman walmakan mithl zilal allay."

The words came from some haunted, ethereal place that stirred my soul.

Where have I heard those words before?

I shook my head to clear it. I had to stay focused while Marcellious kept chanting.

He seemed lost, swept up in the reverie of the words he spoke.

"Where did you learn that song, Marcellious? Is it from your childhood?" I said in a soft voice, not wanting to startle him.

"Yes, it's from my childhood," he said before resuming.

"Do you know what the words mean?"

He didn't reply. He'd already faded into whatever head-space that chant evoked.

The words sparked some long-ago memory in me—some essential place I wanted to explore. But my mind couldn't comprehend all the *wheres*, hows, and *whys* of the mesmer-izing vocalization.

"You've got to let me go, Marcellious." I didn't want to stay here with this madman. I had to find a way to escape and locate Roman. Where was he? What foul circumstances did he have to endure now?

Life here was so very hard. Roman and I had managed to snatch some goodness from our existence through loving each other, but it seemed the 3rd century was not fond of granting favors. People here had to endure their miserable existence until their lives were taken from them.

I understood why people died young in ancient times. The average lifespan for men at this time was about forty-one years of age—if they survived life as a soldier. The way I saw it, why would anyone want to live longer? It wasn't like life got better as you matured. More likely, you endured your life until you could endure it no longer. And, in this situation, death didn't sound entirely unreasonable to me.

Just when I started to slide into despair, Lee's words drifted through my mind.

"Never give up, Olivia. You still have a chance to survive if you have one breath left in your lungs."

I took a long shuddering breath as I listened to Marcellious' repetitive recitation of his chant. And then Roman's voice emerged from my heart.

"My love for you is endless," he'd told me. "Always and forever, you will be mine, no matter what happens to us here."

How could I possibly give up on that kind of reassurance? The love Roman and I shared gave us the courage and the strength to fight the odds. We would *not* go down, either of us —not without a good fight.

I directed my attention to the crazy man who stood swaying several yards away from me.

"Let. Me. Go. If you refuse, I will find a way to escape," I growled.

He snapped out of his sing-song stupor.

"What did you say?"

"I said, if you don't let me go, I'll find a way to escape."

Marcellious threw back his head and howled in laughter. "Says the woman who is bound with chains to my bed."

I writhed and tugged against the chains. "You can't keep me here, Marcellious! You're a sick and twisted man who needs help."

Marcellious sped across the room and climbed onto the bed, straddling me. He pressed his palms on the mattress at either side of my head. "I'm afraid you're stuck here, Olivia. And there is nothing you can do about it."

The spray from his mouth spattered my cheeks.

"You're stuck here, with me. I have no intentions of *ever* letting you go." He caressed the side of my cheek with his slender finger.

I snarled and bit at his hand like a feral dog.

He let out a cold, mocking laugh. "How foolish you are, my sweet, to think that you can best me. No, this has been coming on for years. I've plotted and schemed how to top Roman ever since he won the fight against me. And, when you arrived, my choice was clear. You, Olivia, were meant to be with me."

"You're wrong," I said, fighting against my restraints.

"Am I?" That cruel smile of his spread across his cheeks. "I believe you're wrong. You'll see. After I wear you down."

I lunged and snapped at him.

He placed both palms, one over the other, on my mouth and pressed down hard. "Now I can't hear you, and you can't bite me. See how easy that was? All your bluster and bluff is just that—frivolous folly. I'm in charge now. Me. Not Alexander. I've got what's his, and I intend to use it." His gaze became pinpoint sharp, like a laser. "I'll break you, guaranteed, bitch."

I tried in vain to move my head, open my mouth and bite his palm, but the pressure he exerted was too great.

He lowered himself so his belly pressed against mine and his horrible, rigid erection dug into my thigh. "Here's what's going to happen, my sweet. In two nights, I'm going to fight Roman Alexander to the death. He's being starved as we speak, so he'll be weak. It will be no contest, really, but I'm certain he'll summon some strength from somewhere with which to fight. We wouldn't want it to look too easy, now would we?"

I made a mumbled protest into his flesh.

He nuzzled my nose with his.

I couldn't move away, held fast by his grimy hands.

"So, I'm going to fight Roman to the death, and I will win. I'll place my foot on his dead body, lift my arm high, and declare to all of Rome that I am the most powerful in all the land. And then, you will be mine."

As quick as a snake strike, he released his palms from my mouth and slapped me hard.

He scrambled from my body as my head flew to the side from the impact. Then, he stormed from the room, slamming the door behind him.

I was so screwed. No amount of bluster would save me now.

CHAPTER THIRTY-ONE

OLIVIA

After his outburst, Marcellious never returned to his room. I lay chained to his bed, unable to sleep for hour upon hour, the feather bed turning to steel beneath my body. All I could think about was Roman in the Colosseum dungeon, probably beaten, starved, waiting to fight Marcellious. Did he even know he was to fight Marcellious, or would it be a surprise? What would happen if Marcellious won and plunged his sword through Roman's heart?

The thought was unbearable. That could never happen. If it did, I had every intention of following through with my promise to Marcellious. I'd find a way to kill myself before I'd ever let him put his smarmy hands on me.

Held captive by a madman, what was I to do? Even if I were to escape, I'd no doubt be captured again. I was held prisoner somewhere in the emperor's palace—the emperor's *closely-guarded* palace.

Severus was no fool. He wouldn't leave rooms unwatched or unattended, even a loyal Praetoria's dwelling. Eyes and ears were probably everywhere.

I'd been lying in the same position so long that the bed stabbed me like the feathers had become knives. And, unable to move, I'd soiled myself, which brought enormous shame. However, with no food or drink in my belly, my body was probably consuming muscle or the little fat left on my body. I needn't worry about any act of nature. I was hungry, desperate, and alone. But at least Marcellious wasn't here with his crazy ravings.

What was that song he'd been humming and the words he'd been chanting? As I lay here, I obsessed over it. But each time I thought I might be nearing recall of where I'd heard it, the vague recollection would slip from my mind and slide beyond my awareness.

Finally, exhausted, I fell into a fitful sleep.

Hearing something at the door—a scratching sound or the jangle of metal—I jerked awake. Was Marcellious outside, ready to rape me? I tensed, wondering what manner of assault I could manage, chained as I was by wrist and ankle. The room was dark, and I had no idea what time it was. It could be noon as easily as it could be midnight. There were no windows in this room, and the oil lamps had fizzled long ago.

The door creaked open, and I readied myself for Marcellious.

Instead, a familiar male voice whispered, "Olivia? Olivia, are you in here?"

"Who's asking me?" I hissed. "Who's there?"

I squinted through the gloom seeing only a shadowy shape.

"Olivia. It's me. It's Anthony, the kid you trained."

My heart leaped for joy. "Anthony? How did you get in here?"

Soft footsteps tread across the floor, approaching me.

Embarrassment heated my cheeks as he came closer.

Surely, he'd smell me. I wanted to curl up in shame and self-loathing.

"Don't come too close," I whispered.

"Why? How can I free you if I don't come near you?" he said.

"I'm sure I smell," I replied.

"The scent of freedom must be stronger than any other odors you're worried about. I'm going to set you free."

I smiled. Anthony was right. With every fiber in my body, I longed to be free.

Gentle hands landed on my arm and slid up to my wrists.

"I don't dare light the oil lamps," Anthony said as he fiddled with my wrist restraint.

"Will Marcellious return? What will we do if he does?" I said, feeling too weak to even breathe on Marcellious should he try and grab me. Although it was pitch-black in here, my eyes had adjusted to the atmosphere enough that I could make out shapes.

"We'll fight, of course."

I could hear the smile in Anthony's voice.

"I'm pretty weak at the moment," I admitted.

"I know you, Olivia. Should the need to fight present itself, you'll fight. You are a warrior."

His words gave me courage, and gratitude filled my heart. "Thank you."

Anthony freed one wrist and then worked on the other. "Of course. I can never repay you for teaching me how to defend myself against Marcellious. This is merely a small payback."

As he worked on my ankles, I rubbed my ragged wrists. I'd yanked and pulled against the restraints so much I'd bloodied myself.

"So, what about Marcellious? Is he likely to return?"

Anthony scoffed. "He's so drunk I doubt he can stand. He's not even in this part of the palace—he and the emperor are with whores in the emperor's chambers. Severus likes company when he fucks." He paused before saying, "Excuse my coarse language."

"That's all right," I said, eager for him to free my ankles.

"And then, when he does manage to wake up from his stupor, he'll practice all day. Olivia…" He said my name in a sober, somber tone. "The fight's been moved up. Marcellious doesn't want to wait any longer. He's going to fight Roman tonight."

I gasped. "That son of a bitch. I just want to take a knife and plunge it into his black heart."

"Marcellious can do whatever he likes. He has the emperor's ear, I'm afraid." Anthony let out a sigh while his fingers frantically worked to free me.

In an attempt to calm my nerves, I redirected our conversation. "So, tell me—how did you know to find me here?"

I continued to palpate my poor wrists. They burned with searing pain.

"I saw the whole thing—how you were dragged from the dock, how Roman was taken. I've kept watch on you and Roman both. I just didn't know how I could get to you. But I have a friend in the palace." His voice faltered. "She's one of the servants. She's the one who let me in."

If the situation wasn't so dire, I might have laughed. It sounded like Anthony had a crush on a young woman. And I imagined she was sweet on him, too.

As he worked to free my legs, Anthony's fingers grazed my ankles which felt as bloody raw as my wrists. But I didn't care.

Finally, the chains fell away from my legs and landed on the floor with a tinny clank.

"Give me your hand," he hissed, tugging me to my feet.

We crept across the tile floor.

"I can't be scurrying about like this. I need a cloak or some sort of covering." Besides being soiled, my stola had rips from where it had snagged on the chains as I'd struggled to free myself.

"Don't worry. My friend will help us. She's waiting for us." He cracked open the door and peeked into the hallway.

"What time is it?" I whispered into his back.

"It's dawn. Usually, most of the palace is asleep at this time. That's why I chose this time to free you. I keep a close watch on this place. You never know when you'll need to rescue a friend." He glanced over his shoulder at me, offering a warm smile.

"Well, thank you one thousand times over." I returned the smile.

Anthony looked right, left, and said, "Follow me."

He hurried down the hall, and we entered a vast kitchen.

A pretty young woman with long, straight hair looked over at us from her position at a table. She placed the vegetables she'd been cutting into a ceramic bowl. When her gaze landed on Anthony, she beamed with delight. "Anthony!"

"Cara! I've got her. This is Olivia."

Hurrying toward us, Cara said, "This way. Cook's stepped out to fetch some legumes to prepare the morning meal."

"My friend needs something to wear," Anthony said.

Cara nodded. "I can find something from the laundry. You look to be a similar size to Cook." She scanned me from head to toe. "Let's go."

We followed her down a narrow passageway and into a courtyard. Laundry hung out to dry next to a cistern with running water.

Cara tugged at a stola and handed it to me. "Go ahead and

put it on. Anthony and I will turn around. I'll dispose of your torn garment."

I took the clothing, placed it over my arm, and seized Cara's hands in mine. "Thank you for your kind heart. I pray nothing untoward shall happen to you for your kindness."

"Don't worry. I've got Anthony to protect me." She gave him a dreamy-eyed gaze before saying, "Hurry! We haven't much time."

She and Anthony turned away from me.

I quickly stripped and noticed my gun and daggers were still safely secured around my thigh. My heart soared.

I scooped water from the cistern to hurriedly wash myself. Then, I slipped the garment over my head.

It felt great to be somewhat clean again. "Okay, I'm ready."

Cara gestured with her hand. "This way."

She led me to a doorway that looked out over a quiet street.

Anthony reached inside his loincloth and procured several keys.

"Here, I got these off of a prison guard. Don't ask how I did it." He thrust them into my hand. "These will enable you to free Roman."

He pointed toward the Colosseum that towered in the distance.

I glanced toward the looming structure, noting several guards milling about. "How will I get past those men without fighting and alerting more trouble?"

"Wait! I've got an idea," Cara said. She scurried away from us and disappeared through a door.

"Your friend is too kind to help me," I said.

Anthony's cheeks turned rosy, and he stared at his sandaled feet. "Yes, she's a truly kind person."

"And so, my friend, are you." I patted his forearm.

The hue of his cheeks deepened, and he said nothing.

Cara returned bearing a basket with bunched, dried herbs. "Take this. Tell them you are a healer, and they might grant you passage."

She thrust the basket toward me, and I took it, placing the keys beneath the dried plants.

"One more thing," she said. "Lower yourself, so I can reach your head."

She stood nearly a foot shorter than me. I stooped, and she pulled the abundant fabric of my stola into a hood, shielding my face. "No one as pretty as you should walk about uncloaked. Besides, someone—a Praetoria, perhaps— will recognize you."

"Thank you, Cara." I smiled at her. She couldn't be older than fourteen, but already she showed wisdom and courage beyond her years.

"Cara!" a woman shouted. "Where are you, girl? We've got *ientaculum* to prepare."

"Oh! That's Cook. I've got to run." Cara pulled Anthony's face toward hers and gave him a quick kiss on the cheek. "I'll see you later?"

Anthony nodded, apparently too tongue-tied to speak.

Cara scurried away.

"The guards are minimal at this time," Anthony said to me, shaking off his embarrassment. "Many of them drink to pass the night then fall over, dead drunk, much like Marcellious. Those that you see…" He pointed to the few guards milling about. "Those men probably didn't imbibe last night, so you should avoid them. Head around the back. There's an entrance to the dungeons around there. It's called the Gate of Death." Wincing, he indicated the opposite side of the vast structure.

"The Gate of Death?" I said, taking a step backward.

"Yes. It's the door through which they carry the dead gladiators."

A sick feeling lurched through my belly, imagining my handsome Roman being dragged out of the Colosseum, dead.

"You can do this, Olivia," Anthony said. "You can save Roman."

I nodded. "Thank you, Anthony."

I leaned close and kissed his cheek.

More flames colored his skin a deep pink.

"I don't know if I'll ever see you again, Anthony."

He frowned. "Why not?"

I rolled my lips between my teeth. "Roman and I… we have to leave. It's not safe here for us."

His amber eyes grew watery, but he nodded. "I understand."

"You're a good man, Anthony. You'll do great things in this life. Use everything I taught you to keep yourself and those you care about safe, got it?"

"Understood. Thank you for everything. And you will do great things, too. I have no doubt." He gave me a look of fierce pride, then added, "Good luck, Olivia."

I turned and hurried toward the Colosseum, head down, appearing purposeful. Strike that—I didn't *appear* purposeful. I *was* purposeful.

I had to get Roman out of there.

Just as Anthony had predicted, the lone guard at the back entrance lay sprawled in the dirt, eyes closed, snoring softly. Several amphoras rested on their sides next to him. Large, reddish-purple stains spread across the stone pavers beneath the necks of the amphora, indicating the contents of the bottle.

Guard Number One had a belly full of wine in him.

He blocked the entrance, so I gingerly stepped over him, fit the key in the lock, and let myself into the Colosseum. Once inside, I closed the door behind me. Now all I had to do was find the entrance to the dungeons. I stood still, listening and looking.

A hair-raising snarl washed over me, sounding much like the lions I'd heard at the zoo as a child. Then another rasping growl sounded. And another. I decided to head toward the beasts—no doubt they were trapped in the dungeon, too.

I hurried along the passageway lining the arena's walls until I arrived at a massive door. I fiddled with all the keys until I found the one that unlocked this entrance, then, as before, I let myself inside.

Ahead lay stairs leading into the depths of the building. Taking another deep breath, I began my descent.

Oil lamps lined the walls, but many had burned out, so I had to feel my way along the steep, shadowy corridor.

The snarls and growls grew louder.

Once my feet touched the lower landing, a giant shape lunged toward the metal door lining the massive stone cage. I stifled a yelp and fell back against the opposite wall, staring at the pissed-off lion opposite me. The poor creature lunged at me repeatedly, claws unsheathed, teeth bared.

My heart broke witnessing its suffering. All its ribs showed, and its skin hung from its frame. I wished I could help it, but I had my mission before me—free Roman.

I slunk down the long corridor, peering inside each cage for signs of my man, passing more emaciated lions, a few wolves, and countless criminals. Even though the walls of the underground chambers were made of stone, the smells down here, wafting through the metal bars of the doors, were horrific. Human decay, piss, feces, blood, and vomit assaulted my nostrils. I lifted a sprig of herbs to my nose to try and staunch the smells.

I could not locate Roman.

I rounded the corner to find a guard standing, weapon poised, ready to stab me with his sword.

His eyes widened as he saw me, and a leer spread across his face. "Has my fortune changed today, or what?"

"Hello, good, sir," I said, feigning respect I did not feel. "Severus sent me to tend to Roman Alexander to care for him before tonight's fight."

"Is that so?" He lowered his sword and rested his side against the wall as if preparing for a delightful conversation.

"Yes. Do you know where he is?" I kept my gaze lowered, trying to seem demure. But inside, I was boiling mad.

"What are you going to give me if I tell you?" He practically salivated as he spoke.

"Give you? I only have herbs, good sir." I extended the sprig of herbs I'd held to my nose.

He batted it from my hand and seized my wrist. "Come on, give me some love, honey."

His breath and body stank badly as if he had never washed or brushed a day.

I struggled the way a helpless female might behave. "Let me go."

"Hard to get, eh? I love a good fight before a fuck." He let out a darkly satisfied chuckle.

"Yeah?" I taunted. "How about we get the fight over with and skip the fuck part?"

I tossed the basket of herbs and hooked my foot behind his knee.

His hands flew up, and he fell backward. "You bitch!"

He rolled on his belly to get up.

I straddled him, seized his sword, which had fallen to the floor, and bashed in his head with the hilt.

He let out one last groan before slipping into the fade of silence.

"Olivia?"

An oh, so tantalizingly familiar voice drifted into the hall.

"Roman? Where are you?"

"Down here." His voice emerged as a croak.

I picked up the keys which had fallen from my basket of herbs and followed his voice to find him seated, chained to the wall of his cell. I tried each key with shaking fingers until I located the right one. I rushed inside, straddled him, grabbed his face between my hands, and kissed him over and over.

He crushed his mouth to mine, drinking me in as if I was his nourishment. His hand hooked the back of my neck and drew me closer. If he could have inhaled me, I know he would have—he needed me as much as I needed him.

Our bodies ground together, melding in the heat of our passionate exchange. Together, we were fire and wind, burning in a tempestuous fury.

Insistently, Roman rocked his thick length into me as I widened my legs to receive him. His rigid heat teased the swollen bud between my thighs, stimulating me through his dirty loincloth and my stola, enough to drive me wild.

I felt an orgasm brewing between my legs, just out of reach. It filled me with a primal hunger for this man, this warrior, this fighter. My body's response was unheard of—no one had ever managed to arouse me the way Roman did.

Roman tore his mouth from mine and looked me in the eyes. His poor face was bruised, and angry red marks covered his bare torso.

But, to me, he was as handsome as ever.

"I feared I wouldn't ever see you again," he said. "And now you're here, and I don't want you to ever leave my side."

Before I could reply, he crashed into me with a searing kiss. The taste of him was unlike ever before. He tasted of fear and suffering, hunger and want, strength and muscle. But mostly, he tasted like Roman, the love of my life.

With a groan, I wrenched away, eager to free him. I began to fit keys into the restraints binding him. I only managed to uncuff his right hand when Roman seized my wrist.

"What are you doing?" he said.

My jaw grew slack, and I stared at him uncomprehendingly. "What do you mean? I'm freeing you."

He shook his head. "You can't. You mustn't." His gaze darted toward the door. "I can't risk you being discovered by the guards."

My forehead furrowed. Was he kidding me? My eyes narrowed. Something else was going on with him.

"Roman, this is my decision. There aren't many guards around. I'm going to free you, and we're going to escape."

He kept his attention on me, his eyes bright, but wheels seemed to grind inside his mind.

I paused. "What's going on with you?" I fit the key in his other restraint and unlocked it.

It fell to the ground with a noisy clang.

But then Roman's expression changed to feral and darkly dangerous.

"Come here." He tapped his kissable lips. "Drop the keys."

My hand released, and the keys landed with a soft clunk on the stone floor.

"I can't wait. I want you—*now.*"

My entire body lit up at his words.

His right hand hooked around my neck and drew me close. His other hand snaked around my back.

"I'm so desirous of you, Olivia."

His whispered words blew into my parted lips.

"I want you with a passion that could move mountains." As he spoke, he rolled his hips into mine, letting me feel the rigidity of his passion.

"I want you, too," I said, sliding my arm behind his shoulder. Words conveying the strength of what I felt for him burned in my throat. I had to free them. I had to tell him how I felt.

"I…"

"You." He nuzzled my nose, then brought his mouth to my neck and nipped my skin.

I arched into his love bites.

"What do you have to tell me, my love?" he murmured as he worked his way down my tender neck. As he nibbled, he brought his hands around to my breasts and squeezed and massaged them.

I had to take a deep breath to find the courage to release my feelings. "I love you, Roman Alexander, with every fiber of my being."

He ceased biting me, and I wondered if I shouldn't have said that.

But then he bit hard on my neck, sucking my flesh into his mouth, claiming me.

"Oh, gods," I moaned, my fingernails raking his back. I thrust my hips, rocking into him as a passionate storm swept through me.

Roman let out a low growl, and then his lips found mine.

I was beyond aroused, as if our souls' fires had been ignited. I sucked on his tongue, and he groaned.

He drew my tongue into his mouth and sucked harder, eliciting pain, need, and longing.

I embraced the intensity of his passion, matching it with my savage desire.

He yanked on my stola.

I rose onto my knees, the unforgiving stone beneath me jabbing into my skin.

He tugged the fabric up my body and fingered the slick flesh between my thighs.

I undulated my hips against his fingers, craving more, more, *more*. I was gone, completely lost, drenched by a powerful craving that couldn't be ignored. What this man did to me, the feelings he evoked, was more nourishing than food.

I moaned when he lifted his loincloth, revealing his long, hard length. His stiff erection was pure perfection. The head was swollen and red, while large veins pulsed along his length. He made my mouth water and my sex throb in invitation. Chills coiled inside of me at the anticipation of joining with Roman.

Poised on my knees, I caressed his rock-hard torso and solid abs, tracing the inguinal crease, those V's on either side of his hips that led to his cock.

Roman hissed.

I stroked the coarse black hair on his lower belly, and his cock jerked.

His eyes fiery, gazing at me with pure lust, he grabbed my rump, and said, "Lower onto me, Olivia. Hurry!"

Widening my legs, I slid my juicy sex up and down his length.

"Shh. What if they hear us?"

Roman stopped moving, too, pressing his forehead to mine.

We panted hard.

I cocked my head to listen for guards but heard nothing.

"Okay," I whispered. "Keep going. I *need* you inside of me."

I craved him with unparalleled intensity. It was as if our cells reached out to one another, and alchemy, turning lead into gold, of the dark into light, stirred inside. We were combustible, a chemical reaction ready to explode.

His right hand wriggled between us, grabbing his hard flesh. Grasping my hips with his hand, he impaled me in one strong thrust.

I bit back a groan. This joining of his body with mine was where we escaped all the madness that surrounded us. Even here, where death was a way of life, our lovemaking could set us free for a few beautiful moments.

Two male voices argued down the hall.

"Shit," I breathed.

Roman grunted, his fingers curled against my rear. "I can't stop, Olivia. I think I shall go mad if I don't come inside of you."

Clutching his shoulders, I clenched around his pulsing cock as we listened.

Sweat poured from our bodies, adding to the musky smell.

"Do you think it's safe?" I whispered. "Have they moved away?"

"I don't care. I can't stop now." Roman thrust into me with a fury, his fingernails digging into my flesh.

I bucked against him with abandon, matching his thrusts with my own driving hips.

The voices grew closer.

"Come now, Olivia," Roman hissed into my ear. "Let me feel you milking me."

The orgasm which had been building when we started to kiss begged for release.

"I need your mouth on mine," I whispered. "Kiss me, Roman, or I'll scream. I'm going to climax."

He dropped his lips to mine and consumed me.

We both climaxed simultaneously, like two wild beasts, humming and grunting into one another's mouths.

Tearing his mouth from mine, he let out a growl as he pumped inside me.

"Olivia," he said in a low, guttural tone. "My love."

Ecstasy surged through me as the orgasm rocketed through my body. I took flight, side by side with Roman, our spirits coiled around one another as we sailed into bliss together. Something indescribable pushed me higher and higher. I never wanted to come down. I wanted to fly like this, away from here, with Roman, escaping all the madness of our lives.

Finally, I felt myself drifting back to earth. I relaxed into Roman's hard body, pliant and sated, my arms wrapped around his muscled back.

Still deep inside me, Roman pressed his forehead to mine. After a time, he whispered, "Olivia. That was too swift and far too close for comfort. Had they caught us, they would have sliced off my cock and done who knows what to you. I want to savor you through the night like we did in Caledonia."

"I know. Soon we'll be able to do that." I let myself surrender to Roman, relaxing into his powerful body.

His callused hands stroked my back, up and down, up and down.

I lay against him, listening to his heartbeat. Our breathing slowed, and the world fell away for those few blissful moments.

But now we had to escape.

The anguished cries of a prisoner clawed at my ears. Further away, the lions growled and lunged against the metal bars while the mournful wails of wolves made my heart ache. There was so much suffering in these stone walls. Yet, we had transcended the moment and wrapped ourselves in beauty and magic. Nothing was more powerful than love.

With a sigh, I glanced toward the door. "We should go now. Those guards might return."

I reached out, feeling around the filthy stone floor for the keys

"Tell me," Roman said, his blue eyes piercing me. "How did you get these keys?"

"Anthony rescued me. He and a young woman who works in the emperor's kitchen—I think they're sweet on one another." I smiled at the memory. "Marcellious captured me and locked me in his room. He plans on killing you tonight and had every intention of making me his."

Roman's lip curled in a sneer and his muscles grew rigid. "Did he touch you? Did he lay a hand on you?"

His palms landed on either side of my face, and his eyes looked wild.

I shook my head. "No, he didn't. It was so strange, though. I think he's insane—utterly crazy. He's paranoid and seems to be so lost in this world. He...he had a necklace. It looked like the one Moon Lee had."

Roman shook his head. "Moon Lee's necklace?"

"Yes. He said he stole it from Marcus."

Roman's head fell back.

"Oh, gods almighty! Marcus was my brother! I knew it! We were inseparable. And we looked similar." He lifted his head to gaze into my eyes. "How could I have killed my own brother? I'm going to destroy that bastard. He made me kill my own brother, and he nearly took you away from me. I'm going to slice his head from his body and hold it high in exultation."

"Roman," I said, interrupting his bloodthirsty declarations. "What if Marcellious is your brother? Maybe you shouldn't jump to conclusions about Marcus."

Roman froze. He blinked at me in disbelief. "Why would you say that?"

"He sang a song… even though I couldn't understand the words, they sounded familiar. I *know* those words. I heard them somewhere, and I think they're important."

"That's ridiculous. He must have learned the song from Marcus," he said with conviction.

"No, Roman. Marcellious told me it was from his childhood." Hearing the strength of Roman's beliefs that Marcus was his brother confused me. And the awareness of where we were—in the dungeon beneath the Colosseum—struck me like lightning.

Roman and I were in danger and had to escape *now*.

"I refuse to leave the Colosseum with you until I've killed Marcellious with my bare hands," Roman said. "I'm not a coward. I will fight with honor and respect. And I will not stop until Marcellious is dead."

Mouth open, I stared at him.

"Roman, what if you die? I lost my family. Can you imagine what you will do to me if you get killed? I will lose myself in sorrow and pain. I can't live without you. I want to solve all the mysteries with you. I can't continue living without you by my side."

"My love, I have to do what's right. Marcellious made my life here in Rome hell. Now that I know that Marcus is my brother, I must avenge his death."

I was so frustrated with Roman. I threw my arms into the

air, and my hand struck the back wall, knocking loose a bit of stone.

Roman stared at where my hand hit the wall. "Look!"

I whirled around. Something shiny lay inside a carved opening. The piece of stone that fell free had only been a placeholder.

Roman stepped past me and reached inside the opening. He pulled out a dagger.

"Holy hell, what is that?" I seized the weapon from his palm. I brushed the dust from the hilt and revealed initials carved in the handle. "That's clearly an 'M.' But what's the other initial?"

I held the blade aloft, trying to get it positioned in the dim light coming from the hallway.

"Here." I handed it back to Roman. "What do you think it says? M and a plus sign and a T?"

Roman shook his head. "I think it's an 'L.'" He clutched the dagger to his chest. "Don't you see, Olivia? This dagger must have belonged to Marcus. Those initials are M for Marcus and L for Lydia. I killed my time-traveling twin brother."

He squeezed his eyes shut, and a teardrop appeared in the corner.

My heart shattered for his loss. He must be right. Marcus and Lydia.

His eyelids flew open, and the most feral expression I'd ever seen appeared on his face. His gaze met mine, and I nearly fell backward from his intense scrutiny. "I'm going to destroy Marcellious tonight, mark my words. I'll winnow the sacred words from his throat, and then I'll slice it and drink his blood."

I fisted both hands and hissed, "Roman! Maybe Marcus wasn't your brother. Did Marcellious stay in this prison cell?"

Roman shrugged. "This cell was Marcus' cell when he was a gladiator."

"Well, maybe it was Marcellious' cell, too."

Roman scoffed. "Marcellious stayed on a different side of the hypogeum." A tic pulsed in his jaw, as if he were about to explode. He gripped my shoulders and pinned his gaze to mine. "I need you to leave Rome. It isn't safe. You will time travel tonight since the moon is full."

"What?" Anger roared inside of me. "How can you say that? I will *not* leave without you! I don't even know the words to say!"

"If you don't figure them out by tonight, you must leave Rome. Travel to a different city and find a place that has ancient scriptures. Find the words to time travel. If I survive this fight, I will find you, Olivia." He lifted my hands to my face and regarded me fiercely. "I promise you, Olivia, I will find you and reunite with you. No matter how hard it might be…I will always find you because my heart and soul beats as one with yours."

Tears streamed down my cheeks. After all we'd endured, after everything we'd been through, he wanted me to disappear to who knew where? And, somehow, he would miraculously find me?

The gaze I aimed at him was equally as intense. "No. I refuse to leave without you."

"Olivia," Roman hissed through clenched teeth.

"No way will I leave you." I reached for his arms, and my fingernails dug into his skin.

Roman relented. "Hand me my dagger."

I retrieved it from my thigh and placed it in his palm.

He took it and rested it on a nearby ledge. Then, he placed his hands on either side of my face and kissed me slowly, tenderly, with the softness of feathers and whispers.

How could he do this? How could he devour me with fierce passion and then regale me with tender kisses that spiraled around my heart like soft touches?

Tears slid down my face.

"I won't leave you, Roman," I said when he released me. "Please don't fight Marcellious. We can run away. We can time travel together. Please, Roman."

His face became stoic, a chiseled block. "This I cannot do, Olivia. I must avenge my brother's death. And you must go. It's not safe for you to be here."

I let out a sob, clinging to his wrists.

"I'll find you, Olivia. I found you in this lifetime, and I'll find you in the next." He spoke with such certainty, I actually believed him.

Still, I didn't want to leave him here.

"Olivia, please," he begged. He cupped my face. "Please tell me you understand. I must do what's right. Marcellious wants to fight me tonight. He thinks he will win, but nothing could be further from the truth. I'm going to take his life. And then, my love, I'll find you, even if you're far away in a time I cannot fathom."

Weirdly, we both knew this could be true—either of us could disappear to unknown lands.

CHAPTER THIRTY-TWO

OLIVIA

My nerves were all frayed as I exited the hypogeum. I did not want Roman to fight tonight. But he was staying true to his word—even if it meant his death.

My stomach in knots, I hurried down the hall, staying alert for guards. The smells of decay, human waste, animal dung, and even death filled my nostrils. I'd forgotten my basket of herbs, so I had to cover my nose and mouth with my palm to keep from puking.

The Colosseum hypogeum had been built with massive stones, with insets where the prison cells were located.

At the sound of the same two guards talking around the corner, I slipped into one of the insets near a prisoner's cell.

The man inside the cell looked worse than Roman—dirty, disheveled, bruised, and emaciated. When he saw me, he lurched to his feet and crossed to the edge of his enclosure where I stood. I pivoted, so my back faced him.

"Have you come to free me or fuck me, the way you must have done to the other man?" he said in a tone as dirty as his skin.

"Quiet," I said. "There are guards."

"So? There are always guards. I say we fuck, and then you free me."

I whirled around, reached between the bars, and seized his filthy tunic. "I told you to *shut up*!"

With one quick tug, I yanked his face to the metal where his forehead collided with iron.

He crumpled to the ground, knocked out cold.

The guards' voices grew louder, coming closer.

I backed into the corner where the iron met the stone and stayed still, barely breathing.

The guards sauntered by, engrossed in their conversation.

As soon as they passed, I tiptoed away in the opposite direction. Without further interruption, I managed to step into the morning air without being accosted.

Vendors were starting to set up their wares in the nearby marketplace. I hurried toward one of them, a woman with chickens in stiff fiber cages, and asked, "Good woman, do you know the time of the fight tonight?"

She shrank away from me as if I were the goddess Nyx herself, born of Chaos and bound to bring darkness to her soul. She muttered something about, "Whores who wanted to sleep with the victors."

"It's not like that," I said, spreading my hands wide. "Please, I need to know."

But it was too late—she'd made her judgment of me and held fast to it, her back hunched as she turned away.

I hurried to the next vendor, a man striding down the street with a baby goat on his shoulders.

"Good sir, might you know the time of the fight tonight?"

He brightened. "Yes, I already have a *tessera*. My Guild distributed them to us yesterday."

While in Rome, I'd learned that the tickets to the Colosseum were free, distributed to the Guilds, which, in turn, handed them out to those deemed worthy. The penny-sized clay disks were often sold on the black market, however, much like scalpers did at concerts when I was born.

"That's wonderful," I said. "What time will you arrive?"

"So you haven't seen the announcements painted on the city's walls?" He gestured toward one of the nearby buildings.

"No, I haven't," I said.

"The pre-fighting begins at dusk. But the main event—the fight to the death between Marcellious Demarrias and Roman Alexander—commences at the moonrise. Will you be there?' he asked. His eyes shone with excitement.

His little goat bleated happily, unaware that he would land in someone's stew pot this evening if sold in today's market.

"Of course," I replied.

The man nodded. "Maybe I'll see you there."

A hungry, lecherous light glinted in his gray-green eyes.

"Perhaps," I said, knowing this wasn't likely. With up to fifty-thousand spectators entering through one of eight entrances, the chances of finding anyone you knew was a long shot. "Well, thank you for the information."

I continued on my way.

With no place to go for answers to the sacred script, I decided to head to Roman's home. It seemed a good place to concentrate and plan for the night ahead. I assured myself that no way in hell would Roman die tonight—not if I could help it. I just didn't know what I, a woman deemed beautiful with no other useful traits, could possibly do to save him?

When I entered the home where Amara had once lived, I was assaulted by recollections of her. I fell to my knees in the atrium and sobbed.

"Oh, Amara," I cried, holding my head in my hands. "I

can't believe you're gone. I tried to save you, but nothing I did made a difference. The darkness was too clever for me... and now you're *gone*."

I had no idea her memory would overtake me in such a powerful manner, but I cried until I could cry no more. Then I rose, wiped away my tears with my stola, and proceeded into the house.

Long shadows of memory lingered throughout her and Roman's home, however. This house was like a tomb since every room held stories of things she had done or said. The only place that didn't remind me of Amara was Roman's sleeping quarters. So, I entered his lair and lay on his bed, wrapping myself in a cocoon of our shared love.

I was glad I'd finally told him how I felt. Now, no matter what happened, he'd know. And maybe it would give him the strength he needed to survive.

As I lay there, I closed my eyes, well aware I might never see this place again. I'd hated Rome when I arrived. But here, under the care of Amara, the passion that had first appeared as contentious fighting and belligerence on my part, finally revealed the kind of love Roman and I shared. It was deep and profound, changing both of us in remarkable ways.

Silent tears tracked down my face. Roman's and my heart, mind, and soul were now entwined forever. What kind of god or gods would tear us apart through an untimely death?

With a shake of my head, I opened my eyes and sat up. Wallowing in sorrow would get us nowhere. I untied the sash containing the dagger which had fallen from the wall of Roman's cell, as well as the fragment of stone.

"Where can I find the sacred words to initiate time travel?" I whispered into the empty room. I picked up the dagger by the hilt, turning it over and over in my hand.

Who did this belong to?

Marcellious' insane chants pushed their way into my mind.

"What if Marcellious is the time traveler, not Marcus, the way Roman insists? And what if the words he spoke are really the sacred script used to time travel?" I strained my brain, trying to remember his incantations. "Let's see. What did he say? You'd think it would be burned in my brain; he said it so many times."

When I pictured Marcellious swaying, my torso began to rock, and my eyelids fluttered closed. Words began to roll from my tongue.

"Ya hamiat alqamar fi allayl," I said. "Adeuk 'iitlaq aleinan lilnuwr waturshiduni khilal alzalami."

My eyelids popped open at the presence of light in the room. The dagger was softly glowing!

"Oh, my goodness." I covered my mouth with my hand. "Could the song really be the words of the dagger...?"

Redirecting my attention to remembering the words Marcellious had sang, I closed my eyes and pictured Marcellious humming and chanting. Once again, my eyelids grew heavy.

"Ya hamiat alqamar fi allayl, 'adeuk litutliq aleinan lilnuwr waturshiduni khilal alzalami. Dae alshams aleazimat tarqus min hawlik bialhubi walmawadati. Mean, aftahuu bawaabatikum wamnahwani alsafar eabr alzaman walmakan mithl zilal allay."

When I opened my eyes, the blade was brighter—not as brilliant as my dagger on the night I time-traveled but still…

I glanced down at my stola to find glowing light emanating from my thigh, where my dagger rested, strapped to my leg. I lifted my garment to discover my blade burned brightly, too.

"Oh, my God. I know the words!" I jumped up, placed

my dagger on the bed, and crossed the room to where Roman kept his writing tools. I had to write the script down to see if I could discern its meaning.

I stared at the parchment filled with strange words I'd just written.

"This doesn't look like Arabic, but it sounds like it." I tapped my quill on the paper. "Could it be Aramaic?"

Arabic and Aramaic were similar but not quite. I took a closer look and was right: it appeared to be Aramaic.

Shortly before this whole time travel fiasco had been initi-ated, I'd only had a brief introduction to Aramaic. My grasp of the language was limited. But, after struggling with the words, it looked like the translation went something like, Moon protector of the night, I call on you to unleash the light. Guide me through the dark. Allow the great sun to dance around you with love and passion. Together, open your gates and grant me to travel through time and space like the shadows of the night.

"We travel through time and space like shadows of the night!" I clutched the parchment to my chest. "I can't believe I solved the scripture mystery."

I turned back to the mystery dagger and picked it up again.

I stared at the initials on the hilt. M and T. That has to be a T. I held it toward the dim glow of the dagger and squinted at it. I can't tell. Is the T an L? Marcus and Lydia? Maybe Roman is right—it's an L and Marcus is his brother. I turned it back and forth in the light. No, it has to be a T.

A chill frosted my skin. "What if Marcellious *really* is Roman's twin brother?" This time, the notion slammed into me. I brought my hand to my mouth, unable to stomach this assumption. I shook my head. "No, he had to have heard Marcus say the words."

I refused to believe that Marcellious was Roman's brother. Marcellious was beyond crazy, and Roman and he had nothing in common. My only choice was to return to the prison cell and ask someone for answers. That might solve the remaining pieces, but I didn't want to believe Marcellious was Roman's brother. It made me sick.

Oh, Roman, baby, I think I solved the mystery. I hope I'm right, and I can save you tonight and we can flee Rome together and get away from this miserable place.

CHAPTER THIRTY-THREE

OLIVIA

Realizing I'd uncovered the sacred script gave wings to my feet. I raced around Roman's home, searching for a satchel, intending to head back to the Colosseum and share my good news with Roman. I also had to attach one more final piece to the puzzle and determine if Marcellious was Roman's brother.

When I found a basket, I placed the mystery dagger inside, the stone that had concealed it, and one of Amara's handkerchiefs. I didn't know why, but I wanted to have a keepsake to remember her by. Before leaving, I found another basket, put the satchel at the bottom, and covered it with some of Amara's healing herbs, intending to use the same ruse to get into the dungeon I'd used before.

Then, giving one last look around this precious space where I'd found the love of my life, I let out a deep breath and took my leave through the front door.

The sun was in its usual state of blaze, making its descent toward the horizon as I made my way toward town. Covering my head with the hood of my stola, I hurried through the streets en route to the Colosseum. Once there, I rushed to the entrance where I'd found the drunk guard passed out on the ground. I figured he might be too hungover to give me any grief.

One glance at his expression, however, told me I was wrong—way wrong.

His lip curled in what looked like a perpetual snarl, and his small red eyes gave me the impression that, when awake, he was always angry. No wonder he had to drink himself into a stupor each night.

When I approached him, he put out his hand like a stop sign. "Stop! You're forbidden to enter."

"Good sir, I'm a healer." Keeping my head down, I hefted my basket of herbs in the air.

"I don't care what your excuse is. You're not allowed to enter…especially on a night like tonight. Do you even know what's going down this evening?"

I spared a glance at him. "Why, yes, that's precisely why I'm here. The emperor himself gave me the order to care for whichever man wins tonight. 'He should be treated like royalty.' Those are the emperor's words exactly."

I cast my gaze at the stone pavers again. But in my heart, I wanted to strangle this man. And I could surely do it—but that would draw too much attention.

Looking up at him through my lashes, I saw his squinty-eyed glare as he assessed me and the validity of my words.

"This is a special fight. If the emperor told you to come here, you could enter."

Keeping his gaze pinned to me, he moved aside to let me pass.

"Don't try anything," he called after me as I stepped down the stairs into this hellish landscape.

The hypogeum was like a maze, and as I maneuvered down the connected hallways, I realized I was lost. Frantic, I rushed along past cell after cell until I found the one with the guy whose face I'd smashed into the metal bars. He still lay on the ground, in the same position with flies buzzing around his body.

Oh, no! I killed him.

What choice did I have? I had to survive no matter what. I wished him well on his journey through hell and continued toward Roman's cage.

The metal door lay ajar, and when I peered inside, it was empty. My heart sank.

Where is he? Have they taken him away? I fell back against the stone wall, disheartened.

Pounding footsteps alerted me to look up.

A uniformed guard rushed toward me, his face red with exertion. "Get out! You're not allowed down here!"

I cocked my head and studied him. He appeared to be old by Rome standards—nearly fifty if I guessed right. Instead of getting angry, in a civil tone, I said, "Good sir, I'm sorry for being here, but I was wondering if you could help me. I have a question I hope you can answer."

He held out his open palm. "If I do, what are you going to give me?"

Surprised he didn't ask me for sexual favors, I said, "I only have herbs, good sir. I'm here to treat the winner of tonight's fight."

I held my basket to him, hoping he didn't take it upon himself to root around and discover the satchel containing the dagger.

His face soured, and he let out a grunt. "What's your question?"

"Do you know the names of everyone who has stayed in this prison cell?" I pointed toward Roman's holding chamber with my thumb.

"A few of them, yes. I've been here longer than anyone—nearly twenty years. I've seen more than the heart should bear." He shook his head, a sad expression dragging at his face. "There was Atticus Manius, Felix Appius, Justus Lucius, Titus Gnaeus, Cassius Caeso, Linus Aulus, Magnus…"

I cut him off before he named every gladiator who ever existed. "What about Marcellious? Was he housed here when he was a gladiator?"

The guard squinted at me. "The fellow who's fighting tonight? Marcellious Demarrias?"

"Yes, that's the one."

"Why, yes. He was held here until Roman Alexander arrived. Then he was moved to the other side of the dungeon. He was actually the longest prisoner in this cell. That cell was his home."

"Did Marcus Cassius stay here as a prisoner when he was a gladiator?" I asked.

"Yes, he did. Marcus Cassius was a gladiator who was killed by Roman Alexander. I remember that fight like it was yesterday. Roman and Marcus were inseparable gladiators. Like brothers. I was at a loss when I heard they had to fight each other. It was brutal. But Roman gave him a swift and honorable death. But that cell you're asking about was never Marcus'. He stayed a few cells down. Marcellious was the gladiator that remained in the cell the longest." His weathered face creased in confusion. "Why do you ask?"

I thought quickly for a reasonable response. Unable to find a plausible answer, I went for a redirect. "What I really want to know was whether he had any friends while he was in here."

His face furrowed even more. "Any friends?" He reached up to scratch the wispy stubble on his jaw. "There was Gaius and Amara. He was very close to both of them, especially Amara. She treated him like a mother."

I jerked back at this statement. If Amara treated Marcellious with motherly kindness, what happened to their friendship? And how was that connection made?

"Was there anyone else? A wife, perhaps? Or a lover?"

The guard crossed his arms and appeared to think. Then, his face brightened. "Oh, yes, there was. He loved her very much. And she was beautiful, with hair golden as the sun. I haven't seen that love in his eyes since. They were to be married once he got his freedom."

"What was her name?" I tried to rein in my excitement, but this was huge news.

"Let's see." He stroked his jaw. "It was unique. Something with a Dora. Pandora? No, I don't think that was it. I don't know. It's been too long."

"Did it start with a T?" I asked, leaning forward slightly. I knew I was "leading the witness," but I *had* to find out her name.

"Maybe. I just don't remember. It was too long ago, and many men have passed through the dungeon since. I can't keep up with everyone." He shrugged. "The only reason I remember as much as I do was that she was remarkable, and Marcellious was a different man."

He squeezed the back of his neck. "When she was killed, Marcellious became a madman. He went on a rampage. Nothing could stop him. He was out for blood and would kill anyone he saw. Her death destroyed him."

A shout came from around the corner. "Sirius! Where are you?"

The guard pivoted his head and called back, "I'm here. What do you need?"

"Come quickly. We need help with one of the gladiators. He's gone berserk."

"Good sir, thank you for answering my questions." I remembered tucking a few coins into the sash around my waist before I left, so I fished around and retrieved them. If my plan worked, I wouldn't need them anymore, so I gave him half of what I had, saving the rest for who knew what. "Thank you for your time."

He looked at the coins in my hand and grinned. "Don't have anything but herbs, eh? I see you're skilled with sleight of hand."

He took the coins and jogged away.

I stood in the hall, the smells filling my nose, listening to the prisoners' moans and groans and the animals' snarling and pacing. My heart hammered with everything I'd just learned.

Think, Olivia. You're a clever woman. Put the pieces together—could Marcellious be Roman's brother?

I turned and headed in the opposite direction Sirius had gone. I needed to get out of here.

As I scurried along the packed earth, I continued to fit the pieces together. Marcellious' necklace looked similar to the one Lee had. Coincidence? I don't think so. He said he's been fighting since he was fifteen. He seemed so lost when he said this. And when he sang that song—it came from deep in his memory. And hadn't he spoken of losing her? It had to be the woman Sirius mentioned when Marcellious was happy.

I reached the end of the hall and took the stairs two at a time to get to the massive arched doorway. Thankfully, no guards were about so I slipped out into the late day.

The sun hung on the horizon. Soon it would be dusk, and the fighting would commence.

Hordes of Roman citizens gathered, clutching their small clay disks to enter the arena. An air of excitement was growing and would no doubt continue to build as the night wore on.

My heart thundered so loudly in my ears that I could barely hear anything else. Marcellious *had* to be Roman's twin brother. But they really looked nothing alike. *Could they be fraternal twins? I don't see why not?* But they had nothing in common besides fighting like warriors. Roman was a man of honor and bravery. Marcellious was different, a barbarian.

As this realization sunk in, fear uncoiled in my belly like a snake. If Roman and I could time travel, we could leave all this madness behind. Only I needed Roman's dagger—I'd left it with Roman. Perhaps he left it in the dungeon.

With a sigh, I turned toward the dungeon doorway I'd just exited. I had to go back in and check to see if Roman's dagger was inside. Had to. Did I want to? Not in a million years. With each breach of entry, something awful might occur.

I reached in my basket and took out a piece of dried rosemary. Holding it to my nose to distract me from all the smells down in that fetid place, I made my way down the stairs and hurried toward Roman's prison cell. No one accosted me this time—I'd gotten lucky. But luck would only serve me for a short time. I had to be hasty about my search as well as my exit. And then I had to figure out how to get into the arena to watch the fights.

I made haste to Roman's empty cell. Although the filthy prison chamber was dark, my eyes scanned the floor, lit by torchlight from the hall. No signs of the dagger. Then, my gaze caught on the opening we'd found that held the mysterious blade now tucked safely in my basket. Unable to see inside the carved-out hole, I gingerly felt in there until my hand wrapped around something familiar—a knife handle. I tugged it out.

It was Roman's dagger—he must have put it here for safekeeping.

I slid the dagger beneath the herbs and hurried from the stone cage.

In the hallway, guards led a man who I presumed to be a gladiator.

I ducked into an inset and peeked my head around the corner. Behind me, wolves paced and howled, sending goose-flesh across my skin.

The gladiator, who must have been at least six-foot-five, was tugged by chains. He didn't resist. Fully armored, he carried a lethal-looking double spiked metal mace ball flail. Consisting of two shiny heavy spiked balls made of cast metal suspended from chains and attached to a sturdy wood handle wrapped in leather, the ball flail could do some serious damage. As long as his opponent wasn't wearing a helmet, anyway. Otherwise, the metal spikes would simply bounce off the metal.

Greaves had been strapped to his legs, and his torso and arms were covered by armor. In the hand opposite the hand wielding the ball flail, he carried a six-foot leather shield.

Where are they taking him? Maybe I can slip through the same door that he uses.

They disappeared around a corner.

I slid away from the inset and the worried wolves and, keeping my body pressed to the wall, followed the guards. When I got to the corner where they had disappeared, I took a peek.

A long line of gladiators in various uniforms, from the full armor of the man I'd just seen, to a few wearing only loin-cloths, carrying nets and tridents, stood in a large area near one of the stairways. There were also young women in white tunics and a man in a chariot with zebras harnessed to it. Musicians stood bearing some instruments I didn't recognize.

I'd read about the spectacle of the gladiator fights, and Roman had told me stories, but there was no way to prepare myself for the sight before me.

I scanned the gladiators, searching for Roman. I found him standing near Marcellious.

Both wore loincloths and no armor.

Roman gripped two curved blades, one in each hand.

I gasped. Roman and Marcellious were to fight without shields or protection of any kind.

Roman must have felt my gaze on him because he turned and met my eyes. A scowl formed on his face.

"Go!" he mouthed with a jerk of his head.

I took off running, heading for a stairway, any stairway through which I could slide along with a crowd and enter the Colosseum. Soon the fight would start, and, at the full moon, I was going to time travel Roman, Marcellious, and me to wherever the daggers guided us. If they were brothers, I felt compelled to reunite them.

And if they weren't related? I'd be making the biggest mistake of all time, transporting a deadly enemy with us to an unknown time.

I didn't know if this would be the biggest mistake of all time. It was a huge risk. But the sacred time-traveling words were tucked firmly in my brain, and it was the only chance we might get to escape this hell. Lee had always advised me to take risks.

"You'll never test your power unless you do something that might seem impossible. Then, when you do it success-fully, you'll see there's more to life than most people can even imagine. There are miracles."

That was what it would take to accomplish my task tonight—a miracle. But what if everything went wrong?

CHAPTER THIRTY-FOUR
OLIVIA

Outside the hypogeum, people everywhere were pushing to get inside. Yet, I had no ticket.

A nearby group of men clutched their penny-sized clay tickets.

Quickly devising a plan, I sashayed toward them, then pretended to trip, grabbing the arm of one of the men. "Oh, I'm so sorry," I said demurely as his ticket tumbled from his palm.

He leered at me, patting my hand and saying, "No problem at all, sweetheart. You should watch where you're going."

"I know I should." I batted my eyelashes at him while surreptitiously standing on his ticket. "I can be so clumsy."

He made a heh, heh, heh kind of chuckle and the other men joined in.

I managed to stoop and snatch the ticket from beneath my sandaled foot without anyone noticing.

Then, I said a prayer of thanks to the great whoever. I immersed myself into the multitude of ticket holders, all pushing, shoving, and pressing together in throngs to enter the arena. It was madness surrounding the Colosseum, but I felt sure the insanity would only multiply once we were inside.

I had no idea where my seat was, and a Vigiles, one of the police-type guards watching entrance number eight, stopped me.

"Where did you get this ticket?" he hissed.

"From my husband," I said demurely.

"You can't sit in that section. That's reserved for Rome's noble elite."

"My husband is a wealthy man," I countered. "That's why we're to sit there."

The crowd behind me shifted.

"Let us through," someone shouted.

"Stop holding up progress," another cried.

"Women and slaves sit at the top. Your husband should have known that," the Vigiles said.

"My husband is quite ill, and he gave the ticket to me," I said. "For a game of such importance, he wanted to be alerted immediately. He has wagered much money."

The Vigiles sneered. "Go sit in your section with the slaves."

A man reached over my shoulder. "If she's in my section, she can sit with me."

He waved his clay disk.

The Vigiles eyed the disk, the man behind me, and the surging crowd pushing us forward.

Finally, the Vigiles met my gaze with a contemptuous expression. "Go ahead. Maybe we'll get more entertainment tonight when the men in your section have their way with you." He leered at me and cupped his cock. "Go on, then."

He shoved my companion and me through the arched

gate, and we streamed forward like teeming salmon, rushing through the rapids to their final resting place.

My companion took my arm and said, "Stay close. The Vigiles was right—you are not allowed in the lower section. But I am an Eques—a member of the equestrian class. We rank just below the Senators. I will do my best to protect you, but you may still be sent to the upper levels. It's unheard of for a woman to get a good seat." His ember eyes raked my body. "Even one as fine as yourself."

A wicked leer crossed his face. "But don't worry. I am engaged to be married. If my fiancée finds out I sat with you, though, I might have to come up with a good story of explanation. Oh…" He held out his hand to me. "My name is Titus."

I shook his callused hand. "I'm Olivia."

Titus possessed a certain handsomeness with his chiseled features. He held himself with pride as one of noble birth might do, dressed in his white tunic with a gold-etched purple stripe running the length of the garment.

I grinned at him. "I will pay you handsomely if I survive the night."

"And I will accept your payment." He tucked my arm in the crook of his shoulder, and then we proceeded to our row.

The throngs of men eyed me as we pushed our way to our cushion-covered seats, but no one protested. Instead, I was met with wolfish leers and taunts.

"When you're done with her, Titus, I would like a turn," the fellow next to him said.

"She's a distant cousin, passing through on her travels. My uncle would not look kindly on your actions, Gnaeus," Titus said. "Nor would your wife."

He slapped Gnaeus in a good-natured manner on the back.

Gnaeus lifted a leather wine flagon from his side and offered it to Titus. "I meant no harm."

Titus took a long swig and looked at me inquiringly.

I shook my head and turned to gawk at the arena.

This event had everything a 21st-century sporting event would have, times a thousand. No one came to a Seahawks or a Green Bay Packers game to witness bloodshed and death.

It took about forty-five minutes for the arena to fill with spectators. All the while, Titus ignored me, chatting with his friends.

Finally, when I could spot no more empty seats in the torch-lit arena, the doors to the seventy-six entrances closed.

One of the gates to the corridors of the palace opened. The Roman elite, consisting of the emperor's wife and his whores, senators, and foreign dignitaries, entered, taking their marble, cushion-covered seats in their respective boxes. Several of the emperor's Praetorian Guard filed out and stood at attention around the eye-level boxed seats.

The emperor was nowhere to be seen.

Thrusting his fist into the air, one of the senators shouted, "Let the games begin! Open the Gate of Life!"

All eyes looked east as the massive doors opened.

The man I'd seen below in the chariot appeared, hauled by the zebras. It was Severus himself, wearing a gilded tunic.

I hadn't recognized him from the back.

As he circled the arena, he raised one hand to the crowd.

The crowd roared their approval.

The emperor pumped his palm up and down, waiting until everyone had settled. He brought the prancing zebras to a halt.

"Tonight, we shall witness the fight of fights!" he roared.

Again, everyone cheered and yelled.

"There shall only be *one* victor. Will it be Roman Alexander or Marcellious Demarrias?" Severus called out.

A chill washed down my spine. Please, if anyone in heaven is listening, let neither of them die. I intend to transport us all away from here and prove my theory of Marcellious. I hope I am right about him.

All around me, men shouted, "My money's on Alexander," or, "Marcellious shall win this fight."

"Have you been to the games before?" Titus asked.

"No, I have not."

Titus chuckled. "I thought as much. Otherwise, your eyes would not be so wide." He pointed to Severus. "His role is that of the editor. When it appears that one of the gladiators has won the fight, and he has but to plunge his sword into his opponent's heart, the crowd gives a thumbs-up or a thumbs-down. The editor takes a tally. He might go with the people's decision, or he might not. It's his thumbs-up or down that determines the gladiator's fate."

Another shiver rippled my spine. These games were awful.

"I see," I said to Titus, forcing my lips to smile.

"That is partly why women and slaves are to occupy the upper levels. You can't see well up there and you can't make out the bloodshed. One so delicate as you should not be witness to such savagery." Titus shrugged.

"I'm stronger than I seem," I said, batting my eyelashes at him.

"I imagine you are." He chuckled, then his attention diverted as the Gate of Life opened again.

Young women, who looked no older than late teens, sashayed into the arena. Tittering and giggling, they made their way toward the emperor. He handed his reins to a Praetorian, stepped from his chariot, and held out his hands to two of the teens.

They escorted him to his seat, cooing and fawning over him.

"Those are the vestal virgins. They guard the Temple of Vestas and maintain her fire, ensuring Rome's safety and very existence is secure." Titus's bare arms pressed close to mine as he spoke. "They will perform a sacred ceremony next."

A man dressed in a long tunic carried a goat around his shoulder, much like the vendor in the marketplace who had given me the time of tonight's event.

My stomach sickened. I had a feeling I knew what they would do.

Grasping the goat's ankles, the man lifted the animal high before the emperor and intoned a Latin chant.

One of the vestal virgins procured a knife from her long robe. She looked expectantly at the man until he nodded, knelt, and pinned the goat to the ground.

The poor animal bleated and writhed.

My heart broke.

The knife-wielding virgin stepped toward the goat, two-handed the hilt, and lifted her arms high. With practiced ease, she plunged the blade into the goat's torso.

The goat screamed, and the crowd went wild.

The man picked the goat up and held it in the air. Blood dripped from the gaping gash, right into the man's mouth.

The goat writhed violently and then grew limp.

Another virgin caught the dripping blood in a silver goblet. With pomp and flourish, she walked toward the emperor and handed it to him.

He took it, either sipped or pretended to sip, then raised the goblet in the air.

The audience whooped and cheered.

Titus leaned toward me and shouted over the din. "The goat will be roasted in the hypogeum and served to the emperor and his guest."

"I see," I said, feeling queasy at what I'd just witnessed. I didn't have time to dwell on the bloodletting, though, as the Gate of Life cracked open once again and acrobats, dancers, and musicians tromped across the sandy arena floor.

They sang, danced, and pranced with the kind of gaiety it didn't deserve. We were here to celebrate death, not rejoice in beauty and wonder. My nerves were frayed, and my stomach threatened to expel the contents of my last meal. I honestly didn't know how I could endure what was to come.

After the dancers passed, a line of drummers appeared. They circled the arena, found their positions, and began to drum.

Once more, the Gate of Life opened, and the gladiators appeared—but Roman and Marcellious were nowhere in sight.

The audience got to its feet, cheering and shouting.

The gladiators reveled in all the attention. This could herald their last moments on earth and they wanted to eat it up. They stalked through the arena baring their teeth and taunting the crowd.

The noise was deafening.

I couldn't imagine it getting any louder until those fighters disappeared through the Gate of Life and two other gladiators appeared in their wake—Roman and Marcellious.

A manic hysteria overtook the audience as they screamed and roared.

Marcellious and Roman each strode in opposite directions.

I'd imagined them being hauled in here in chains, but they were unencumbered.

And Roman...my eyes were riveted to his every move. He stalked like a lion, his expression fierce, never making eye contact with Marcellious. He seemed to eye every person in the crowd, all fifty thousand. But when he came to stand before the level where I sat, his eyes landed on mine.

And, the world fell away for a second that lasted a lifetime. There was only the two of us—no cheering crowd, no Titus, no emperor, and all his debauchery. Just us.

My heart swelled, and I pressed my hand to my chest.

Roman inclined his head, subtly acknowledging the gesture.

But all too soon, Roman yanked his gaze away and continued his stalking. Then, he and Marcellious disappeared, swallowed in the depths of the hypogeum.

Titus gave me a curious stare. "Do you know him? It looks like you share a special connection with Alexander."

"It's not like that." I shook my head in protest.

"Isn't it?" he said, but his conjecture was interrupted by the first gladiator, a man in partial armor covering his torso but not his arms, entering the arena.

He stalked the sand pit, waving his sword in elaborate circles and flashing his teeth.

An air of expectancy hushed the crowd as everyone watched the fighter make his rounds.

Then, a trap door opened, and two lions rushed from the dungeon, all claws and teeth, and snarls. They launched themselves at the gladiator.

A collective "Oh," filled the stands.

The man fought valiantly, but the two starving lions were probably desperate for a meal. Their desperation won.

Many of the audience groaned.

"We like a fight drawn out," Titus said with a chuckle. "This one passed too quickly."

"I see," I said, the phrase the only thing I could think to say when faced with such bloodthirst and violence.

Several more animal versus man fights ensued.

The score so far was lions, wolves, and a Bengal tiger, one point each; gladiators zero.

Darkness fell like black oil smearing the sky. The torches lighting the arena blazed brightly, filling the air with unctuous smoke. The moon appeared, a giant golden orb pushing its way into the sky. As the moon ascended, I watched countless men hack at one another brutally and fall to their knees when they could take no more. Fight after fight, each lasting a mere fifteen minutes ended with one of the gladiators receiving the emperor's thumbs-down.

Then, the man was quickly dispatched, much to the audience's delight. After his demise, he would be hauled through the Gate of Death while the victor pranced around the arena, receiving cries of adoration.

Finally, the main event was announced as the full moon rose higher.

Titus glanced at me. "You don't look so well. Are you okay?"

"No." I clutched my queasy stomach. "I'm not. I can't bear to watch this next fight. I need some air."

"Suit yourself," he said. "If this battle goes in my favor, I will be a richer man."

He chuckled in a *heh, heh, heh* sort of way.

"And who do you have your money on?" I said before taking my leave.

"Alexander, of course. He's the fittest of the two."

His friend, Gnaeus, interrupted him. "Not a chance. Demarrias wants blood. He won't stop until Alexander is dead. Even if Demarrias is the victor and the emperor gave the thumbs-up to Alexander, I heard Demarrias will defy the emperor's orders and strike. He's declared no chance in hell that Alexander will live to see another day. One of my friends partied with Demarrias last night. Said he acted like one insane."

My mind reeled. My God. The Romans are a brutal culture, but especially Marcellious.

I touched Titus's biceps. "Thank you for keeping me safe."

I snatched my basket from where it sat next to me.

He gave me his attention, frowning slightly. "My pleasure. Come back if you want to."

I shook my head. "I can't."

I hope to never see your face again, nor any audience member.

I scurried down the steps as Roman and Marcellious rose from the dungeon on platforms attached to an elaborate pulley system.

Once more, the din from the audience no doubt reached the stars.

I pressed my hands to my ears and walked closer to the sand pit where Marcellious and Roman were fighting. How could I get into the arena and make all of this disappear?

I paused at the bottom of the steps, eyes glued to the sand-filled arena.

Marcellious and Roman stepped from their respective platforms and circled one another. They bared their teeth like snarling animals, parrying and thrusting with their scythe-like curved weapons without making contact.

Marcellious lunged on the offense, and Roman stumbled backward.

The crowd groaned.

Before Roman could fall, he got his feet under him and charged Marcellious. His arm was outstretched, the blade gripped in his hand aimed for Marcellious' chest.

Marcellious barely managed to get out of the way and avoid being skewered. He sprinted behind Roman and snaked his arm around Roman's neck.

Roman's hands flew upward, curved blades heading toward Marcellious' eyes.

Marcellious released Roman and arched backward, avoiding the blades.

Roman let out a wicked laugh. Then, he swooped his arm in a mighty arc. The blade sliced a path along Marcellious' torso.

The spectators both cheered and hissed.

Marcellious paused, wiped two fingers through the crimson liquid, and sucked on his bloody digits. Fire in his eyes, he charged once more. He slashed at Roman's neck, drawing an angry gash.

Roman let out a war cry.

I gasped, glued to my spot on the stone steps. *Please don't let his carotid artery be cut.*

The audience shrieked their approval.

Side gates opened, and several snarling wolves charged into the arena. The ravenous wolves split into two groups and circled the men.

Roman and Marcellious had to keep watch on their opponent and the wolf pack.

Every muscle in my body tightened in fear.

The wolves circled, moving in harmony with one another.

The largest wolf, the leader, circled the two men, and the others followed.

Roman kept one of his blades outstretched toward Marcellious and one aimed at the wolves.

One of the animals lunged for Roman's ankle. It sank its fangs into his flesh.

Roman slashed at the beast's neck as Marcellious charged, knife extended.

Marcellious sliced his blade across Roman's arm.

Roman hooked his bleeding foot behind Marcellious' shin, and Marcellious' leg buckled, sending him to the ground.

Two of the wolves raced for the fallen man, snarling and growling. They bit at Marcellious' belly, nipping away small chunks of skin and muscle as Roman fought off the attacks of the other wolves.

Marcellious kicked his legs, trying to scramble away from the hungry beasts. The tip of one of his blades sank into the wolf's belly, and it let out a cry of pain. Marcellious seized the other wolf's neck and twisted, snapping the bones until the head hung limply.

Marcellious jack-knifed to his feet. Blood dripped from his belly, stained his loincloth, and ran down his legs.

Roman grabbed the tail of one of the animals and swung it around and around. He let it go, and it flew toward Marcellious, knocking him to the ground.

Marcellious landed with a grunt and shoved the dying beast to the side. With a roar, he darted behind Roman, seized his arms behind his back, and bit Roman's ear.

Roman bent forward, flinging Marcellious to the ground over his head. Blood trickled down his neck and torso like a tiny river when he stood.

Marcellious landed with a thud, letting out a wheeze. He

lay on the ground gasping as Roman ran toward him, his blades lifted high.

The remaining wolves circled the arena, cowering away from Roman and Marcellious.

When Roman skidded to a stop at Marcellious' side, he lifted his foot, ready to stomp. Just as Roman's sandaled foot was about to crush Marcellious's windpipe, Marcellious managed to roll out of the way.

He leaped to his feet and powered toward Roman. Like a baseball player diving for home plate, he flung himself forward and grabbed Roman's calves.

Roman hurtled to the ground with a bone-cracking whomp. He let out a long groan.

Marcellious seized his advantage and straddled him, holding his blade to Roman's neck.

The crowd was on their feet now.

I glanced at the moon, which drifted upward like a helium balloon. I had to act soon.

I urged my legs to move, but they wouldn't.

The audience members lifted their thumbs up and down, jeering, catcalling, and contributing to the overall mayhem.

I unglued my feet from the stone and hurried to the ground floor. Once there, I exited the Colosseum and went back into the dungeon.

The sounds of moans and groans filled the hallway, probably from those who had won tonight's fight at the expense of their own bodies. But at least no guards were insight—they were all probably watching the main event.

As I scurried through the dank, smelly hallway, I became overpowered by doubt. All the "what ifs" collided in my brain. What if my plan doesn't work? What if Marcellious isn't the owner of the third dagger? What if Marcellious isn't Roman's brother? What if I have the time-

traveling scriptures wrong? What if we all land somewhere worse?

What if, what if, what if…

I wished I had Lee's guidance at that moment. I felt utterly alone.

I found the corridor leading to one of the trap doors, which had catapulted the wild animals into the arena. No way could I figure out how to use that entrance in time. I hurried toward another door that lay ajar. I could use that one to get into the sand pit.

As I climbed the stairs to the open door, a guard apprehended me, seizing my arm with his filthy hand.

"Where do you think you're going?" he said.

"I have to get out there," I said. "I'm a healer."

I lifted my little basket.

"No one enters the arena without my permission," he snapped.

He lunged to grab my shoulders.

I skirted out of his way, dropping my basket. The herbs tumbled out, along with the satchel.

The guard scrambled to pick them up. I kicked him hard in the stomach, and he fell backward. Then, in a snap decision, I lifted my stola, removed my Glock, and said, "You're dead in three, two, one."

I took aim and fired.

Brain matter exploded from his skull. The guard's body jerked as blood bubbled from the wound onto his forehead.

I'd shot him right between the eyes.

Stooping, I fished the daggers and the stone piece free from the satchel and shoved them in the basket so I could easily access them. Then, Glock in hand, I tiptoed toward the door and peeked around the corner, fearing that Roman would be dead.

Instead, Roman held Marcellious firmly on the ground with his foot.

Happiness filled me. He'd turned the tables against Marcellious.

Marcellious wheezed and gasped as he gripped Roman's ankle.

Roman kicked free of Marcellious' grip and jumped. His knee crashed down on Marcellious' ribcage.

Even from where I stood, I heard Marcellious' ribs crack.

Roman straddled Marcellious and held the blade to his neck.

Every person in the arena got to his feet, shouting, "Roman, Roman, Roman, Roman."

"No!" I screamed and pushed open the massive door, sprinting into the arena.

Roman and Marcellious' gazes both snapped to me.

Rage flashed across Marcellious' face.

Roman shouted, "Get back, Olivia!"

The emperor yelled, "Seize her!"

Two Praetorians rushed at me.

I jerked up my gun and shot them both.

They flew backward and crashed to the ground.

Someone in the audience cried, "She's a witch!"

The crowd took up a chant. "She's a witch! Get her!"

Roman focused on Marcellious once more. With gritted teeth, he gripped Marcellious' neck and placed the blade of his curved knife above his hand. His arm shook with exertion.

"Roman, stop! He's your brother!"

Roman whipped up his head to look at me and then dropped his gaze back at Marcellious.

The moon disappeared behind a cloud.

"What is she doing? Is she a sorceress? What mad spell is she casting?" someone shouted.

A strange wind began to blow. Torches flickered and extinguished.

Using the remaining light, I called "Roman!" and hurled the dagger at him.

He caught the blade with his palm, slicing his skin.

I grabbed the mystery dagger and prayed my theory about him was correct. I heaved it toward Marcellious with all my strength.

He gave me a vicious, snarling look and caught the dagger before it struck his neck. Blood dripped from his skin as he gripped the hilt.

Roman still held fast to Marcellious' neck, staring at the dagger in his hand.

From the top rows came the sounds of screams. In lower rows, men shouted and yelled.

The Colosseum was plunged into chaos as darkness consumed us all.

I stood tall and grabbed my dagger from my thigh. Then, in one swift move, I sliced my hand. As blood spurted from the wound, I closed my eyes. The sacred words streamed from my mouth, loud and clear.

"Ya hamiat alqamar fi allayl, 'adeuk litutliq aleinan lilnuwr waturshiduni khilal alzalami. Dae alshams aleazimat tarqus min hawlik bialhubi walmawadati. Mean, aftahuu bawaabatikum wamnahwani alsafar eabr alzaman walmakan mithl zilal allay." I repeated the words over and over.

Each dagger began to glow, illuminating the wide-eyed faces of Roman and Marcellious.

A huge black darkness, darker than the night if that were even possible, rolled toward us.

As the shadowy shapes of men thundered toward me, weapons drawn, I felt blanketed by a buzzing, vibrating, overwhelming sensation. I'd felt this the first time I had time traveled.

Rome disappeared into the darkness, but my only thoughts were if Roman and Marcellious were with me and if I had done everything correctly, without leaving anyone behind....

And where on earth would we end up?

The Journey Continues...
Blade of Shadows Book 2: Darkness of Time

THANK YOU FOR READING!

Enjoy *Timeborne*? Please take a second to leave a review!

OTHER BOOKS IN THE BLADE OF SHADOWS SERIES

TIMEBORNE (BOOK 1)

DARKNESS OF TIME (BOOK 2)

TIMEBOUND (BOOK 3)

WICKED LOVERS OF TIME (BOOK 3.5)

Balthazar and Alina's Story

TIMEHUNTERS (BOOK 4)

COMING SOON 2025

(FINAL SAGA BOOK 5) (COMING SOON 2025)

JOIN THE BLADE OF SHADOWS!

https://www.authorsarasamuels.com/

Join the Club!

Blade of Shadows Book Club

(Facebook Group)

TikTok

Instagram

Facebook

BookBub

APPRECIATION

I am immensely grateful to everyone who has supported me on this journey, especially my parents. Their constant encouragement to pursue my dreams and follow my heart has been a guiding force in my life. Their faith in me has been the foundation of everything I've achieved.

A special thank you goes to Chaela, who has been more than just a book adviser throughout this process—you've been my rock and best friend. Having you in my life is a blessing, and I'm incredibly grateful for your guidance and friendship.

To Rainy, my exceptional editor, your keen eye and thoughtful feedback have transformed my manuscript into something truly special. I'm so fortunate to have had your expertise in refining this story, and I deeply appreciate your dedication.

Thank you, Charity, for your meticulous proofreading and valuable comments that have significantly enhanced this book. Your precision and dedication have not gone unnoticed.

My beta readers, your enthusiastic and insightful comments have not only improved this book but have also fueled my excitement and confidence in this project. Thank you for your amazing support and energy.

A HUGE shout-out to my street team, and ARC team,—your constant support, love, and encouragement have empowered me to publish this book. I couldn't have reached this point without you.

Lastly, to everyone who has picked up a copy of this

book, thank you from the bottom of my heart. Releasing my debut series was incredibly nerve-wracking, and your support has been a comfort and a joy. I hope you'll stay with me on this adventure, eager to see where our beloved characters end up next and what secrets they uncover.

ABOUT THE AUTHOR

SARA SAMUELS is the author of the Blade of Shadow series. When Sara isn't daydreaming about her stories and time travel, she spends her day reading romance, cooking and baking, spending time with family, and enjoying life. Sara loves to connect with readers on Instagram, TikTok or by email, so feel free to email her, or message her on social media because she will reply back! Follow her on Instagram or TikTok @storytellersarasamuels to get related updates and posts. Email her at sara@authorsarasamuels.com

Visit her website at https://www.authorsarasamuels.com/ and sign up for the mailing list to stay informed about new releases, contests and more!

Made in the USA
Middletown, DE
25 July 2024

57994026R00203